50
Inspirational Speeches

50 Inspirational Speeches

RUPA

First published by
Rupa Publications India Pvt. Ltd 2023
7/16, Ansari Road, Daryaganj
New Delhi 110002

Sales Centres:
Bengaluru Chennai
Hyderabad Jaipur Kathmandu
Kolkata Mumbai Prayagraj

P-ISBN: 978-93-5702-549-2
E-ISBN: 978-93-5702-550-8

First impression 2023

10 9 8 7 6 5 4 3 2 1

Printed in India

Contents

1

THE THIRD PHILIPPIC

Demosthenes

Demosthenes, the Greek politician who overcame a speech defect in his childhood to become one of the most acclaimed orators of Ancient Greece, delivered 'The Third Philippic' in 341 BC. The speech, which was his third out of four attempts to rally the Athenians against Philip II of Macedon, lamented the complacency and lack of unity among Greeks, urged the Athenians to take Philip's threat seriously and to get ready for an armed resistance by reminding them of their glorious past. It remains his most famous and successful address.

Many speeches are made, men of Athens, at almost every meeting of the Assembly, with reference to the aggressions which Philip has been committing, ever since he concluded the Peace, not only against yourselves but against all other peoples.

And I am sure that all would agree, however little they may act on their belief, that our aim, both in speech and in action, should be to cause him to cease from his insolence and to pay the penalty for it. And yet I see that in fact the treacherous sacrifice of our interests has gone on, until what seems an ill-omened saying may, I fear, be really true—that if all who came forward desired to propose, and you desired to carry, the measures which would make your position as pitiful as it could possibly be, it could not, so I believe, be made worse than it is now.

It may be that there are many reasons for this, and that our affairs did not reach their present condition from any one or two causes. But if you examine the matter aright, you will find that the chief responsibility rests with those whose aim is to win your favour, not to propose what is best. Some of them, men of Athens, so long as they can maintain the conditions which bring them reputation and influence, take no thought for the future and therefore think that you also should take none, while others, by accusing and slandering those who are actively at work, are simply trying to make the city spend its energies in punishing the members of its own body, and so leave Philip free to say and do what he likes.

Such political methods as these, familiar to you as they are, are the real causes of the evil. And I beg you, men of Athens, if I tell you certain truths outspokenly, to let no resentment on your part fall upon me on this account. Consider the matter in this light. In every other sphere of life, you believe that the right of free speech ought to be so universally shared by all who are in the city, that you have extended it both to foreigners and to slaves; and one may see many a servant in Athens speaking his mind with greater liberty than is granted to citizens in some other states: but from the sphere of political counsel you have utterly banished this liberty.

The result is that in your meetings you give yourselves airs and enjoy their flattery, listening to nothing but what is meant to please you, while in the world of facts and events, you are in the last extremity of peril. If then you are still in this mood to-day, I do not know what I can say; but if you are willing to listen while I tell you, without flattery, what your interest requires, I am prepared to speak. For though our position is very bad indeed, and much has been sacrificed, it is still possible, even now, if you will do your duty, to set all right once more.

It is a strange thing, perhaps, that I am about to say, but it is true. The worst feature in the past is that in which lies our best hope for the future. And what is this? It is that you are in your present plight because you do not do any part of your duty, small or great; for of course, if you were doing all that you should do, and were still in this evil case, you could not even hope for any improvement. As it is, Philip has conquered your indolence and your indifference; but he has not conquered Athens. You have not been vanquished, you have never even stirred.

Now if it was admitted by us all that Philip was at war with Athens, and was transgressing the Peace, a speaker would have to do nothing but to advise you as to the safest and easiest method of resistance to him. But since there are some who are in so extraordinary a frame of mind that, though he is capturing cities, though many of your possessions are in his hands, and though he is committing aggressions against all men, they still tolerate certain speakers, who constantly assert at your meetings that it is some of us who are provoking the war, it is necessary to be on our guard and come to a right understanding on the matter.

For there is a danger lest any one who proposes or advises resistance should find himself accused of having brought about the war. Well, I say this first of all, and lay it down as a principle, that if it is open to us to deliberate whether we should remain at peace or should go to war...

Now if it is possible for the city to remain at peace, if the decision rests with us that I may make this my starting-point, then I say that we ought to do so, and I call upon any one who says that it is so to move his motion, and to act and not to defraud us. But if another with weapons in his hands and a large force about him holds out to you the name of peace while his own acts are acts of war what course remains open to us but that of resistance?

Though if you wish to profess peace in the same manner as he, I have no quarrel with you. But if any man's conception of peace is that it is a state in which Philip can master all that intervenes till at last he comes to attack ourselves, such a conception, in the first place, is madness; and, in the second place, this peace that he speaks of is a peace which you are to observe towards Philip, while he does not observe it towards you: and this it is, this power to carry on war against you, without being met by any hostilities on your part, that Philip is purchasing with all the money that he is spending.

Indeed, if we intend to wait till the time comes when he admits that he is at war with us, we are surely the most innocent persons in the world. Why, even if he comes to Attica itself, to the very Peiraeus, he will never make such an admission, if we are to judge by his dealings with others.

For, to take one instance, he told the Olynthians, when he was five miles from the city, that there were only two alternatives, either they must cease to live in Olynthus, or he to live in Macedonia: but during the whole time before that, whenever any one accused him of any such sentiments, he was indignant and sent envoys to answer the charge. Again, he marched into the Phocians' country, as though visiting his allies. It was by Phocian envoys that he was escorted on the march; and most people in Athens contended strongly that his crossing the Pass would bring no good to Thebes.

Worse still, he has lately seized Pherae and still holds it, though he went to Thessaly as a friend and an ally. And, latest of all, he told those unhappy citizens of Oreus that he had sent his soldiers to visit them and to make kind inquiries; he had heard that they were sick, and suffering from faction, and it was right for an ally and a true friend to be present at such a time.

Now if, instead of giving them warning and using open force, he deliberately chose to deceive these men, who could have done him no harm, though they might have taken precautions against suffering any themselves, do you imagine that he will make a formal declaration of war upon you before he commences hostilities, and that, so long as you are content to be deceived? Impossible! For so long as you, though you are the injured party, make no complaint against him, but accuse some of your own body, he would be the most fatuous man on earth if he were to interrupt your strife and contentions with one another, to bid you turn upon himself, and so to cut away the ground from the arguments by which his hirelings put you off, when they tell you that he is not at war with Athens.

In God's name, is there a man in his senses who would judge by words, and not by facts, whether another was at peace or at war with him? Of course there is not. Why, from the very first, when the Peace had only just been made, before those who are now in the Chersonese had been sent out, Philip was taking Serrhium and Doriscus, and expelling the soldiers who were in the castle of Serrhium and the Sacred Mountain, where they had been placed by your general. But what was he doing, in acting thus? For he had sworn to a Peace. And let no one ask, what do these things amount to? What do they matter to Athens?

For whether these acts were trifles which could have no interest for you is another matter; but the principles of religion and justice, whether a man transgress them in small things or great, have always the same force. What? When he is sending mercenaries into the Chersonese, which the king and all the Hellenes have acknowledged to be yours; when he openly avows that he is going to the rescue, and states it in his letter, what is it that he is doing?

He tells you, indeed, that he is not making war upon you. But so far am I from admitting that one who acts in this manner is observing the Peace which he made with you, that I hold that in grasping at Megara, in setting up tyrants in Euboea, in advancing against Thrace at the present moment, in pursuing his machinations in the Peloponnese, and in carrying out his entire policy with the help of his army, he is violating the Peace and is making war against you. Unless you mean to say that even to bring up engines to besiege you is no breach of the Peace, until they are actually planted against your walls. But you will not say this; for the man who is taking the steps and contriving the means which will lead to my capture is at war with me, even though he has not yet thrown a missile or shot an arrow.

Now what are the things which would imperil your safety, if anything should happen? The alienation of the Hellespont, the placing of Megara and Euboea in the power of the enemy, and the attraction of Peloponnesian sympathy to his cause. Can I then say that one who is erecting such engines of war as these against the city is at peace with you?

Far from it! For from the very day when he annihilated the Phocians, from that very day, I say, I date the beginning of his hostilities against you. And for your part, I think that you will be wise if you resist him at once; but that if you let him be, you will find that, when you wish to resist, resistance itself is impossible. Indeed, so widely do I differ, men of Athens, from all your other advisers, that I do not think there is any room for discussion to-day in regard to the Chersonese or Byzantium.

We must go to their defence and take every care that they do not suffer and we must send all that they need to the soldiers who are at present there. But we have to take counsel for the good of all the Hellenes, in view of the grave peril in which they stand. And I wish to tell you on what grounds I am so alarmed at the situation, in order that if my reasoning is correct, you may share my conclusions, and exercise some forethought for yourselves at least, if you are actually unwilling to do so for the Hellenes as a whole; but that if you think that I am talking nonsense, and am out of my senses, you may both now and hereafter decline to attend to me as though I were a sane man.

The rise of Philip to greatness from such small and humble beginnings; the mistrustful and quarrelsome attitude of the Hellenes towards one another; the fact that his growth out of what he was into what he is was a far more extraordinary thing than would be his subjugation of all that remains, when he has already secured so much. All this and all similar themes, upon which I might speak at length, I will pass over.

But I see that all men, beginning with yourselves, have conceded to him the very thing which has been at issue in every Hellenic war during the whole of the past. And what is this? It is the right to act as he pleases, to mutilate and to strip the Hellenic peoples, one by one, to attack and to enslave their cities.

For 73 years you were the leading people of Hellas, and the

Spartans for 30 years save one; and in these last times, after the battle of Leuctra, the Thebans too acquired some power: yet neither to you nor to Thebes nor to Sparta was such a right ever conceded by the Hellenes, as the right to do whatever you pleased. Far from it!

First of all it was your own behavior, or rather that of the Athenians of that day, which some thought immoderate; and all, even those who had no grievance against Athens, felt bound to join the injured parties, and to make war upon you. Then, in their turn, the Spartans, when they had acquired an empire and succeeded to a supremacy like your own, attempted to go beyond all bounds and to disturb the established order to an unjustifiable extent; and once more, all, even those who had no grievance against them, had recourse to war.

Why mention the others? For we ourselves and the Spartans, though we could originally allege no injury done by the one people to the other, nevertheless felt bound to go to war on account of the wrongs which we saw the rest suffering. And yet all the offences of the Spartans in those 30 years of power, and of your ancestors in their 70 years, were less, men of Athens, than the wrongs inflicted upon the Greeks by Philip, in the 13 years, not yet completed, during which he has been to the fore. Less do I say?

They are not a fraction of them. A few words will easily prove this. I say nothing of Olynthus, and Methone, and Apollonia, and 32 cities in the Thracian region, all annihilated by him with such savagery, that a visitor to the spot would find it difficult to tell that they had ever been inhabited. I remain silent in regard to the extirpation of the great Phocian race. But what is the condition of Thessaly? Has he not robbed their very cities of their governments and set up tetrarchies, that they may be enslaved, not merely by whole cities, but by whole tribes at a time?

Are not the cities of Euboea even now ruled by tyrants, and that in an island that is neighbour to Thebes and Athens? Does he not write expressly in his letters, 'I am at peace with those who choose to obey me?' And what he thus writes he does not fail to act upon; for he is gone to invade the Hellespont; he previously went to attack Ambracia; the great city of Elis in the Peloponnese is his; he has recently intrigued against Megara; and neither Hellas nor the world beyond it is large enough to contain the man's ambition.

But though all of us, the Hellenes, see and hear these things, we send no representatives to one another to discuss the matter; we show no indignation; we are in so evil a mood, so deep have the lines been dug which sever city from city, that up to this very day we are unable to act as either our interest or our duty require.

We cannot unite; we can form no combination for mutual support or friendship; but we look on while the man grows greater, because every one has made up his mind, as it seems to me, to profit by the time during which his neighbour is being ruined, and no one cares or acts for the safety of the Hellenes. For we all know that Philip is like the recurrence or the attack of a fever or other illness, in his descent upon those who fancy themselves for the present well out of his reach.

And further, you must surely realize that all the wrongs that the Hellenes suffered from the Spartans or ourselves they at least suffered at the hands of true-born sons of Hellas; and, one might conceive, it was as though a lawful son, born to a great estate, managed his affairs in some wrong or improper way. His conduct would in itself deserve blame and denunciation, but at least it could not be said that he was not one of the family, or was not the heir to the property.

But had it been a slave or a supposititious son that was thus ruining and spoiling an inheritance to which he had no title, why, good Heavens! how infinitely more scandalous and reprehensible all would have declared it to be. And yet they show no such feeling in regard to Philip, although not only is he no Hellene, not only has he no kinship with Hellenes, but he is not even a barbarian from a country that one could acknowledge with credit.

He is a pestilent Macedonian, from whose country it used not to be possible to buy even a slave of any value.

And in spite of this, is there any degree of insolence to which he does not proceed? Not content with annihilating cities, does he not manage the Pythian games, the common meeting of the Hellenes, and send his slaves to preside over the competition in his absence? Is he not master of Thermopylae, and of the passes which lead into Hellenic territory? Does he not hold that district with garrisons and mercenaries? Has he not taken the precedence in consulting the oracle, and thrust aside ourselves and the Thessalians and Dorians and the rest of the Amphictyons, though the right is not one which is given even to all of the Hellenes?

Does he not write to the Thessalians to prescribe the constitution under which they are to live? Does he not send one body of mercenaries to Porthmus, to expel the popular party of Eretria, and another to Oreus, to set up Philistides as tyrant? And yet the Hellenes see these things and endure them, gazing, it seems to me, as they would gaze at a hailstorm, each people praying that it may not come their way, but no one trying to prevent it. Nor is it only his outrages upon Hellas that go unresisted.

No one resists even the aggressions which are committed against himself. Ambracia and Leucas belong to the Corinthians. He has attacked them: Naupactus to the Achaeans. He has sworn to hand it over to the Aetolians: Echinus to the Thebans. He has taken it from them, and is now marching against their allies the Byzantines, is it not so? And of our own possessions, to pass by all the rest, is not Cardia, the greatest city in the Chersonese, in his hands? Thus are we treated. And we are all hesitating and torpid, with our eyes upon our neighbours, distrusting one another, rather than the man whose victims we all are.

But if he treats us collectively in this outrageous fashion, what do you think he will do, when he has become master of each of us separately? What then is the cause of these things? For as it was not without reason and just cause that the Hellenes in old days were so prompt for freedom, so it is not without reason or cause that they are now so prompt to be slaves. There was a spirit, men of Athens, a spirit in the minds of the people in those days, which is absent to-day, the spirit which vanquished the wealth of Persia, which led Hellas in the path of freedom, and never gave way in face of battle by sea or by land; a spirit whose extinction to-day has brought universal ruin and turned Hellas upside down. What was this spirit? It was nothing subtle nor clever.

It meant that men who took money from those who aimed at dominion or at the ruin of Hellas were execrated by all; that it was then a very grave thing to be convicted of bribery; that the punishment for the guilty man was the heaviest that could be inflicted; that for him there could be no plea for mercy, nor hope of pardon.

No orator, no general, would then sell the critical opportunity whenever it arose—the opportunity so often offered to men by fortune, even when they are careless and their foes are on their guard. They did not barter away the harmony between people and people, nor their own mistrust of the tyrant and the foreigner, nor any of these high sentiments.

Where are such sentiments now? They have been sold in the market and are gone; and those have been imported in their stead, through which the nation lies ruined and plague-stricken, the envy of the man who has received his hire; the amusement which accompanies his avowal, the pardon granted to those whose guilt is proved, the hatred of one who censures the crime; and all the appurtenances of corruption.

For as to ships, numerical strength, unstinting abundance of funds and all other material of war, and all the things by which the strength of cities is estimated, every people can command these in greater plenty and on a larger scale by far than in old days. But all these resources are rendered unserviceable, ineffectual, unprofitable, by those who traffic in them.

That these things are so to-day, you doubtless see, and need no testimony of mine: and that in times gone by the opposite was true, I will prove to you, not by any words of my own, but by the record inscribed by your ancestors on a pillar of bronze, and placed on the Acropolis, not to be a lesson to themselves, they needed no such record to put them in a right mind, but to be a reminder and an example to you of the zeal that you ought to display in such a cause.

What then is the record? 'Arthmius, son of Pythonax, of Zeleia, is an outlaw, and is the enemy of the Athenian people and their allies, he and his house.' Then follows the reason for which this step was taken, 'because he brought the gold from the Medes into the Peloponnese.' Such is the record.

Consider, in Heaven's name, what must have been the mind of the Athenians of that day, when they did this, and their conception of their position. They set up a record, that because a man of Zeleia, Arthmius by name, a slave of the King of Persia, for Zeleia is in Asia, as part of his service to the king, had brought gold, not to Athens, but to the Peloponnese, he should be an enemy of Athens and her allies, he and his house, and that they should be outlaws.

And this outlawry is no such disfranchisement as we ordinarily mean by the word. For what would it matter to a man of Zeleia, that he might have no share in the public life of Athens? But there is a clause in the Law of Murder, dealing with those in connection with whose death the law does not allow a prosecution for murder but the slaying of them is to be a holy act: 'And let him die an outlaw,' it runs. The meaning, accordingly, is this that the slayer of such a man is to be pure from all guilt.

They thought, therefore, that the safety of all the Hellenes was a matter which concerned themselves, apart from this belief, it could not have mattered to them whether any one bought or corrupted men in the Peloponnese; and whenever they detected such offenders, they carried their punishment and their vengeance so far as to pillory their names for ever. As the natural consequence, the Hellenes were a terror to the foreigner, not the foreigner to the Hellenes. It is not so now. Such is not your attitude in these or in other matters.

But what is it? You know it yourselves; for why should I accuse you explicitly on every point? And that of the rest of the Hellenes is like your own, and no better; and so I say that the present situation demands our utmost earnestness and good counsel. And what counsel? Do you bid me tell you, and will you not be angry if I do so?

[He reads from the document.]

Now there is an ingenuous argument, which is used by those who would reassure the city, to the effect that, after all, Philip is not yet in the position once held by the Spartans, who ruled everywhere over sea and land, with the king for their ally, and nothing to withstand them; and that, none the less, Athens defended herself even against them, and was not swept away. Since that time the progress in every direction, one may say, has been great, and has made the world to-day very different from what it was then; but I believe that in no respect has there been greater progress or development than in the art of war.

In the first place, I am told that in those days the Spartans and all our other enemies would invade us for four or five months during, that is, the actual summer, and would damage Attica with infantry and citizen-troops, and then return home again. And so old-fashioned were the men of that day, nay rather, such true citizens, that no one ever purchased any object from another for money, but their warfare was of a legitimate and open kind.

But now, as I am sure you see, most of our losses are the result of treachery, and no issue is decided by open conflict or battle; while you are told that it is not because he leads a column of heavy infantry that Philip can march wherever he chooses, but because he has attached to himself a force of light infantry, cavalry, archers, mercenaries and similar troops.

And whenever, with such advantages, he falls upon a State

which is disordered within, and in their distrust of one another no one goes out in defence of its territory, he brings up his engines and besieges them. I pass over the fact that summer and winter are alike to him, that there is no close season during which he suspends operations.

But if you all know these things and take due account of them, you surely must not let the war pass into Attica, nor be dashed from your seat through looking back to the simplicity of those old hostilities with Sparta. You must guard against him, at the greatest possible distance, both by political measures and by preparations; you must prevent his stirring from home, instead of grappling with him at close quarters in a struggle to the death.

For, men of Athens, we have many natural advantages for a war, if we are willing to do our duty. There is the character of his country, much of which we can harry and damage, and a thousand other things. But for a pitched battle he is in better training than we.

Nor have you only to recognize these facts, and to resist him by actual operations of war. You must also by reasoned judgment and of set purpose come to execrate those who address you in his interest, remembering that it is impossible to master the enemies of the city, until you punish those who are serving them in the city itself.

And this, before God and every Heavenly Power, this you will not be able to do. For you have reached such a pitch of folly or distraction or, I know not what to call it, for often has the fear actually entered my mind that some more than mortal power may be driving our fortunes to ruin, that to enjoy their abuse, or their malice, or their jests, or whatever your motive may chance to be, you call upon men to speak who are hirelings, and some of whom would not even deny it; and you laugh to hear their abuse of others.

And terrible as this is, there is yet worse to be told. For you have actually made political life safer for these men, than for those who uphold your own cause. And yet observe what calamities the willingness to listen to such men lays up in store. I will mention facts known to you all.

In Olynthus, among those who were engaged in public affairs, there was one party who were on the side of Philip, and served his interests in everything; and another whose aim was their city's real good, and the preservation of their fellow citizens from bondage. Which were the destroyers of their country? which betrayed the cavalry, through whose betrayal Olynthus perished? Those whose sympathies were with Philip's cause; those who, while the city still existed brought such dishonest and slanderous charges against the speakers whose advice was for the best, that, in the case of Apollonides at least, the people of Olynthus was even induced to banish the accused.

Nor is this instance of the unmixed evil wrought by these practices in the case of the Olynthians an exceptional one, or without parallel elsewhere. For in Eretria, when Plutarchus and the mercenaries had been got rid of, and the people had control of the city and of Porthmus, one party wished to entrust the State to you, the other to entrust it to Philip. And through listening mainly, or rather entirely, to the latter, these poor luckless Eretrians were at last persuaded to banish the advocates of their own interests.

For, as you know, Philip, their ally, sent Hipponicus with a thousand mercenaries, stripped Porthmus of its walls, and set up three tyrants—Hipparchus, Automedon and Cleitarchus. And since then he has already twice expelled them from the country when they wished to recover their position sending on the first occasion the mercenaries commanded by Eurylochus, on the second, those under Parmenio.

And why go through the mass of the instances? Enough to mention how in Oreus Philip had, as his agents, Philistides, Menippus, Socrates, Thoas and Agapaeus—the very men who are now in possession of the city—and every one knew the fact; while a certain Euphraeus, who once lived here in Athens, acted in the interests of freedom, to save his country from bondage.

To describe the insults and the contumely with which he met would require a long story; but a year before the capture of the town he laid an information of treason against Philistides and his party, having perceived the nature of their plans. A number of men joined forces, with Philip for their paymaster and director, and haled Euphraeus off to prison as a disturber of the peace.

Seeing this, the democratic party in Oreus, instead of coming to the rescue of Euphraeus, and beating the other party to death, displayed no anger at all against them, and agreed with a malicious pleasure that Euphraeus deserved his fate. After this the conspirators worked with all the freedom they desired for the capture of the city, and made arrangements for the execution of the scheme; while any of the democratic party, who perceived what was going on, maintained a panic-stricken silence, remembering the fate of Euphraeus. So wretched was their condition, that though this dreadful calamity was confronting them, no one dared open his lips, until all was ready and the enemy was advancing up to the walls. Then the one party set about the defence, the other about the betrayal of the city.

And when the city had been captured in this base and shameful manner, the successful party governed despotically: and of those who had been their own protectors, and had been ready to treat Euphraeus with all possible harshness, they expelled some and murdered others; while the good Euphraeus killed himself, thus testifying to the righteousness and purity of his motives in opposing Philip on behalf of his countrymen.

Now for what reason, you may be wondering, were the peoples of Olynthus and Eretria and Oreus more agreeably disposed towards Philip's advocates than towards their own? The reason was the same as it is with you, that those who speak for your true good can never, even if they would, speak to win popularity with you. They are constrained to inquire how the State may be saved: while their opponents, in the very act of seeking popularity, are cooperating with Philip.

The one party said, 'You must pay taxes.' The other, 'There is no need to do so.' The one said, 'Go to war, and do not trust him.' The other, 'Remain at peace'—until they were in the toils. And, not to mention each separately, I believe that the same thing was true of all. The one side said what would enable them to win favour; the other, what would secure the safety of their State. And at last the main body of the people accepted much that they proposed, not now from any such desire for gratification, nor from ignorance, but as a concession to circumstances, thinking that their cause was now wholly lost.

It is this fate, I solemnly assure you, that I dread for you, when the time comes that you make your reckoning, and realize that there is no longer anything that can be done. May you never find yourselves, men of Athens, in such a position! Yet in any case, it were better to die ten thousand deaths, than to do anything out of servility towards Philip or to sacrifice any of those who speak for your good. A noble recompense did the people in Oreus receive, for entrusting themselves to Philip's friends, and thrusting Euphraeus aside! And a noble recompense the democracy of Eretria, for driving away your envoys, and surrendering to Cleitarchus! They are slaves, scourged and butchered! A noble clemency did he show to the Olynthians, who elected Lasthenes to command the cavalry, and banished Apollonides!

It is folly, and it is cowardice, to cherish hopes like these, to give way to evil counsels, to refuse to do anything that you should do, to listen to the advocates of the enemy's cause, and to fancy that you dwell in so great a city that, whatever happens, you will not suffer any harm.

Aye, and it is shameful to exclaim after the event, 'Why, who would have expected this? Of course, we ought to have done, or not to have done, such and such things!' The Olynthians could tell you of many things, to have foreseen which in time would have saved them from destruction. So too could the people of Oreus, and the Phocians, and every other people that has been destroyed.

But how does that help them now? So long as the vessel is safe, be it great or small, so long must the sailor and the pilot and every man in his place exert himself and take care that no one may capsize it by design or by accident: but when the seas have overwhelmed it, all their efforts are in vain.

So it is, men of Athens, with us. While we are still safe, with our great city, our vast resources, our noble name, what are we to do? Perhaps some one sitting here has long been wishing to ask this question. Aye, and I will answer it, and will move my motion; and you shall carry it, if you wish. We ourselves, in the first place, must conduct the resistance and make preparation for it with ships, that is, and money, and soldiers. For though all but ourselves give way and become slaves, we at least must contend for freedom.

And when we have made all these preparations ourselves, and let them be seen, then let us call upon the other states for aid, and send envoys to carry our message in all directions, to the Peloponnese, to Rhodes, to Chios, to the king. For it is not unimportant for his interests either that Philip should be prevented from subjugating the world, that so, if you persuade them, you may have partners to share the danger and the expense, in case of need; and if you do not, you may at least delay the march of events.

For since the war is with a single man, and not against the strength of a united state, even delay is not without its value, any more than were those embassies of protest which last year went round the Peloponnese, when I and Polyeuctus, that best of men, and Hegesippus and the other envoys went on our tour, and forced him to halt, so that he neither went to attack Acarnania, nor set out for the Peloponnese.

But I do not mean that we should call upon the other states, if we are not willing to take any of the necessary steps ourselves. It is folly to sacrifice what is our own, and then pretend to be anxious for the interests of others, to neglect the present, and alarm others in regard to the future. I do not propose this. I say that we must send money to the forces in the Chersonese, and do all that they ask of us. That we must make preparation ourselves, while we summon, convene, instruct and warn the rest of the Hellenes.

That is the policy for a city with a reputation such as yours. But if you fancy that the people of Chalcis or of Megara will save Hellas, while you run away from the task, you are mistaken. They may well be content if they can each save themselves. The task is yours. It is the prerogative that your forefathers won, and through many a great peril bequeathed to you.

But if each of you is to sit and consult his inclinations, looking for some way by which he may escape any personal action, the first consequence will be that you will never find any one who will act; and the second, I fear, that the day will come when we shall be forced to do, at one and the same time, all the things we wish to avoid.

This then is my proposal, and this I move. If the proposal is carried out, I think that even now the state of our affairs may be remedied. But if any one has a better proposal to make, let him make it, and give us his advice. And I pray to all the gods that whatever be the decision that you are about to make, it may be for your good.

2

WAR

Alexander the Great

After a decade of warfare and being far from their homeland, Alexander's soldiers lacked the desire to engage in further combat, particularly against formidable adversaries like King Porus and his army. Leveraging his skills in persuasive speaking, which he honed during his education under Aristotle, Alexander instilled his troops with the inspiration required to persevere, fight and emerge victorious.

I observe, gentlemen, that when I would lead you on a new venture you no longer follow me with your old spirit. I have asked you to meet me that we may come to a decision together: are we, upon my advice, to go forward, or, upon yours, to turn back?

If you have any complaint to make about the results of your efforts hitherto, or about myself as your commander, there is no more to say. But let me remind you: through your courage and endurance you have gained possession of Ionia, the Hellespont, both Phrygias, Cappadocia, Paphlagonia, Lydia, Caria, Lycia, Pamphylia, Phoenicia and Egypt; the Greek part of Libya is now yours, together with much of Arabia, lowland Syria, Mesopotamia, Babylon and Susia; Persia and Media with all the territories either formerly controlled by them or not are in your hands; you have made yourselves masters of the lands beyond the Caspian Gates, beyond the Caucasus, beyond the Tanais, of Bactria, Hyrcania and the Hyrcanian Sea; we have driven the Scythians back into the desert; and Indus and Hydaspes, Acesines and Hydraotes flow now through country which is ours. With all that accomplished, why do you hesitate to extend the power of Macedon—your power—to the Hyphasis and the tribes on the other side? Are you afraid that a few natives who may still be left will offer opposition? Come, come! These natives either surrender without a blow or are caught on the run—or leave their country undefended for your taking; and when we take it, we make a present of it to those who have joined us of their own free will and fight on our side.

For a man who is a man, work, in my belief, if it is directed to noble ends, has no object beyond itself; none the less, if any of you wish to know what limit may be set to this particular campaign, let me tell you that the area of country still ahead of us, from here to the Ganges and the Eastern Ocean, is comparatively small. You will undoubtedly find that this ocean is connected with the Hyrcanian Sea, for the great Stream of Ocean encircles the earth. Moreover I shall prove to you, my friends, that the Indian and Persian Gulfs and the Hyrcanian Sea are all three connected and continuous. Our ships will sail round from the Persian Gulf to Libya as far as the Pillars of Hercules, whence all Libya to the eastward will soon be ours, and all Asia too, and to this empire there will be no boundaries but what God Himself has made for the whole world.

But if you turn back now, there will remain unconquered many warlike peoples between the Hyphasis and the Eastern Ocean, and many more to the northward and the Hyrcanian Sea, with the Scythians, too, not far away; so that if we withdraw now there is a danger that the territory which we do not yet securely hold may be stirred to revolt by some nation or other we have not yet forced into submission. Should that happen, all that we have done and suffered will have proved fruitless—or we shall be faced with the task of doing it over again from the beginning. Gentlemen of Macedon, and you, my friends and allies, this must not be. Stand firm; for well you know that hardship and danger are the price of glory, and that sweet is the savour of a life of courage and of deathless renown beyond the grave.

Are you not aware that if Heracles, my ancestor, had gone no further than Tiryns or Argos—or even than the Peloponnese or Thebes—he could never have won the glory which changed him from a man into a god, actual or apparent? Even Dionysus, who is a god indeed, in a sense beyond what is applicable to Heracles, faced not a few laborious tasks; yet we have done more: we have passed beyond Nysa and we have taken the rock of Aornos which Heracles himself could not take. Come, then; add the rest of Asia to what you already possess—a small addition to the great sum of your conquests. What great or noble work could we ourselves have achieved had we thought it enough, living at ease in Macedon, merely to guard our homes, accepting no burden beyond checking the encroachment of the Thracians on our borders, or the Illyrians and Triballians, or perhaps such Greeks as might prove a menace to our comfort?

I could not have blamed you for being the first to lose heart if I, your commander, had not shared in your exhausting marches and your perilous campaigns; it would have been natural enough if you had done all the work merely for others to reap the reward. But it is not so. You and I, gentlemen, have shared the labour and shared the danger, and the rewards are for us all. The conquered territory belongs to you; from your ranks the governors of it are chosen; already the greater part of its treasure passes into your hands, and when all Asia is overrun, then indeed I will go further than the mere satisfaction of our ambitions: the utmost hopes of riches or power which each one of you cherishes will be far surpassed, and whoever wishes to return home will be allowed to go, either with me or without me. I will make those who stay the envy of those who return.

3

SPEECH TO THE TROOPS AT TILBURY

Elizabeth I

The Spanish Armada was a formidable fleet sent by Spain in an attempt to invade England and overthrow Queen Elizabeth I. In 1588, as the English forces prepared for a potential invasion, Queen Elizabeth I delivered a powerful and stirring speech to rally her troops at Tilbury, a fort on the river Thames. In her address, Queen Elizabeth I exhibited remarkable courage and determination, standing before her army and delivering a resolute call to action. She expressed her unwavering faith in the resilience and fighting spirit of her soldiers and reassured them of her commitment to their cause.

My loving people:

We have been persuaded by some that are careful of our safety, to take heed how we commit ourselves to armed multitudes for fear of treachery; but I assure you, I do not desire to live to distrust my faithful and loving people. Let tyrants fear. I have always so behaved myself that, under God, I have placed my chiefest strength and safeguard in the loyal hearts and goodwill of my subjects; and therefore I am come amongst you, as you see, at this time, not for my recreation and disport, but being resolved, in the midst and heat of the battle, to live and die amongst you all; to lay down for my God, and for my kingdom, and my people, my honour and my blood, even in the dust.

I know I have the body of a weak, feeble woman; but I have the heart and stomach of a king, and of a king of England too, and think foul scorn that Parma or Spain, or any prince of Europe, should dare to invade the borders of my realm; to which rather than any dishonour shall grow by me, I myself will take up arms, I myself will be your general, judge and rewarder of every one of your virtues in the field.

I know already, for your forwardness you have deserved rewards and crowns; and we do assure you on a word of a prince, they shall be duly paid. In the meantime, my lieutenant general shall be in my stead, than whom never prince commanded a more noble or worthy subject; not doubting but by your obedience to my general, by your concord in the camp, and your valour in the field, we shall shortly have a famous victory over these enemies of my God, of my kingdom and of my people.

4

GIVE ME LIBERTY OR GIVE ME DEATH

Patrick Henry

The 'Give me liberty or give me death' speech, delivered on 23 March 1775, during the Virginia Convention, has become one of the most renowned and impactful speeches in American history. Patrick Henry, a prominent figure in the American Revolution, delivered the speech as tensions between the American colonies and Great Britain were escalating. In his speech, Henry passionately argued for the need to resist British oppression and fight for American independence.

No man thinks more highly than I do of the patriotism, as well as abilities, of the very worthy gentlemen who have just addressed the House. But different men often see the same subject in different lights; and, therefore, I hope it will not be thought disrespectful to those gentlemen if, entertaining as I do opinions of a character very opposite to theirs, I shall speak forth my sentiments freely and without reserve. This is no time for ceremony. The question before the House is one of awful moment to this country. For my own part, I consider it as nothing less than a question of freedom or slavery; and in proportion to the magnitude of the subject ought to be the freedom of the debate. It is only in this way that we can hope to arrive at truth, and fulfill the great responsibility which we hold to God and our country. Should I keep back my opinions at such a time, through fear of giving offense, I should consider myself as guilty of treason towards my country, and of an act of disloyalty toward the Majesty of Heaven, which I revere above all earthly kings.

Mr President, it is natural to man to indulge in the illusions of hope. We are apt to shut our eyes against a painful truth, and listen to the song of that siren till she transforms us into beasts. Is this the part of wise men, engaged in a great and arduous struggle for liberty? Are we disposed to be of the number of those who, having eyes, see not, and, having ears, hear not, the things which so nearly concern their temporal salvation? For my part, whatever anguish of spirit it may cost, I am willing to know the whole truth; to know the worst, and to provide for it.

I have but one lamp by which my feet are guided, and that is the lamp of experience. I know of no way of judging of the future but by the past. And judging by the past, I wish to know what there has been in the conduct of the British ministry for the last ten years to justify those hopes with which gentlemen have been pleased to solace themselves and the House. Is it that insidious smile with which our petition has been lately received? Trust it not, sir; it will prove a snare to your feet. Suffer not yourselves to be betrayed with a kiss. Ask yourselves how this gracious reception of our petition comports with those warlike preparations which cover our waters and darken our land. Are fleets and armies necessary to a work of love and reconciliation? Have we shown ourselves so unwilling to be reconciled that force must be called in to win back our love? Let us not deceive ourselves, sir. These are the implements of war and subjugation; the last arguments to which kings resort. I ask gentlemen, sir, what means this martial array, if its purpose be not to force us to submission? Can gentlemen assign any other possible motive for it? Has Great Britain any enemy, in this quarter of the world, to call for all this accumulation of navies and armies? No, sir, she has none. They are meant for us: they can be meant for no other. They are sent over to bind and rivet upon us those chains which the British ministry have been so long forging. And what have we to oppose to them? Shall we try argument? Sir, we have been trying that for the last ten years. Have we anything new to offer upon the subject? Nothing. We have held the subject up in every light of which it is capable; but it has been all in vain. Shall we resort to entreaty and humble supplication? What terms shall we find which have not been already exhausted? Let us not, I beseech you, sir, deceive ourselves. Sir, we have done everything that could be done to avert the storm which is now coming on. We have petitioned; we have remonstrated; we have supplicated; we have prostrated ourselves before the throne, and have implored its interposition to arrest the tyrannical hands of the ministry and Parliament. Our petitions have been slighted; our remonstrances have produced additional violence and insult; our supplications have been disregarded; and we have been spurned, with contempt, from the foot of the throne! In vain, after these things, may we indulge the fond hope of peace and reconciliation. There is no longer any room for hope. If we wish to be free—if we mean to preserve inviolate those inestimable privileges for which we have been so long contending—if we mean not basely to abandon the noble struggle in which we have been so long engaged, and which we have pledged ourselves never to abandon until the glorious object of our contest shall be obtained—we must fight! I repeat it, sir, we must fight! An appeal to arms and to the God of hosts is all that is left us!

They tell us, sir, that we are weak; unable to cope with so formidable an adversary. But when shall we be stronger? Will it be the next week, or the next year? Will it be when we are totally disarmed, and when a British guard shall be stationed in every house? Shall we gather strength by irresolution and inaction? Shall we acquire the means of effectual resistance by lying supinely on our backs and hugging the delusive phantom of hope, until our enemies shall have bound us hand and foot? Sir, we are not weak if we make a proper use of those means which the God of nature hath placed in our power. The millions of people, armed in the holy cause of liberty, and in such a country as that which we possess, are invincible by any force which our enemy can send against us. Besides, sir, we shall not fight our battles alone. There is a just

God who presides over the destinies of nations, and who will raise up friends to fight our battles for us. The battle, sir, is not to the strong alone; it is to the vigilant, the active, the brave. Besides, sir, we have no election. If we were base enough to desire it, it is now too late to retire from the contest. There is no retreat but in submission and slavery! Our chains are forged! Their clanking may be heard on the plains of Boston! The war is inevitable—and let it come! I repeat it, sir, let it come.

It is in vain, sir, to extenuate the matter. Gentlemen may cry, Peace, Peace—but there is no peace. The war is actually begun! The next gale that sweeps from the north will bring to our ears the clash of resounding arms! Our brethren are already in the field! Why stand we here idle? What is it that gentlemen wish? What would they have? Is life so dear, or peace so sweet, as to be purchased at the price of chains and slavery? Forbid it, Almighty God! I know not what course others may take; but as for me, give me liberty or give me death!

5

NEWBURGH ADDRESS

George Washington

The 'Newburgh Address' refers to the speech George Washington gave on 15 March 1783 in Newburgh. He spoke to a gathering of military officers, who, incited by unpaid wages at the close of the Revolutionary War, were considering rebellion against the Congress. In the handwritten rendition included here, he asked the soldiers to trust him and be patient, resisting the impulse to disrupt the country's progress towards peace. Eye-witness accounts underscore how the speech moved the soldiers to tears, evoking memories of Washington's enduring commitment in the war, leading to the revolt being immediately called off.

Gentlemen,

By an anonymous summons, an attempt has been made to convene you together—how inconsistent with the rules of propriety! how unmilitary! and how subversive of all order and discipline—let the good sense of the Army decide.

In the moment of this summons, another anonymous production was sent into circulation; addressed more to the feelings & passions, than to the reason & judgment of the Army. The Author of the piece, is entitled to much credit for the goodness of his Pen: and I could wish he had as much credit for the rectitude of his Heart—for, as Men see thro' different Optics, and are induced by the reflecting faculties of the Mind, to use different means to attain the same end; the Author of the Address, should have had more charity, than to mark for Suspicion, the Man who should recommend Moderation and longer forbearance—or, in other words, who should not think as he thinks, and act as he advises. But he had another plan in view, in which candor and liberality of Sentiment, regard to justice, and love of Country, have no part; and he was right, to insinuate the darkest suspicion, to effect the blackest designs.

That the Address is drawn with great art, and is designed to answer the most insidious purposes. That it is calculated to impress the Mind, with an idea of premeditated injustice in the Sovereign power of the United States, and rouse all those resentments which must unavoidably flow from such a belief. That the secret Mover of this Scheme (whoever he may be) intended to take advantage of the passions, while they were warmed by the recollection of past distresses, without giving time for cool, deliberative thinking, & that composure of Mind which is so necessary to give dignity & stability to measures, is rendered too obvious, by the mode of conducting the business, to need other proof than a reference to the proceeding.

Thus much, Gentlemen, I have thought it incumbent on me to observe to you, to shew upon what principles I opposed the irregular and hasty meeting which was proposed to have been held on Tuesday last: and not because I wanted a disposition to give you every opportunity, consistent with your own honor, and the dignity of the Army, to make known your grievances. If my conduct heretofore, has not evinced to you, that I have been a faithful friend to the Army; my declaration of it at this time wd be equally unavailing & improper—But as I was among the first who embarked in the cause of our common Country—As I have never left your side one moment, but when called from you, on public duty—As I have been the constant companion & witness of your Distresses, and not among the last to feel, & acknowledge your Merits—As I have ever considered my own Military reputation as inseperably connected with that of the Army—As my Heart has ever expanded wth joy, when I have heard its praises—and my indignation has arisen, when the Mouth of detraction has been opened against it—it can scarcely be supposed, at this late stage of the War, that I am indifferent to its interests.

But—how are they to be promoted? The way is plain, says the anonymous Addresser—If War continues, remove into the unsettled Country—there establish yourselves, and leave an ungrateful Country to defend itself—But who are they to defend? Our Wives, our Children, our Farms and other property which we leave behind us. or—in this state of hostile seperation, are we to take the two first (the latter cannot be removed) to perish in a Wilderness, with hunger cold & nakedness? If Peace takes place, never sheath your Sword says he untill you have obtained full and ample Justice—this dreadful alternative, of either deserting our Country in the extremest hour of her distress, or turning our Army against it, (which is the apparent object, unless Congress can be compelled into an instant compliance) has something so shocking in it, that humanity revolts at the idea. My God! What can this Writer have in view, by recommending such measures? Can he be a friend to the Army? Can he be a friend to this Country? Rather, is he not an insidious Foe? Some Emissary, perhaps, from New York, plotting the ruin of both, by sowing the seeds of discord & seperation between the Civil & Military powers of the Continent? And what a Compliment does he pay to our understandings, when he recommends measures in either alternative, impracticable in their nature?

But here, Gentlemen, I will drop the curtain; because it wd be as imprudent in me to assign my reasons for this opinion, as it would be insulting to your conception, to suppose you stood in need of them. A moments reflection will convince every dispassionate Mind of the physical impossibility of carrying either proposal into execution.

There might, Gentlemen, be an impropriety in my taking notice, in this Address to you, of an anonymous production—but the manner in which that performance has been introduced to the Army—the effect it was intended to have, together with some other circumstances, will amply justify my observations on the tendency of that Writing. With respect to the advice given by the Author—to suspect the Man, who shall recommend moderate measures and longer forbearance—I spurn it—as every Man, who regards that liberty, & reveres that Justice for which we contend, undoubtedly must—for if Men are to be precluded from offering their sentiments on a matter, which may involve the most serious and alarming consequences, that can invite the consideration of Mankind; reason is of no use to us—the freedom of Speech may be taken away—and, dumb & silent we may be led, like sheep, to the Slaughter.

I cannot, in justice to my own belief, & what I have great reason to conceive is the intention of Congress, conclude this Address, without giving it as my decided opinion; that that Honble Body, entertain exalted sentiments of the Services of the Army; and, from a full conviction of its Merits & sufferings, will do it compleat Justice: That their endeavors, to discover & establish funds for this purpose, have been unwearied, and will not cease, till they have succeeded, I have not a doubt. But, like all other large Bodies, where there is a variety of different Interests to reconcile, their deliberations are slow. Why then should we distrust them? and, in consequence of that distrust, adopt measures, which may cast a shade over that glory which, has been so justly acquired; and tarnish the reputation of an Army which is celebrated thro' all Europe, for its fortitude and Patriotism? and for what is this done? to bring the object we seek for nearer? No! most certainly, in my opinion, it will cast it at a greater distance.

For myself (and I take no merit in giving the assurance, being induced to it from principles of gratitude, veracity & justice)—a grateful sence of the confidence you have ever placed in me—a recollection of the Chearful assistance, & prompt obedience I have experienced from you, under every vicisitude of Fortune, and the sincere affection I feel for an Army, I have so long had the honor to Command, will oblige me to declare, in this public & solemn manner, that, in the attainment of compleat justice for all your toils & dangers, and in the gratification of every wish, so far as may be done consistently with the great duty I owe my Country, and those powers we are bound to respect, you may freely command my services to the utmost of my abilities.

While I give you these assurances, and pledge my self in the most unequivocal manner, to exert whatever ability I am possesed of, in your favor—let me entreat you, Gentlemen, on your part, not to take any measures, which, viewed in the calm light of reason, will lessen the dignity, & sully the glory you have hitherto maintained—let me request you to rely on the plighted faith of your Country, and place a full confidence in the purity of the intentions of Congress; that, previous to your dissolution as an Army they will cause all your Accts to be fairly liquidated, as directed in their resolutions, which were published to you two days ago—and that they will adopt the most effectual measures in their power, to render ample justice to you, for your faithful and meritorious Services. And let me conjure you, in the name of our common Country—as you value your own sacred honor—as you respect the rights of humanity, & as you regard the Military & national character of America, to express your utmost horror & detestation of the Man who wishes, under any specious pretences, to overturn the liberties of our Country, & who wickedly attempts to open the flood Gates of Civil discord, & deluge our rising Empire in Blood.

By thus determining—& thus acting, you will pursue the plain & direct Road to the attainment of your wishes. You will defeat the insidious designs of our Enemies, who are compelled to resort from open force to secret Artifice. You will give one more distinguished proof of unexampled patriotism & patient virtue, rising superior to the pressure of the most complicated sufferings; And you will, by the dignity of your Conduct, afford occasion for Posterity to say, when speaking of the glorious example you have exhibited to man kind, 'had this day been wanting, the World had never seen the last stage of perfection to which human nature is capable of attaining.'

6

INAUGURAL ADDRESS

Thomas Jefferson

Thomas Jefferson delivered his first inaugural address on 4 March 1801. He was declared president after a tense election which saw the government change hands for the first time in the USA, from the Federalist Party to the Democratic-Republican Party. Unlike the two presidents before him, Jefferson chose to walk to and from the inauguration venue and donned common clothes rather than a formal suit. The moving address reflected Jefferson's humble and democratic ideals, advocating unity and harmony between the two political factions and all Americans.

Friends and fellow-citizens,

Called upon to undertake the duties of the first executive office of our country, I avail myself of the presence of that portion of my fellow-citizens which is here assembled to express my grateful thanks for the favor with which they have been pleased to look toward me, to declare a sincere consciousness that the task is above my talents, and that I approach it with those anxious and awful presentiments which the greatness of the charge and the weakness of my powers so justly inspire. A rising nation, spread over a wide and fruitful land, traversing all the seas with the rich productions of their industry, engaged in commerce with nations who feel power and forget right, advancing rapidly to destinies beyond the reach of mortal eye—when I contemplate these transcendent objects, and see the honor, the happiness and the hopes of this beloved country committed to the issue and the auspices of this day, I shrink from the contemplation, and humble myself before the magnitude of the undertaking. Utterly, indeed, should I despair did not the presence of many whom I here see remind me that in the other high authorities provided by our Constitution I shall find resources of wisdom, of virtue and of zeal on which to rely under all difficulties. To you, then, gentlemen, who are charged with the sovereign functions of legislation, and to those associated with you, I look with encouragement for that guidance and support which may enable us to steer with safety the vessel in which we are all embarked amidst the conflicting elements of a troubled world.

During the contest of opinion through which we have passed the animation of discussions and of exertions has sometimes worn an aspect which might impose on strangers unused to think freely and to speak and to write what they think; but this being now decided by the voice of the nation, announced according to the rules of the Constitution, all will, of course, arrange themselves under the will of the law, and unite in common efforts for the common good. All, too, will bear in mind this sacred principle, that though the will of the majority is in all cases to prevail, that will to be rightful must be reasonable; that the minority possess their equal rights, which equal law must protect, and to violate would be oppression. Let us, then, fellow-citizens, unite with one heart and one mind. Let us restore to social intercourse that harmony and affection without which liberty and even life itself are but dreary things. And let us reflect that, having banished from our land that religious intolerance under which mankind so long bled and suffered, we have yet gained little if we countenance a political intolerance as despotic, as wicked, and capable of as bitter and bloody persecutions. During the throes and convulsions of the ancient world, during the agonizing spasms of infuriated man, seeking through blood and slaughter his long-lost liberty, it was not wonderful that the agitation of the billows should reach even this distant and peaceful shore; that this should be more felt and feared by some and less by others, and should divide opinions as to measures of safety. But every difference of opinion is not a difference of principle. We have called by different names brethren of the same principle. We are all Republicans, we are all Federalists. If there be any among us who would wish to dissolve this Union or to change its republican form, let them stand undisturbed as monuments of the safety with which error of opinion may be tolerated where reason is left free to combat it. I know, indeed, that some honest men fear that a republican government can not be strong, that this Government is not strong enough; but would the honest patriot, in the full tide of successful experiment, abandon a government which has so far kept us free and firm on the theoretic and visionary fear that this Government, the world's best hope, may by possibility want energy to preserve itself? I trust not. I believe this, on the contrary, the strongest Government on earth. I believe it the only one where every man, at the call of the law, would fly to the standard of the law, and would meet invasions of the public order as his own personal concern. Sometimes it is said that man can not be trusted with the government of himself. Can he, then, be trusted with the government of others? Or have we found angels in the forms of kings to govern him? Let history answer this question.

Let us, then, with courage and confidence pursue our own federal and republican principles, our attachment to union and representative government. Kindly separated by nature and a wide ocean from the exterminating havoc of one quarter of the globe; too high-minded to endure the degradations of the others; possessing a chosen country, with room enough for our descendants to the thousandth and thousandth generation; entertaining a due sense of our equal right to the use of our own faculties, to the acquisitions of our own industry, to honor and confidence from our fellow-citizens, resulting not from birth, but from our actions and their sense of them; enlightened by a benign religion, professed, indeed, and practiced in various forms, yet all of them inculcating honesty, truth, temperance, gratitude and the love of man; acknowledging and adoring an overruling Providence, which by all its dispensations proves that it delights in the happiness of man here and his greater happiness hereafter—with all these blessings, what more is necessary to make us a happy and a prosperous people? Still one thing more, fellow-citizens—a wise and frugal government, which shall restrain men from injuring one another, shall leave them otherwise free to regulate their own pursuits of industry and improvement, and shall not take from the mouth of labor the bread it has earned. This is the sum of good government, and this is necessary to close the circle of our felicities.

About to enter, fellow-citizens, on the exercise of duties which comprehend everything dear and valuable to you, it is proper you should understand what I deem the essential principles of our government, and consequently those which ought to shape its administration. I will compress them within the narrowest compass they will bear, stating the general principle, but not all its limitations. Equal and exact justice to all men, of whatever state or persuasion, religious or political; peace, commerce and honest friendship with all nations, entangling alliances with none; the support of the state governments in all their rights, as the most competent administrations for our domestic concerns and the surest bulwarks against antirepublican tendencies; the preservation of the general government in its whole constitutional vigor, as the sheet anchor of our peace at home and safety abroad; a jealous care of the right of election by the people—a mild and safe corrective of abuses which are lopped by the sword of revolution where peaceable remedies are unprovided; absolute acquiescence in the decisions of the majority, the vital principle of republics, from which is no appeal but to force, the vital principle and immediate parent of despotism; a well-disciplined militia, our best reliance in peace and for the first moments of war till regulars may relieve them; the supremacy of the civil over the military authority; economy in the public expense, that labor may be lightly burthened; the honest payment of our debts and sacred preservation of the public faith;

encouragement of agriculture, and of commerce as its handmaid; the diffusion of information and arraignment of all abuses at the bar of the public reason; freedom of religion; freedom of the press, and freedom of person under the protection of the habeas corpus, and trial by juries impartially selected. These principles form the bright constellation which has gone before us and guided our steps through an age of revolution and reformation. The wisdom of our sages and blood of our heroes have been devoted to their attainment. They should be the creed of our political faith, the text of civic instruction, the touchstone by which to try the services of those we trust; and should we wander from them in moments of error or of alarm, let us hasten to retrace our steps and to regain the road which alone leads to peace, liberty and safety.

I repair, then, fellow-citizens, to the post you have assigned me. With experience enough in subordinate offices to have seen the difficulties of this the greatest of all, I have learnt to expect that it will rarely fall to the lot of imperfect man to retire from this station with the reputation and the favor which bring him into it. Without pretensions to that high confidence you reposed in our first and greatest revolutionary character, whose preeminent services had entitled him to the first place in his country's love and destined for him the fairest page in the volume of faithful history, I ask so much confidence only as may give firmness and effect to the legal administration of your affairs. I shall often go wrong through defect of judgment. When right, I shall often be thought wrong by those whose positions will not command a view of the whole ground. I ask your indulgence for my own errors, which will never be intentional, and your support against the errors of others, who may condemn what they would not if seen in all its parts. The approbation implied by your suffrage is a great consolation to me for the past, and my future solicitude will be to retain the good opinion of those who have bestowed it in advance, to conciliate that of others by doing them all the good in my power, and to be instrumental to the happiness and freedom of all.

Relying, then, on the patronage of your good will, I advance with obedience to the work, ready to retire from it whenever you become sensible how much better choice it is in your power to make. And may that Infinite Power which rules the destinities of the universe lead our councils to what is best, and give them a favorable issue for your peace and prosperity.

7

OF FREE ENQUIRY

Frances Wright

'Of Free Enquiry' is a speech delivered by Frances Wright, a Scottish-American social reformer, feminist and abolitionist, in 1829. This speech serves as a powerful testament to Wright's commitment to intellectual freedom, critical thinking and the pursuit of truth.

There is a common error that I feel myself called upon to notice; nor know I the country in which it is more prevalent than in this. Whatever indifference may generally prevail among men, still there are many eager for the acquisition of knowledge; willing to enquire, and anxious to base their opinions upon correct principles. In the curiosity which motives their exertions, however, the vital principle is but too often wanting. They come selfishly, and not generously, to the tree of knowledge. They eat, but care not to impart of the fruit to others. Nay, there are who, having leaped the briar fence of prejudice themselves, will heap new thorns in the way of those who would venture the same...

But will this imputation startle my hearers? Will they say, America is the home of liberty, and Americans brethren in equality. Is it so? and may we not ask here, as elsewhere, how many are there, not anxious to monopolize, but to universalize knowledge? How many, that consider their own improvement in relation always with that of their fellow beings, and who feel the imparting of truth to be not a work of supererogation, but a duty; the withholding it, not a venial omission, but a treachery to the race. Which of us have not seen fathers of families pursuing investigations themselves, which they hide from their sons, and, more especially, from their wives and daughters? As if truth could be of less importance to the young than to the old; or as if the sex which in all ages has ruled the destinies of the world, could be less worth enlightening than that which only follows its lead!

The observation I have hazarded may require some explanation. Those who arrogate power usually think themselves superior de facto and de jure. Yet justly might it be made a question whether those who ostensibly govern are not always unconsciously led. Should we examine closely into the state of things, we might find that, in all countries, the governed decide the destinies of the governors, more than the governors those of the governed; even as the labouring classes influence more directly the fortunes of a nation than does the civil officer, the aspiring statesman, the rich capitalist or the speculative philosopher.

However novel it may appear, I shall venture the assertion, that, until women assume the place in society which good sense and good feeling alike assign to them, human improvement must advance but feebly. It is in vain that we would circumscribe the power of one half of our race, and that half by far the most important and influential. If they exert it not for good, they will for evil; if they advance not knowledge, they will perpetuate ignorance. Let women stand where they may in the scale of improvement, their position decides that of the race. Are they cultivated?—so is society polished and enlightened. Are they ignorant?—so is it gross and insipid. Are they wise?—so is the human condition prosperous. Are they foolish?—so is it unstable and unpromising. Are they free?—so is the human character elevated. Are they enslaved?—so is the whole race degraded...

...It is my object to show, that, before we can engage successfully in the work of enquiry, we must engage in a body; we must engage collectively; as human beings desirous of attaining the highest excellence of which our nature is capable; as children of one family, anxious to discover the true and the useful for the common advantage of all. It is my farther object to show that no co-operation in this matter can be effective which does not embrace the two sexes on a footing of equality; and, again, that no co-operation in this matter can be effective, which does not embrace human beings on a footing of equality. Is this a republic—a country whose affairs are governed by the public voice—while the public mind is unequally enlightened? Is this a republic, where the interests of the many keep in check those of the few—while the few hold possession of the courts of knowledge, and the many stand as suitors at the door? Is this a republic, where the rights of all are equally respected, the interests of all equally secured, the ambitions of all equally regulated, the services of all equally rendered? Is this such a republic—while we see endowed colleges for the rich, and barely common schools for the poor; while but one drop of colored blood shall stamp a fellow creature for a slave, or, at the least, degrade him below sympathy; and while one half of the whole population is left in civil bondage, and, as it were, sentenced to mental imbecility?

Let us pause to enquire if this be consistent with the being of a republic. Without knowledge, could your fathers have conquered liberty? and without knowledge, can you retain it? Equality! where is it, if not in education? Equal rights! they cannot exist without equality of instruction. 'All men are born free and equal!' they are indeed so born, but do they so live? Are they educated as equals? and, if not, can they be equal? and, if not equal, can they be free? Do not the rich command instruction? and they who have instruction, must they not possess the power? and when they have the power, will they not exert it in their own favor? I will ask more; I will ask, do they not exert it in their own favor? I will ask if two professions do not now rule the land and its inhabitants? I will ask, whether your legislatures are not governed by lawyers and your households by priests? And I will farther ask, whether the deficient instruction of the mass of your population does not give to lawyers their political ascendancy; and whether the ignorance of women be not the cause that your domestic hearths are invaded by priests?...

...Your political institutions have taken equality for their basis; your declaration of rights, upon which your institutions rest, sets forth this principle as vital and inviolate. Equality is the soul of liberty; there is, in fact, no liberty without it—none that cannot be overthrown by the violence of ignorant anarchy, or sapped by the subtilty of professional craft. That this is the case your reasons will admit; that this is the case your feelings do admit—even those which are the least amiable and the least praiseworthy. The jealousy betrayed by the uncultivated against those of more polished address and manners, has its source in the beneficial principle to which we advert, however, (in this, as in many other cases,) misconceived and perverted. Cultivation of mind will ever lighten the countenance and polish the exterior. This external superiority, which is but a faint emanation of the superiority within, vulgar eyes can see and ignorant jealousy will resent. This, in a republic, leads to brutality; and, in aristocracies, where this jealously is restrained by fear, to servility. Here it will lead the wagoner to dispute the road with a carriage; and, in Europe, will make the foot passenger doff his hat to the lordly equipage which spatters him with mud, while there he mutters curses only in his heart. The unreasoning observer will refer the conduct of the first to the republican institutions—the reflecting observer, to the anti-republican education. The instruction befitting free men is that which gives the sun of knowledge to shine on all; and which at once secures the liberties of each individual, and disposes each individual to make a proper use of them.

Equality, then, we have shown to have its seat in the mind. A proper cultivation of the faculties would ensure a sufficiency of that equality for all the ends of republican government, and for all the modes of social enjoyment. The diversity in the natural powers of different minds, as decided by physical organization, would be then only a source of interest and agreeable variety. All would be capable of appreciating the peculiar powers of each; and each would perceive that his interests, well understood, were in unison with the interests of all. Let us now examine whether liberty, properly interpreted, does not involve, among your unalienable rights as citizens and human beings, the right of equal means of instruction.

Have ye given a pledge, sealed with the blood of your fathers, for the equal rights of all human kind sheltered within your confines? What means the pledge? or what understand ye by human rights? But understand them as ye will, define them as ye will, how are men to be secured in any rights without instruction? how to be secured in the equal exercise of those rights without equality of instruction? By instruction understand me to mean, knowledge—just knowledge; not talent, not genius, not inventive mental powers. These will vary in every human being; but knowledge is the same for every mind, and every mind may and ought to be trained to receive it. If, then, ye have pledged, at each anniversary of your political independence, your lives, properties and honor, to the securing your common liberties, ye have pledged your lives, properties and honor, to the securing of your common instruction. Or will you secure the end without securing the means? ye shall do it, when ye reap the harvest without planting the seed...

All men are born free and equal! That is: our moral feelings acknowledge it to be just and proper, that we respect those liberties in others, which we lay claim to for ourselves; and that we permit the free agency of every individual, to any extent which violates not the free agency of his fellow creatures.

There is but one honest limit to the rights of a sentient being; it is where they touch the rights of another sentient being. Do we exert our own liberties without injury to others—we exert them justly; do we exert them at the expense of others—unjustly. And, in thus doing, we step from the sure platform of liberty upon the uncertain threshold of tyranny. Small is the step; to the unreflecting so imperceptibly small, that they take it every hour of their lives as thoughtlessly as they do it unfeelingly...

Who among us but has had occasion to remark the ill-judged,

however well intentioned government of children by their teachers; and, yet more especially, by their parents? In what does this mismanagement originate? In a misconception of the relative position of the parent or guardian, and of the child; in a departure, by the parent, from the principle of liberty, in his assumption of rights destructive of those of the child; in his exercise of authority, as by right divine, over the judgment, actions and person of the child; in his forgetfulness of the character of the child, as a human being, born 'free and equal' among his compeers; that is, having equal claims to the exercise and development of all his senses, faculties and powers, with those who brought him into existence, and with all sentient beings who tread the earth. Were a child thus viewed by his parent, we should not see him, by turns, made a plaything and a slave; we should not see him commanded to believe, but encouraged to reason; we should not see him trembling under the rod, nor shrinking from a frown, but reading the wishes of others in the eye, gathering knowledge wherever he threw his glance, rejoicing in the present hour and treasuring up sources of enjoyment for future years. We should not then see the youth launching into life without compass or quadrant. We should not see him doubting at each emergency how to act, shifting his course with the shifting wind, and, at last, making shipwreck of mind and body on the sunken rocks of hazard and dishonest speculation, nor on the foul quicksands of debasing licentiousness.

What, then, has the parent to do, if he would conscientiously discharge that most sacred of all duties, that weightiest of all responsibilities, which ever did or ever will devolve on a human being? What is he to do, who, having brought a creature into existence, endowed with varied faculties, with tender susceptibilities, capable of untold wretchedness or equally of unconceived enjoyment; what is he to do, that he may secure the happiness of that creature, and make the life he has given blessing and blessed, instead of cursing and cursed? What is he to do?—he is to encourage in his child a spirit of enquiry, and equally to encourage it in himself. He is never to advance an opinion without showing the facts upon which it is grounded; he is never to assert a fact, without proving it to be a fact. He is not to teach a code of morals any more than a creed of doctrines; but he is to direct his young charge to observe the consequences of actions on himself and on others; and to judge of the propriety of those actions by their ascertained consequences. He is not to command his feelings any more than his opinions or his actions; but he is to assist him in the analysis of his feelings, in the examination of their nature, their tendencies, their effects. Let him do this, and have no anxiety for the result. In the free exercise of his senses, in the fair development of his faculties, in a course of simple and unrestrained enquiry, he will discover truth, for he will ascertain facts; he will seize upon virtue, for he will have distinguished beneficial from injurious actions; he will cultivate kind, generous, just and honourable feelings, for he will have proved them to contribute to his own happiness and to shed happiness around him.

Who, then, shall say, enquiry is good for him and not good for his children? Who shall cast error from himself, and allow it to be grafted on the minds he has called into being? Who shall break the chains of his own ignorance, and fix them, through his descendants, on his race? But, there are some who, as parents, make one step in duty, and halt at the second. We see men who will aid the instruction of their sons, and condemn only their daughters to ignorance. 'Our sons,' they say, 'will have to exercise political rights, may aspire to public offices, may fill some learned profession, may struggle for wealth and acquire it. It is well that we give them a helping hand; that we assist them to such knowledge as is going, and make them as sharp witted as their neighbors. But for our daughters,' they say—if indeed respecting them they say any thing—'for our daughters, little trouble or expense is necessary. They can never be any thing; in fact, they are nothing. We had best give them up to their mothers, who may take them to Sunday's preaching; and, with the aid of a little music, a little dancing and a few fine gowns, fit them out for the market of marriage.'

Am I severe? It is not my intention. I know that I am honest, and I fear that I am correct. Should I offend, however I may regret, I shall not repent it; satisfied to incur displeasure, so that I render service.

But to such parents I would observe, that with regard to their sons, as to their daughters, they are about equally mistaken. If it be their duty, as we have seen, to respect in their children the same natural liberties which they cherish for themselves—if it be their duty to aid as guides, not to dictate as teachers—to lend assistance to the reason, not to command its prostration,—then have they nothing to do with the blanks or the prizes in store for them, in the wheel of worldly fortune. Let possibilities be what they may in favor of their sons, they have no calculations to make on them. It is not for them to ordain their sons magistrates nor statesmen; nor yet even lawyers, physicians or merchants. They have only to improve the one character which they receive at the birth. They have only to consider them as human beings, and to ensure them the fair and thorough development of all the faculties, physical, mental and moral, which distinguish their nature. In like manner, as respects their daughters, they have nothing to do with the injustice of laws, nor the absurdities of society. Their duty is plain, evident, decided. In a daughter they have in charge a human being; in a son, the same. Let them train up these human beings, under the expanded wings of liberty. Let them seek for them and with them just knowledge; encouraging, from the cradle upwards, that useful curiosity which will lead them unbidden in the paths of free enquiry; and place them, safe and superior to the storms of life, in the security of well regulated, self-possessed minds, well grounded, well reasoned, conscientious opinions and self-approved, consistent practice.

I have as yet, in this important matter, addressed myself only to the reason and moral feelings of my audience; I could speak also to their interests. Easy were it to show, that in proportion as your children are enlightened, will they prove blessings to society and ornaments to their race. But if this be true of all, it is more especially true of the now more neglected half of the species. Were it only in our power to enlighten part of the rising generation, and should the interests of the whole decide our choice of the portion, it were the females, and not the males, we should select. When, now a twelvemonth since, the friends of liberty and science pointed out to me, in London, the walls of the rising university, I observed, with a smile, that they were beginning at the wrong end: 'Raise such an edifice for your young women, and ye have enlightened the nation.' It has already been observed, that women, wherever placed, however high or low in the scale of cultivation, hold the destinies of humankind. Men will ever rise or fall to the level of the other sex; and from some causes in their conformation, we find them, however armed with power or enlightened with knowledge, still held in leading strings even by the least cultivated female. Surely, then, if they knew their interests, they would desire the improvement of those who, if they do not advantage, will injure them; who, if they elevate not their minds and meliorate not their hearts, will debase the one and harden the other; and who, if they endear not existence, most assuredly will dash it with poison. How many, how omnipotent are the interests which engage men to break the mental chains of women! How many, how dear are the interests which engage them to exalt rather than lower their condition, to multiply their solid acquirements, to respect their liberties, to make them their equals, to wish them even their superiors! Let them enquire into these things. Let them examine the relation in which the two sexes stand, and ever must stand, to each other. Let them perceive, that, mutually dependent, they must ever be giving and receiving, or they must be losing;—receiving or losing in knowledge, in virtue, in enjoyment. Let them perceive how immense the loss, or how immense the gain. Let them not imagine that they know aught of the delights which intercourse with the other sex can give, until they have felt the sympathy of mind with mind, and heart with heart; until they bring into that intercourse every affection, every talent, every confidence, every refinement, every respect. Until power is annihilated on one side, fear and obedience on the other, and both restored to their birthright—equality. Let none think that affection can reign without it; or friendship, or esteem. Jealousies, envyings, suspicions, reserves, deceptions—these are the fruits of inequality. Go, then! and remove the evil first from the minds of women, then from their condition, and then from your laws. Think it no longer indifferent whether the mothers of the rising generation are wise or foolish...

There is a vulgar persuasion, that the ignorance of women, by favoring their subordination, ensures their utility. 'Tis the same argument employed by the ruling few against the subject many in aristocracies; by the rich against the poor in democracies; by the learned professions against the people in all countries. And let us observe, that if good in one case, it should be good in all; and that, unless you are prepared to admit that you are yourselves less industrious in proportion to your intelligence, you must abandon the position with respect to others. But, in fact, who is it among men that best struggle with difficulties?—the strong minded or the weak? Who meet with serenity adverse fortune?—the wise or the foolish? Who accommodate themselves to irremediable circumstances? or, when remediable, who control and mould them at will?—the intelligent or the ignorant? Let your answer in your own case, be your answer in that of women...

Let us understand what knowledge is. Let us clearly perceive that accurate knowledge regards all equally; that truth, or fact, is the same thing for all human-kind; that there are not truths for the rich and truths for the poor, truths for men and truths for women; there are simply truths, that is, facts, which all who open their eyes and their ears and their understandings can perceive.

There is no mystery in these facts. There is no witchcraft in knowledge. Science is not a trick; not a puzzle. The philosopher is not a conjuror. The observer of nature who envelopes his discoveries in mystery, either knows less than he pretends, or feels interested in withholding his knowledge. The teacher whose lessons are difficult of comprehension, is either clumsy or he is dishonest.

We observed...that it was the evident interest of our appointed teachers to disguise the truth. We discovered this to be a matter of necessity, arising out of their dependence upon the public favor. We may observe yet another cause, now operating far and wide—universally, omnipotently—a cause pervading the whole mass of society, and springing out of the existing motive principle of human action—competition. Let us examine, and we shall discover it to be the object of each individual to obscure the first elements of the knowledge he professes—be that knowledge mechanical and operative, or intellectual and passive. It is thus that we see the simple manufacture of a pair of shoes magnified into an art, demanding a seven years apprenticeship, when all its intricacies might be mastered in as many months. It is thus that cutting out a coat after just proportions is made to involve more science, and to demand more study, than the anatomy of the body it is to cover. And it is thus, in like manner, that all the branches of knowledge, involved in what is called scholastic learning, are wrapped in the fogs of pompous pedantry; and that every truth, instead of being presented in naked innocence, is obscured under a weight of elaborate words, and lost and buried in a medley of irrelevant ideas, useless amplifications and erroneous arguments. Would we unravel this confusion—would we distinguish the true from the false, the real from the unreal, the useful from the useless—would we break our mental leading strings—would we know the uses of all our faculties—would we be virtuous, happy and intelligent beings—would we be useful in our generation—would we possess our own minds in peace, be secure in our opinions, be just in our feelings, be consistent in our practice—would we command the respect of others, and—far better—would we secure our own—let us enquire.

Let us enquire! What mighty consequences, are involved in these little words! Whither have they not led? To what are they not yet destined to lead? Before them thrones have given way. Hierarchies have fallen, dungeons have disclosed their secrets. Iron bars, and iron laws, and more iron prejudices, have given way; the prison house of the mind hath burst its fetters; science disclosed her treasures; truth her moral beauties; and civil liberty, sheathing her conquering sword, hath prepared her to sit down in peace at the feet of knowledge...

Did the knowledge of each individual embrace all the discoveries made by science, all the truths extracted by philosophy from the combined experience of ages, still would enquiry be in its infancy, improvement in its dawn. Perfection for man is in no time, in no place. The law of his being, like that of the earth he inhabits, is to move always, to stop never. From the earliest annals of tradition, his movement has been in advance. The tide of his progress hath had ebbs and flows, but hath left a thousand marks by which to note its silent but tremendous influx...

If this be so—and who that looks abroad shall gainsay the assertion?—if this be so—and who that looks to your jails, to your penitentiaries, to your houses of refuge, to your hospitals, to your asylums, to your hovels of wretchedness, to your haunts of intemperance, to your victims lost in vice and hardened in profligacy, to childhood without protection, to youth without guidance, to the widow without sustenance, to the female destitute and female outcast, sentenced to shame and sold to degradation—who that looks to these shall say, that enquiry hath not a world to explore, and improvement yet a world to reform!

8

AIN'T I A WOMAN?

Sojourner Truth

'Ain't I a Woman?' is a famous speech delivered by Sojourner Truth, a prominent African American abolitionist and women's rights activist, during the Women's Rights Convention in Akron, Ohio, in 1851. In her speech, Sojourner Truth advocated for the equal rights of women, particularly African American women who faced intersecting challenges of racism and sexism. She addressed the prevailing arguments at the time that women were weak and needed to be protected, asserting her own strength and resilience as a woman and as a former slave.

Well, children, where there is so much racket there must be something out of kilter. I think that 'twixt the Negroes of the South and the women at the North, all talking about rights, the white men will be in a fix pretty soon. But what's all this here talking about?

That man over there says that women need to be helped into carriages, and lifted over ditches, and to have the best place everywhere. Nobody ever helps me into carriages, or over mud-puddles, or gives me any best place! And ain't I a woman? Look at me! Look at my arm! I have ploughed and planted, and gathered into barns, and no man could head me! And ain't I a woman? I could work as much and eat as much as a man—when I could get it—and bear the lash as well! And ain't I a woman? I have borne thirteen children, and seen most all sold off to slavery, and when I cried out with my mother's grief, none but Jesus heard me! And ain't I a woman?

Then they talk about this thing in the head; what's this they call it? [member of audience whispers, 'intellect'] That's it, honey. What's that got to do with women's rights or Negroes' rights? If my cup won't hold but a pint, and yours holds a quart, wouldn't you be mean not to let me have my little half measure full?

Then that little man in black there, he says women can't have as much rights as men, 'cause Christ wasn't a woman! Where did your Christ come from? Where did your Christ come from? From God and a woman! Man had nothing to do with Him.

If the first woman God ever made was strong enough to turn the world upside down all alone, these women together ought to be able to turn it back, and get it right side up again! And now they is asking to do it, the men better let them.

Obliged to you for hearing me, and now old Sojourner ain't got nothing more to say.

9

WHAT TO THE AMERICAN SLAVE IS THE FOURTH OF JULY?

Frederick Douglass

'What to the American Slave is the Fourth of July?' is a speech delivered by Frederick Douglass, an African American abolitionist and former slave, on 5 July 1852. This powerful and provocative excerpt from the speech challenges the hypocrisy and injustice of celebrating American independence while millions of African Americans remained enslaved.

Fellow citizens, pardon me, and allow me to ask, why am I called upon to speak here today? What have I or those I represent to do with your national independence? Are the great principles of political freedom and of natural justice, embodied in that Declaration of Independence, extended to us? And am I, therefore, called upon to bring our humble offering to the national altar, and to confess the benefits, and express devout gratitude for the blessings resulting from your independence to us?

Would to God, both for your sakes and ours, that an affirmative answer could be truthfully returned to these questions. Then would my task be light, and my burden easy and delightful. For who is there so cold that a nation's sympathy could not warm him? Who so obdurate and dead to the claims of gratitude, that would not thankfully acknowledge such priceless benefits? Who so stolid and selfish that would not give his voice to swell the hallelujahs of a nation's jubilee, when the chains of servitude had been torn from his limbs? I am not that man. In a case like that, the dumb might eloquently speak, and the 'lame man leap as an hart.' But such is not the state of the case. I say it with a sad sense of disparity between us. I am not included within the pale of this glorious anniversary! Your high independence only reveals the immeasurable distance between us. The blessings in which you this day rejoice are not enjoyed in common. The rich inheritance of justice, liberty, prosperity, and independence bequeathed by your fathers is shared by you, not by me. The sunlight that brought life and healing to you has brought stripes and death to me. This Fourth of July is yours, not mine. You may rejoice, I must mourn. To drag a man in fetters into the grand illuminated temple of liberty, and call upon him to join you in joyous anthems, were inhuman mockery and sacrilegious irony. Do you mean, citizens, to mock me, by asking me to speak today? If so, there is a parallel to your conduct. And let me warn you, that it is dangerous to copy the example of a nation (Babylon) whose crimes, towering up to heaven, were thrown down by the breath of the Almighty, burying that nation in irrecoverable ruin.

Fellow citizens, above your national, tumultuous joy, I hear the mournful wail of millions, whose chains, heavy and grievous yesterday, are today rendered more intolerable by the jubilant shouts that reach them. If I do forget, if I do not remember those bleeding children of sorrow this day, 'may my right hand forget her cunning, and may my tongue cleave to the roof of my mouth!'

To forget them, to pass lightly over their wrongs and to chime in with the popular theme would be treason most scandalous and shocking, and would make me a reproach before God and the world.

My subject, then, fellow citizens, is 'American Slavery.' I shall see this day and its popular characteristics from the slave's point of view. Standing here, identified with the American bondman, making his wrongs mine, I do not hesitate to declare, with all my soul, that the character and conduct of this nation never looked blacker to me than on this Fourth of July.

Whether we turn to the declarations of the past, or to the professions of the present, the conduct of the nation seems equally hideous and revolting. America is false to the past, false to the present and solemnly binds herself to be false to the future. Standing with God and the crushed and bleeding slave on this occasion, I will, in the name of humanity, which is outraged, in the name of liberty, which is fettered, in the name of the Constitution and the Bible, which are disregarded and trampled upon, dare to call in question and to denounce, with all the emphasis I can command, everything that serves to perpetuate slavery—the great sin and shame of America! 'I will not equivocate—I will not excuse.' I will use the severest language I can command, and yet not one word shall escape me that any man, whose judgment is not blinded by prejudice, or who is not at heart a slave-holder, shall not confess to be right and just.

But I fancy I hear some of my audience say it is just in this circumstance that you and your brother Abolitionists fail to make a favorable impression on the public mind. Would you argue more and denounce less, would you persuade more and rebuke less, your cause would be much more likely to succeed. But, I submit, where all is plain there is nothing to be argued. What point in the anti-slavery creed would you have me argue? On what branch of the subject do the people of this country need light? Must I undertake to prove that the slave is a man? That point is conceded already. Nobody doubts it. The slave-holders themselves acknowledge it in the enactment of laws for their government. They acknowledge it when they punish disobedience on the part of the slave. There are 72 crimes in the State of Virginia, which, if committed by a black man (no matter how ignorant he be), subject him to the punishment of death; while only two of these same crimes will subject a white man to like punishment.

What is this but the acknowledgment that the slave is a moral, intellectual and responsible being? The manhood of the slave is conceded. It is admitted in the fact that Southern statute books are covered with enactments, forbidding, under severe fines and penalties, the teaching of the slave to read and write. When you can point to any such laws in reference to the beasts of the field, then I may consent to argue the manhood of the slave. When the dogs in your streets, when the fowls of the air, when the cattle on your hills, when the fish of the sea, and the reptiles that crawl, shall be unable to distinguish the slave from a brute, then I will argue with you that the slave is a man!

For the present it is enough to affirm the equal manhood of the Negro race. Is it not astonishing that, while we are plowing, planting, and reaping, using all kinds of mechanical tools, erecting houses, constructing bridges, building ships, working in metals of brass, iron, copper, silver and gold; that while we are reading, writing and ciphering, acting as clerks, merchants and secretaries, having among us lawyers, doctors, ministers, poets, authors, editors, orators and teachers; that we are engaged in all the enterprises common to other men—digging gold in California, capturing the whale in the Pacific, feeding sheep and cattle on the hillside, living, moving, acting, thinking, planning, living in families as husbands, wives and children, and above all, confessing and worshipping the Christian God and looking hopefully for life and immortality beyond the grave—we are called upon to prove that we are men?

Would you have me argue that man is entitled to liberty? That he is the rightful owner of his own body? You have already declared it. Must I argue the wrongfulness of slavery? Is that a question for republicans? Is it to be settled by the rules of logic and argumentation, as a matter beset with great difficulty, involving a doubtful application of the principle of justice, hard to understand? How should I look today in the presence of Americans, dividing and subdividing a discourse, to show that men have a natural right to freedom, speaking of it relatively and positively, negatively and affirmatively? To do so would be to make myself ridiculous, and to offer an insult to your understanding. There is not a man beneath the canopy of heaven who does not know that slavery is wrong for him.

What! Am I to argue that it is wrong to make men brutes, to rob them of their liberty, to work them without wages, to keep them ignorant of their relations to their fellow men, to beat them with sticks, to flay their flesh with the lash, to load their limbs with irons, to hunt them with dogs, to sell them at auction, to sunder their families, to knock out their teeth, to burn their flesh, to starve them into obedience and submission to their masters? Must I argue that a system thus marked with blood and stained with pollution is wrong? No—I will not. I have better employment for my time and strength than such arguments would imply.

What, then, remains to be argued? Is it that slavery is not divine; that God did not establish it; that our doctors of divinity are mistaken? There is blasphemy in the thought. That which is inhuman cannot be divine. Who can reason on such a proposition? They that can, may—I cannot. The time for such argument is past.

At a time like this, scorching irony, not convincing argument, is needed. Oh! Had I the ability, and could I reach the nation's ear, I would today pour out a fiery stream of biting ridicule, blasting reproach, withering sarcasm and stern rebuke. For it is not light that is needed, but fire; it is not the gentle shower, but thunder. We need the storm, the whirlwind and the earthquake. The feeling of the nation must be quickened; the conscience of the nation must be roused; the propriety of the nation must be startled; the hypocrisy of the nation must be exposed; and its crimes against God and man must be denounced.

What to the American slave is your Fourth of July? I answer, a day that reveals to him more than all other days of the year, the gross injustice and cruelty to which he is the constant victim. To him your celebration is a sham; your boasted liberty an unholy license; your national greatness, swelling vanity; your sounds of rejoicing are empty and heartless; your shouts of liberty and equality, hollow mock; your prayers and hymns, your sermons and thanks givings, with all your religious parade and solemnity, are to him mere bombast, fraud, deception, impiety and hypocrisy—a thin veil to cover up crimes which would disgrace a nation of savages. There is not a nation of the earth guilty of practices more shocking and bloody than are the people of these United States at this very hour.

Go search where you will, roam through all the monarchies and despotisms of the Old World, travel through South America, search out every abuse and when you have found the last, lay your facts by the side of the everyday practices of this nation, and you will say with me that, for revolting barbarity and shameless hypocrisy, America reigns without a rival.

10

GETTYSBURG ADDRESS

Abraham Lincoln

The Gettysburg Address is a famous speech delivered by President Abraham Lincoln during the American Civil War. Lincoln gave the speech on 19 November 1863, at the dedication of the Soldiers' National Cemetery in Gettysburg, Pennsylvania, where one of the bloodiest battles of the war had taken place several months earlier. The speech is considered one of the most iconic speeches in American history and is known for its brevity and powerful message. It lasted only about two minutes and consisted of just 272 words. Despite its short length, the Gettysburg Address encapsulates the principles of human equality and the significance of the Civil War in a profound manner.

Four score and seven years ago our fathers brought forth on this continent a new nation, conceived in liberty, and dedicated to the proposition that all men are created equal.

Now we are engaged in a great civil war, testing whether that nation, or any nation so conceived and so dedicated, can long endure. We are met on a great battlefield of that war. We have come to dedicate a portion of that field as a final resting place for those who here gave their lives that that nation might live. It is altogether fitting and proper that we should do this.

But in a larger sense we cannot dedicate, we cannot consecrate, we cannot hallow this ground. The brave men, living and dead, who struggled here have consecrated it, far above our poor power to add or detract. The world will little note, nor long remember, what we say here, but it can never forget what they did here. It is for us the living, rather, to be dedicated here to the unfinished work which they who fought here have thus far so nobly advanced. It is rather for us to be here dedicated to the great task remaining before us, that from these honored dead we take increased devotion to that cause for which they gave the last full measure of devotion, that we here highly resolve that these dead shall not have died in vain, that this nation, under God, shall have a new birth of freedom, and that government of the people, by the people, for the people, shall not perish from the earth.

11

IS IT A CRIME TO VOTE?

Susan Brownell Anthony

'Is It a Crime to Vote?' is a speech delivered by Susan B. Anthony, a prominent American suffragist and women's rights activist, in 1873. This speech reflects Anthony's unwavering commitment to fighting for women's suffrage and her willingness to challenge societal norms and laws that denied women the right to vote.

Friends and fellow citizens:

I stand before you tonight under indictment for the alleged crime of having voted at the last presidential election, without having a lawful right to vote. It shall be my work this evening to prove to you that in thus voting, I not only committed no crime, but, instead, simply exercised my citizen's rights, guaranteed to me and all United States citizens by the National Constitution, beyond the power of any state to deny.

The preamble of the Federal Constitution says:

'We, the people of the United States, in order to form a more perfect union, establish justice, insure domestic tranquillity, provide for the common defence, promote the general welfare, and secure the blessings of liberty to ourselves and our posterity, do ordain and establish this Constitution for the United States of America.'

It was we, the people; not we, the white male citizens; nor yet we, the male citizens; but we, the whole people, who formed the Union. And we formed it, not to give the blessings of liberty, but to secure them; not to the half of ourselves and the half of our posterity, but to the whole people—women as well as men. And it is a downright mockery to talk to women of their enjoyment of the blessings of liberty while they are denied the use of the only means of securing them provided by this democratic-republican government—the ballot.

For any state to make sex a qualification that must ever result in the disfranchisement of one entire half of the people, is to pass a bill of attainder, or, an ex post facto law, and is therefore a violation of the supreme law of the land. By it the blessings of liberty are forever withheld from women and their female posterity.

To them this government has no just powers derived from the consent of the governed. To them this government is not a democracy. It is not a republic. It is an odious aristocracy; a hateful oligarchy of sex; the most hateful aristocracy ever established on the face of the globe; an oligarchy of wealth, where the rich govern the poor. An oligarchy of learning, where the educated govern the ignorant, or even an oligarchy of race, where the Saxon rules the African, might be endured; but this oligarchy of sex, which makes father, brothers, husband, sons, the oligarchs over the mother and sisters, the wife and daughters, of every household, which ordains all men sovereigns, all women subjects, carries dissension, discord, and rebellion into every home of the nation.

Webster, Worcester and Bouvier all define a citizen to be a person in the United States, entitled to vote and hold office.

The only question left to be settled now is: Are women persons? And I hardly believe any of our opponents will have the hardihood to say they are not. Being persons, then, women are citizens; and no state has a right to make any law, or to enforce any old law, that shall abridge their privileges or immunities. Hence, every discrimination against women in the constitutions and laws of the several states is today null and void, precisely as is every one against Negroes.

12

THE DEATH KNELL OF FANATICISM

Swami Vivekananda

During 11–27 September 1893, Swami Vivekananda delivered six addresses at the World's Parliament of Religions in Chicago. Presented here are his initial and concluding addresses, which posit religious harmony and universal tolerance as the beacons of hope in a world torn by bigotry and fanaticism.

Welcome Session Address

Sisters and Brothers of America,

It fills my heart with joy unspeakable to rise in response to the warm and cordial welcome which you have given us. I thank you in the name of the most ancient order of monks in the world; I thank you in the name of the mother of religions; and I thank you in the name of the millions and millions of Hindu people of all classes and sects.

My thanks, also, to some of the speakers on this platform who, referring to the delegates from the Orient, have told you that these men from far-off nations may well claim the honour of bearing to different lands the idea of toleration. I am proud to belong to a religion which has taught the world both tolerance and universal acceptance. We believe not only in universal toleration, but we accept all religions as true. I am proud to belong to a nation which has sheltered the persecuted and the refugees of all religions and all nations of the earth. I am proud to tell you that we have gathered in our bosom the purest remnant of the Israelites, who came to southern India and took refuge with us in the very year in which their holy temple was shattered to pieces by Roman tyranny. I am proud to belong to the religion which has sheltered and is still fostering the remnant of the grand Zoroastrian nation. I will quote to you, brethren, a few lines from a hymn which I remember to have repeated from my earliest boyhood, which is every day repeated by millions of human beings: 'As the different streams having their sources in different places all mingle their water in the sea, so, O Lord, the different paths which men take through different tendencies, various though they appear, crooked or straight, all lead to Thee.'

The present convention, which is one of the most august assemblies ever held, is in itself a vindication, a declaration to the world, of the wonderful doctrine preached in the Gita: 'Whosoever comes to Me, through whatsoever form, I reach him; all men are struggling through paths which in the end lead to Me.' Sectarianism, bigotry and its horrible descendant, fanaticism, have long possessed this beautiful earth. They have filled the earth with violence, drenched it often and often with human blood, destroyed civilization and sent whole nations to despair. Had it not been for these horrible demons, human society would be far more advanced than it is now. But their time is come; and I fervently hope that the bell that tolled this morning in honour of this convention may be the death-knell of all fanaticism, of all persecutions with the sword or with the pen, and of all uncharitable feelings between persons wending their way to the same goal.

Final Session Address

The World's Parliament of Religions has become an accomplished fact, and the merciful Father has helped those who laboured to bring it into existence, and crowned with success their most unselfish labour.

My thanks to those noble souls whose large hearts and love of truth first dreamed this wonderful dream and then realized it. My thanks to the shower of liberal sentiments that has overflowed this platform. My thanks to this enlightened audience for their uniform kindness to me and for their appreciation of every thought that tends to smooth the friction of religions. A few jarring notes were heard from time to time in this harmony. My special thanks to them, for they have, by their striking contrast, made the general harmony the sweeter.

Much has been said of the common ground of religious unity. I am not going just now to venture my own theory. But if anyone here hopes that this unity will come by the triumph of any one of the religions and the destruction of the others, to him I say, 'Brother, yours is an impossible hope.' Do I wish that the Christian would become Hindu? God forbid. Do I wish that the Hindu or Buddhist would become Christian? God forbid.

The seed is put in the ground, and earth and air and water are placed around it. Does the seed become the earth, or the air, or the water? No. It becomes a plant, it develops after the law of its own growth, assimilates the air, the earth, and the water, converts them into plant substance, and grows into a plant.

Similar is the case with religion. The Christian is not to become a Hindu or a Buddhist, nor a Hindu or a Buddhist to become a Christian. But each must assimilate the spirit of the others and yet preserve his individuality and grow according to his own law of growth.

If the Parliament of Religions has shown anything to the world it is this: it has proved to the world that holiness, purity and charity are not the exclusive possessions of any church in the world, and that every system has produced men and women of the most exalted character. In the face of this evidence, if anybody dreams of the exclusive survival of his own religion and the destruction of the others, I pity him from the bottom of my heart, and point out to him that upon the banner of every religion will soon be written, in spite of resistance: 'Help and not Fight', 'Assimilation and not Destruction', 'Harmony and Peace and not Dissension'.

13

THE STRENUOUS LIFE

Theodore Roosevelt

'The Strenuous Life' is a speech given by Theodore Roosevelt on 10 April 1899 in Chicago. Roosevelt had resolved to live a life of struggle, toil and activity despite suffering from physical ailments from a young age. His speech was a reflection of this belief and advocated for Americans to follow this doctrine for the success and progress of the nation.

In speaking to you, men of the greatest city of the West, men of the State which gave to the country Lincoln and Grant, men who pre-eminently and distinctly embody all that is most American in the American character, I wish to preach, not the doctrine of ignoble ease, but the doctrine of the strenuous life, the life of toil and effort, of labor and strife; to preach that highest form of success which comes, not to the man who desires mere easy peace, but to the man who does not shrink from danger, from hardship or from bitter toil, and who out of these wins the splendid ultimate triumph.

A life of ignoble ease, a life of that peace which springs merely from lack either of desire or of power to strive after great things, is as little worthy of a nation as of an individual. I ask only that what every self-respecting American demands from himself and from his sons shall be demanded of the American nation as a whole. Who among you would teach your boys that ease, that peace, is to be the first consideration in their eyes—to be the ultimate goal after which they strive? You men of Chicago have made this city great, you men of Illinois have done your share, and more than your share, in making America great, because you neither preach nor practice such a doctrine. You work yourselves, and you bring up your sons to work. If you are rich and are worth your salt, you will teach your sons that though they may have leisure, it is not to be spent in idleness; for wisely used leisure merely means that those who possess it, being free from the necessity of working for their livelihood, are all the more bound to carry on some kind of non-remunerative work in science, in letters, in art, in exploration, in historical research—work of the type we most need in this country, the successful carrying out of which reflects most honor upon the nation.

We do not admire the man of timid peace. We admire the man who embodies victorious effort; the man who never wrongs his neighbor, who is prompt to help a friend, but who has those virile qualities necessary to win in the stern strife of actual life. It is hard to fail, but it is worse never to have tried to succeed. In this life we get nothing save by effort. Freedom from effort in the present merely means that there has been stored up effort in the past. A man can be freed from the necessity of work only by the fact that he or his fathers before him have worked to good purpose. If the freedom thus purchased is used aright, and the man still does actual work, though of a different kind, whether as a writer or a General, whether in the field of politics or in the field of exploration and adventure, he shows he deserves his good fortune. But if he treats this period of freedom from the need of actual labor as a period not of preparation, but of mere enjoyment, he shows that he is simply a cumberer of the earth's surface, and he surely unfits himself to hold his own with his fellows if the need to do so should again arise. A mere life of ease is not in the end a very satisfactory life, and, above all, it is a life which ultimately unfits those who follow it for serious work in the world.

As it is with the individual, so it is with the nation. It is a base untruth to say that happy is the nation that has no history. Thrice happy is the nation that has a glorious history. Far better it is to dare mighty things, to win glorious triumphs, even though checkered by failure, than to take rank with those poor spirits who neither enjoy much nor suffer much, because they live in the gray twilight that knows not victory nor defeat. If in 1861 the men who loved the Union had believed that peace was the end of all things, and war and strife the worst of all things, and had acted up to their belief, we would have saved hundreds of thousands of lives, we would have saved hundreds of millions of dollars. Moreover, besides saving all the blood and treasure we then lavished, we would have prevented the heartbreak of many women, the dissolution of many homes, and we would have spared the country those months of gloom and shame when it seemed as if our armies marched only to defeat. We could have avoided all this suffering simply by shrinking from strife. And if we had thus avoided it, we would have shown that we were weaklings, and that we were unfit to stand among the great nations of the earth. Thank God for the iron in the blood of our fathers, the men who upheld the wisdom of Lincoln, and bore sword or rifle in the armies of Grant! Let us, the children of the men who proved themselves equal to the mighty days—let us, the children of the men who carried the great Civil War to a triumphant conclusion, praise the God of our fathers that the ignoble counsels of peace were rejected; that the suffering and loss, the blackness of sorrow and despair, were unflinchingly faced, and the years of strife endured; for in the end the slave was freed, the Union restored and the mighty American republic placed once more as a helmeted queen among nations.

We of this generation do not have to face a task such as that our fathers faced, but we have our tasks, and woe to us if we fail to perform them! We cannot, if we would, play the part of China, and be content to rot by inches in ignoble ease within our borders, taking no interest in what goes on beyond them, sunk in a scrambling commercialism; heedless of the higher life, the life of aspiration, of toil and risk, busying ourselves only with the wants of our bodies for the day, until suddenly we should find, beyond a shadow of question, what China has already found, that in this world the nation that has trained itself to a career of unwarlike and isolated ease is bound, in the end, to go down before other nations which have not lost the manly and adventurous qualities. If we are to be a really great people, we must strive in good faith to play a great part in the world. We cannot avoid meeting great issues. All that we can determine for ourselves is whether we shall meet them well or ill. Last year we could not help being brought face to face with the problem of war with Spain. All we could decide was whether we should shrink like cowards from the contest, or enter into it as beseemed a brave and high-spirited people; and; once in, whether failure or success should crown our banners. So it is now. We cannot avoid the responsibilities that confront us in Hawaii, Cuba, Porto Rico and the Philippines. All we can decide is whether we shall meet them in a way that will redound to the national credit, or whether we shall make of our dealings with these new problems a dark and shameful page in our history. To refuse to deal with them at all merely amounts to dealing with them badly. We have a given problem to solve. If we undertake the solution, there is, of course, always danger that we may not solve it aright; but to refuse to undertake the solution simply renders it certain that we cannot possibly solve it aright.

The timid man, the lazy man, the man who distrusts his country, the over-civilized man, who has lost the great fighting, masterful virtues, the ignorant man, and the man of dull mind, whose soul is incapable of feeling the mighty lift that thrills 'stern men with empires in their brains'—all these, of course, shrink from seeing the nation undertake its new duties; shrink from seeing us build a navy and an army adequate to our needs; shrink from seeing us do our share of the world's work, by bringing order out of chaos in the great, fair tropic islands from which the valor of our soldiers and sailors has driven the Spanish flag. These are the men who fear the strenuous life, who fear the only national life which is really worth leading. They believe in that cloistered life which saps the hardy virtues in a nation, as it saps them in the individual; or else they are wedded to that base spirit of gain and greed which recognizes in commercialism the be-all and end-all of national life, instead of realizing that, though an indispensable element, it is, after all, but one of the many elements that go to make up true national greatness. No country can long endure if its foundations are not laid deep in the material prosperity which comes from thrift, from business energy and enterprise, from hard, unsparing effort in the fields of industrial activity; but neither was any nation ever yet truly great if it relied upon material prosperity alone. All honor must be paid to the architects of our material prosperity, to the great captains of industry who have built our factories and our railroads, to the strong men who toil for wealth with brain or hand; for great is the debt of the nation to these and their kind. But our debt is yet greater to the men whose highest type is to be found in a statesman like Lincoln, a soldier like Grant. They showed by their lives that they recognized the law of work, the law of strife; they toiled to win a competence for themselves and those dependent upon them; but they recognized that there were yet other and even loftier duties—duties to the nation and duties to the race.

We cannot sit huddled within our own borders and avow ourselves merely an assemblage of well-to-do hucksters who care nothing for what happens beyond. Such a policy would defeat even its own end; for as the nations grow to have ever wider and wider interests, and are brought into closer and closer contact, if we are to hold our own in the struggle for naval and commercial supremacy, we must build up our power without our own borders. We must build the Isthmian Canal, and we must grasp the points of vantage which will enable us to have our say in deciding the destiny of the oceans of the East and the West.

So much for the commercial side. From the standpoint of international honor the argument is even stronger. The guns that thundered off Manila and Santiago, left us echoes of glory, but they also left us a legacy of duty. If we drove out a medieval tyranny only to make room for savage anarchy, we had better not have begun the task at all. It is worse than idle to say that we have no duty to perform, and can leave to their fates the islands we have conquered. Such a course would be the course of infamy. It would be followed at once by utter chaos in the wretched islands themselves. Some stronger, manlier power would have to step in and do the work, and we would have shown ourselves weaklings, unable to carry to successful completion the labors that great and high-spirited nations are eager to undertake.

The work must be done; we cannot escape our responsibility; and if we are worth our salt, we shall be glad of the chance to do the work—glad of the chance to show ourselves equal to one of the great tasks set modern civilization. But let us not deceive ourselves as to the importance of the task. Let us not be misled by vainglory into underestimating the strain it will put on our powers. Above all, let us, as we value our own self-respect, face the responsibilities with proper seriousness, courage and high resolve. We must demand the highest order of integrity and ability in our public men who are to grapple with these new problems. We must hold to a rigid accountability those public servants who show unfaithfulness to the interests of the nation or inability to rise to the high level of the new demands upon our strength and our resources.

Of course we must remember not to judge any public servant by any one act, and especially should we beware of attacking the men who are merely the occasions and not the causes of disaster. Let me illustrate what I mean by the army and the navy. If 20 years ago we had gone to war, we should have found the navy as absolutely unprepared as the army. At that time our ships could not have encountered with success the fleets of Spain any more than nowadays we can put untrained soldiers, no matter how brave, who are armed with archaic black-powder weapons, against well-drilled regulars armed with the highest type of modern repeating rifle. But in the early eighties the attention of the nation became directed to our naval needs. Congress most wisely made a series of appropriations to build up a new navy, and under a succession of able and patriotic secretaries, of both political parties, the navy was gradually built up, until its material became equal to its splendid personnel, with the result that last summer it leaped to its proper place as one of the most brilliant and formidable fighting navies in the entire world. We rightly pay all honor to the men controlling the navy at the time it won these great deeds, honor to Secretary Long and Admiral Dewey, to the captains who handled the ships in action, to the daring lieutenants who braved death in the smaller craft, and to the heads of bureaus at Washington who saw that the ships were so commanded, so armed, so equipped, so well engined, as to insure the best results. But let us also keep ever in mind that all of this would not have availed if it had not been for the wisdom of the men who during the preceding fifteen years had built up the navy. Keep in mind the secretaries of the navy during those years; keep in mind the senators and congressmen who by their votes gave the money necessary to build and to armor the ships, to construct the great guns and to train the crews; remember also those who actually did build the ships, the armor and the guns; and remember the admirals and captains who handled battle-ship, cruiser and torpedo-boat on the high seas, alone and in squadrons, developing the seamanship, the gunnery and the power of acting together, which their successors utilized so gloriously at Manila and off Santiago.

And, gentlemen, remember the converse, too. Remember that justice has two sides. Be just to those who built up the navy, and, for the sake of the future of the country, keep in mind those who opposed its building up. Read the Congressional Record. Find out the senators and congressmen who opposed the grants for building the new ships; who opposed the purchase of armor, without which the ships were worthless; who opposed any adequate maintenance for the Navy Department, and strove to cut down the number of men necessary to man our fleets. The men who did these things were one and all working to bring disaster on the country. They have no share in the glory of Manila, in the honor of Santiago. They have no cause to feel proud of the valor of our sea-captains, of the renown of our flag. Their motives may or may not have been good, but their acts were heavily fraught with evil. They did ill for the national honor, and we won in spite of their sinister opposition.

Now, apply all this to our public men of to-day. Our army has never been built up as it should be built up. I shall not discuss with an audience like this the puerile suggestion that a nation of seventy millions of freemen is in danger of losing its liberties from the existence of an army of 100,000 men, three-fourths of whom will be employed in certain foreign islands, in certain coast fortresses and on Indian reservations. No man of good sense and stout heart can take such a proposition seriously. If we are such weaklings as the proposition implies, then we are unworthy of freedom in any event. To no body of men in the United States is the country so much indebted as to the splendid officers and enlisted men of the regular army and navy. There is no body from which the country has less to fear, and none of which it should be prouder, none which it should be more anxious to upbuild.

Our army needs complete reorganization—not merely enlarging—and the reorganization can only come as the result of legislation. A proper general staff should be established, and the positions of ordinance, commissary and quartermaster officers should be filled by detail from the line. Above all, the army must be given the chance to exercise in large bodies. Never again should we see, as we saw in the Spanish war, major-generals in command of divisions who had never before commanded three companies together in the field. Yet, incredible to relate, the recent Congress has shown a queer inability to learn some of the lessons of the war. There were large bodies, of men in both branches who opposed the declaration of war, who opposed the ratification of peace, who opposed the upbuilding of the army, and who even opposed the purchase of armor at a reasonable price for the battle-ships and cruisers, thereby putting an absolute stop to the building of any new fighting-ships for the navy. If, during the years to come, any disaster should befall our arms, afloat or ashore, and thereby any shame come to the United States, remember that the blame will lie upon the men whose names appear upon the roll-calls of Congress on the wrong side of these great questions. On them will lie the burden of any loss of our soldiers and sailors, of any dishonor to the flag; and upon you and the people of this country will lie the blame if you do not repudiate, in no unmistakable way, what these men have done. The blame will not rest upon the untrained commander of untried troops, upon the civil officers of a department the organization of which has been left utterly inadequate, or upon the admiral with an insufficient number of ships; but upon the public men who have so lamentably failed in forethought as to refuse to remedy these evils long in advance, and upon the nation that stands behind those public men.

So, at the present hour, no small share of the responsibility for the blood shed in the Philippines, the blood of our brothers and the blood of their wild and ignorant foes, lies at the thresholds of those who so long delayed the adoption of the treaty of peace, and of those who by their worse than foolish words deliberately invited a savage people to plunge into a war fraught with sure disaster for them—a war, too, in which our own brave men who follow the flag must pay with their blood for the silly, mock humanitarianism of the prattlers who sit at home in peace.

The army and the navy are the sword and the shield which this nation must carry if she is to do her duty among the nations of the earth—if she is not to stand merely as the China of the western hemisphere. Our proper conduct toward the tropic islands we have wrested from Spain is merely the form which our duty has taken at the moment. Of course we are bound to handle the affairs of our own household well. We must see that there is civic honesty, civic cleanliness, civic good sense in our home administration of city, state and nation. We must strive for honesty in office, for honesty toward the creditors of the nation and of the individual; for the widest freedom of individual initiative where possible, and for the wisest control of individual initiative where it is hostile to the welfare of the many. But because we set our own household in order we are not thereby excused from playing our part in the great affairs of the world. A man's first duty is to his own home, but he is not thereby excused from doing his duty to the state; for if he fails in this second duty it is under the penalty of ceasing to be a free man. In the same way, while a nation's first duty is within its own borders, it is not thereby absolved from facing its duties in the world as a whole; and if it refuses to do so, it merely forfeits its right to struggle for a place among the peoples that shape the destiny of mankind.

In the West Indies and the Philippines alike we are confronted by most difficult problems. It is cowardly to shrink from solving them in the proper way; for solved they must be, if not by us, then by some stronger and more manful race. If we are too weak, too selfish, or too foolish to solve them, some bolder and abler people must undertake the solution. Personally, I am far too firm a believer in the greatness of my country and the power of my countrymen to admit for one moment that we shall ever be driven to the ignoble alternative.

The problems are different for the different islands. Porto Rico is not large enough to stand alone. We must govern it wisely and well, primarily in the interest of its own people. Cuba is, in my judgment, entitled ultimately to settle for itself whether it shall be an independent state or an integral portion of the mightiest of republics. But until order and stable liberty are secured, we must remain in the island to insure them, and infinite tact, judgment, moderation and courage must be shown by our military and civil representatives in keeping the island pacified, in relentlessly stamping out brigandage, in protecting all alike, and yet in showing proper recognition to the men who have fought for Cuban liberty. The Philippines offer a yet graver problem. Their population includes half-caste and native Christians, warlike Moslems and wild pagans. Many of their people are utterly unfit for self-government, and show no signs of becoming fit. Others may in time become fit but at present can only take part in self-government under a wise supervision, at once firm and beneficent. We have driven Spanish tyranny from the islands. If we now let it be replaced by savage anarchy, our work has been for harm and not for good. I have scant patience with those who fear to undertake the task of governing the Philippines, and who openly avow that they do fear to undertake it, or that they shrink from it because of the expense and trouble; but I have even scanter patience with those who make a pretense of humanitarianism to hide and cover their timidity, and who cant about 'liberty' and the 'consent of the governed,' in order to excuse themselves for their unwillingness to play the part of men. Their doctrines, if carried out, would make it incumbent upon us to leave the Apaches of Arizona to work out their own salvation, and to decline to interfere in a single Indian reservation. Their doctrines condemn your forefathers and mine for ever having settled in these United States.

England's rule in India and Egypt has been of great benefit to England, for it has trained up generations of men accustomed to look at the larger and loftier side of public life. It has been of even greater benefit to India and Egypt. And finally, and most of all, it has advanced the cause of civilization. So, if we do our duty aright in the Philippines, we will add to that national renown which is the highest and finest part of national life, will greatly benefit the people of the Philippine Islands, and, above all, we will play our part well in the great work of uplifting mankind. But to do this work, keep ever in mind that we must show in a high degree the qualities of courage, of honesty and of good judgment. Resistance must be stamped out. The first and all-important work to be done is to establish the supremacy of our flag. We must put down armed resistance before we can accomplish anything else, and there should be no parleying, no faltering, in dealing with our foe. As for those in our own country who encourage the foe, we can afford contemptuously to disregard them; but it must be remembered that their utterances are not saved from being treasonable merely by the fact that they are despicable.

When once we have put down armed resistance, when once our rule is acknowledged, then an even more difficult task will begin, for then we must see to it that the islands are administered with absolute honesty and with good judgment. If we let the public service of the islands be turned into the prey of the spoils politician, we shall have begun to tread the path which Spain trod to her own destruction. We must send out there only good and able men, chosen for their fitness, and not because of their partisan service, and these men must not only administer impartial justice to the natives and serve their own government with honesty and fidelity, but must show the utmost tact and firmness, remembering that, with such people as those with whom we are to deal, weakness is the greatest of crimes, and that next to weakness comes lack of consideration for their principles and prejudices.

I preach to you, then, my countrymen, that our country calls not for the life of ease but for the life of strenuous endeavor. The twentieth century looms before us big with the fate of many nations. If we stand idly by, if we seek merely swollen, slothful ease and ignoble peace, if we shrink from the hard contests where men must win at hazard of their lives and at the risk of all they hold dear, then the bolder and stronger peoples will pass us by, and will win for themselves the domination of the world. Let us therefore boldly face the life of strife, resolute to do our duty well and manfully; resolute to uphold righteousness by deed and by word; resolute to be both honest and brave, to serve high ideals, yet to use practical methods. Above all, let us shrink from no strife, moral or physical, within or without the nation, provided we are certain that the strife is justified, for it is only through strife, through hard and dangerous endeavor, that we shall ultimately win the goal of true national greatness.

14

VOTES FOR WOMEN

Mark Twain

American author Mark Twain delivered this speech on 20 January 1901 at the annual meeting of the Hebrew Technical School for Girls. The speech, in which Twain stated he was 'a woman's rights man,' supported women's suffrage and argued that women's judgment skills were on par, if not better than men, and as such their contribution to political decision-making was necessary for the nation's well-being.

Ladies and Gentlemen, it is a small help that I can afford, but it is just such help that one can give as coming from the heart through the mouth. The report of Mr Meyer was admirable, and I was as interested in it as you have been. Why, I'm twice as old as he, and I've had so much experience that I would say to him, when he makes his appeal for help: 'Don't make it for today or tomorrow, but collect the money on the spot.'

We are all creatures of sudden impulse. We must be worked up by steam, as it were. Get them to write their wills now, or it may be too late by-and-by. 15 or 20 years ago I had an experience I shall never forget. I got into a church which was crowded by a sweltering and panting multitude. The city missionary of our town—Hartford—made a telling appeal for help. He told of personal experiences among the poor in cellars and top lofts requiring instances of devotion and help. The poor are always good to the poor. When a person with his millions gives $100,000 it makes a great noise in the world, but he does not miss it; it's the widow's mite that makes no noise but does the best work.

I remember on that occasion in the Hartford church the collection was being taken up. The appeal had so stirred me that I could hardly wait for the hat or plate to come my way. I had $400 in my pocket, and I was anxious to drop it in the plate and wanted to borrow more. But the plate was so long in coming my way that the fever-heat of beneficence was going down lower and lower—going down at the rate of $100 a minute. The plate was passed too late. When it finally came to me, my enthusiasm had gone down so much that I kept my $400—and stole a dime from the plate. So, you see, time sometimes leads to crime. Oh, many a time have I thought of that and regretted it, and I adjure you all to give while the fever is on you.

Referring to woman's sphere in life, I'll say that woman is always right. For 25 years I've been a woman's rights man. I have always believed, long before my mother died, that, with her gray hairs and admirable intellect, perhaps she knew as much as I did. Perhaps she knew as much about voting as I.

I should like to see the time come when women shall help to make the laws. I should like to see that whiplash, the ballot, in the hands of women. As for this city's government, I don't want to say much, except that it is a shame—a shame; but if I should live 25 years longer—and there is no reason why I shouldn't—I think I'll see women handle the ballot. If women had the ballot today, the state of things in this town would not exist.

If all the women in this town had a vote today they would elect a mayor at the next election, and they would rise in their might and change the awful state of things now existing here.

15

WOMEN, IDEALS AND THE NATION

Constance Markievicz

On 28 March 1909, Constance Markievicz addressed the Students' National Literary Society in Dublin, Ireland. This speech represents an early example of Markievicz's passionate advocacy for Irish nationalism and her commitment to social justice. In her address, Markievicz spoke about the importance of youth engagement in the struggle for Irish independence. She highlighted the role of students and young intellectuals in shaping the future of Ireland and fostering a sense of national identity.

I take it as a great compliment that so many of you, the rising young women of Ireland, who are distinguishing yourselves every day and coming more and more to the front, should give me this opportunity. We older people look to you with great hopes and a great confidence that in your gradual emancipation you are bringing fresh ideas, fresh energies and above all a great genius for sacrifice into the life of the nation.

In Ireland the women seem to have taken less part in public life, and to have had less share in the struggle for liberty, than in other nations. In Russia, among the people who are working to overthrow the tyrannical and unjust government of the Czar and his officials, and in Poland where, to be a nationalist, men and women must take their lives in their hands, women work as comrades, shoulder to shoulder, with their men. No duty is too hard, no act too dangerous for them to undertake. Many a woman has been incarcerated in the dungeons under St Peter and St Paul—

to sit in the damp and mouldy gloom and watch—perhaps for a week, perhaps for a year—the little gate high up on the wall, where one day or other, sure enough, she would see a little stream of dirty water begin to trickle through, which would tell her that soon that which once had been her would drift out into the world again.

Many another woman has dropped exhausted on the long, weary march through the snow-covered steppes to the land of exile. Weighed down by her chains, unable to stir herself, scarcely a groan escapes her, even under the lash of the knout—freely applied by the soldier in charge—she has sunk down hopeless and helpless, alone on the dreary plain, to watch for a few short hours the big black birds circling nearer and nearer, borne up and sustained by the knowledge that 'no sacrifice is ever in vain,' and that as the death of Christ brought a new hope and a new life to an old world, so the blood of each martyr shed in the cause of liberty will give a new impetus to the comrades who are left behind to continue the work.

Now, England in this twentieth century is much more civilized, and much more subtle than Russia in her methods for subjugating a nation; therefore, more difficult to fight; and much more difficult to realize as an enemy. She deals out pennies liberally and noisily with her right hand, shouting into our ears all the time how good and how liberal she is to the mere Irish, while her left hand is busily engaged in feeling in our pockets and abstracting as many as she can of the few gold pieces we have earned by the sweat of our brows. She trumpets her own praise loudly through the world—John Bull's bluntness, honesty, truth and bravery, his nobleness in dealing with his enemies—all this has been sung, shouted and declaimed throughout civilization, so that Irish people, being very simple and honest themselves, have often taken a very long time to realize that we are being governed—not as we are told for the ultimate good of the Irish nation, but as an alien province that must be prevented from interfering with the commerce of, and whose interest must always be kept subservient to, England.

She has systematically overtaxed us for our own good; she has depopulated our country—and it is for our own good; she has tried to kill our language—for our own good; she entices our young men into her armies, to fight her battles for her—and still it is for our own good. She began this policy in 1800 when—entirely for our own good—our Parliament was disbanded, and we were given instead the great privilege of sending to Westminster a small band of representatives to make the best fight they could for Irish rights against an overwhelming majority; which, of course, while causing but a small annoyance to England, brought there with the representatives of Ireland, their families and the whole of the society in which they moved. In fact the wealthiest and most influential section of the Irish nation was, at one fell swoop, transferred to London, there to spend its money, and to learn to talk about the 'Empire.' The immense privilege of belonging to the 'greatest Empire in the world' of being one with 'the greatest people in the world,' has since been shouted and preached and sung to us, till many of us have been beguiled into believing this story of fairy gold only to be lost—lost to our country in her direst need!

In this desertion our women participated quite as much as our men, they abandoned their Dublin mansions, to hire or buy houses in London, they followed the English Court about and joined the English ranks of toadies and placehunters, bringing up their daughters in English ways and teaching them to make English ideals their ideals, and when possible marrying them to Englishmen.

Of course this could not go on for ever, and the Irish nation, at last realizing that they and their interests had been sold for years, refused to be represented by them any longer...but it was too late—the rich and the aristocratic section of the men and women of Ireland had been lost to their country for years, if not for all eternity.

Now, I am not going to discuss the subtle psychological question of why it was that so few women in Ireland have been prominent in the national struggle, or try to discover how they lost in the dark ages of persecution the magnificent legacy of Maeve, Fleas, Macha and their other great fighting ancestors. True, several women distinguished themselves on the battlefields of '98, and we have the women of the *Nation* newspaper, of the Ladies' Land League, also in our own day the few women who have worked their hardest in the Sinn Féin movement and in the Gaelic League, and we have the woman who won a battle for Ireland, by preventing a wobbly Corporation from presenting King Edward of England with a loyal address. But for the most part our women, though sincere, steadfast Nationalists at heart, have been content to remain quietly at home, and leave all the fighting and striving to the men.

Lately things seem to be changing. As in the last century, during the sixties, a strong tide of liberty swept over the world, so now again a strong tide of liberty seems to be coming towards us, swelling and growing and carrying before it all the outposts that hold women enslaved and bearing them triumphantly into the life of the nations to which they belong.

We are in a very difficult position here, as so many Unionist women would fain have us work together with them for the emancipation of their sex and votes—obviously to send a member to Westminster. But I would ask every Nationalist woman to pause before she joined a Suffrage Society or Franchise League that did not include in their Programme the Freedom of their nation. 'A Free Ireland with No Sex Disabilities in her Constitution' should be the motto of all Nationalist women. And a grand motto it is.

There are great possibilities, in the hands and the hearts of the young women of Ireland—great possibilities indeed, and great responsibilities. For as you are born a woman, so you are born an Irelander, with all the troubles and responsibilities of both. You may shirk or deny them, but they are there, and some day—as a woman and as an Irelander—you will have to face the question of how your life has been spent, and how have you served your sex and your nation?

The greatest gifts that the young women of Ireland can bring into public life with them, are ideals and principles. Ideals, that are but the Inward Vision, that will show them their nation glorious and free, no longer a reproach to her sons and daughters; and principles that will give them courage and strength—the patient toil of the worker, the brilliant inspiration of the leader.

Women, from having till very recently stood so far removed from all politics, should be able to formulate a much clearer and more incisive view of the political situation than men. For a man from the time he is a mere lad is more or less in touch with politics, and has usually the label of some party attached to him, long before he properly understands what it really means.

We all know that when you get quite close to a rock or to a waterfall you lose the general effect of the mountain of which it is only a small part; and it is just the same with politics. Men all their lives are so occupied in examining closely, from a narrow party point of view all the little Bills 'relating to Ireland'—that all parties in the British Houses of Parliament are so constantly throwing them, to fight and squabble over—that they often quite lose sight of their 'mountain' and forget that—as the greater contains the less, as the mountain contains the rocks and the waterfalls, so does the lost nationhood of their country contain class legislation, sex legislation, trade legislation.

Now, here is a chance for our women. Let them remind their men, that their first duty is to examine any legislation proposed not from a party point of view, not from the point of view of a sex, a trade or a class, but simply and only from the standpoint of their Nation. Let them learn to be statesmen and not merely politicians. Let them consider how their action with regard to it may help or hinder their national struggle for independence and nothing else, and then let them act accordingly.

Taking my simile from another point of view, as surely that a few stones, and a few pails of water, though improving our garden, are but a poor substitute for our great mysterious mountain, so these little Bills, though improving the conditions of our people, are at the best but a poor substitute for our Nation's freedom, which in the meantime has been shelved and almost forgotten. Now, let our women come forward with the determination that we must obtain possession of the mountain itself—not contenting ourselves with buying or stealing bits of rock and pails of water.

Fix your mind on the ideal of Ireland free, with her women enjoying the full rights of citizenship in their own nation, and no one will be able to side-track you, and so make use of you to use up the energies of the nation in obtaining all sorts of concessions—concessions, too, that for the most part were coming in the natural course of evolution, and were perhaps just hastened a few years by the fierce agitations to obtain them.

Catholic emancipation must have come; it has come even in Russian Poland, where the whole nation was in arms against Russia as late as '63, and where it stands for a much greater thing than it does here.

Catholicism is an integral part of a Pole's Nationality, the Orthodox religion an integral part of a Russian's, for all Poles are Catholic, all Russians Orthodox—and a Pole of the Orthodox religion would even now be regarded with suspicion in Poland and could not possibly enter any Polish National Movement; while a Russian who was a Catholic would find it difficult even to live in his country.

Tenant right and peasant proprietorship, extension of the franchise and universal suffrage, are all but steps in the evolution of the world; for, as education and with it the knowledge of the rights of a man or a woman to live, is gained by the masses of mankind, so gradually they push their way—individually and collectively—into the life of their nation, and being in the majority, the moment they realize their power, the world may be theirs for the taking.

But our national freedom cannot, and must not, be left to evolution. If we look around us, we will find that evolution—as far as Ireland is concerned—is tending rather to annihilate us as a nation altogether. We seem day by day to be brought more and more in touch with England, and little by little to be losing all that distinctiveness which pertains to a nation, and which may be called nationality. London seems to be coming nearer and nearer to us till quite imperceptibly it has become the centre of the universe to even many good Irishmen.

Of course all modern inventions have helped England in the task of submerging our interests in hers—trains, the penny post, the telegraph system, have all brought her nearer, and given her more power over us. More especially the daily papers, forcing England upon us as the headquarters of our politics, our society, our stock exchange, our sport, teaching us to regard her foreign policy and her wars from the point of view of one or other of her political parties—all this, I say, wears away the rock of our national pride, and little by little we drift nearer to the conventional English views on life.

The educational systems through the country have also been used to work for the destruction of our nationality, from the smart English governess who despised the mere Irish, to the village schoolmaster forced to train up his scholars in ignorance of Ireland's wrongs, in ignorance of Ireland's language and history.

The schools, too, were usually under the patronage of the priest or parson of the district, and therefore very naturally concentrated on developing strong sectarian feelings in the children, instead of the broader creed of nationalism.

Every right granted to us by England has been done in such a way that it helped to split us up into divisions and sub-divisions. That policy is being continued now. We have had landlords and tenants, Catholics and Protestants, North and South, besides the sub-divisions into the different sections of the English political parties. We are rapidly adding graziers and peasants, farmers and labourers, to the list of Irishmen who are all losing sight of their ideal, and sordidly scrambling for what they hope to get. They are curiously blind and inconsistent, too, for no great and real prosperity can be ours, while our interests are always the very last to be considered in an Empire.

To prove this, take a glance at two of the Bills that are being very much discussed at this moment.

The Liberals are talking of Land Tax. This may suit the needs of England very well, with her big, rich proprietors, who can well afford to pay it; but over here, where the land is at this moment gradually becoming the property of the farmer, big and small, through a system of paying a certain rent to the Government, it will mean that this rent has been raised, and nothing more, and that, in spite of England's promises. The rent goes into England's pockets, so also does the Land Tax. Therefore, except in the terms, where is the difference? And who cares whether the extra charge is called rent or Land Tax? It will have to be paid, and that is the only point of any importance to the farmer.

Then take the great Conservative cry of Tariff Reform. We are all told that Cobden ruined Ireland's milling industry with Free Trade, and we are all familiar with the pitiful ruins of mills, great and small, through the country. Round Dublin, along the Dodder banks, one ruin after another, tells its sad tale of unemployment and emigration to the holiday wanderer. In Sligo—my own county—every little stream has the same tale to tell; and where, even the bleak walls have vanished, you often find a record of bygone prosperity in names such as Milltown or Millbrook.

But conditions have changed all over the world since Cobden's day, and tax on flour now would only mean that the wheat-growing industry of Canada would benefit largely. 'Colonial Preference' would mean that Canada would get every advantage over Russia and other wheat-growing countries in our markets, while Ireland would possibly have to pay more for bread.

In the ready-made clothing trades, England with her Black Country, with her great manufacturing towns, has always been our worst enemy, and a tax on foreign ready-made clothes would tend to close the markets to all but English goods—the very ones (that once grant we require Protection at all) we require to be protected the most against. England's greatest rival in ready-mades is Germany. We, at present, count for nothing, and, of course, German goods excluded by a prohibitary tariff, England would do practically what she liked with the markets over here. Her firms would be in the position of a certain English boot factory which established a shop in Limerick in competition to a Limerick boot factory. Being a rich firm, they were able to sell their wares under cost price to the unsuspicious people of Limerick, till the day when the Limerick factory closed its doors, unable to stand up against the competition, and from that day the people of Limerick have had to pay through the boots they wear—the expenses of the fight, and a huge dividend to the English company, as well as having the unemployed from the ruined industry to support, unless they emigrate.

All this points to the one way in which the women of Ireland can help their country; and, indeed, many of them are already doing so; and it is a movement too that all creeds, all classes and all politics can join in. We have the Irish Industrial Development Associations, and the Sinn Féin organizations both working very hard for this object, but still there is much to be done.

It is not enough just vaguely to buy Irish goods where you can do so without trouble, just in a sort of sentimental way. No; you must make Irish goods as necessary to your daily life, as your bath or your breakfast. Say to you yourselves, 'We must establish here a Voluntary Protection against foreign goods.' By this I mean that we must not resent sometimes having to pay an extra penny for an Irish-made article—which is practically protection—as the result of protection is that native manufacturers are enabled to charge the extra penny that will enable their infant factory to live and grow strong, and finally to compete on absolutely equal terms with the foreign-made article.

Every Irish industry that we manage even to keep in existence is an added wealth to our nation, and therefore indirectly to ourselves.

It employs labour which serves to keep down the poor rates, and to check emigration. The large sums of money it turns over benefits every other trade in the country. So you also will benefit, for the richer the country, the better price you will be able to command for your services in the professions and trades, and the more positions will be created to which you may aspire.

Besides, as in the case of the boot factory in Limerick, so in the other industries. If we allow England to ruin them, it is we that will have to pay up in the end.

An Irishman is but a poor match for an Englishman in trade, because he is such an extraordinary good hand in driving a bargain.

This may sound paradoxical, but you will find that nevertheless it is true. Who can sell a horse better at a fair than an Irishman?—abstracting the uttermost farthing from his English customer. But in his heated arguments, and in his gentle persuasiveness, he entirely omits to mention that his animal has staggers, is a crib-biter, or some other such trifle. The Irishman will tell you with pride for years after of the wonderful bargain he struck, but he will draw a veil over the fact that he has lost his best customer, and a good market for many horses in the succeeding years.

Now, it is the same spirit that prompts us to glory in bargains we make when we are buying, and boast when we return home one shilling the richer than we expected from buying foreign-made articles, forgetting that the shillings spent on foreign goods and the shillings saved are both robbed from our Nation—our Nation is the poorer for them, and we as parts of our nation are the poorer for them too.

If the women of Ireland would organize the movement for buying Irish goods more, they might do a great deal to help their country. If they would make it the fashion to dress in Irish clothes, feed on Irish food—in fact, in this as in everything, LIVE REALLY IRISH LIVES, they would be doing something great, and don't let our clever Irish colleens rest content with doing this individually, but let them go out and speak publicly about it, form leagues, of which 'No English Goods' is the war-cry. Let them talk, and talk, publicly and privately, never minding how they bore people—till not one even of the peasants in the wilds of Galway but has heard and approved of the movement.

I daresay you will think this all very obvious and very dull, but Patriotism and Nationalism and all great things are made up of much that is obvious and dull, and much that in the beginning is small, but that will be found to lead out into fields that are broader and full of interest. You will go out into the world and get elected on to as many public bodies as possible, and by degrees through your exertions no public institution—whether hospital, workhouse, asylum or any other, and no private house—but will be supporting the industries of your country.

Ireland wants her girls to help her to build up her national life. Their fresh, clean views of life, their young energies, have been long too hidden away and kept separate in their different homes. Bring them out and organize them, and lo! you will find a great new army ready to help the national cause. The old idea that a woman can only serve her nation through her home is gone, so now is the time; on you the responsibility rests. No one can help you but yourselves alone; you must make the world look upon you as citizens first, as women after. For each one of you there is a niche waiting—your place in the nation. Try and find it. It may be as a leader, it may be as a humble follower—perhaps in a political party, perhaps in a party of your own—but it is there, and if you cannot find it for yourself, no one can find it for you.

If you are fitted for public work take up any that is within your reach, so long as you feel that you can do it. Ireland wants reforming, sweeping clean from ocean to ocean; and it is only the young people can do it.

Since the Union we have been steadily deteriorating; all our ideals have been gradually slipping from us. Let us look all these facts bravely in the face, and make up our minds to change them.

We know that the Government of England is responsible for

all this. First, for the famine, with its deaths and desolations, by which our people were taught to beg and to appeal and to look to England, and our fine national spirit was taught to be submissive.

Emigration—another policy sent to us from England—has helped to build up another great nation at Ireland's expense. The men and women whom she could least afford to lose were the ones who so often had to go, leaving the weak and the feeble to continue their own race.

But what has done us most harm of all is a system of Government calculated to foster all that was low or mean in our nature—treachery, place-hunting, besides all the petty, mean vices that follow on the idea that commercial prosperity and nothing else is the highest ideal of life. These ideas, and many more, we have been allowing a subtle foe to graft on our national character at her will.

But we have seen it in time; and a nation of idealists and soldiers has only to see it, and she will prune off the bad growths, as a strong nature will throw off an unclean sickness.

Drunkenness is one of the great national evils for us to fight. It has caused more harm to our nation than at first seems possible. Many and many a defeat and massacre in '98 were facilitated by the drunkenness of the patriot army. To quote 'The Boys of Wexford:'

'We bravely fought and conquered
At Ross and Wexford town;
And if we failed to keep them,
'Twas drink that brought us down.
We had no drink beside us
On Tubberneering's day,
Depending on the long bright pike,
And well it won its way.'

Again, another way of helping Ireland—make this country untenable for the British Army—let them be taught to paraphrase the Cromwellian cry and say when ordered to Ireland, 'To Hell or Ireland.' Take a leaf from the book of the Italian ladies in their treatment of the armies of the Austrian usurper. Boycott them, men and officers, let them realize what the sight of a red or khaki coat means to a right-thinking Irishman or woman; let them feel that you would force them to leave, that you would fain see in their place the gorgeous uniforms of an Irish army, the brilliant ranks of regiments like the Volunteers of '82. Make public opinion so strong that no Irish lad will ever again join the army of his country's enemies, to be at any moment called upon to 'quell sedition' in his own country or to fight against other noble nations in the same plight as themselves.

If Irish boys could realize the contempt the British Army is held in abroad, if they heard it talked of as the last relic of barbarism, a 'mercenary army' and, as the most immoral army in the world, they would indeed hesitate before they entered it.

Then, again, you can educate your universities, colleges and schools. Don't permit pro-English propaganda, vice-regal patronage. I saw the other day a lecture advertised to be given by Father Maturin, Dr Delany, SJ, in the chair, under the patronage of Her Excellency, the Countess of Aberdeen. How long are the students of Ireland going silently to acquiesce in insults such as these? Many of us had great hopes of a new order of things when 'God Save the King' was rioted down by some brave young men, but that protest does not seem to have lead to anything more.

The '63 revolution in Poland was chiefly organized by students. Cannot the young men and women realize their strength? It is they who are the universities and colleges of the country; without them the schools would cease to be. Let them force their senates or governing bodies into line and not allow them to tolerate, or worse still, to solicit any English patronage however they may be tempted. Let the maiden of Ireland, fleet as Atalanta, never pause in the race for freedom; let her shut her eyes to the golden apples that England will strew on her path, wisely understanding the bitter disappointment that must have been the lot of the other Atalanta, when she had realized that she had lost her race, her great prestige, her sex's prowess. And all for what? For some fruit to eat.

As I write this a couple of lines from a Scotch poet are running in my head, which apply very aptly to us and to Ireland—

> 'Breathes there a man with soul so dead,
> Who never to himself has said,
> This is my own my Native Land?'

I think that there are very few Irishwomen whose souls are so dead that they would answer that question in the negative, but how many of them have realized the responsibility they have admitted when they say, 'My own, my native land?' Those words applied to our nation exclude all other nations from your possession. No man can apply the words, 'My native land' to two countries—to Ireland and England, or to Ireland and any other country. That we still can use those words proves that our souls incorporate in the soul of our nation are free still. The great soul of Ireland is still unconquered, and it is to the free souls of her sons and her daughters that she looks to free her body.

Each one of us has a soul, an Irish soul, a tiny atom of the great national soul of Ireland. Let us give that soul her chance; let us listen to her lofty aspirations, to the truth and justice of her claims. Ireland's soul was born free; it is we must free her body too.

In every action we do in life, the idea behind it is the thing that counts—if you go deep enough—the soul as it were. And so it is only by realizing that unless the ideal, the spirit of self-sacrifice and love of country, is at the back of our work for commercial prosperity, sex emancipation, and other practical reforms, that we can hope to help our land. Every little act 'for Ireland's sake' will help to build up a great nation, noble and self-sacrificing, industrious and free.

Do you think that Christ would have conquered so much of the world, and held it for nearly 2,000 years, with a selfish practical policy and nothing more? No; Christianity, and other religions which have prevailed, have done so through their ideals, for which men and women were not afraid to die. Why did the Macedonian Empire break up? Why have we nothing left of the glories of the great Kingdom of Spain? What was the cause of the fall of Napoleon, and why did the French Empire crumble away? Because they were founded upon usurpation and sustained by physical force, that most unstable of human powers, and no physical force can hold forever a free-souled and steadfast people.

England is now holding by force three civilized nations—nations whose ideals are Freedom, Justice and Nationhood—Ireland, India and Egypt, not to consider her savage territories and South Africa. Her colonies have to be coaxed into loyalty, and her House of Commons goes into hysterics over the news that Germany is building ships. Does that look like an Empire that is replete with a great National confidence, that is going to last for all eternity?

Wherever Ireland is known in the world, she is known by the great legacy her martyrs have left her, tales of noble deeds, of fearless deaths, of lives of self-denial and renunciation. Her name stands for the emblem of all that is brave and true, while England, her conqueror, has but gained for herself universally among the nations, the sobriquet of 'La Perfide Albion.'

To sum up in a few words what I want the Young Ireland women to remember from me. Regard yourselves as Irish, believe in yourselves as Irish, as units of a nation distinct from England, your conqueror, and as determined to maintain your distinctiveness and gain your deliverance. Arm yourselves with weapons to fight your nation's cause. Arm your souls with noble and free ideas. Arm your minds with the histories and memories of your country and her martyrs, her language, and a knowledge of her arts, and her industries. And if in your day the call should come for your body to arm, do not shirk that either.

May this aspiration towards life and freedom among the women of Ireland bring forth a Joan of Arc to free our nation!

16

THE MAN IN THE ARENA

Theodore Roosevelt

'The Man in the Arena' is a powerful speech given by Theodore Roosevelt in 1910. It is often cited as an inspirational call to action and a reminder of the importance of courage, resilience and active engagement in life. Although it is commonly known as 'The Man in the Arena', a phrase taken from its most popular excerpt, the larger speech is called 'Citizenship in a Republic', delivered by Roosevelt at the Sorbonne in Paris.

Strange and impressive associations rise in the mind of a man from the New World who speaks before this august body in this ancient institution of learning. Before his eyes pass the shadows of mighty kings and war-like nobles, of great masters of law and theology; through the shining dust of the dead centuries he sees crowded figures that tell of the power and learning and splendor of times gone by; and he sees also the innumerable host of humble students to whom clerkship meant emancipation, to whom it was well-nigh the only outlet from the dark thraldom of the Middle Ages.

This was the most famous university of mediaeval Europe at a time when no one dreamed that there was a New World to discover. Its services to the cause of human knowledge already stretched far back into the remote past at a time when my forefathers, three centuries ago, were among the sparse bands of traders, ploughmen, wood-choppers and fisherfolk who, in hard struggle with the iron unfriendliness of the Indian-haunted land, were laying the foundations of what has now become the giant republic of the West. To conquer a continent, to tame the shaggy roughness of wild nature, means grim warfare; and the generations engaged in it cannot keep, still less add to, the stores of garnered wisdom which were once theirs, and which are still in the hands of their brethren who dwell in the old land. To conquer the wilderness means to wrest victory from the same hostile forces with which mankind struggled on the immemorial infancy of our race. The primaeval conditions must be met by the primaeval qualities which are incompatible with the retention of much that has been painfully acquired by humanity as through the ages it has striven upward toward civilization. In conditions so primitive there can be but a primitive culture. At first only the rudest school can be established, for no others would meet the needs of the hard-driven, sinewy folk who thrust forward the frontier in the teeth of savage men and savage nature; and many years elapse before any of these schools can develop into seats of higher learning and broader culture.

The pioneer days pass; the stump-dotted clearings expand into vast stretches of fertile farm land; the stockaded clusters of log cabins change into towns; the hunters of game, the fellers of trees, the rude frontier traders and tillers of the soil, the men who wander all their lives long through the wilderness as the heralds and harbingers of an oncoming civilization, themselves vanish before the civilization for which they have prepared the way. The children of their successors and supplanters, and then their children and their children and children's children, change and develop with extraordinary rapidity. The conditions accentuate vices and virtues, energy and ruthlessness, all the good qualities and all the defects of an intense individualism, self-reliant, self-centered, far more conscious of its rights than of its duties and blind to its own shortcomings. To the hard materialism of the frontier days succeeds the hard materialism of an industrialism even more intense and absorbing than that of the older nations; although these themselves have likewise already entered on the age of a complex and predominantly industrial civilization.

As the country grows, its people, who have won success in so many lines, turn back to try to recover the possessions of the mind and the spirit, which perforce their fathers threw aside in order better to wage the first rough battles for the continent their children inherit. The leaders of thought and of action grope their way forward to a new life, realizing, sometimes dimly, sometimes clear-sightedly, that the life of material gain, whether for a nation or an individual, is of value only as a foundation, only as there is added to it the uplift that comes from devotion to loftier ideals. The new life thus sought can in part be developed afresh from what is roundabout in the New World; but it can developed in full only by freely drawing upon the treasure-houses of the Old World, upon the treasures stored in the ancient abodes of wisdom and learning, such as this is where I speak to-day. It is a mistake for any nation to merely copy another; but it is even a greater mistake, it is a proof of weakness in any nation, not to be anxious to learn from one another and willing and able to adapt that learning to the new national conditions and make it fruitful and productive therein. It is for us of the New World to sit at the feet of Gamaliel of the Old; then, if we have the right stuff in us, we can show that Paul in his turn can become a teacher as well as a scholar.

Today I shall speak to you on the subject of individual citizenship, the one subject of vital importance to you, my hearers, and to me and my countrymen, because you and we are great citizens of great democratic republics. A democratic republic such as ours—an effort to realize in its full sense government by, of and for the people—represents the most gigantic of all possible social experiments, the one fraught with great responsibilities alike for good and evil. The success of republics like yours and like ours means the glory, and our failure the despair, of mankind; and for you and for us the question of the quality of the individual citizen is supreme. Under other forms of government, under the rule of one man or very few men, the quality of the leaders is all-important. If, under such governments, the quality of the rulers is high enough, then the nations for generations lead a brilliant career, and add substantially to the sum of world achievement, no matter how low the quality of the average citizen; because the average citizen is an almost negligible quantity in working out the final results of that type of national greatness. But with you and us the case is different. With you here, and with us in my own home, in the long run, success or failure will be conditioned upon the way in which the average man, the average women, does his or her duty, first in the ordinary, every-day affairs of life, and next in those great occasional cries which call for heroic virtues. The average citizen must be a good citizen if our republics are to succeed. The stream will not permanently rise higher than the main source; and the main source of national power and national greatness is found in the average citizenship of the nation. Therefore it behooves us to do our best to see that the standard of the average citizen is kept high; and the average cannot be kept high unless the standard of the leaders is very much higher.

It is well if a large proportion of the leaders in any republic, in any democracy, are, as a matter of course, drawn from the classes represented in this audience to-day; but only provided that those classes possess the gifts of sympathy with plain people and of devotion to great ideals. You and those like you have received special advantages; you have all of you had the opportunity for mental training; many of you have had leisure; most of you have had a chance for enjoyment of life far greater than comes to the majority of your fellows. To you and your kind much has been given, and from you much should be expected. Yet there are certain failings against which it is especially incumbent that both men of trained and cultivated intellect, and men of inherited wealth and position should especially guard themselves, because to these failings they are especially liable; and if yielded to, their—your—chances of useful service are at an end. Let the man of learning, the man of lettered leisure, beware of that queer and cheap temptation to pose to himself and to others as a cynic, as the man who has outgrown emotions and beliefs, the man to whom good and evil are as one. The poorest way to face life is to face it with a sneer. There are many men who feel a kind of twister pride in cynicism; there are many who confine themselves to criticism of the way others do what they themselves dare not even attempt. There is no more unhealthy being, no man less worthy of respect, than he who either really holds, or feigns to hold, an attitude of sneering disbelief toward all that is great and lofty, whether in achievement or in that noble effort which, even if it fails, comes to second achievement. A cynical habit of thought and speech, a readiness to criticize work which the critic himself never tries to perform, an intellectual aloofness which will not accept contact with life's realities—all these are marks, not as the possessor would fain to think, of superiority but of weakness. They mark the men unfit to bear their part painfully in the stern strife of living, who seek, in the affection of contempt for the achievements of others, to hide from others and from themselves in their own weakness. The role is easy; there is none easier, save only the role of the man who sneers alike at both criticism and performance.

It is not the critic who counts; not the man who points out how the strong man stumbles, or where the doer of deeds could have done them better. The credit belongs to the man who is actually in the arena, whose face is marred by dust and sweat and blood; who strives valiantly; who errs, who comes short again and again, because there is no effort without error and shortcoming; but who does actually strive to do the deeds; who knows great enthusiasms, the great devotions; who spends himself in a worthy cause; who at the best knows in the end the triumph of high achievement, and who at the worst, if he fails, at least fails while daring greatly, so that his place shall never be with those cold and timid souls who neither know victory nor defeat. Shame on the man of cultivated taste who permits refinement to develop into fastidiousness that unfits him for doing the rough work of a workaday world. Among the free peoples who govern themselves there is but a small field of usefulness open for the men of cloistered life who shrink from contact with their fellows. Still less room is there for those who deride of slight what is done by those who actually bear the brunt of the day; nor yet for those others who always profess that they would like to take action, if only the conditions of life were not exactly what they actually are. The man who does nothing cuts the same sordid figure in the pages of history, whether he be a cynic, or fop, or voluptuary. There is little use for the being whose tepid soul knows nothing of great and generous emotion, of the high pride, the stern belief, the lofty enthusiasm, of the men who quell the storm and ride the thunder. Well for these men if they succeed; well also, though not so well, if they fail, given only that they have nobly ventured, and have put forth all their heart and strength. It is war-worn Hotspur, spent with hard fighting, he of the many errors and valiant end, over whose memory we love to linger, not over the memory of the young lord who 'but for the vile guns would have been a valiant soldier.'

France has taught many lessons to other nations: surely one of the most important lessons is the lesson her whole history teaches, that a high artistic and literary development is compatible with notable leadership in arms and statecraft. The brilliant gallantry of the French soldier has for many centuries been proverbial; and during these same centuries at every court in Europe the 'freemasons of fashion' have treated the French tongue as their common speech; while every artist and man of letters, and every man of science able to appreciate that marvelous instrument of precision, French prose, had turned toward France for aid and inspiration. How long the leadership in arms and letters has lasted is curiously illustrated by the fact that the earliest masterpiece in a modern tongue is the splendid French epic which tells of Roland's doom and the vengeance of Charlemange when the lords of the Frankish hosts were stricken at Roncesvalles. Let those who have, keep, let those who have not, strive to attain, a high standard of cultivation and scholarship. Yet let us remember that these stand second to certain other things. There is need of a sound body, and even more of a sound mind. But above mind and above body stands character—the sum of those qualities which we mean when we speak of a man's force and courage, of his good faith and sense of honor. I believe in exercise for the body, always provided that we keep in mind that physical development is a means and not an end. I believe, of course, in giving to all the people a good education. But the education must contain much besides book-learning in order to be really good. We must ever remember that no keenness and subtleness of intellect, no polish, no cleverness, in any way make up for the lack of the great solid qualities. Self-restraint, self-mastery, common sense, the power of accepting individual responsibility and yet of acting in conjunction with others, courage and resolution—these are the qualities which mark a masterful people. Without them no people can control itself, or save itself from being controlled from the outside. I speak to brilliant assemblage; I speak in a great university which represents the flower of the highest intellectual development; I pay all homage to intellect and to elaborate and specialized training of the intellect; and yet I know I shall have the assent of all of you present when I add that more important still are the commonplace, every-day qualities and virtues.

Such ordinary, every-day qualities include the will and the power to work, to fight at need and to have plenty of healthy children. The need that the average man shall work is so obvious as hardly to warrant insistence. There are a few people in every country so born that they can lead lives of leisure. These fill a useful function if they make it evident that leisure does not mean idleness; for some of the most valuable work needed by civilization is essentially non-remunerative in its character, and of course the people who do this work should in large part be drawn from those to whom remuneration is an object of indifference. But the average man must earn his own livelihood. He should be trained to do so, and he should be trained to feel that he occupies a contemptible position if he does not do so; that he is not an object of envy if he is idle, at whichever end of the social scale he stands, but an object of contempt, an object of derision. In the next place, the good man should be both a strong and a brave man; that is, he should be able to fight, he should be able to serve his country as a soldier, if the need arises. There are well-meaning philosophers who declaim against the unrighteousness of war. They are right only if they lay all their emphasis upon the unrighteousness. War is a dreadful thing, and unjust war is a crime against humanity. But it is such a crime because it is unjust, not because it is a war. The choice must ever be in favor of righteousness, and this is whether the alternative be peace or whether the alternative be war. The question must not be merely, is there to be peace or war? The question must be, is it right to prevail? Are the great laws of righteousness once more to be fulfilled? And the answer from a strong and virile people must be 'Yes,' whatever the cost. Every honorable effort should always be made to avoid war, just as every honorable effort should always be made by the individual in private life to keep out of a brawl, to keep out of trouble; but no self-respecting individual, no self-respecting nation, can or ought to submit to wrong.

Finally, even more important than ability to work, even more important than ability to fight at need, is it to remember that the chief of blessings for any nation is that it shall leave its seed to inherit the land. It was the crown of blessings in Biblical times and it is the crown of blessings now. The greatest of all curses in is the curse of sterility, and the severest of all condemnations should be that visited upon willful sterility. The first essential in any civilization is that the man and women shall be father and mother of healthy children, so that the race shall increase and not decrease. If that is not so, if through no fault of the society there is failure to increase, it is a great misfortune. If the failure is due to the deliberate and willful fault, then it is not merely a misfortune, it is one of those crimes of ease and self-indulgence, of shrinking from pain and effort and risk, which in the long run Nature punishes more heavily than any other. If we of the great republics, if we, the free people who claim to have emancipated ourselves form the thraldom of wrong and error, bring down on our heads the curse that comes upon the willfully barren, then it will be an idle waste of breath to prattle of our achievements, to boast of all that we have done. No refinement of life, no delicacy of taste, no material progress, no sordid heaping up riches, no sensuous development of art and literature, can in any way compensate for the loss of the great fundamental virtues; and of these great fundamental virtues the greatest is the race's power to perpetuate the race. Character must show itself in the man's performance both of the duty he owes himself and of the duty he owes the state. The man's foremost duty is owed to himself and his family; and he can do this duty only by earning money, by providing what is essential to material well-being; it is only after this has been done that he can hope to build a higher superstructure on the solid material foundation; it is only after this has been done that he can help in his movements for the general well-being. He must pull his own weight first, and only after this can his surplus strength be of use to the general public. It is not good to excite that bitter laughter which expresses contempt; and contempt is what we feel for the being whose enthusiasm to benefit mankind is such that he is a burden to those nearest him; who wishes to do great things for humanity in the abstract, but who cannot keep his wife in comfort or educate his children.

Nevertheless, while laying all stress on this point, while not merely acknowledging but insisting upon the fact that there must be a basis of material well-being for the individual as for the nation, let us with equal emphasis insist that this material well-being represents nothing but the foundation, and that the foundation, though indispensable, is worthless unless upon it is raised the superstructure of a higher life. That is why I decline to recognize the mere multimillionaire, the man of mere wealth, as an asset of value to any country; and especially as not an asset to my own country. If he has earned or uses his wealth in a way that makes him a real benefit, of real use—and such is often the case—why, then he does become an asset of real worth. But it is the way in which it has been earned or used, and not the mere fact of wealth, that entitles him to the credit. There is need in business, as in most other forms of human activity, of the great guiding intelligences. Their places cannot be supplied by any number of lesser intelligences. It is a good thing that they should have ample recognition, ample reward. But we must not transfer our admiration to the reward instead of to the deed rewarded; and if what should be the reward exists without the service having been rendered, then admiration will only come from those who are mean of soul. The truth is that, after a certain measure of tangible material success or reward has been achieved, the question of increasing it becomes of constantly less importance compared to the other things that can be done in life. It is a bad thing for a nation to raise and to admire a false standard of success; and there can be no falser standard than that set by the deification of material well-being in and for itself. But the man who, having far surpassed the limits of providing for the wants; both of the body and mind, of himself and of those depending upon him, then piles up a great fortune, for the acquisition or retention of which he returns no corresponding benefit to the nation as a whole, should himself be made to feel that, so far from being desirable, he is an unworthy citizen of the community: that he is to be neither admired nor envied; that his right-thinking fellow countrymen put him low in the scale of citizenship, and leave him to be consoled by the admiration of those whose level of purpose is even lower than his own.

My position as regards the moneyed interests can be put in a few words. In every civilized society property rights must be carefully safeguarded; ordinarily, and in the great majority of cases, human rights and property rights are fundamentally and in the long run identical; but when it clearly appears that there is a real conflict between them, human rights must have the upper hand, for property belongs to man and not man to property. In fact, it is essential to good citizenship clearly to understand that there are certain qualities which we in a democracy are prone to admire in and of themselves, which ought by rights to be judged admirable or the reverse solely from the standpoint of the use made of them. Foremost among these I should include two very distinct gifts—the gift of money-making and the gift of oratory. Money-making, the money touch I have spoken of above. It is a quality which in a moderate degree is essential. It may be useful when developed to a very great degree, but only if accompanied and controlled by other qualities; and without such control the possessor tends to develop into one of the least attractive types produced by a modern industrial democracy. So it is with the orator. It is highly desirable that a leader of opinion in democracy should be able to state his views clearly and convincingly. But all that the oratory can do of value to the community is enable the man thus to explain himself; if it enables the orator to put false values on things, it merely makes him a power for mischief. Some excellent public servants have not that gift at all, and must merely rely on their deeds to speak for them; and unless oratory does represent genuine conviction based on good common sense and able to be translated into efficient performance, then the better the oratory the greater the damage to the public it deceives. Indeed, it is a sign of marked political weakness in any commonwealth if the people tend to be carried away by mere oratory, if they tend to value words in and for themselves, as divorced from the deeds for which they are supposed to stand. The phrase-maker, the phrase-monger, the ready talker, however great his power, whose speech does not make for courage, sobriety and right understanding, is simply a noxious element in the body politic, and it speaks ill for the public if he has influence over them. To admire the gift of oratory without regard to the moral quality behind the gift is to do wrong to the republic.

Of course all that I say of the orator applies with even greater force to the orator's latter-day and more influential brother, the journalist. The power of the journalist is great, but he is entitled neither to respect nor admiration because of that power unless it is used aright. He can do, and often does, great good. He can do, and he often does, infinite mischief. All journalists, all writers, for the very reason that they appreciate the vast possibilities of their profession, should bear testimony against those who deeply discredit it. Offenses against taste and morals, which are bad enough in a private citizen, are infinitely worse if made into instruments for debauching the community through a newspaper. Mendacity, slander, sensationalism, inanity, vapid triviality, all are potent factors for the debauchery of the public mind and conscience. The excuse advanced for vicious writing, that the public demands it and that demand must be supplied, can no more be admitted than if it were advanced by purveyors of food who sell poisonous adulterations. In short, the good citizen in a republic must realize that they ought to possess two sets of qualities, and that neither avails without the other. He must have those qualities which make for efficiency; and that he also must have those qualities which direct the efficiency into channels for the public good. He is useless if he is inefficient. There is nothing to be done with that type of citizen of whom all that can be said is that he is harmless. Virtue which is dependent upon a sluggish circulation is not impressive. There is little place in active life for the timid good man. The man who is saved by weakness from robust wickedness is likewise rendered immune from robuster virtues. The good citizen in a republic must first of all be able to hold his own. He is no good citizen unless he has the ability which will make him work hard and which at need will make him fight hard. The good citizen is not a good citizen unless he is an efficient citizen.

But if a man's efficiency is not guided and regulated by a moral sense, then the more efficient he is the worse he is, the more dangerous to the body politic. Courage, intellect, all the masterful qualities, serve but to make a man more evil if they are merely used for that man's own advancement, with brutal indifference to the rights of others. It speaks ill for the community if the community worships these qualities and treats their possessors as heroes regardless of whether the qualities are used rightly or wrongly. It makes no difference as to the precise way in which this sinister efficiency is shown. It makes no difference whether such a man's force and ability betray themselves in a career of money-maker or politician, soldier or orator, journalist or popular leader. If the man works for evil, then the more successful he is the more he should be despised and condemned by all upright and far-seeing men. To judge a man merely by success is an abhorrent wrong; and if the people at large habitually so judge men, if they grow to condone wickedness because the wicked man triumphs, they show their inability to understand that in the last analysis free institutions rest upon the character of citizenship, and that by such admiration of evil they prove themselves unfit for liberty. The homely virtues of the household, the ordinary workaday virtues which make the woman a good housewife and housemother, which make the man a hard worker, a good husband and father, a good soldier at need, stand at the bottom of character. But of course many other must be added thereto if a state is to be not only free but great. Good citizenship is not good citizenship if only exhibited in the home. There remains the duties of the individual in relation to the State, and these duties are none too easy under the conditions which exist where the effort is made to carry on the free government in a complex industrial civilization. Perhaps the most important thing the ordinary citizen, and, above all, the leader of ordinary citizens, has to remember in political life is that he must not be a sheer doctrinaire. The closest philosopher, the refined and cultured individual who from his library tells how men ought to be governed under ideal conditions, is of no use in actual governmental work; and the one-sided fanatic, and still more the mob-leader, and the insincere man who to achieve power promises what by no possibility can be performed, are not merely useless but noxious.

The citizen must have high ideals, and yet he must be able to achieve them in practical fashion. No permanent good comes from aspirations so lofty that they have grown fantastic and have become impossible and indeed undesirable to realize. The impractical visionary is far less often the guide and precursor than he is the embittered foe of the real reformer, of the man who, with stumblings and shortcoming, yet does in some shape, in practical fashion, give effect to the hopes and desires of those who strive for better things. Woe to the empty phrase-maker, to the empty idealist, who, instead of making ready the ground for the man of action, turns against him when he appears and hampers him when he does work! Moreover, the preacher of ideals must remember how sorry and contemptible is the figure which he will cut, how great the damage that he will do, if he does not himself, in his own life, strive measurably to realize the ideals that he preaches for others. Let him remember also that the worth of the ideal must be largely determined by the success with which it can in practice be realized. We should abhor the so-called 'practical' men whose practicality assumes the shape of that peculiar baseness which finds its expression in disbelief in morality and decency, in disregard of high standards of living and conduct. Such a creature is the worst enemy of the body politic. But only less desirable as a citizen is his nominal opponent and real ally, the man of fantastic vision who makes the impossible better forever the enemy of the possible good.

We can just as little afford to follow the doctrinaires of an extreme individualism as the doctrinaires of an extreme socialism. Individual initiative, so far from being discouraged, should be stimulated; and yet we should remember that, as society develops and grows more complex, we continually find that things which once it was desirable to leave to individual initiative can, under changed conditions, be performed with better results by common effort. It is quite impossible, and equally undesirable, to draw in theory a hard-and-fast line which shall always divide the two sets of cases. This every one who is not cursed with the pride of the closet philosopher will see, if he will only take the trouble to think about some of our commonest phenomena. For instance, when people live on isolated farms or in little hamlets, each house can be left to attend to its own drainage and water-supply; but the mere multiplication of families in a given area produces new problems which, because they differ in size, are found to differ not only in degree, but in kind from the old; and the questions of drainage and water-supply have to be considered from the common standpoint. It is not a matter for abstract dogmatizing to decide when this point is reached; it is a matter to be tested by practical experiment. Much of the discussion about socialism and individualism is entirely pointless, because of the failure to agree on terminology. It is not good to be a slave of names. I am a strong individualist by personal habit, inheritance and conviction; but it is a mere matter of common sense to recognize that the State, the community, the citizens acting together, can do a number of things better than if they were left to individual action. The individualism which finds its expression in the abuse of physical force is checked very early in the growth of civilization, and we of to-day should in our turn strive to shackle or destroy that individualism which triumphs by greed and cunning, which exploits the weak by craft instead of ruling them by brutality. We ought to go with any man in the effort to bring about justice and the equality of opportunity, to turn the tool-user more and more into the tool-owner, to shift burdens so that they can be more equitably borne. The deadening effect on any race of the adoption of a logical and extreme socialistic system could not be overstated; it would spell sheer destruction; it would produce grosser wrong and outrage, fouler immortality, than any existing system. But this does not mean that we may not with great advantage adopt certain of the principles professed by some given set of men who happen to call themselves Socialists; to be afraid to do so would be to make a mark of weakness on our part.

But we should not take part in acting a lie any more than in telling a lie. We should not say that men are equal where they are not equal, nor proceed upon the assumption that there is an equality where it does not exist; but we should strive to bring about a measurable equality, at least to the extent of preventing the inequality which is due to force or fraud. Abraham Lincoln, a man of the plain people, blood of their blood and bone of their bone, who all his life toiled and wrought and suffered for them, at the end died for them, who always strove to represent them, who would never tell an untruth to or for them, spoke of the doctrine of equality with his usual mixture of idealism and sound common sense. He said (I omit what was of merely local significance):

'I think the authors of the Declaration of Independence intended to include all men, but they did not mean to declare all men equal in all respects. They did not mean to say all men were equal in color, size, intellect, moral development or social capacity. They defined with tolerable distinctness in what they did consider all men created equal—equal in certain inalienable rights, among which are life, liberty and pursuit of happiness. This they said, and this they meant. They did not mean to assert the obvious untruth that all were actually enjoying that equality, or yet that they were about to confer it immediately upon them. They meant to set up a standard maxim for free society which should be familiar to all—constantly looked to, constantly labored for and, even though never perfectly attained, constantly approximated, and thereby constantly spreading and deepening its influence, and augmenting the happiness and value of life to all people, everywhere.'

We are bound in honor to refuse to listen to those men who would make us desist from the effort to do away with the inequality which means injustice; the inequality of right, opportunity, of privilege. We are bound in honor to strive to bring ever nearer the day when, as far is humanly possible, we shall be able to realize the ideal that each man shall have an equal opportunity to show the stuff that is in him by the way in which he renders service. There should, so far as possible, be equal of opportunity to render service; but just so long as there is inequality of service there should and must be inequality of reward. We may be sorry for the general, the painter, the artists, the worker in any profession or of any kind, whose misfortune rather than whose fault it is that he does his work ill. But the reward must go to the man who does his work well; for any other course is to create a new kind of privilege, the privilege of folly and weakness; and special privilege is injustice, whatever form it takes.

To say that the thriftless, the lazy, the vicious, the incapable, ought to have reward given to those who are far-sighted, capable and upright, is to say what is not true and cannot be true. Let us try to level up, but let us beware of the evil of leveling down. If a man stumbles, it is a good thing to help him to his feet. Every one of us needs a helping hand now and then. But if a man lies down, it is a waste of time to try and carry him; and it is a very bad thing for every one if we make men feel that the same reward will come to those who shirk their work and those who do it. Let us, then, take into account the actual facts of life, and not be misled into following any proposal for achieving the millennium, for recreating the golden age, until we have subjected it to hardheaded examination. On the other hand, it is foolish to reject a proposal merely because it is advanced by visionaries. If a given scheme is proposed, look at it on its merits, and, in considering it, disregard formulas. It does not matter in the least who proposes it, or why. If it seems good, try it. If it proves good, accept it; otherwise reject it. There are plenty of good men calling themselves Socialists with whom, up to a certain point, it is quite possible to work. If the next step is one which both we and they wish to take, why of course take it, without any regard to the fact that our views as to the tenth step may differ. But, on the other hand, keep clearly in mind that, though it has been worth while to take one step, this does not in the least mean that it may not be highly disadvantageous to take the next. It is just as foolish to refuse all progress because people demanding it desire at some points to go to absurd extremes, as it would be to go to these absurd extremes simply because some of the measures advocated by the extremists were wise.

The good citizen will demand liberty for himself, and as a matter of pride he will see to it that others receive liberty which he thus claims as his own. Probably the best test of true love of liberty in any country is the way in which minorities are treated in that country. Not only should there be complete liberty in matters of religion and opinion, but complete liberty for each man to lead his life as he desires, provided only that in so doing he does not wrong his neighbor. Persecution is bad because it is persecution, and without reference to which side happens at the moment to be the persecutor and which the persecuted. Class hatred is bad in just the same way, and without regard to the individual who, at a given time, substitutes loyalty to a class for loyalty to a nation, or substitutes hatred of men because they happen to come in a certain social category, for judgement awarded them according to their conduct. Remember always that the same measure of condemnation should be extended to the arrogance which would look down upon or crush any man because he is poor and to envy and hatred which would destroy a man because he is wealthy. The overbearing brutality of the man of wealth or power, and the envious and hateful malice directed against wealth or power, are really at root merely different manifestations of the same quality, merely two sides of the same shield. The man who, if born to wealth and power, exploits and ruins his less fortunate brethren is at heart the same as the greedy and violent demagogue who excites those who have not property to plunder those who have. The gravest wrong upon his country is inflicted by that man, whatever his station, who seeks to make his countrymen divide primarily in the line that separates class from class, occupation from occupation, men of more wealth from men of less wealth, instead of remembering that the only safe standard is that which judges each man on his worth as a man, whether he be rich or whether he be poor, without regard to his profession or to his station in life. Such is the only true democratic test, the only test that can with propriety be applied in a republic. There have been many republics in the past, both in what we call antiquity and in what we call the Middle Ages. They fell, and the prime factor in their fall was the fact that the parties tended to divide along the line that separates wealth from poverty. It made no difference which side was successful; it made no difference whether the republic fell under the rule of an oligarchy or the rule of a mob. In either case, when once loyalty to a class had been substituted for loyalty to the republic, the end of the republic was at hand. There is no greater need to-day than the need to keep ever in mind the fact that the cleavage between right and wrong, between good citizenship and bad citizenship, runs at right angles to, and not parallel with, the lines of cleavage between class and class, between occupation and occupation. Ruin looks us in the face if we judge a man by his position instead of judging him by his conduct in that position.

In a republic, to be successful we must learn to combine intensity of conviction with a broad tolerance of difference of conviction. Wide differences of opinion in matters of religious, political and social belief must exist if conscience and intellect alike are not be stunted, if there is to be room for healthy growth. Bitter internecine hatreds, based on such differences, are signs, not of earnestness of belief, but of that fanaticism which, whether religious or anti-religious, democratic or anti-democratic, is itself but a manifestation of the gloomy bigotry which has been the chief factor in the downfall of so many, many nations.

Of one man in especial, beyond any one else, the citizens of a republic should beware, and that is of the man who appeals to them to support him on the ground that he is hostile to other citizens of the republic, that he will secure for those who elect him, in one shape or another, profit at the expense of other citizens of the republic. It makes no difference whether he appeals to class hatred or class interest, to religious or anti-religious prejudice. The man who makes such an appeal should always be presumed to make it for the sake of furthering his own interest. The very last thing an intelligent and self-respecting member of a democratic community should do is to reward any public man because that public man says that he will get the private citizen something to which this private citizen is not entitled, or will gratify some emotion or animosity which this private citizen ought not to possess. Let me illustrate this by one anecdote from my own experience. A number of years ago I was engaged in cattle-ranching on the great plains of the western United States. There were no fences. The cattle wandered free, the ownership of each one was determined by the brand; the calves were branded with the brand of the cows they followed. If on a round-up and animal was passed by, the following year it would appear as an unbranded yearling, and was then called a maverick. By the custom of the country these mavericks were branded with the brand of the man on whose range they were found. One day I was riding the range with a newly hired cowboy, and we came upon a maverick. We roped and threw it; then we built a fire, took out a cinch-ring, heated it in the fire; and then the cowboy started to put on the brand. I said to him, 'It so-and-so's brand,' naming the man on whose range we happened to be. He answered: 'That's all right, boss; I know my business.' In another moment I said to him: 'Hold on, you are putting on my brand!' To which he answered: 'That's all right; I always put on the boss's brand.' I answered: 'Oh, very well. Now you go straight back to the ranch and get whatever is owing to you; I don't need you any longer.' He jumped up and said: 'Why, what's the matter? I was putting on your brand.' And I answered: 'Yes, my friend, and if you will steal for me then you will steal from me.'

Now, the same principle which applies in private life applies also in public life. If a public man tries to get your vote by saying that he will do something wrong in your interest, you can be absolutely certain that if ever it becomes worth his while he will do something wrong against your interest. So much for the citizenship to the individual in his relations to his family, to his neighbor, to the State. There remain duties of citizenship which the State, the aggregation of all the individuals, owes in connection with other States, with other nations. Let me say at once that I am no advocate of a foolish cosmopolitanism. I believe that a man must be a good patriot before he can be, and as the only possible way of being, a good citizen of the world. Experience teaches us that the average man who protests that his international feeling swamps his national feeling, that he does not care for his country because he cares so much for mankind, in actual practice proves himself the foe of mankind; that the man who says that he does not care to be a citizen of any one country, because he is the citizen of the world, is in fact usually and exceedingly undesirable citizen of whatever corner of the world he happens at the moment to be in. In the dim future all moral needs and moral standards may change; but at present, if a man can view his own country and all others countries from the same level with tepid indifference, it is wise to distrust him, just as it is wise to distrust the man who can take the same dispassionate view of his wife and mother. However broad and deep a man's sympathies, however intense his activities, he need have no fear that they will be cramped by love of his native land.

Now, this does not mean in the least that a man should not wish to do good outside of his native land. On the contrary, just as I think that the man who loves his family is more apt to be a good neighbor than the man who does not, so I think that the most useful member of the family of nations is normally a strongly patriotic nation. So far from patriotism being inconsistent with a proper regard for the rights of other nations, I hold that the true patriot, who is as jealous of the national honor as a gentleman of his own honor, will be careful to see that the nations neither inflict nor suffer wrong, just as a gentleman scorns equally to wrong others or to suffer others to wrong him. I do not for one moment admit that a man should act deceitfully as a public servant in his dealing with other nations, any more than he should act deceitfully in his dealings as a private citizen with other private citizens. I do not for one moment admit that a nation should treat other nations in a different spirit from that in which an honorable man would treat other men.

In practically applying this principle to the two sets of cases there is, of course, a great practical difference to be taken into account. We speak of international law; but international law is something wholly different from private or municipal law, and the capital difference is that there is a sanction for the one and no sanction for the other; that there is an outside force which compels individuals to obey the one, while there is no such outside force to compel obedience as regards to the other. International law will, I believe, as the generations pass, grow stronger and stronger until in some way or other there develops the power to make it respected. But as yet it is only in the first formative period. As yet, as a rule, each nation is of necessity to judge for itself in matters of vital importance between it and its neighbors, and actions must be of necessity, where this is the case, be different from what they are where, as among private citizens, there is an outside force whose action is all-powerful and must be invoked in any crisis of importance. It is the duty of wise statesmen, gifted with the power of looking ahead, to try to encourage and build up every movement which will substitute or tend to substitute some other agency for force in the settlement of international disputes. It is the duty of every honest statesman to try to guide the nation so that it shall not wrong any other nation. But as yet the great civilized peoples, if they are to be true to themselves and to the cause of humanity and civilization, must keep in mind that in the last resort they must possess both the will and the power to resent wrong-doings from others. The men who sanely believe in a lofty morality preach righteousness; but they do not preach weakness, whether among private citizens or among nations. We believe that our ideals should be so high, but not so high as to make it impossible measurably to realize them. We sincerely and earnestly believe in peace; but if peace and justice conflict, we scorn the man who would not stand for justice though the whole world came in arms against him.

And now, my hosts, a word in parting. You and I belong to the only two republics among the great powers of the world. The ancient friendship between France and the United States has been, on the whole, a sincere and disinterested friendship. A calamity to you would be a sorrow to us. But it would be more than that. In the seething turmoil of the history of humanity certain nations stand out as possessing a peculiar power or charm, some special gift of beauty or wisdom of strength, which puts them among the immortals, which makes them rank forever with the leaders of mankind. France is one of these nations. For her to sink would be a loss to all the world. There are certain lessons of brilliance and of generous gallantry that she can teach better than any of her sister nations. When the French peasantry sang of Malbrook, it was to tell how the soul of this warrior-foe took flight upward through the laurels he had won. Nearly seven centuries ago, Froissart, writing of the time of dire disaster, said that the realm of France was never so stricken that there were not left men who would valiantly fight for it. You have had a great past. I believe you will have a great future. Long may you carry yourselves proudly as citizens of a nation which bears a leading part in the teaching and uplifting of mankind.

17

FREEDOM OR DEATH

Emmeline Pankhurst

'Freedom or Death' is a speech delivered by Emmeline Pankhurst, a leading figure in the suffragette movement in the United Kingdom, in Hartford, Connecticut in 1913. This powerful speech encapsulates Pankhurst's fierce determination and unwavering commitment to women's suffrage. In her address, Pankhurst passionately advocates for women's right to vote, emphasizing the urgent need for equality and justice.

I do not come here as an advocate, because whatever position the suffrage movement may occupy in the United States of America, in England it has passed beyond the realm of advocacy and it has entered into the sphere of practical politics. It has become the subject of revolution and civil war, and so tonight I am not here to advocate woman suffrage. American suffragists can do that very well for themselves.

I am here as a soldier who has temporarily left the field of battle in order to explain—it seems strange it should have to be explained—what civil war is like when civil war is waged by women. I am not only here as a soldier temporarily absent from the field at battle; I am here—and that, I think, is the strangest part of my coming—I am here as a person who, according to the law courts of my country, it has been decided, is of no value to the community at all; and I am adjudged because of my life to be a dangerous person, under sentence of penal servitude in a convict prison.

It is not at all difficult if revolutionaries come to you from Russia, if they come to you from China, or from any other part of the world, if they are men. But since I am a woman it is necessary to explain why women have adopted revolutionary methods in order to win the rights of citizenship. We women, in trying to make our case clear, always have to make as part of our argument, and urge upon men in our audience the fact—a very simple fact—that women are human beings.

Suppose the men of Hartford had a grievance, and they laid that grievance before their legislature, and the legislature obstinately refused to listen to them, or to remove their grievance, what would be the proper and the constitutional and the practical way of getting their grievance removed? Well, it is perfectly obvious at the next general election the men of Hartford would turn out that legislature and elect a new one.

But let the men of Hartford imagine that they were not in the position of being voters at all, that they were governed without their consent being obtained, that the legislature turned an absolutely deaf ear to their demands, what would the men of Hartford do then? They couldn't vote the legislature out. They would have to choose; they would have to make a choice of two evils: they would either have to submit indefinitely to an unjust state of affairs, or they would have to rise up and adopt some of the antiquated means by which men in the past got their grievances remedied.

Your forefathers decided that they must have representation for taxation, many, many years ago. When they felt they couldn't wait any longer, when they laid all the arguments before an obstinate British government that they could think of, and when their arguments were absolutely disregarded, when every other means had failed, they began by the tea party at Boston, and they went on until they had won the independence of the United States of America. It is about eight years since the word militant was first used to describe what we were doing. It was not militant at all, except that it provoked militancy on the part of those who were opposed to it. When women asked questions in political meetings and failed to get answers, they were not doing anything militant. In Great Britain it is a custom, a time-honoured one, to ask questions of candidates for parliament and ask questions of members of the government. No man was ever put out of a public meeting for asking a question. The first people who were put out of a political meeting for asking questions, were women; they were brutally ill-used; they found themselves in jail before 24 hours had expired.

We were called militant, and we were quite willing to accept the name. We were determined to press this question of the enfranchisement of women to the point where we were no longer to be ignored by the politicians.

You have two babies very hungry and wanting to be fed. One baby is a patient baby, and waits indefinitely until its mother is ready to feed it. The other baby is an impatient baby and cries lustily, screams and kicks and makes everybody unpleasant until it is fed. Well, we know perfectly well which baby is attended to first. That is the whole history of politics. You have to make more noise than anybody else, you have to make yourself more obtrusive than anybody else, you have to fill all the papers more than anybody else, in fact you have to be there all the time and see that they do not snow you under.

When you have warfare things happen; people suffer; the noncombatants suffer as well as the combatants. And so it happens in civil war. When your forefathers threw the tea into Boston Harbour, a good many women had to go without their tea. It has always seemed to me an extraordinary thing that you did not follow it up by throwing the whiskey overboard; you sacrificed the women; and there is a good deal of warfare for which men take a great deal of glorification which has involved more practical sacrifice on women than it has on any man. It always has been so. The grievances of those who have got power, the influence of those who have got power commands a great deal of attention; but the wrongs and the grievances of those people who have no power at all are apt to be absolutely ignored. That is the history of humanity right from the beginning. Well, in our civil war people have suffered, but you cannot make omelettes without breaking eggs; you cannot have civil war without damage to something. The great thing is to see that no more damage is done than is absolutely necessary, that you do just as much as will arouse enough feeling to bring about peace, to bring about an honourable peace for the combatants; and that is what we have been doing.

We entirely prevented stockbrokers in London from telegraphing to stockbrokers in Glasgow and vice versa: for one whole day telegraphic communication was entirely stopped. I am not going to tell you how it was done. I am not going to tell you how the women got to the mains and cut the wires; but it was done. It was done, and it was proved to the authorities that weak women, suffrage women, as we are supposed to be, had enough ingenuity to create a situation of that kind. Now, I ask you, if women can do that, is there any limit to what we can do except the limit we put upon ourselves?

If you are dealing with an industrial revolution, if you get the men and women of one class rising up against the men and women of another class, you can locate the difficulty; if there is a great industrial strike, you know exactly where the violence is and how the warfare is going to be waged; but in our war against the government you can't locate it. We wear no mark; we belong to every class; we permeate every class of the community from the highest to the lowest; and so you see in the woman's civil war the dear men of my country are discovering it is absolutely impossible to deal with it: you cannot locate it, and you cannot stop it. 'Put them in prison,' they said, 'that will stop it.' But it didn't stop it at all: instead of the women giving it up, more women did it, and more and more and more women did it until there were 300 women at a time, who had not broken a single law, only 'made a nuisance of themselves' as the politicians say. Then they began to legislate. The British government has passed more stringent laws to deal with this agitation than it ever found necessary during all the history of political agitation in my country. They were able to deal with the revolutionaries of the Chartists' time; they were able to deal with the trades union agitation; they were able to deal with the revolutionaries later on when the Reform Acts were passed: but the ordinary law has not sufficed to curb insurgent women. They had to dip back into the Middle Ages to find a means of repressing the women in revolt.

They have said to us, government rests upon force, the women haven't force, so they must submit. Well, we are showing them that government does not rest upon force at all: it rests upon consent. As long as women consent to be unjustly governed, they can be, but directly women say: 'We withhold our consent, we will not be governed any longer so long as that government is unjust.' Not by the forces of civil war can you govern the very weakest woman. You can kill that woman, but she escapes you then; you cannot govern her. No power on earth can govern a human being, however feeble, who withholds his or her consent. When they put us in prison at first, simply for taking petitions, we submitted; we allowed them to dress us in prison clothes; we allowed them to put us in solitary confinement; we allowed them to put us amongst the most degraded of criminals; we learned of some of the appalling evils of our so-called civilization that we could not have learned in any other way. It was valuable experience, and we were glad to get it.

I have seen men smile when they heard the words 'hunger strike', and yet I think there are very few men today who would be prepared to adopt a 'hunger strike' for any cause. It is only people who feel an intolerable sense of oppression who would adopt a means of that kind. It means you refuse food until you are at death's door, and then the authorities have to choose between letting you die, and letting you go; and then they let the women go.

Now, that went on so long that the government felt that they were unable to cope. It was [then] that, to the shame of the British government, they set the example to authorities all over the world of feeding sane, resisting human beings by force. There may be doctors in this meeting: if so, they know it is one thing to feed by force an insane person; but it is quite another thing to feed a sane, resisting human being who resists with every nerve and with every fibre of her body the indignity and the outrage of forcible feeding. Now, that was done in England, and the government thought they had crushed us. But they found that it did not quell the agitation, that more and more women came in and even passed that terrible ordeal, and they were obliged to let them go. Then came the legislation—the 'Cat and Mouse Act'. The home secretary said, 'Give me the power to let these women go when they are at death's door, and leave them at liberty under license until they have recovered their health again and then bring them back.' It was passed to repress the agitation, to make the women yield—because that is what it has really come to, ladies and gentlemen. It has come to a battle between the women and the government as to who shall yield first, whether they will yield and give us the vote, or whether we will give up our agitation.

Well, they little know what women are. Women are very slow to rouse, but once they are aroused, once they are determined, nothing on earth and nothing in heaven will make women give way; it is impossible. And so this 'Cat and Mouse Act' which is being used against women today has failed. There are women lying at death's door, recovering enough strength to undergo operations who have not given in and won't give in, and who will be prepared, as soon as they get up from their sick beds, to go on as before. There are women who are being carried from their sick beds on stretchers into meetings. They are too weak to speak, but they go amongst their fellow workers just to show that their spirits are unquenched, and that their spirit is alive, and they mean to go on as long as life lasts.

Now, I want to say to you who think women cannot succeed, we have brought the government of England to this position, that it has to face this alternative: either women are to be killed or women are to have the vote. I ask American men in this meeting, what would you say if in your state you were faced with that alternative, that you must either kill them or give them their citizenship? Well, there is only one answer to that alternative, there is only one way out—you must give those women the vote.

You won your freedom in America when you had the revolution, by bloodshed, by sacrificing human life. You won the civil war by the sacrifice of human life when you decided to emancipate the negro. You have left it to women in your land, the men of all civilized countries have left it to women, to work out their own salvation. That is the way in which we women of England are doing. Human life for us is sacred, but we say if any life is to be sacrificed it shall be ours; we won't do it ourselves, but we will put the enemy in the position where they will have to choose between giving us freedom or giving us death.

So here am I. I come in the intervals of prison appearance. I come after having been four times imprisoned under the 'Cat and Mouse Act', probably going back to be rearrested as soon as I set my foot on British soil. I come to ask you to help to win this fight. If we win it, this hardest of all fights, then, to be sure, in the future it is going to be made easier for women all over the world to win their fight when their time comes.

18

STRIKE AGAINST WAR

Helen Keller

'Strike Against War' was a speech given by disability rights activist and writer Helen Keller on 5 January 1916 to the Women's Peace Party at Carnegie Hall, New York. The speech was an appeal to the workforce to protest against American participation in World War I, foreseeing it as a path to increased exploitation by the US government.

To begin with, I have a word to say to my good friends, the editors, and others who are moved to pity me. Some people are grieved because they imagine I am in the hands of unscrupulous persons who lead me astray and persuade me to espouse unpopular causes and make me the mouthpiece of their propaganda. Now, let it be understood once and for all that I do not want their pity; I would not change places with one of them. I know what I am talking about. My sources of information are as good and reliable as anybody else's. I have papers and magazines from England, France, Germany and Austria that I can read myself. Not all the editors I have met can do that. Quite a number of them have to take their French and German second hand. No, I will not disparage the editors. They are an overworked, misunderstood class. Let them remember, though, that if I cannot see the fire at the end of their cigarettes, neither can they thread a needle in the dark. All I ask, gentlemen, is a fair field and no favor. I have entered the fight against preparedness and against the economic system under which we live. It is to be a fight to the finish, and I ask no quarter.

The future of the world rests in the hands of America. The future of America rests on the backs of 80 million working men and women and their children. We are facing a grave crisis in our national life. The few who profit from the labor of the masses want to organize the workers into an army which will protect the interests of the capitalists. You are urged to add to the heavy burdens you already bear the burden of a larger army and many additional warships. It is in your power to refuse to carry the artillery and the dread-noughts and to shake off some of the burdens, too, such as limousines, steam yachts and country estates. You do not need to make a great noise about it. With the silence and dignity of creators you can end wars and the system of selfishness and exploitation that causes wars. All you need to do to bring about this stupendous revolution is to straighten up and fold your arms.

We are not preparing to defend our country. Even if we were as helpless as Congressman Gardner says we are, we have no enemies foolhardy enough to attempt to invade the United States. The talk about attack from Germany and Japan is absurd. Germany has its hands full and will be busy with its own affairs for some generations after the European war is over.

With full control of the Atlantic Ocean and the Mediterranean Sea, the allies failed to land enough men to defeat the Turks at Gallipoli; and then they failed again to land an army at Salonica in time to check the Bulgarian invasion of Serbia. The conquest of America by water is a nightmare confined exclusively to ignorant persons and members of the Navy League.

Yet, everywhere, we hear fear advanced as argument for armament. It reminds me of a fable I read. A certain man found a horseshoe. His neighbor began to weep and wail because, as he justly pointed out, the man who found the horseshoe might someday find a horse. Having found the shoe, he might shoe him. The neighbor's child might some day go so near the horse's hells as to be kicked, and die. Undoubtedly the two families would quarrel and fight, and several valuable lives would be lost through the finding of the horseshoe. You know the last war we had we quite accidentally picked up some islands in the Pacific Ocean which may some day be the cause of a quarrel between ourselves and Japan. I'd rather drop those islands right now and forget about them than go to war to keep them. Wouldn't you?

Congress is not preparing to defend the people of the United States. It is planning to protect the capital of American speculators and investors in Mexico, South America, China and the Philippine Islands. Incidentally this preparation will benefit the manufacturers of munitions and war machines.

Until recently there were uses in the United States for the money taken from the workers. But American labor is exploited almost to the limit now, and our national resources have all been appropriated. Still the profits keep piling up new capital. Our flourishing industry in implements of murder is filling the vaults of New York's banks with gold. And a dollar that is not being used to make a slave of some human being is not fulfilling its purpose in the capitalistic scheme. That dollar must be invested in South America, Mexico, China or the Philippines.

It was no accident that the Navy League came into prominence at the same time that the National City Bank of New York established a branch in Buenos Aires. It is not a mere coincidence that six business associates of J.P. Morgan are officials of defense leagues. And chance did not dictate that Mayor Mitchel should appoint to his Committee of Safety a thousand men that represent a fifth of the wealth of the United States. These men want their foreign investments protected.

Every modern war has had its root in exploitation. The Civil War was fought to decide whether the slaveholders of the South or the capitalists of the North should exploit the West. The Spanish-American War decided that the United States should exploit Cuba and the Philippines. The South African War decided that the British should exploit the diamond mines. The Russo-Japanese War decided that Japan should exploit Korea. The present war is to decide who shall exploit the Balkans, Turkey, Persia, Egypt, India, China, Africa. And we are whetting our sword to scare the victors into sharing the spoils with us. Now, the workers are not interested in the spoils; they will not get any of them anyway.

The preparedness propagandists have still another object, and a very important one. They want to give the people something to think about besides their own unhappy condition. They know the cost of living is high, wages are low, employment is uncertain and will be much more so when the European call for munitions stops. No matter how hard and incessantly the people work, they often cannot afford the comforts of life; many cannot obtain the necessities.

Every few days we are given a new war scare to lend realism to their propaganda. They have had us on the verge of war over the *Lusitania*, the *Gulflight*, the *Ancona*, and now they want the workingmen to become excited over the sinking of the *Persia*. The workingman has no interest in any of these ships. The Germans might sink every vessel on the Atlantic Ocean and the Mediterranean Sea, and kill Americans with every one—the American workingman would still have no reason to go to war.

All the machinery of the system has been set in motion. Above the complaint and din of the protest from the workers is heard the voice of authority.

'Friends,' it says, 'fellow workmen, patriots; your country is in danger! There are foes on all sides of us. There is nothing between us and our enemies except the Pacific Ocean and the Atlantic Ocean. Look at what has happened to Belgium. Consider the fate of Serbia. Will you murmur about low wages when your country, your very liberties, are in jeopardy? What are the miseries you endure compared to the humiliation of having a victorious German army sail up the East River? Quit your whining, get busy and prepare to defend your firesides and your flag. Get an army, get a navy; be ready to meet the invaders like the loyal-hearted freemen you are.'

Will the workers walk into this trap? Will they be fooled again? I am afraid so. The people have always been amenable to oratory of this sort. The workers know they have no enemies except their masters. They know that their citizenship papers are no warrant for the safety of themselves or their wives and children. They know that honest sweat, persistent toil and years of struggle bring them nothing worth holding on to, worth fighting for. Yet, deep down in their foolish hearts they believe they have a country. Oh blind vanity of slaves!

The clever ones, up in the high places know how childish and silly the workers are. They know that if the government dresses them up in khaki and gives them a rifle and starts them off with a brass band and waving banners, they will go forth to fight valiantly for their own enemies. They are taught that brave men die for their country's honor. What a price to pay for an abstraction—the lives of millions of young men; other millions crippled and blinded for life; existence made hideous for still more millions of human beings; the achievement and inheritance of generations swept away in a moment—and nobody better off for all the misery! This terrible sacrifice would be comprehensible if the thing you die for and call country fed, clothed, housed and warmed you, educated and cherished your children. I think the workers are the most unselfish of the children of men; they toil and live and die for other people's country, other people's sentiments, other people's liberties and other people's happiness! The workers have no liberties of their own; they are not free when they are compelled to work twelve or ten or eight hours a day. they are not free when they are ill paid for their exhausting toil. They are not free when their children must labor in mines, mills and factories or starve, and when their women may be driven by poverty to lives of shame. They are not free when they are clubbed and imprisoned because they go on strike for a raise of wages and for the elemental justice that is their right as human beings.

We are not free unless the men who frame and execute the

laws represent the interests of the lives of the people and no other interest. The ballot does not make a free man out of a wage slave. there has never existed a truly free and democratic nation in the world. From time immemorial men have followed with blind loyalty the strong men who had the power of money and of armies. Even while battlefields were piled high with their own dead they have tilled the lands of the rulers and have been robbed of the fruits of their labor. They have built palaces and pyramids, temples and cathedrals that held no real shrine of liberty.

As civilization has grown more complex the workers have become more and more enslaved, until today they are little more than parts of the machines they operate. Daily they face the dangers of railroad, bridge, skyscraper, freight train, stokehold, stockyard, lumber raft and mine. Panting and training at the docks, on the railroads and underground and on the seas, they move the traffic and pass from land to land the precious commodities that make it possible for us to live. And what is their reward? A scanty wage, often poverty, rents, taxes, tributes and war indemnities.

The kind of preparedness the workers want is reorganization and reconstruction of their whole life, such as has never been attempted by statesmen or governments. The Germans found out years ago that they could not raise good soldiers in the slums so they abolished the slums. They saw to it that all the people had at least a few of the essentials of civilization—decent lodging, clean streets, wholesome if scanty food, proper medical care and proper safeguards for the workers in their occupations. That is only a small part of what should be done, but what wonders that one step toward the right sort of preparedness has wrought for Germany! For 18 months it has kept itself free from invasion while carrying on an extended war of conquest, and its armies are still pressing on with unabated vigor. It is your business to force these reforms on the administration. Let there be no more talk about what a government can or cannot do. All these things have been done by all the belligerent nations in the hurly-burly of war. Every fundamental industry has been managed better by the governments than by private corporations.

It is your duty to insist upon still more radical measure. It is your business to see that no child is employed in an industrial establishment or mine or store, and that no worker in needlessly exposed to accident or disease. It is your business to make them give you clean cities, free from smoke, dirt and congestion. It is your business to make them pay you a living wage. It is your business to see that this kind of preparedness is carried into every department on the nation, until everyone has a chance to be well born, well nourished, rightly educated, intelligent and serviceable to the country at all times.

Strike against all ordinances and laws and institutions that continue the slaughter of peace and the butcheries of war. Strike against war, for without you no battles can be fought. Strike against manufacturing shrapnel and gas bombs and all other tools of murder. Strike against preparedness that means death and misery to millions of human beings. Be not dumb, obedient slaves in an army of destruction. Be heroes in an army of construction.

19

SPEECH AT BANARAS HINDU UNIVERSITY

Mohandas Karamchand Gandhi

Mahatma Gandhi's speech on 4 February 1916 at the inauguration of the Banaras Hindu University was one of his first public orations in India, and caused enough of a stir for him to have to leave it unfinished. The speech attacked the imposition of the English language on Indians and the elitist nature of the freedom movement, emphasizing the importance of uplifting the common people and farmers to secure self-government through ethical, non-violent means.

I wish to tender my humble apology for the long delay that took place before I was able to reach this place. And you will readily accept the apology when I tell you that I am not responsible for the delay nor is any human agency responsible for it. The fact is that I am like an animal on show, and my keepers in their over-kindness always manage to neglect a necessary chapter in this life, and, that is, pure accident. In this case, they did not provide for the series of accidents that happened to us—to me, keepers, and my carriers. Hence this delay.

Friends, under the influence of the matchless eloquence of Mrs Besant who has just sat down, pray, do not believe that our university has become a finished product, and that all the young men who are to come to the university, that has yet to rise and come into existence, have also come and returned from it finished citizens of a great empire. Do not go away with any such impression, and if you, the student world to which my remarks are supposed to be addressed this evening, consider for one moment that the spiritual life, for which this country is noted and for which this country has no rival, can be transmitted through the lip, pray, believe me, you are wrong. You will never be able merely through the lip, to give the message that India, I hope, will one day deliver to the world. I myself have been fed up with speeches and lectures. I except the lectures that have been delivered here during the last two days from this category, because they are necessary. But I do venture to suggest to you that we have now reached almost the end of our resources in speech-making; it is not enough that our ears are feasted, that our eyes are feasted, but it is necessary that our hearts have got to be touched and that our hands and feet have got to be moved.

We have been told during the last two days how necessary it is, if we are to retain our hold upon the simplicity of Indian character, that our hands and feet should move in unison with our hearts. But this is only by way of preface. I wanted to say it is a matter of deep humiliation and shame for us that I am compelled this evening under the shadow of this great college, in this sacred city, to address my countrymen in a language that is foreign to me. I know that if I was appointed an examiner, to examine all those who have been attending during these two days this series of lectures, most of those who might be examined upon these lectures would fail. And why? Because they have not been touched.

I was present at the sessions of the great Congress in the month of December. There was a much vaster audience, and will you believe me when I tell you that the only speeches that touched the huge audience in Bombay were the speeches that were delivered in Hindustani? In Bombay, mind you, not in Banaras where everybody speaks Hindi. But between the vernaculars of the Bombay Presidency on the one hand and Hindi on the other, no such great dividing line exists as there does between English and the sister language of India; and the Congress audience was better able to follow the speakers in Hindi. I am hoping that this university will see to it that the youths who come to it will receive their instruction through the medium of their vernaculars. Our languages are the reflection of ourselves, and if you tell me that our languages are too poor to express the best thought, then say that the sooner we are wiped out of existence the better for us. Is there a man who dreams that English can ever become the national language of India? Why this handicap on the nation? Just consider for one moment what an equal race our lads have to run with every English lad.

I had the privilege of a close conversation with some Poona professors. They assured me that every Indian youth, because he reached his knowledge through the English language, lost at least six precious years of life. Multiply that by the numbers of students turned out by our schools and colleges, and find out for yourselves how many thousand years have been lost to the nation. The charge against us is that we have no initiative. How can we have any, if we are to devote the precious years of our life to the mastery of a foreign tongue? We fail in this attempt also. Was it possible for any speaker yesterday and today to impress his audience as was possible for Mr Higginbotham? It was not the fault of the previous speakers that they could not engage the audience. They had more than substance enough for us in their addresses. But their addresses could not go home to us. I have heard it said that after all it is English-educated India which is leading and which is leading and which is doing all the things for the nation. It would be monstrous if it were otherwise. The only education we receive is English education. Surely we must show something for it. But suppose that we had been receiving during the past 50 years education through our vernaculars, what should we have today? We should have today a free India, we should have our educated men, not as if they were foreigners in their own land but speaking to the heart of the nation; they would be working amongst the poorest of the poor, and whatever they would have gained during these

50 years would be a heritage for the nation. Today even our wives are not the sharers in our best thought. Look at Professor Bose and Professor Ray and their brilliant researches. Is it not a shame that their researches are not the common property of the masses? Let us now turn to another subject.

The Congress has passed a resolution about self-government, and I have no doubt that the All-India Congress Committee and the Muslim League will do their duty and come forward with some tangible suggestions. But I, for one, must frankly confess that I am not so much interested in what they will be able to produce as I am interested in anything that the student world is going to produce or the masses are going to produce. No paper contribution will ever give us self-government. No amount of speeches will ever make us fit for self-government. It is only our conduct that will fit for us it. And how are we trying to govern ourselves?

I want to think audibly this evening. I do not want to make a speech and if you find me this evening speaking without reserve, pray, consider that you are only sharing the thoughts of a man who allows himself to think audibly, and if you think that I seem to transgress the limits that courtesy imposes upon me, pardon me for the liberty I may be taking. I visited the Vishwanath temple last evening, and as I was walking through those lanes, these were the thoughts that touched me. If a stranger dropped from above on to this great temple, and he had to consider what we as Hindus were, would he not be justified in condemning us? Is not this great temple a reflection of our own character? I speak feelingly, as a Hindu. Is it right that the lanes of our sacred temple should be as dirty as they are? The houses round about are built anyhow. The lanes are tortuous and narrow. If even our temples are not models of roominess and cleanliness, what can our self-government be? Shall our temples be abodes of holiness, cleanliness and peace as soon as the English have retired from India, either of their own pleasure or by compulsion, bag and baggage?

I entirely agree with the President of the Congress that before we think of self-government, we shall have to do the necessary plodding. In every city there are two divisions, the cantonment and the city proper. The city mostly is a stinking den. But we are a people unused to city life. But if we want city life, we cannot reproduce the easy-going hamlet life. It is not comforting to think that people walk about the streets of Indian Bombay under the perpetual fear of dwellers in the storeyed building spitting upon them. I do a great deal of railway traveling. I observe the difficulty of third-class passengers. But the railway administration is by no means to blame for all their hard lot. We do not know the elementary laws of cleanliness. We spit anywhere on the carriage floor, irrespective of the thoughts that it is often used as sleeping space. We do not trouble ourselves as to how we use it; the result is indescribable filth in the compartment. The so-called better class passengers overawe their less fortunate brethren. Among them I have seen the student world also; sometimes they behave no better. They can speak English and they have worn Norfolk jackets and, therefore, claim the right to force their way in and command seating accommodation.

I have turned the searchlight all over, and as you have given me the privilege of speaking to you, I am laying my heart bare. Surely we must set these things right in our progress towards self-government. I now introduce you to another scene. His Highness the Maharaja who presided yesterday over our deliberations spoke about the poverty of India. Other speakers laid great stress upon it. But what did we witness in the great pandal in which the foundation ceremony was performed by the Viceroy? Certainly a most gorgeous show, an exhibition of jewellery, which made a splendid feast for the eyes of the greatest jeweller who chose to come from Paris. I compare with the richly bedecked noble men the millions of the poor. And I feel like saying to these noble men, 'There is no salvation for India unless you strip yourselves of this jewellery and hold it in trust for your countrymen in India.' I am sure it is not the desire of the King-Emperor or Lord Hardinge that in order to show the truest loyalty to our King-Emperor, it is necessary for us to ransack our jewellery boxes and to appear bedecked from top to toe. I would undertake, at the peril of my life, to bring to you a message from King George himself that he excepts nothing of the kind.

Sir, whenever I hear of a great palace rising in any great city of India, be it in British India or be it in India which is ruled by our great chiefs, I become jealous at once, and say, 'Oh, it is the money that has come from the agriculturists.' Over 75 per cent of the population are agriculturists and Mr Higginbotham told us last night in his own felicitous language, that they are the men who grow two blades of grass in the place of one. But there cannot be much spirit of self-government about us, if we take away or allow others to take away from them almost the whole of the results of their labour. Our salvation can only come through the farmer. Neither the lawyers, nor the doctors, nor the rich landlords are going to secure it.

Now, last but not the least, it is my bounden duty to refer to what agitated our minds during these two or three days. All of us have had many anxious moments while the Viceroy was going through the streets of Banaras. There were detectives stationed in many places. We were horrified. We asked ourselves, 'Why this distrust?' Is it not better that even Lord Hardinge should die than live a living death? But a representative of a mighty sovereign may not. He might find it necessary to impose these detectives on us? We may foam, we may fret, we may resent, but let us not forget that India of today in her impatience has produced an army of anarchists. I myself am an anarchist, but of another type. But there is a class of anarchists amongst us, and if I was able to reach this class, I would say to them that their anarchism has no room in India, if India is to conquer. It is a sign of fear. If we trust and fear God, we shall have to fear no one, not the Maharajas, not the Viceroys, not the detectives, not even King George.

I honour the anarchist for his love of the country. I honour him for his bravery in being willing to die for his country; but I ask him—is killing honourable? Is the dagger of an assassin a fit precursor of an honourable death? I deny it. There is no warrant for such methods in any scriptures. If I found it necessary for the salvation of India that the English should retire, that they should be driven out, I would not hesitate to declare that they would have to go, and I hope I would be prepared to die in defence of that belief. That would, in my opinion, be an honourable death. The bomb-thrower creates secret plots, is afraid to come out into the open, and when caught pays the penalty of misdirected zeal.

I have been told, 'Had we not done this, had some people not thrown bombs, we should never have gained what we have got with reference to the partition movement.'

[Mrs Besant: 'Please stop it.']

This was what I said in Bengal when Mr Lyon presided at the meeting. I think what I am saying is necessary. If I am told to stop I shall obey.

[Turning to the Chairman] I await your orders. If you consider that by my speaking as I am, I am not serving the country and the empire I shall certainly stop.

[Cries of 'Go on.']

[The Chairman: 'Please, explain your object.']

I am simply... [another interruption]

My friends, please do not resent this interruption. If Mrs Besant this evening suggests that I should stop, she does so because she loves India so well, and she considers that I am erring in thinking audibly before you young men. But even so, I simply say this, that I want to purge India of this atmosphere of suspicion on either side, if we are to reach our goal; we should have an empire which is to be based upon mutual love and mutual trust. Is it not better that we talk under the shadow of this college than that we should be talking irresponsibly in our homes? I consider that it is much better that we talk these things openly. I have done so with excellent results before now. I know that there is nothing that the students do not know. I am, therefore, turning the searchlight towards ourselves. I hold the name of my country so dear to me that I exchange these thoughts with you, and submit to you that there is no room for anarchism in India. Let us frankly and openly say whatever we want to say our rulers, and face the consequences if what we have to say does not please them. But let us not abuse.

I was talking the other day to a member of the much-abused civil service. I have not very much in common with the members of that service, but I could not help admiring the manner in which he was speaking to me. He said: 'Mr Gandhi, do you for one moment suppose that all we, civil servants, are a bad lot, that we want to oppress the people whom we have come to govern?' 'No,' I said. 'Then if you get an opportunity put in a word for the much-abused civil service.' And I am here to put in that word. Yes, many members of the Indian Civil Service are most decidedly overbearing; they are tyrannical, at times thoughtless. Many other adjectives may be used. I grant all these things and I grant also that after having lived in India for a certain number of years some of them become somewhat degraded. But what does that signify? They were gentlemen before they came here, and if they have lost some of the moral fibre, it is a reflection upon ourselves.

Just think out for yourselves, if a man who was good yesterday has become bad after having come in contact with me, is he responsible that he has deteriorated or am I? The atmosphere of sycophancy and falsity that surrounds them on their coming to India demoralizes them, as it would many of us. It is well to take the blame sometimes. If we are to receive self-government, we shall have to take it. We shall never be granted self-government. Look at the history of the British Empire and the British nation; freedom-loving as it is, it will not be a party to give freedom to a people who will not take it themselves. Learn your lesson if you wish to from the Boer War. Those who were enemies of that empire only a few years ago have now become friends...

[At this point there was an interruption and a movement on the platform to leave. The speech, therefore, ended here abruptly.]

20

WAR MESSAGE

Thomas Woodrow Wilson

Woodrow Wilson, War Message to Congress, 1917. Wilson's re-election in 1916 owed a great deal to the campaign slogan, 'He kept us out of war.' But the resumption of unrestricted submarine warfare by Germany in 1917 significantly changed the international situation. Several US merchant ships were sunk in March by German U-boats. That April, Wilson called Congress into extraordinary session to ask for a declaration of war against Germany. Within four days both the Senate and the House voted overwhelmingly to support the president.

Gentlemen of the Congress:

I have called the Congress into extraordinary session because there are serious, very serious, choices of policy to be made, and made immediately, which it was neither right nor constitutionally permissible that I should assume the responsibility of making.

On the third of February last I officially laid before you the extraordinary announcement of the Imperial German Government that on and after the first day of February it was its purpose to put aside all restraints of law or of humanity and use its submarines to sink every vessel that sought to approach either the ports of Great Britain and Ireland or the western coasts of Europe or any of the ports controlled by the enemies of Germany within the Mediterranean. That had seemed to be the object of the German submarine warfare earlier in the war, but since April of last year the imperial government had somewhat restrained the commanders of its undersea craft in conformity with its promise then given to us that passenger boats should not be sunk and that due warning would be given to all other vessels which its submarines might seek to destroy, when no resistance was offered or escape attempted, and care taken that their crews were given at least a fair chance to save their lives in their open boats. The precautions taken were meager and haphazard enough, as was proved in distressing instance after instance in the progress of the cruel and unmanly business, but a certain degree of restraint was observed. The new policy has swept every restriction aside. Vessels of every kind, whatever their flag, their character, their cargo, their destination, their errand, have been ruthlessly sent to the bottom without warning and without thought of help or mercy for those on board, the vessels of friendly neutrals along with those of belligerents. Even hospital ships and ships carrying relief to the sorely bereaved and stricken people of Belgium, though the latter were provided with safe conduct through the proscribed areas by the German government itself and were distinguished by unmistakable marks of identity, have been sunk with the same reckless lack of compassion or of principle. I was for a little while unable to believe that such things would in fact be done by any government that had hitherto subscribed to the humane practices of civilized nations. International law had its origin in the attempt to set up some law which would be respected and observed upon the seas, where no nation had right of dominion and where lay the free highways of the world... This minimum of right the German government has swept aside under the plea of retaliation and necessity and because it had no weapons which it could use at sea except these which it is impossible to employ as it is employing them without throwing to the winds all scruples of humanity or of respect for the understandings that were supposed to underlie the intercourse of the world. I am not now thinking of the loss of property involved, immense and serious as that is, but only of the wanton and wholesale destruction of the lives of non-combatants, men, women and children, engaged in pursuits which have always, even in the darkest periods of modern history, been deemed innocent and legitimate. Property can be paid for, the lives of peaceful and innocent people cannot be. The present German submarine warfare against commerce is a warfare against mankind.

It is a war against all nations. American ships have been sunk, American lives taken, in ways which it has stirred us very deeply to learn of, but the ships and people of other neutral and friendly nations have been sunk and overwhelmed in the waters in the same way. There has been no discrimination. The challenge is to all mankind. Each nation must decide for itself how it will meet it. The choice we make for ourselves must be made with a moderation of counsel and a temperateness of judgment befitting our character and our motives as a nation. We must put excited feeling away. Our motive will not be revenge or the victorious assertion of the physical might of the nation, but only the vindication of right, of human right, of which we are only a single champion.

When I addressed the Congress on 26 February last I thought that it would suffice to assert our neutral rights with arms, our right to use the seas against unlawful interference, our right to keep our people safe against unlawful violence. But armed neutrality, it now appears, is impracticable. Because submarines are in effect outlaws when used as the German submarines have been used against merchant shipping, it is impossible to defend ships against their attacks as the law of nations has assumed that merchantmen would defend themselves against privateers or cruisers, visible craft giving chase upon the open sea. It is common prudence in such circumstances, grim necessity indeed, to endeavor to destroy them before they have shown their own intention. They must be dealt with upon sight, if dealt with at all. The German government denies the right of neutrals to use arms at all within the areas of the sea which it has proscribed, even in the defense of rights which no modern publicist has ever before questioned their right to defend. The intimation is conveyed that the armed guards which we have placed on our merchant ships will be treated as beyond the pale of law and subject to be dealt with as pirates would be. Armed neutrality is ineffectual enough at best; in such circumstances and in the face of such pretensions it is worse than ineffectual: it is likely only to produce what it was meant to prevent; it is practically certain to draw us into the war without either the rights or the effectiveness of belligerents. There is one choice we cannot make, we are incapable of making: we will not choose the path of submission and suffer the most sacred rights of our nation and our people to be ignored or violated. The wrongs against which we now array ourselves are no common wrongs; they cut to the very roots of human life.

With a profound sense of the solemn and even tragical character of the step I am taking and of the grave responsibilities which it involves, but in unhesitating obedience to what I deem my constitutional duty, I advise that the Congress declare the recent course of the Imperial German Government to be in fact nothing less war against the government and people of the United States; that it formally accept the status of belligerent which has thus been thrust upon it; and that it take immediate steps not only to put the country in a more thorough state of defense but also to exert all its power and employ all its resources to bring the government of the German empire to terms and end the war.

What this will involve is clear. It will involve the utmost practicable cooperation in counsel and action with the governments now at war with Germany, and, as incident to that, the extension to those governments of the most liberal financial credit, in order that our resources may so far as possible be added to theirs. It will involve the organization and mobilization of all the material resources of the country to supply the materials of war and serve the incidental needs of the nation in the most abundant and yet the most economical and efficient way possible. It will involve the immediate full equipment of the navy in all respects but particularly in supplying it with the best means of dealing with the enemy's submarines. It will involve the immediate addition to the armed forces of the United States already provided for by law in case of war at least five hundred thousand men, who should, in my opinion, be chosen upon the principle of universal liability to service, and also the authorization of subsequent additional increments of equal force so soon as they may be needed and can be handled in training. It will involve also, of course, the granting of adequate credits to the government, sustained, I hope, so far as they can equitably be sustained by the present generation, by well conceived taxation. I say sustained so far as may be equitable by taxation because it seems to me that it would be most unwise to base the credits which will now be necessary entirely on money borrowed. It is our duty, I most respectfully urge, to protect our people so far as we may against the very serious hardships and evils which would be likely to arise out of the inflation which would be produced by vast loans.

In carrying out the measures by which these things are to be accomplished we should keep constantly in mind the wisdom of interfering as little as possible in our own preparation and in the equipment of our own military forces with the duty—for it will be a very practical duty—of supplying the nations already at war with Germany with the materials which they can obtain only from us or by our assistance. They are in the field and we should help them in every way to be effective there.

I shall take the liberty of suggesting, through the several executive departments of the government, for the consideration of your committees, measures for the accomplishment of the several objects I have mentioned. I hope that it will be your pleasure to deal with them as having been framed after very careful thought by the branch of the government upon which the responsibility of conducting the war and safeguarding the nation will most directly fall.

While we do these things, these deeply momentous things, let us be very clear, and make very clear to all the world what our motives and our objects are. My own thought has not been driven from its habitual and normal course by the unhappy events of the last two months, and I do not believe that the thought of the nation has been altered or clouded by them. I have exactly the same things in mind now that I had in mind when I addressed the Senate on 22 January last; the same that I had in mind when I addressed the Congress on 3 February and on 26 February. Our object now, as then, is to vindicate the principles of peace and justice in the life of the world as against selfish and autocratic power and to set up amongst the really free and self-governed peoples of the world such a concert of purpose and of action as will henceforth insure the observance of those principles. Neutrality is no longer feasible or desirable where the peace of the world is involved and the freedom of its peoples, and the menace to that peace and freedom lies in the existence of autocratic governments backed by organized force which is controlled wholly by their will, not by the will of their people. We have seen the last of neutrality in such circumstances. We are at the beginning of an age in which it will be insisted that the same standards of conduct and of responsibility for wrong done shall be observed among nations and their governments that are observed among the individual citizens of civilized states.

We have no quarrel with the German people. We have no feeling towards them but one of sympathy and friendship. It was not upon their impulse that their government acted in entering this war. It was not with their previous knowledge or approval. It was a war determined upon as wars used to be determined upon in the old, unhappy days when peoples were nowhere consulted by their rulers and wars were provoked and waged in the interest of dynasties or of little groups of ambitious men who were accustomed to use their fellow men as pawns and tools.

Self governed nations do not fill their neighbor states with spies or set the course of intrigue to bring about some critical posture of affairs which will give them an opportunity to strike and make conquest. Such designs can be successfully worked out only under cover and where no one has the right to ask questions. Cunningly contrived plans of deception or aggression, carried, it may be, from generation to generation, can be worked out and kept from the light only within the privacy of courts or behind the carefully guarded confidences of a narrow and privileged class. They are happily impossible where public opinion commands and insists upon full information concerning all the nation's affairs.

A steadfast concert for peace can never be maintained except by a partnership of democratic nations. No autocratic government could be trusted to keep faith within it or observe its covenants. It must be a league of honor, a partnership of opinion. Intrigue would eat its vitals away; the plottings of inner circles who could plan what they would and render account to no one would be a corruption seated at its very heart. Only free peonies can hold their purpose and their honor steady to a common end and prefer the interests of mankind to any narrow interest of their own.

Does not every American feel that assurance has been added to our hope for the future peace of the world by the wonderful and heartening things that have been happening within the last few weeks in Russia? Russia was known by those who knew it best to have been always in fact democratic at heart, in all the vital habits of her thought, in all the intimate relationships of her people that spoke their natural instinct, their habitual attitude towards life. The autocracy that crowned the summit of her political structure, long as it had stood and terrible as was the reality of its power, was not in fact Russian in origin, character, or purpose; and now it has been shaken off and the great, generous Russian people have been added in all their naive majesty and might to the forces that are fighting for freedom in the world, for justice, and for peace. Here is a fit partner for a League of Honor.

One of the things that has served to convince us that the Prussian autocracy was not and could never be our friend is that from the very outset of the present war it has filled our unsuspecting communities and even our offices of government with spies and set criminal intrigues everywhere afoot against our national unity of counsel, our peace within and without, our industries and our commerce. Indeed it is now evident that its spies were here even before the war began; and it is unhappily not a matter of conjecture but a fact proved in our courts of justice that the intrigues which have more than once come perilously near to disturbing the peace and dislocating the industries of the country have been carried on at the instigation, with the support, and even under the personal direction of official agents of the Imperial Government accredited to the Government of the United States. Even in checking these things and trying to extirpate them we have sought to put the most generous interpretation possible upon them because we knew that their source lay, not in any hostile feeling or purpose of the German people towards us (who were, no doubt, as ignorant of them as we ourselves were), but only in the selfish designs of a government that did what it pleased and told its people nothing. But they have played their part in serving to convince us at last that that government entertains no real friendship for us and means to act against our peace and security at its convenience. That it means to stir up enemies against us at our very doors the intercepted note to the German minister at Mexico City is eloquent evidence.

We are accepting this challenge of hostile purpose because we know that in such a government, following such methods, we can never have a friend; and that in the presence of its organized power, always lying in wait to accomplish we know not what purpose, there can be no assured security for the democratic governments of the world. We are now about to accept gauge of battle with this natural foe to liberty and shall, if necessary, spend the whole force of the nation to check and nullify its pretensions and its power. We are glad, now that we see the facts with no veil of false pretense about them, to fight thus for the ultimate peace of the world and for the liberation of its peoples, the German peoples included: for the rights of nations great and small and the privilege of men everywhere to choose their way of life and of obedience.

The world must be made safe for democracy. Its peace must be planted upon the tested foundations of political liberty. We have no selfish ends to serve. We desire no conquest, no dominion. We seek no indemnities for ourselves, no material compensation for the sacrifices we shall freely make. We are but one of the champions of the rights of mankind. We shall be satisfied when those rights have been made as secure as the faith and the freedom of nations can make them. Just because we fight without rancor and without selfish object, seeking nothing for ourselves but what we shall wish to share with all free peoples, we shall, I feel confident, conduct our operations as belligerents without passion and ourselves observe with proud punctilio the principles of right and of fair play we profess to be fighting for.

I have said nothing of the governments allied with the Imperial Government of Germany because they have not made war upon us or challenged us to defend our right and our honor. The Austro-Hungarian government has, indeed, avowed its unqualified endorsement and acceptance of the reckless and lawless submarine warfare adopted now without disguise by the Imperial German Government, and it has therefore not been possible for this government to receive Count Tarnowski, the ambassador recently accredited to this government by the Imperial and Royal Government of Austria-Hungary; but that government has not actually engaged in warfare against citizens of the United States on the seas, and I take the liberty, for the present at least, of postponing a discussion of our relations with the authorities at Vienna. We enter this war only where we are clearly forced into it because there are no other means of defending our rights.

It will be all the easier for us to conduct ourselves as belligerents in a high spirit of right and fairness because we act without animus, not in enmity towards a people or with the desire to bring any injury or disadvantage upon them, but only in armed opposition to an irresponsible government which has thrown aside all considerations of humanity and of right and is running amuck. We are, let me say again, the sincere friends of the German people, and shall desire nothing so much as the early reestablishment of intimate relations of mutual advantage between us—however hard it may be for them, for the time being, to believe that this is spoken from our hearts. We have borne with their present government through all these bitter months because of that friendship—exercising a patience and forbearance which would otherwise have been impossible. We shall, happily, still have an opportunity to prove that friendship in our daily attitude and actions towards the millions of men and women of German birth and native sympathy who live amongst us and share our life, and we shall be proud to prove it towards all who are in fact loyal to their neighbors and to the government in the hour of test. They are, most of them, as true and loyal Americans as if they had never known any other fealty or allegiance. They will be prompt to stand with us in rebuking and restraining the few who may be of a different mind and purpose. If there should be disloyalty, it will be dealt with with a firm hand of stern repression; but, if it lifts its head at all, it will lift it only here and there and without countenance except from a lawless and malignant few.

It is a distressing and oppressive duty, gentlemen of the Congress, which I have performed in thus addressing you. There are, it may be, many months of fiery trial and sacrifice ahead of us. It is a fearful thing to lead this great peaceful people into war, into the most terrible and disastrous of all wars, civilization itself seeming to be in the balance. But the right is more precious than peace, and we shall fight for the things which we have always carried nearest our hearts—for democracy, for the right of those who submit to authority to have a voice in their own governments, for the fights and liberties of small nations, for a universal dominion of right by such a concert of free peoples as shall bring peace and safety to all nations and make the world itself at last free. To such a task we can dedicate our lives and our fortunes, everything that we are and everything that we have, with the pride of those who know that the day has come when America is privileged to spend her blood and her might for the principles that gave her birth and happiness and the peace which she has treasured. God helping her, she can do no other.

21

FREEDOM IS MY BIRTHRIGHT

Bal Gangadhar Tilak

Bal Gangadhar Tilak, a prominent leader in India's freedom struggle, delivered a historic speech in Nasik, Maharashtra in 1917, famously known as the 'Freedom is my birthright' speech. This powerful and impassioned address encapsulated Tilak's unwavering belief in the inherent right of every Indian to be free from British colonial rule.

I am young in spirit though old in body. I do not wish to lose this privilege of youth. To deny the growing capacity to my thinking power is to admit that I have no right to speak on this resolution. Whatever I am going to speak today is eternally young. The body might grow old, decrepit and it might perish, but the soul is immortal. Similarly, if there might be an apparent lull in our Home Rule activities, the freedom of the spirit behind it is eternal and indestructible, and it will secure liberty for us.

The Soul means Parameshwar and the mind will not get peace till it gets identified with Him. If one body is worn out the soul will take another: so assures the Gita. This philosophy is quite old. Freedom is my birthright. So long as it is awake within me, I am not old. No weapon can cut this spirit, no fire can burn it, no water can wet it, no wind can dry it. I say further that no CID can burn it. I declare the same principle to the Superintendent of Police who is sitting before me, to the Collector who had been invited to attend this meeting and to the government shorthand writer who is busy taking down notes of our speeches.

This principle will not disappear even if it seems to be killed. We ask for Home Rule and we must get it. The Science which ends in Home Rule is the Science of Politics and not the one which ends in slavery. The Science of Politics is the 'Vedas' of the country. You have a soul and I only want to wake it up. I want to tear off the blind that has been let down by ignorant, designing and selfish people. The Science of Politics consists of two parts. The first is Divine and the second is Demonic. The slavery of a Nation comes into the latter part. There cannot be a moral justification for the Demonic part of the Science of Politics. A Nation which might justify this is guilty of sin in the sight of God. Some people have the courage to declare what is harmful to them and some have not that courage. The political and religious teaching consists in giving the knowledge of this principle. Religious and political teachings are not separate, though they appear to be so on account of foreign rule. All philosophies are included in the Science of Politics.

Who does not know the meaning of Home Rule? Who does not want it? Would you like it, if I enter your house and take possession of your cooking department? I must have the right to manage the affairs in my own house. It is only lunatics and children who do not know how to manage their own affairs.

The cardinal creed of the conferences is that a member must be above 21 years of age; do you not, therefore, think that you want your own rights? Not being lunatics or children you understand your own business, your own rights and, therefore, you know Home Rule. We are told we are not fit for Home Rule. A century has passed away and the British Rule has not made us fit for Home Rule; now we will make our own efforts and fit ourselves for it.

To offer irrelevant excuses, to hold out any temptation and to make other offers will be putting a stigma on the English policy. England is trying to protect the small state of Belgium with the help of India; how can it then say that we should not have Home Rule? Those who find fault with us are avaricious people. But there are people who find fault even with the All-Merciful God. We must work hard to save the soul of our Nation without caring for anything. The good of our country consists in guarding this—our birthright. The Congress has passed this Home Rule resolution. The Provincial Conference is only a child of the Congress, which submits to mandates of its father. We will follow Shri Ramachandra in obeying the order of our father the Congress. We are determined to make efforts to get this resolution enforced even if the effort leads us to the desert, compels us to live incognito, makes us suffer any hardship and even if it finally brings us to death. Shri Ramachandra did it. Do not pass this resolution by merely clapping your hands but by taking a solemn vow that you will work for it. We will work for it by every possible constitutional and law-abiding method to get Home Rule.

Through the grace of God, England has changed its mind towards us. We feel our efforts will not be without success. England proudly thought that a tiny nation might be able to protect the Empire by itself. This pride has gone down. England has now begun to feel that it must make changes in the constitution of the Empire. Lloyd George has openly confessed that England cannot go on without the help of India. All notions about a Nation of a thousand years old have to be changed. The English people have discovered that the wisdom of all their parties is not sufficient. The Indian soldiers have saved the lives of the British soldiers on the French battlefield and have showed their bravery. Those who once considered us as slaves have begun now to call us brothers. God has brought about all these changes. We must push our demands while the notion of this brotherhood is existing in the minds of the English. We must inform them that we, 30 crores of the Indian people, are ready to lay down our lives for the Empire; and that while we are with them none shall dare cast an evil glance at the Empire.

22

STATEMENT IN THE GREAT TRIAL OF 1922

Mohandas Karamchand Gandhi

On 18 March 1922, Mahatma Gandhi and Shankerlal G. Banker, the publisher of Young India, *were tried under Section 124A for sedition due to Gandhi's political articles. They pleaded guilty and Gandhi, in his statement, reaffirmed his belief in non-violent non-cooperation as vital to dismantle the oppressive British Raj.*

Before I read this statement I would like to state that I entirely endorse the learned Advocate General's remarks in connection with my humble self. I think that he has made, because it is very true and I have no desire whatsoever to conceal from this court the fact that to preach disaffection towards the existing system of government has become almost a passion with me, and the Advocate General is entirely in the right when he says that my preaching of disaffection did not commence with my connection with Young India but that it commenced much earlier, and in the statement that I am about to read, it will be my painful duty to admit before this court that it commenced much earlier than the period stated by the Advocate General. It is a painful duty with me but I have to discharge that duty knowing the responsibility that rests upon my shoulders, and I wish to endorse all the blame that the learned Advocate General has thrown on my shoulders in connection with the Bombay occurrences, Madras occurrences and the Chauri Chaura occurrences. Thinking over these things deeply and sleeping over them night after night, it is impossible for me to dissociate myself from the diabolical crimes of Chauri Chaura or the mad outrages of Bombay. He is quite right when he says, that as a man of responsibility, a man having received a fair share of education, having had a fair share of experience of this world, I should have known the consequences of every one of my acts. I know them. I knew that I was playing with fire. I ran the risk and if I was set free I would still do the same. I have felt it this morning that I would have failed in my duty, if I did not say what I said here just now.

I wanted to avoid violence. Non-violence is the first article of my faith. It is also the last article of my creed. But I had to make my choice. I had either to submit to a system which I considered had done an irreparable harm to my country, or incur the risk of the mad fury of my people bursting forth when they understood the truth from my lips. I know that my people have sometimes gone mad. I am deeply sorry for it and I am, therefore, here to submit not to a light penalty but to the highest penalty. I do not ask for mercy. I do not plead any extenuating act. I am here, therefore, to invite and cheerfully submit to the highest penalty that can be inflicted upon me for what in law is a deliberate crime, and what appears to me to be the highest duty of a citizen. The only course open to you, the Judge, is, as I am going to say in my statement, either to resign your post, or inflict on me the severest penalty if you believe that the system and law you are assisting to administer are good for the people. I do not except that kind of conversion. But by the time I have finished with my statement you will have a glimpse of what is raging within my breast to run this maddest risk which a sane man can run.

[He then read out the written statement:] I owe it perhaps to the Indian public and to the public in England, to placate which this prosecution is mainly taken up, that I should explain why from a staunch loyalist and cooperator, I have become an uncompromising disaffectionist and non-cooperator. To the court too I should say why I plead guilty to the charge of promoting disaffection towards the government established by law in India.

My public life began in 1893 in South Africa in troubled weather. My first contact with British authority in that country was not of a happy character. I discovered that as a man and an Indian, I had no rights. More correctly I discovered that I had no rights as a man because I was an Indian.

But I was not baffled. I thought that this treatment of Indians was an excrescence upon a system that was intrinsically and mainly good. I gave the government my voluntary and hearty cooperation, criticizing it freely where I felt it was faulty but never wishing its destruction.

Consequently when the existence of the Empire was threatened in 1899 by the Boer challenge, I offered my services to it, raised a volunteer ambulance corps and served at several actions that took place for the relief of Ladysmith. Similarly in 1906, at the time of the Zulu 'revolt', I raised a stretcher bearer party and served till the end of the 'rebellion'. On both the occasions I received medals and was even mentioned in dispatches. For my work in South Africa I was given by Lord Hardinge a Kaisar-i-Hind gold medal. When the war broke out in 1914 between England and Germany, I raised a volunteer ambulance cars in London, consisting of the then resident Indians in London, chiefly students. Its work was acknowledged by the authorities to be valuable. Lastly, in India when a special appeal was made at the War Conference in Delhi in 1918 by Lord Chelmsford for recruits, I struggled at the cost of my health to raise a corps in Kheda, and the response was being made when the hostilities ceased and orders were received that no more recruits were wanted. In all these efforts at service, I was actuated by the belief that it was possible by such services to gain a status of full equality in the Empire for my countrymen.

The first shock came in the shape of the Rowlatt Act—a law designed to rob the people of all real freedom. I felt called upon to lead an intensive agitation against it. Then followed the Punjab horrors beginning with the massacre at Jallianwala Bagh and culminating in crawling orders, public flogging and other indescribable humiliations. I discovered too that the plighted word of the Prime Minister to the Mussalmans of India regarding the integrity of Turkey and the holy places of Islam was not likely to be fulfilled. But in spite of the forebodings and the grave warnings of friends, at the Amritsar Congress in 1919, I fought for cooperation and working of the Montagu–Chelmsford reforms, hoping that the Prime Minister would redeem his promise to the Indian Mussalmans, that the Punjab wound would be healed, and that the reforms, inadequate and unsatisfactory though they were, marked a new era of hope in the life of India.

But all that hope was shattered. The Khilafat promise was not to be redeemed. The Punjab crime was whitewashed and most culprits went not only unpunished but remained in service, and some continued to draw pensions from the Indian revenue and in some cases were even rewarded. I saw too that not only did the reforms not mark a change of heart, but they were only a method of further raining India of her wealth and of prolonging her servitude.

I came reluctantly to the conclusion that the British connection had made India more helpless than she ever was before, politically and economically. A disarmed India has no power of resistance against any aggressor if she wanted to engage, in an armed conflict with him. So much is this the case that some of our best men consider that India must take generations, before she can achieve Dominion Status. She has become so poor that she has little power of resisting famines. Before the British advent India spun and wove in her millions of cottages, just the supplement she needed for adding to her meagre agricultural resources. This cottage industry, so vital for India's existence, has been ruined by incredibly heartless and inhuman processes as described by English witness. Little do town dwellers know how the semi-starved masses of India are slowly sinking to lifelessness. Little do they know that their miserable comfort represents the brokerage they get for their work they do for the foreign exploiter, that the profits and the brokerage are sucked from the masses. Little do they realize that the government established by law in British India is carried on for this exploitation of the masses. No sophistry, no jugglery in figures, can explain away the evidence that the skeletons in many villages present to the naked eye. I have no doubt whatsoever that both England and the town dweller of India will have to answer, if there is a God above, for this crime against humanity, which is perhaps unequalled in history. The law itself in this country has been used to serve the foreign exploiter. My unbiased examination of the Punjab Marital Law cases has led me to believe that at least 95 per cent of convictions were wholly bad. My experience of political cases in India leads me to the conclusion, in nine out of every ten, the condemned men were totally innocent. Their crime consisted in the love of their country. In 99 cases out of 100, justice has been denied to Indians as against Europeans in the courts of India. This is not an exaggerated picture. It is the experience of almost every Indian who has had anything to do with such cases. In my opinion, the administration of the law is thus prostituted, consciously or unconsciously, for the benefit of the exploiter.

The greater misfortune is that the Englishmen and their Indian associates in the administration of the country do not know that they are engaged in the crime I have attempted to describe. I am satisfied that many Englishmen and Indian officials honestly believe that they are administering one of the best systems devised in the world, and that India is making steady, though, slow progress. They do not know that a subtle but effective system of terrorism and an organized display of force on the one hand, and the deprivation of all powers of retaliation or self-defence on the other, have emasculated the people and induced in them the habit of simulation. This awful habit has added to the ignorance and the self-deception of the administrators. Section 124A, under which

I am happily charged, is perhaps the prince among the political sections of the Indian Penal Code designed to suppress the liberty of the citizen. Affection cannot be manufactured or regulated by law. If one has no affection for a person or system, one should be free to give the fullest expression to his disaffection, so long as he does not contemplate, promote or incite to violence. But the section under which Mr Banker and I are charged is one under which mere promotion of disaffection is a crime.

I have studied some of the cases tried under it; I know that some of the most loved of India's patriots have been convicted under it. I consider it a privilege, therefore, to be charged under that section. I have endeavored to give in their briefest outline the reasons for my disaffection. I have no personal ill-will against any single administrator, much less can I have any disaffection towards the King's person. But I hold it to be a virtue to be disaffected towards a government which in its totality has done more harm to India than any previous system. India is less manly under the British rule than she ever was before. Holding such a belief, I consider it to be a sin to have affection for the system. And it has been a precious privilege for me to be able to write what I have in the various articles tendered in evidence against me.

In fact, I believe that I have rendered a service to India and England by showing in non-cooperation the way out of the unnatural state in which both are living. In my opinion, non-cooperation with evil is as much a duty as is cooperation with good. But in the past, non-cooperation has been deliberately expressed in violence to the evil-doer. I am endeavoring to show to my countrymen that violent non-cooperation only multiples evil, and that as evil can only be sustained by violence, withdrawal of support of evil requires complete abstention from violence. Non-violence implies voluntary submission to the penalty for non-cooperation with evil. I am here, therefore, to invite and submit cheerfully to the highest penalty that can be inflicted upon me for what in law is deliberate crime, and what appears to me to be the highest duty of a citizen. The only course open to you, the Judge and the assessors, is either to resign your posts and thus dissociate yourselves from evil, if you feel that the law you are called upon to administer is an evil, and that in reality I am innocent, or to inflict on me the severest penalty, if you believe that the system and the law you are assisting to administer are good for the people of this country, and that my activity is, therefore, injurious to the common weal.

23

DANDI MARCH

Mohandas Karamchand Gandhi

Throughout the Dandi March that began on 12 March 1930, Gandhi addressed the crowds that gathered along the route, emphasizing the principles of non-violence, self-reliance and unity. His message centered on the power of civil disobedience as a means to challenge unjust laws and demand independence.

In all probability this will be my last speech to you. Even if the Government allow me to march tomorrow morning, this will be my last speech on the sacred bank of the Sabarmati. Possibly these may be the last words of my life here.

I have already told you yesterday what I had to say. Today I shall confine myself to what you should do after I and my companions are arrested. The programme of the march to Jalalpur must be fulfilled as originally settled. The enlistment of volunteers for this purpose should be confined to Gujarat. From what I have seen and heard during the last fortnight I am inclined to believe that the stream of civil resisters will flow unbroken.

But let there be not a semblance of breach of peace even after all of us have been arrested. We have resolved to utilize all our resources in the pursuit of an exclusively non-violent struggle. Let no one commit a wrong in anger. This is my hope and prayer. I wish these words of mine reached every nook and corner of the land. My task shall be done if I perish and so do my comrades. It will then be for the Working Committee of the Congress to show you the way and it will be up to you to follow its lead. That is the only meaning of the Working Committee's resolution. The reins of the movement will still remain in the hands of those of my associates who believe in non-violence as an article of faith. Of course, the Congress will be free to chalk out what course of action commands itself to it. So long as I have not reached Jalalpur, let nothing be done in contravention to the authority vested in me by the Congress. But once I am arrested, the whole general responsibility shifts to the Congress. No one who believes in non-violence, as a creed, need therefore sit still. My compact with the Congress ends as soon as I am arrested. In that case, there should be no slackness in the enrolment of volunteers. Wherever possible, civil disobedience of salt laws should be started. These laws can be violated in three ways. It is an offence to manufacture salt wherever there are facilities for doing so. The possession and sale of contraband salt (which includes natural salt or earth salt) is also an offence. The purchasers of such salt will be equally guilty. To carry away the natural salt depots on the seashore is likewise a violation of law. So is the hawking of such salt. In short, you may choose anyone or all of these devices to break the salt monopoly.

We are however, not to be content with this alone. Wherever there are Congress Committees there is no ban by the Congress and wherever the local workers have self-confidence, other suitable means may be adopted. I prescribe only one condition, viz. let our pledge of truth and non-violence as the only means for the attainment of swaraj be faithfully kept. For the rest, everyone has a free hand. But that does not give a licence to all and sundry to carry on their individual responsibility. Where there are no leaders and only a handful of men, have faith in the program, they may do what they can, if they have enough self-confidence. They have a right, nay it is their duty to do so. The history of the world is full of instances of men who rose to leadership by sheer force of self-confidence, bravery and tenacity. We too, if we aspire to swaraj and are impatient to attain it, should have similar self-confidence. Our ranks will swell and our hearts strengthen as the number of our arrests by Government increases.

Let nobody assume that after I am arrested there will be no one left to guide them. It is not I but Pandit Jawaharlal who is your guide. He has the capacity to lead. Though the fact is that those who have learnt the lesson of fearlessness and self-effacement need no leader, but if we lack these virtues, not even Jawaharlal will be able to produce them in us.

Much can be done in other ways besides these. Liquor and foreign cloth shops can be picketed. We can refuse to pay taxes if we have the requisite strength. The lawyers can give up practice. The public can boycott the courts by refraining from litigation. Government servants can resign their posts. This is the easiest solution of the problem of freedom. Let all who are cooperating with the Government in one way or another, be it by paying taxes, keeping titles, or sending children to official schools, etc., withdraw their cooperation in all or as many ways as possible. One can devise other methods, too, of non-cooperation with the Government. And then there are women who can stand shoulder to shoulder with men in this struggle.

You may take it as my will. It was the only message that I desired to impart to you before starting on the march or for the jail. I wish there to be no suspension or abandonment of the war that commences tomorrow morning or earlier if I am arrested before that time. I shall eagerly await the news that ten batches are ready as soon as my batch is arrested. I believe there are men in India to complete the work begun by me today. I have faith in the righteousness of our cause and the purity of our weapons. And where the means are clean, there God is undoubtedly present with His blessings. And where these three combine, there defeat is an impossibility. A satyagrahi, whether free or incarcerated, is ever victorious. He is vanquished only when he forsakes truth and non-violence and turns a deaf ear to the inner voice. If, therefore, there is such a thing as defeat for even a satyagrahi, he alone is the cause of it. God bless you all and keep off all obstacles from the path in the struggle that begins tomorrow. Let this be our prayer.

24

PROFESSIONS FOR WOMEN

Virginia Woolf

In this speech, delivered on 21 January 1931 before a branch of the National Society for Women's Service, Woolf shares her personal experiences as a female writer and the internal and external obstacles she had to overcome. She addresses the various roles assigned to women, such as being wives, mothers and caretakers, which often limited their opportunities for professional growth and individual expression.

When your secretary invited me to come here, she told me that your Society is concerned with the employment of women and she suggested that I might tell you something about my own professional experiences. It is true I am a woman; it is true I am employed; but what professional experiences have I had? It is difficult to say. My profession is literature; and in that profession there are fewer experiences for women than in any other, with the exception of the stage—fewer, I mean, that are peculiar to women. For the road was cut many years ago—by Fanny Burney, by Aphra Behn, by Harriet Martineau, by Jane Austen, by George Eliot—many famous women, and many more unknown and forgotten, have been before me, making the path smooth, and regulating my steps. Thus, when I came to write, there were very few material obstacles in my way. Writing was a reputable and harmless occupation. The family peace was not broken by the scratching of a pen. No demand was made upon the family purse. For ten and sixpence one can buy paper enough to write all the plays of

Shakespeare—if one has a mind that way. Pianos and models, Paris, Vienna and Berlin, masters and mistresses, are not needed by a writer. The cheapness of writing paper is, of course, the reason why women have succeeded as writers before they have succeeded in the other professions.

But to tell you my story—it is a simple one. You have only got to figure to yourselves a girl in a bedroom with a pen in her hand. She had only to move that pen from left to right—from ten o'clock to one. Then it occurred to her to do what is simple and cheap enough after all—to slip a few of those pages into an envelope, fix a penny stamp in the corner, and drop the envelope into the red box at the corner. It was thus that I became a journalist; and my effort was rewarded on the first day of the following month—a very glorious day it was for me—by a letter from an editor containing a cheque for one pound ten shillings and sixpence. But to show you how little I deserve to be called a professional woman, how little I know of the struggles and difficulties of such lives, I have to admit that instead of spending that sum upon bread and butter, rent, shoes and stockings, or butcher's bills, I went out and bought a cat—a beautiful cat, a Persian cat, which very soon involved me in bitter disputes with my neighbours.

What could be easier than to write articles and to buy Persian cats with the profits? But wait a moment. Articles have to be about something. Mine, I seem to remember, was about a novel by a famous man. And while I was writing this review, I discovered that if I were going to review books I should need to do battle with a certain phantom. And the phantom was a woman, and when I came to know her better I called her after the heroine of a famous poem, The Angel in the House. It was she who used to come between me and my paper when I was writing reviews. It was she who bothered me and wasted my time and so tormented me that at last I killed her. You who come of a younger and happier generation may not have heard of her—you may not know what I mean by the Angel in the House. I will describe her as shortly as I can. She was intensely sympathetic. She was immensely charming. She was utterly unselfish. She excelled in the difficult arts of family life. She sacrificed herself daily. If there was chicken, she took the leg; if there was a draught she sat in it—in short she was so constituted that she never had a mind or a wish of her own, but preferred to sympathize always with the minds and wishes of others. Above all—I need not say it—she was pure. Her purity was supposed to be her chief beauty—her blushes, her great grace. In those days—the last of Queen Victoria—every house had its Angel. And when I came to write I encountered her with the very first words. The shadow of her wings fell on my page; I heard the rustling of her skirts in the room. Directly, that is to say, I took my pen in my hand to review that novel by a famous man, she slipped behind me and whispered: 'My dear, you are a young woman. You are writing about a book that has been written by a man. Be sympathetic; be tender; flatter; deceive; use all the arts and wiles of our sex. Never let anybody guess that you have a mind of your own. Above all, be pure.' And she made as if to guide my pen. I now record the one act for which I take some credit to myself, though the credit rightly belongs to some excellent ancestors of mine who left me a certain sum of money—shall we say £500 a year?—so that it was not necessary for me to depend solely on charm for my living. I turned upon her and caught her by the throat. I did my best to kill her. My excuse, if I were to be had up in a court of law, would be that I acted in self-defence. Had I not killed her she would have killed me. She would have plucked the heart out of my writing. For, as I found, directly I put pen to paper, you cannot review even a novel without having a mind of your own, without expressing what you think to be the truth about human relations, morality, sex. And all these questions, according to the Angel of the House, cannot be dealt with freely and openly by women; they must charm, they must conciliate, they must—to put it bluntly—tell lies if they are to succeed. Thus, whenever I felt the shadow of her wing or the radiance of her halo upon my page, I took up the inkpot and flung it at her. She died hard. Her fictitious nature was of great assistance to her. It is far harder to kill a phantom than a reality. She was always creeping back when I thought I had despatched her. Though I flatter myself that I killed her in the end, the struggle was severe; it took much time that had better have been spent upon learning Greek grammar; or in roaming the world in search of adventures. But it was a real experience; it was an experience that was bound to befall all women writers at that time. Killing the Angel in the House was part of the occupation of a woman writer.

But to continue my story. The Angel was dead; what then remained? You may say that what remained was a simple and common object—a young woman in a bedroom with an inkpot. In other words, now that she had rid herself of falsehood, that young woman had only to be herself. Ah, but what is 'herself'? I mean, what is a woman? I assure you, I do not know. I do not believe that you know. I do not believe that anybody can know until she has expressed herself in all the arts and professions open to human skill. That indeed is one of the reasons why I have come here out of respect for you, who are in process of showing us by your experiments what a woman is, who are in process of providing us, by your failures and successes, with that extremely important piece of information.

But to continue the story of my professional experiences. I made one pound ten and six by my first review; and I bought a Persian cat with the proceeds. Then I grew ambitious. A Persian cat is all very well, I said; but a Persian cat is not enough. I must have a motor car. And it was thus that I became a novelist—for it is a very strange thing that people will give you a motor car if you will tell them a story. It is a still stranger thing that there is nothing so delightful in the world as telling stories. It is far pleasanter than writing reviews of famous novels. And yet, if I am to obey your secretary and tell you my professional experiences as a novelist, I must tell you about a very strange experience that befell me as a novelist. And to understand it you must try first to imagine a novelist's state of mind. I hope I am not giving away professional secrets if I say that a novelist's chief desire is to be as unconscious as possible. He has to induce in himself a state of perpetual lethargy. He wants life to proceed with the utmost quiet and regularity. He wants to see the same faces, to read the same books, to do the same things day after day, month after month, while he is writing, so that nothing may break the illusion in which he is living—so that nothing may disturb or disquiet the mysterious nosings about, feelings round, darts, dashes and sudden discoveries of that very shy and illusive spirit, the imagination. I suspect that this state is the same both for men and women. Be that as it may, I want you to imagine me writing a novel in a state of trance. I want you to figure to yourselves a girl sitting with a pen in her hand, which for minutes, and indeed for hours, she never dips into the inkpot. The image that comes to my mind when I think of this girl is the image of a fisherman lying sunk in dreams on the verge of a deep lake with a rod held out over the water. She was letting her imagination sweep unchecked round every rock and cranny of the world that lies submerged in the depths of our unconscious being. Now came the experience, the experience that I believe to be far commoner with women writers than with men. The line raced through the girl's fingers. Her imagination had rushed away. It had sought the pools, the depths, the dark places where the largest fish slumber. And then there was a smash. There was an explosion. There was foam and confusion. The imagination had dashed itself against something hard. The girl was roused from her dream. She was indeed in a state of the most acute and difficult distress. To speak without figure she had thought of something, something about the body, about the passions which it was unfitting for her as a woman to say. Men, her reason told her, would be shocked. The consciousness of—what men will say of a woman who speaks the truth about her passions had roused her from her artist's state of unconsciousness. She could write no more. The trance was over.

Her imagination could work no longer. This I believe to be a very common experience with women writers—they are impeded by the extreme conventionality of the other sex. For though men sensibly allow themselves great freedom in these respects, I doubt that they realize or can control the extreme severity with which they condemn such freedom in women.

These then were two very genuine experiences of my own. These were two of the adventures of my professional life. The first—killing the Angel in the House—I think I solved. She died. But the second, telling the truth about my own experiences as a body, I do not think I solved. I doubt that any woman has solved it yet. The obstacles against her are still immensely powerful—and yet they are very difficult to define. Outwardly, what is simpler than to write books? Outwardly, what obstacles are there for a woman rather than for a man? Inwardly, I think, the case is very different; she has still many ghosts to fight, many prejudices to overcome. Indeed it will be a long time still, I think, before a woman can sit down to write a book without finding a phantom to be slain, a rock to be dashed against. And if this is so in literature, the freest of all professions for women, how is it in the new professions which you are now for the first time entering?

Those are the questions that I should like, had I time, to ask you. And indeed, if I have laid stress upon these professional experiences of mine, it is because I believe that they are, though in different forms, yours also. Even when the path is nominally open—when there is nothing to prevent a woman from being a doctor, a lawyer, a civil servant—there are many phantoms and obstacles, as I believe, looming in her way. To discuss and define them is I think of great value and importance; for thus only can the labour be shared, the difficulties be solved. But besides this, it is necessary also to discuss the ends and the aims for which we are fighting, for which we are doing battle with these formidable obstacles. Those aims cannot be taken for granted; they must be perpetually questioned and examined. The whole position, as I see it—here in this hall surrounded by women practicing for the first time in history I know not how many different professions—is one of extraordinary interest and importance. You have won rooms of your own in the house hitherto exclusively owned by men. You are able, though not without great labour and effort, to pay the rent. You are earning your £500 a year. But this freedom is only a beginning—the room is your own, but it is still bare. It has to be furnished; it has to be decorated; it has to be shared. How are you going to furnish it, how are you going to decorate it? With whom are you going to share it, and upon what terms? These, I think are questions of the utmost importance and interest. For the first time in history you are able to ask them; for the first time you are able to decide for yourselves what the answers should be. Willingly would I stay and discuss those questions and answers—but not to-night. My time is up; and I must cease.

25

THE BOMBER WILL ALWAYS GET THROUGH

Stanley Baldwin

Stanley Baldwin addressed the British Parliament on 10 November 1932 during a debate on disarmament. Baldwin contended that no defence was possible against air warfare, and any such attempt would only result in retaliation against the innocent. In the speech, he reflected on the complexities of disarmament amid the contemporary climate, urging nations across the world to deliberate eliminating air forces and regulating civil aviation. He entreated the youth to seriously assess the utilization and implication of air weaponry.

I find myself at the close of a most interesting debate which has been well worth while—I myself should not have regretted a second day—in which there have been a number of most interesting contributions, in profound agreement with one of two of the opening observations of Mr Lansbury. Disarmament, in my view, will not stop war; it is a matter of the will to peace.

It is often said that two natural instincts make for the preservation of the race—reproduction of the species and the preservation of the species by fighting for safety. The right honourable gentleman is perfectly right. That fighting instinct, although he did not say it, is the oldest instinct we have in our nature; and that is what we are up against. I agree with him that the highest duty of statesmanship is to work to remove the causes of war. That is the difficult and the constant duty of statesmen, and that is where true statesmanship is shown.

But what you can do by disarmament, and what we all hope to do, is to make war more difficult. It is to make it more difficult to start; it is to make it pay less to continue; and to that I think we ought to direct our minds.

I have studied these matters myself for many years. My duty has made me chairman for five years of the Committee of Imperial Defence. I have sat continuously for 10 years on that committee, except during the period when the present Opposition were in power, and there is no subject that interests me more deeply nor which is more fraught with the ultimate well or ill being of the human race.

What the world suffers from is a sense of fear, a want of confidence; and it is a fear held instinctively and without knowledge very often. But my own view—and I have slowly and deliberately come to this conclusion—is that there is no one thing that is more responsible for that fear—I am speaking of what the honourable Gentleman of Limehouse [Clement Attlee, who proposed the debate's original motion] called the common people, of whom I am chief—there is no greater cause of that fear than the fear of the air.

Up to the time of the last War civilians were exempt from the worst perils of war. They suffered sometimes from hunger, sometimes from the loss of sons and relatives serving in the Army. But now, in addition to this, they suffered from the constant fear not only of being killed themselves, but, what is perhaps worse for a man, of seeing his wife and children killed from the air. These feelings exist among ordinary people throughout the whole civilized world, but I doubt if many of those who have that fear realize one or two things with reference to its cause.

One is the appalling speed which the air has brought into modern warfare; the speed of the attack. The speed of the attack, compared with the attack of an army, is as the speed of a motor-car to that of a four-in-hand. In the next war you will find that any town within reach of an aerodrome can be bombed within the first five minutes of war to an extent inconceivable in the last War, and the question is, whose morale will be shattered quickest by that preliminary bombing?

I think it is well also for the man in the street to realize that there is no power on earth that can protect him from being bombed, whatever people may tell him. The bomber will always get through, and it is very easy to understand that if you realize the area of space. Take any large town you like on this island or on the Continent within reach of an aerodrome. For the defence of that town and its suburbs you have to split up the air into sectors for defence. Calculate that the bombing aeroplanes will be at least 20,000 feet high in the air, and perhaps higher, and it is a matter of mathematical calculation that you will have sectors of from 10 to hundreds of cubic miles.

Imagine 100 cubic miles covered with cloud and fog, and you can calculate how many aeroplanes you would have to throw into that to have much chance of catching odd aeroplanes as they fly through it. It cannot be done, and there is no expert in Europe who will say that it can. The only defence is in offence, which means that you have got to kill more women and children more quickly than the enemy if you want to save yourselves. I mention that so that people may realize what is waiting for them when the next war comes.

The knowledge of this is probably more widespread on the Continent than in these islands. I am told that in many parts of the Continent open preparations are being made to educate the population how best to seek protection. They are being told by lectures; they have considered, I understand, the evacuation of whole populated areas which may find themselves in the zone of fire; and I think I remember to have seen in some of our English illustrated papers pictures of various experiments in protection that are being made on the Continent. There was the Geneva Gas Protocol, signed by 28 countries in June 1925, and yet I find that in these experiments on the Continent people are being taught the necessary precautions to take against the use of gas dropped from the air.

I will not pretend that we are not taking our precautions in this country. We have done it. We have made our investigations much more quietly, and hitherto without any publicity, but considering the years that are required to make preparations any government of this country in the present circumstances of the world would have been guilty of criminal negligence had they neglected to make their preparations.

[House: 'Hear, hear.']

The same is true of other nations. What more potent cause of fear can there be than this kind of thing that is going on on the Continent? And fear is a very dangerous thing. It is quite true that it may act as a deterrent in people's minds against war, but it is much more likely to make them want to increase armaments to protect them against the terrors that they know may be launched against them.

We have to remember that aerial warfare is still in its infancy, and its potentialities are incalculable and inconceivable. How have the nations tried to deal with this terror of the air? I confess that the more I have studied this question the more depressed I have been at the perfectly futile attempts that have been made to deal with this problem.

The amount of time that has been wasted at Geneva in discussing questions such as the reduction of the size of aeroplanes, the prohibition of bombardment of the civil population, the prohibition of bombing, has really reduced me to despair. What would be the only object of reducing the size of aeroplanes? So long as we are working at this form of warfare every scientific man in the country will immediately turn to making a high-explosive bomb about the size of a walnut and as powerful as a bomb of big dimensions, and our last fate may be just as bad as the first.

The prohibition of the bombardment of the civil population, the next thing talking about, is impracticable so long as any bombing exists at all. In the last War there were areas where munitions were made. They now play a part in war that they never played in previous wars, and it is essential to an enemy to knock these out. And so long as they can be knocked out by bombing and no other way, you will never in the practice of war stop that form of bombing.

The prohibition of bombing aeroplanes, or of bombing, leads you to two very obvious considerations when you have examined the question. The first difficulty about that is this:

Will any form of prohibition, whether by convention, treaty, agreement or anything you like not to bomb be effective in war? Quite frankly, I doubt it. And, in doubting it, I make no reflection on the good faith of either ourselves or any other country. If a man has a potential weapon and has his back to the wall and is going to be killed, he will use that weapon whatever it is and whatever undertaking he has given about it. The experience has shown us that the stern test of war will break down all conventions.

[House: 'Hear, hear.']

I will remind the House of the instance which I gave a few weeks ago of the preparations that are being made in the case of bombing with gas, a material forbidden by the Geneva Protocol of 1925. To go a little more closely home, let me remind the House of the Declaration of London, which was in existence in 1914, and which was whittled away bit by bit until the last fragment dropped into the sea in the early spring of 1916.

[Sir Austen Chamberlain: 'It was never ratified.']

No, but we regarded it as binding. Let me also remind the House what I reminded them of before—of two things in the last War. We all remember the cry that was raised when gas was first used, and it was not long before we used it. We remember also the cry that was raised when civilian towns were first bombed. It was not long before we replied, and quite naturally. No one regretted seeing it done more than I did. It was an extraordinary instance of the psychological change that comes over all of us in times of war. So I rule out any prospect of relief from these horrors by any agreement of what I may call local restraint of that kind.

As far as the air is concerned there is, as has been most truly said, no way of complete disarmament except the abolition of flying. We have never known mankind to go back on a new invention. It might be a good thing for this world, as I heard some of the most distinguished men in the air service say, if men had never learned to fly.

[House: 'Hear, hear.']

There is no more important question before every man, woman and child in Europe than what we are going to do with this power now that we have got it. I make no excuse for bringing before the House tonight this subject, to ventilate it in this first assembly of the world, in the hope that what is said here may be read in other countries and may be considered and pondered, because on the solution of this question not only hangs our civilization, but before that terrible day comes, there hangs a lesser question but a difficult one, and that is the possible rearmament of Germany with an air force.

There have been some paragraphs in the Press which looked as though they were half inspired, by which I mean they look as though somebody had been talking about something he had no right to, to someone who did not quite comprehend it.

[House: Laughter]

There have been paragraphs on this subject in which the suggestion was put forward for the abolition of the air forces of the world and the international control of civil aviation. Let me put that in a slightly different way. I am firmly convinced, and have been for some time, that if it is possible the air forces of the world ought to be abolished. But if they are, you have got civil aviation, and in civil aviation you have your potential bombers. It is all very well using the phrase 'international control,' but nobody knows quite what it means, and the subject has never been investigated. That is my answer to Captain Guest.

In my view, it is necessary for the nations of the world

concerned to devote the whole of their mind to this question of civil aviation, to see if it is possible so to control civil aviation that such disarmament would be feasible. I say the nations concerned, because this is a subject on which no nation that has no air force or no air sense has any qualification to express a view; and I think that such an investigation should only be made by the nations which have air forces and who possess an air sense.

Undoubtedly, although she has not an air force, Germany should be a participant in any such discussion which might take place. Such an investigation under the most favourable circumstances would be bound to last a long time, for there is no more difficult or more intricate subject, even assuming that all the participants were desirous of coming to a conclusion.

So in the meantime there will arise the question of disarmament only, and on that I would only say a word. Captain Guest raised a point there and pointed out quite truly that this country had never even carried out the programme of the Bonar Law Government in 1922–23 as the minimum for the safety of this country. He expressed a fear—a very natural and proper fear—lest we, with a comparatively small air force among the large air forces of the world, should disarm from that point, and the vast difference between our strength and that of some other countries would remain relatively as great as it was today. That kind of disarmament does not recommend itself to the government.

[House: 'Hear, hear.']

I assure my right honourable friend that the point which he raised has been very present to our minds, and, in my view, the position is amply safeguarded. I would make only one or two other observations; my desire having been to direct the minds of people to this subject. It has never really been much discussed or thought out, and yet to my mind it is far the most important of all the questions of disarmament, for all disarmament hangs on the air, and as long as the air exists you cannot get rid of that fear of which I spoke and which I believe to be the parent of many troubles.

[House: 'Hear, hear.']

One cannot help reflecting that during the tens or hundreds of millions of years in which the human race has been on this earth, it is only within our generation that we have secured the mastery of the air, and, I do not know how the youth of the world may feel, but it is no cheerful thought to the older men that having got that mastery of the air we are going to defile the earth from the air as we have defiled the soil for nearly all the years that mankind has been on it.

This is a question for young men far more than it is for us. They are the men who fly in the air, and future generations will fly in the air more and more. Few of my colleagues around me here will see another great war. I do not think that we have seen the last great war, but I do not think that there will be one just yet. At any rate, if it does come we shall be too old to be of use to anyone. But what about the younger men, they who will have to fight out this bloody issue of warfare; it is really for them to decide. They are the majority on the earth. It touches them more closely. The instrument is in their hands.

[House: 'Hear, hear.']

There are some instruments so terrible that mankind has resolved not to use them. I happen to know myself of at least three inventions deliberately proposed for use in the last War and which were never used. Potent to a degree and, indeed, I wondered at the conscience of the world.

If the conscience of the young men will ever come to feel that in regard to this one instrument the thing will be done. But if they do not feel like that... As I say, the future is in their hands, but when the next war comes and European civilization is wiped out, as it will be and by no force more than by that force, then do not let them lay the blame on the old men, but let them remember that they principally and they alone are responsible for the terrors that have fallen on the earth.

[House: Loud and prolonged cheers.]

26

THE ONLY THING WE HAVE TO FEAR IS FEAR ITSELF

Franklin Delano Roosevelt

Franklin D. Roosevelt was first inaugurated as president of the United States on 4 March 1933, when the country was in the throes of the Great Depression. This speech was his inaugural address, and it impressed upon the audience his willingness to take drastic action in dire straits. He likened the financial crisis to a wartime situation and resolved to spearhead employment generation and rein in financial institutions, urging the country and administration not to fear, but to act.

This is a day of national consecration, and I am certain that my fellow Americans expect that on my induction into the presidency I will address them with a candor and a decision which the present situation of our nation impels. This is pre-eminently the time to speak the truth, the whole truth, frankly and boldly. Nor need we shrink from honestly facing conditions in our country today. This great nation will endure as it has endured, will revive and will prosper. So, first of all, let me assert my firm belief that the only thing we have to fear is fear itself—nameless, unreasoning, unjustified terror which paralyzes needed efforts to convert retreat into advance. In every dark hour of our national life a leadership of frankness and vigor has met with that understanding and support of the people themselves which is essential to victory. I am convinced that you will again give that support to leadership in these critical days.

In such a spirit on my part and on yours we face our common difficulties. They concern, thank God, only material things. Values have shrunken to fantastic levels; taxes have risen; our ability to pay has fallen; government of all kinds is faced by serious curtailment of income; the means of exchange are frozen in the currents of trade; the withered leaves of industrial enterprise lie on every side; farmers find no markets for their produce; the savings of many years in thousands of families are gone.

More important, a host of unemployed citizens face the grim problem of existence, and an equally great number toil with little return. Only a foolish optimist can deny the dark realities of the moment.

Yet our distress comes from no failure of substance. We are stricken by no plague of locusts. Compared with the perils which our forefathers conquered because they believed and were not afraid, we have still much to be thankful for. Nature still offers her bounty and human efforts have multiplied it. Plenty is at our doorstep, but a generous use of it languishes in the very sight of the supply. Primarily this is because the rulers of the exchange of mankind's goods have failed, through their own stubbornness and their own incompetence, have admitted their failure, and abdicated. Practices of the unscrupulous money changers stand indicted in the court of public opinion, rejected by the hearts and minds of men.

True they have tried, but their efforts have been cast in the pattern of an outworn tradition. Faced by failure of credit they have proposed only the lending of more money. Stripped of the lure of profit by which to induce our people to follow their false leadership, they have resorted to exhortations, pleading tearfully for restored confidence. They know only the rules of a generation of self-seekers. They have no vision, and when there is no vision the people perish.

The money changers have fled from their high seats in the temple of our civilization. We may now restore that temple to the ancient truths. The measure of the restoration lies in the extent to which we apply social values more noble than mere monetary profit.

Happiness lies not in the mere possession of money; it lies in the joy of achievement, in the thrill of creative effort. The joy and moral stimulation of work no longer must be forgotten in the mad chase of evanescent profits. These dark days will be worth all they cost us if they teach us that our true destiny is not to be ministered unto but to minister to ourselves and to our fellow men.

Recognition of the falsity of material wealth as the standard of success goes hand in hand with the abandonment of the false belief that public office and high political position are to be valued only by the standards of pride of place and personal profit; and there must be an end to a conduct in banking and in business which too often has given to a sacred trust the likeness of callous and selfish wrongdoing. Small wonder that confidence languishes, for it thrives only on honesty, on honor, on the sacredness of obligations, on faithful protection, on unselfish performance; without them it cannot live.

Restoration calls, however, not for changes in ethics alone. This nation asks for action, and action now.

Our greatest primary task is to put people to work. This is no unsolvable problem if we face it wisely and courageously. It can be accomplished in part by direct recruiting by the government itself, treating the task as we would treat the emergency of a war, but at the same time, through this employment, accomplishing greatly needed projects to stimulate and reorganize the use of our natural resources.

Hand in hand with this we must frankly recognize the overbalance of population in our industrial centers and, by engaging on a national scale in a redistribution, endeavor to provide a better use of the land for those best fitted for the land. The task can be helped by definite efforts to raise the values of agricultural products and with this the power to purchase the output of our cities. It can be helped by preventing realistically the tragedy of the growing loss through foreclosure of our small homes and our farms. It can be helped by insistence that the federal, state and local governments act forthwith on the demand that their cost be drastically reduced. It can be helped by the unifying of relief activities which today are often scattered, uneconomical and unequal. It can be helped by national planning for and supervision of all forms of transportation and of communications and other utilities which have a definitely public character. There are many ways in which it can be helped, but it can never be helped merely by talking about it. We must act and act quickly.

Finally, in our progress toward a resumption of work we require two safeguards against a return of the evils of the old order; there must be a strict supervision of all banking and credits and investments; there must be an end to speculation with other people's money, and there must be provision for an adequate but sound currency.

There are the lines of attack. I shall presently urge upon a new Congress in special session detailed measures for their fulfillment, and I shall seek the immediate assistance of the several states.

Through this program of action we address ourselves to putting our own national house in order and making income balance outgo. Our international trade relations, though vastly important, are in point of time and necessity secondary to the establishment of a sound national economy. I favor as a practical policy the putting of first things first. I shall spare no effort to restore world trade by international economic readjustment, but the emergency at home cannot wait on that accomplishment.

The basic thought that guides these specific means of national recovery is not narrowly nationalistic. It is the insistence, as a first consideration, upon the interdependence of the various elements in all parts of the United States—a recognition of the old and permanently important manifestation of the American spirit of the pioneer. It is the way to recovery. It is the immediate way. It is the strongest assurance that the recovery will endure.

In the field of world policy I would dedicate this nation to the policy of the good neighbor—the neighbor who resolutely respects himself and, because he does so, respects the rights of others—the neighbor who respects his obligations and respects the sanctity of his agreements in and with a world of neighbors.

If I read the temper of our people correctly, we now realize as we have never realized before our interdependence on each other; that we can not merely take but we must give as well; that if we are to go forward, we must move as a trained and loyal army willing to sacrifice for the good of a common discipline, because without such discipline no progress is made, no leadership becomes effective. We are, I know, ready and willing to submit our lives and property to such discipline, because it makes possible a leadership which aims at a larger good. This I propose to offer, pledging that the larger purposes will bind upon us all as a sacred obligation with a unity of duty hitherto evoked only in time of armed strife.

With this pledge taken, I assume unhesitatingly the leadership of this great army of our people dedicated to a disciplined attack upon our common problems.

Action in this image and to this end is feasible under the form of government which we have inherited from our ancestors. Our Constitution is so simple and practical that it is possible always to meet extraordinary needs by changes in emphasis and arrangement without loss of essential form. That is why our constitutional system has proved itself the most superbly enduring political mechanism the modern world has produced. It has met every stress of vast expansion of territory, of foreign wars, of bitter internal strife, of world relations.

It is to be hoped that the normal balance of executive and legislative authority may be wholly adequate to meet the unprecedented task before us. But it may be that an unprecedented demand and need for undelayed action may call for temporary departure from that normal balance of public procedure.

I am prepared under my constitutional duty to recommend the measures that a stricken nation in the midst of a stricken world may require. These measures, or such other measures as the Congress may build out of its experience and wisdom, I shall seek, within my constitutional authority, to bring to speedy adoption.

But in the event that the Congress shall fail to take one of these two courses, and in the event that the national emergency is still critical, I shall not evade the clear course of duty that will then confront me. I shall ask the Congress for the one remaining instrument to meet the crisis—broad Executive power to wage a war against the emergency, as great as the power that would be given to me if we were in fact invaded by a foreign foe.

For the trust reposed in me I will return the courage and the devotion that befit the time. I can do no less.

We face the arduous days that lie before us in the warm courage of the national unity; with the clear consciousness of seeking old and precious moral values; with the clean satisfaction that comes from the stem performance of duty by old and young alike. We aim at the assurance of a rounded and permanent national life.

We do not distrust the future of essential democracy. The people of the United States have not failed. In their need they have registered a mandate that they want direct, vigorous action. They have asked for discipline and direction under leadership. They have made me the present instrument of their wishes. In the spirit of the gift I take it.

In this dedication of a nation we humbly ask the blessing of God. May He protect each and every one of us. May He guide me in the days to come.

27

EVERY MAN A KING

Huey Pierce Long Jr

'Every Man a King' was a radio address given by Huey P. Long on 23 February 1934, as part of Long's efforts to promote his populist agenda and garner support for his political platform. Long passionately advocated for economic justice and equality. He outlined his vision of redistributing wealth and power to uplift the working class and alleviate poverty.

Is that a right of life, when the young children of this country are being reared into a sphere which is more owned by 12 men than it is by 120 million people?

Ladies and gentlemen, I have only 30 minutes in which to speak to you this evening, and I, therefore, will not be able to discuss in detail so much as I can write when I have all of the time and space that is allowed me for the subjects, but I will undertake to sketch them very briefly without manuscript or preparation, so that you can understand them so well as I can tell them to you tonight.

I contend, my friends, that we have no difficult problem to solve in America, and that is the view of nearly everyone with whom I have discussed the matter here in Washington and elsewhere throughout the United States—that we have no very difficult problem to solve.

It is not the difficulty of the problem which we have; it is the fact that the rich people of this country—and by rich people I mean the super-rich—will not allow us to solve the problems, or rather the one little problem that is afflicting this country, because in order to cure all of our woes it is necessary to scale down the big fortunes, that we may scatter the wealth to be shared by all of the people.

We have a marvelous love for this government of ours; in fact, it is almost a religion, and it is well that it should be, because we have a splendid form of government and we have a splendid set of laws. We have everything here that we need, except that we have neglected the fundamentals upon which the American government was principally predicated.

How may of you remember the first thing that the Declaration of Independence said? It said, 'We hold these truths to be self-evident, that there are certain inalienable rights of the people, and among them are life, liberty, and the pursuit of happiness'; and it said, further, 'We hold the view that all men are created equal.'

Now, what did they mean by that? Did they mean, my friends, to say that all men were created equal and that that meant that any one man was born to inherit $10 billion and that another child was to be born to inherit nothing?

Did that mean, my friends, that someone would come into this world without having had an opportunity, of course, to have hit one lick of work, should be born with more than it and all of its children and children's children could ever dispose of, but that another one would have to be born into a life of starvation?

That was not the meaning of the Declaration of Independence when it said that all men are created equal of 'That we hold that all men are created equal.'

Nor was it the meaning of the Declaration of Independence when it said that they held that there were certain rights that were inalienable—the right of life, liberty, and the pursuit of happiness. Is that right of life, my friends, when the young children of this country are being reared into a sphere which is more owned by 12 men than it is by 120 million people?

Is that, my friends, giving them a fair shake of the dice or anything like the inalienable right of life, liberty, and the pursuit of happiness, or anything resembling the fact that all people are created equal; when we have today in America thousands and hundreds of thousands and millions of children on the verge of starvation in a land that is overflowing with too much to eat and too much to wear? I do not think you will contend that, and I do not think for a moment that they will contend it.

Now let us see if we cannot return this government to the Declaration of Independence and see if we are going to do anything regarding it. Why should we hesitate or why should we quibble or why should we quarrel with one another to find out what the difficulty is, when we know what the Lord told us what the difficulty is, and Moses wrote it out so a blind man could see it, then Jesus told us all about it, and it was later written in the Book of James, where everyone could read it?

I refer to the Scriptures, now, my friends, and give you what it says not for the purpose of convincing you of the wisdom of myself, not for the purpose ladies and gentlemen, of convincing you of the fact that I am quoting the Scripture means that I am to be more believed than someone else; but I quote you the Scripture, rather refer you to the Scripture, because whatever you see there you may rely upon will never be disproved so long as you or your children or anyone may live; and you may further depend upon the fact that not one historical fact that the Bible has ever contained has ever yet been disproved by any scientific discovery or by reason of anything that has been disclosed to man through his own individual mind or through the wisdom of the Lord which the Lord has allowed him to have.

But the Scripture says, ladies and gentlemen, that no country can survive, or for a country to survive it is necessary that we keep the wealth scattered among the people, that nothing should be held permanently by any one person, and that 50 years seems to be the year of jubilee in which all property would be scattered about and returned to the sources from which it originally came, and every seventh year debt should be remitted.

Those two things the Almighty said to be necessary—I should say He knew to be necessary, or else He would not have so prescribed that the property would be kept among the general run of the people and that everyone would continue to share in it; so that no one man would get half of it and hand it down to a son, who takes half of what was left, and that son hand it down to another one, who would take half of what was left, until, like a snowball going downhill, all of the snow was off of the ground except what the snowball had.

I believe that was the judgment and the view and the law of the Lord, that we would have to distribute wealth every so often, in order that there could not be people starving to death in a land of plenty, as there is in America today. We have in American today more wealth, more goods, more food, more clothing, more houses than we have ever had. We have everything in abundance here. We have the farm problem, my friends, because we have too much cotton, because we have too much wheat, and have too much corn, and too much potatoes.

We have a home-loan problem because we have too many houses, and yet nobody can buy them and live in them.

We have trouble, my friends, in the country, because we have too much money owing, the greatest indebtedness that has ever been given to civilization, where it has been shown that we are incapable of distributing to the actual things that are here, because the people have not money enough to supply themselves with them, and because the greed of a few men is such that they think it is necessary that they own everything, and their pleasure consists in the starvation of the masses, and in their possessing things they cannot use, and their children cannot use, but who bask in the splendor of sunlight and wealth, casting darkness and despair and impressing it on everyone else.

'So, therefore,' said the Lord, in effect, 'if you see these things that now have occurred and exist in this and other countries, there must be a constant scattering of wealth in any country if this country is to survive.'

'Then,' said the Lord, in effect, 'every seventh year there shall be a remission of debts; there will be no debts after seven years.' That was the law.

Now, let us take America today. We have in American today, ladies and gentlemen, $272 billion of debt. Two hundred and seventy-two thousand millions of dollars of debts are owed by the various people of this country today. Why, my friends, that cannot be paid. It is not possible for that kind of debt to be paid.

The entire currency of the United States is only $6 billion. That is all of the money that we have got in America today. All the actual money you have got in all of your banks, all that you have got in the Government Treasury, is $6 billion; and if you took all that money and paid it out today you would still owe $266 billion; and if you took all that money and paid again you would still owe $260 billion; and if you took it, my friends, 20 times and paid it you would still owe $150 billion.

You would have to have 45 times the entire money supply of the United States today to pay the debts of the people of America, and then they would just have to start out from scratch, without a dime to go on with.

So, my friends, it is impossible to pay all of these debts, and you might as well find out that it cannot be done. The United States Supreme Court has definitely found out that it could not be done, because, in a Minnesota case, it held that when a State has postponed the evil day of collecting a debt it was a valid and constitutional exercise of legislative power.

Now, ladies and gentlemen, if I may proceed to give you some other words that I think you can understand—I am not going to belabor you by quoting tonight—I am going to tell you what the wise men of all ages and all times, down even to the present day, have all said: that you must keep the wealth of the country scattered, and you must limit the amount that any one man can own. You cannot let any man own $300 billion or $400 billion. If you do, one man can own all of the wealth that the United States has in it.

Now, my friends, if you were off on an island where there were hundred lunches, you could not let one man eat up the hundred lunches, or take the hundred lunches and not let anybody else eat any of them. If you did, there would not be anything else for the balance of the people to consume.

So, we have in America today, my friends, a condition by which about 10 men dominate the means of activity in at least 85 per cent of the activities that you own. They either own directly everything or they have got some kind of mortgage on it, with a very small percentage to be excepted. They own the banks, they own the steel mills, they own the railroads, they own the bonds, they own the mortgages, they own the stores and they have chained the country from one end to the other, until there is not any kind of business that a small, independent man could go into today and make a living, and there is not any kind of business that an independent man can go into and make any money to buy an automobile with; and they have finally and gradually and steadily eliminated everybody from the fields in which there is a living to be made, and still they have got little enough sense to think they ought to be able to get more business out of it anyway.

If you reduce a man to the point where he is starving to death and bleeding and dying, how do you expect that man to get hold of any money to spend with you? It is not possible. Then, ladies and gentlemen, how do you expect people to live, when the wherewith cannot be had by the people?

In the beginning I quoted from the Scriptures. I hope you will understand that I am not quoting Scripture to convince you of my goodness personally, because that is a thing between me and my Maker, that is something as to how I stand with my Maker and as to how you stand with your Maker. That is not concerned with this issue, except and unless there are those of you who would be so good as to pray for the souls of some of us. But the Lord gave his law, and in the Book of James they said so, that the rich should weep and howl for the miseries that had come upon them; and, therefore, it was written that when the rich hold goods they could not use and could not consume, you will inflict punishment on them, and nothing but days of woe ahead of them.

Then we have heard of the great Greek philosopher, Socrates, and the greater Greek philosopher, Plato, and we have read the dialog between Plato and Socrates, in which one said that great riches brought on great poverty, and would be destructive of a country. Read what they said. Read what Plato said; that you must not let any one man be too poor, and you must not let any one man be too rich; that the same mill that grinds out the extra rich is the mill that will grind out the extra poor, because, in order that the extra rich can become so affluent, they must necessarily take more of what ordinarily would belong to the average man.

It is a very simple process of mathematics that you do not have to study, and that no one is going to discuss with you.

So that was the view of Socrates and Plato. That was the view of the English statesmen. That was the view of American statesmen. That was the view of American statesmen like Daniel Webster, Thomas Jefferson, Abraham Lincoln, William Jennings Bryan and Theodore Roosevelt, and even as late as Herbert Hoover and Franklin D. Roosevelt.

Both of these men, Mr Hoover and Mr Roosevelt, came out and said there had to be a decentralization of wealth, but neither one of them did anything about it. But, nevertheless, they recognized the principle. The fact that neither one of them ever did anything about it is their own problem that I am not undertaking to criticize; but had Mr Hoover carried out what he says ought to be done, he would be retiring from the president's office, very probably, three years from now, instead of one year ago; and had Mr Roosevelt proceeded along the lines that he stated were necessary for the decentralization of wealth, he would have gone, my friends, a long way already, and within a few months he would have probably reached a solution of all of the problems that afflict this country.

But I wish to warn you now that nothing that has been done up to this date has taken one dime away from these big-fortune holders; they own just as much as they did, and probably a little bit more; they hold just as many of the debts of the common people as they ever held, and probably a little bit more; and unless we, my friends, are going to give the people of this country a fair shake of the dice, by which they will all get something out of the funds of this land, there is not a chance on the topside of this God's eternal earth by which we can rescue this country and rescue the people of this country.

It is necessary to save the government of the country, but is much more necessary to save the people of America. We love this country. We love this government. It is a religion, I say. It is a kind of religion people have read of when women, in the name of religion, would take their infant babes and throw them into the burning flame, where they would be instantly devoured by the all-consuming fire, in days gone by; and there probably are some people of the world even today, who, in the name of religion, throw their tear-dimmed eyes into the sad faces of their fathers and mothers, who cannot given them food and clothing they both needed, and which is necessary to sustain them, and that goes on day after day, and night after night, when day gets into darkness and blackness, knowing those children would arise in the morning without being fed, and probably to bed at night without being fed.

Yet in the name of our government, and all alone, those people undertake and strive as hard as they can to keep a good government alive, and how long they can stand that no one knows. If I were in their place tonight, the place where millions are, I hope that I would have what I might say—I cannot give you the word to express the kind of fortitude they have; that is the word—I hope that I might have the fortitude to praise and honor my government that had allowed me here in this land, where there is too much to eat and too much to wear, to starve in order that a handful of men can have so much more than they can ever eat or they can ever wear.

Now, we have organized a society, and we call it 'Share Our Wealth Society,' a society with the motto 'every man a king.'

Every man a king, so there would be no such thing as a man or woman who did not have the necessities of life, who would not be dependent upon the whims and caprices and ipse dixit of the financial martyrs for a living. What do we propose by this society? We propose to limit the wealth of big men in the country. There is an average of $15,000 in wealth to every family in America. That is right here today.

We do not propose to divide it up equally. We do not propose a division of wealth, but we propose to limit poverty that we will allow to be inflicted upon any man's family. We will not say we are going to try to guarantee any equality, or $15,000 to families. No; but we do say that one-third of the average is low enough for any one family to hold, that there should be a guaranty of a family wealth of around $5,000; enough for a home, and automobile, a radio, and the ordinary conveniences and the opportunity to educate their children; a fair share of the income of this land thereafter to that family so there will be no such thing as merely the select to have those things, and so there will be no such thing as a family living in poverty and distress.

We have to limit fortunes. Our present plan is that we will allow no one man to own more than $50 million. We think that with that limit we will be able to carry out the balance of the program. It may be necessary that we limit it to less than $50 million. It may be necessary, in working out of the plans, that no man's fortune would be more than $10 million or $15 million. But be that as it may, it will still be more than any one man, or any one man and his children and their children, will be able to spend in their lifetimes; and it is not necessary or reasonable to have wealth piled up beyond that point where we cannot prevent poverty among the masses.

Another thing we propose is old-age pension of $30 a month for everyone that is 60 years old. Now, we do not give this pension to a man making $1,000 a year, and we do not give it to him if he has $10,000 in property, but outside of that we do.

We will limit hours of work. There is not any necessity of having over-production. I think all you have got to do, ladies and gentlemen, is just limit the hours of work to such an extent as people will work only so long as is necessary to produce enough for all of the people to have what they need. Why, ladies and gentleman, let us say that all of these labor-saving devices reduce hours down to where you do not have to work but 4 hours a day; that is enough for these people, and then praise be the name of the Lord, if it gets that good. Let it be good and not a curse, and then we will have 5 hours a day and 5 days a week, or even less than that, and we might give a man a whole month off during a year, or give him two months; and we might do what other countries have seen fit to do, and what I did in Louisiana, by having schools by which adults could go back and learn the things that have been discovered since they went to school.

We will not have any trouble taking care of the agricultural situation. All you have to do is balance your production with your consumption. You simply have to abandon a particular crop that you have too much of, and all you have to do is store the surplus for the next year, and the government will take it over. When you have good crops in the area in which the crops that have been planted are sufficient for another year, put in your public works in the particular year when you do not need to raise any more, and by that means you get everybody employed. When the government has enough of any particular crop to take care of all of the people, that will be all that is necessary; and in order to do all of this, our taxation is going to be to take the billion-dollar fortunes and strip them down to frying size, not to exceed $50 million, and it is necessary to come to $10 million, we will come to $10 million. We have worked the proposition out to guarantee a limit upon property (and no man will own less than one-third the average), and guarantee a reduction of fortunes and a reduction of hours to spread wealth throughout this country. We would care for the old people above 60 and take them away from this thriving industry and given them a chance to enjoy the necessities and live in ease, and thereby lift from the market the labor which would probably create a surplus of commodities.

Those are the things we propose to do. 'Every man a king.' Every man to eat when there is something to eat; all to wear something when there is something to wear. That makes us all sovereign.

You cannot solve these things through these various and sundry alphabetical codes. You can have the NRA and PWA and CWA and the UUG and GIN and any other kind of 'dad-gummed' lettered code. You can wait until doomsday and see 25 more alphabets, but that is not going to solve this proposition. Why hide? Why quibble? You know what the trouble is. The man that says he does not know what the trouble is just hiding his face to keep from seeing the sunlight.

God told you what the trouble was. The philosophers told you what the trouble was; and when you have a country where one man owns more than a hundred thousand people, or a million people, and when you have a country where there are four men, as in America, that have got more control over things than all the 120 million people together, you know what the trouble is.

We had these great incomes in this country; but the farmer, who plowed from sunup to sundown, who labored here from sunup to sundown for six days a week, wound up at the end of the with practically nothing.

And we ought to take care of the veterans of the wars in this program. That is a small matter. Suppose it does cost a billion dollars a year—that means that the money will be scattered throughout this country. We ought to pay them a bonus. We can do it. We ought to take care of every single one of the sick and disabled veterans. I do not care whether a man got sick on the battlefield or did not; every man that wore the uniform of this country is entitled to be taken care of, and there is money enough to do it; and we need to spread the wealth of the country, which you did not do in what you call the NRA.

If the NRA has done any good, I can put it all in my eye without having it hurt. All I can see that NRA has done is to put the little man out of business—the little merchant in his store, the little Dago that is running a fruit stand, or the Greek shoe-shining stand, who has to take hold of a code of 275 pages and study with a spirit level and compass and looking-glass; he has to hire a Philadelphia lawyer to tell him what is in the code; and by the time he learns what the code is, he is in jail or out of business; and they have got a chain code system that has already put him out of business. The NRA is not worth anything, and I said so when they put it through.

Now, my friends, we have got to hit the root with the axe. Centralized power in the hands of a few, with centralized credit in the hands of a few, is the trouble.

Get together in your community tonight or tomorrow and organize one of our Share Our Wealth societies. If you do not understand it, write me and let me send you the platform; let me give you the proof of it.

This is Huey P. Long talking, United States senator, Washington, DC. Write me and let me send you the data on this proposition. Enroll with us. Let us make known to the people what we are going to do. I will send you a button, if I have got enough of them left. We have got a little button that some of our friends designed, with our message around the rim of the button, and in the center 'Every man a king.' Many thousands of them are meeting through the United States, and every day we are getting hundreds and hundreds of letters. Share Our Wealth societies are now being organized, and people have it within their power to relieve themselves from this terrible situation.

Look at what the Mayo brothers announced this week, these greatest scientists of all the world today, who are entitled to have more money than all the Morgans and the Rockefellers, or anyone else, and yet the Mayos turn back their big fortunes to be used for treating the sick, and said they did not want to lay up fortunes in this earth, but wanted to turn them back where they would do some good; but the other big capitalists are not willing to do that, are not willing to do what these men, 10 times more worthy, have already done, and it is going to take a law to require them to do it.

Organize your Share Our Wealth society and get your people to meet with you, and make known your wishes to your senators and representatives in Congress.

Now, my friends, I am going to stop. I thank you for this opportunity to talk to you. I am having to talk under the auspices and by the grace and permission of the National Broadcasting System tonight, and they are letting me talk free. If I had the money, and I wish I had the money, I would like to talk to you more often on this line, but I have not got it, and I cannot expect these people to give it to me free except on some rare instance. But, my friends, I hope to have the opportunity to talk with you, and I am writing to you, and I hope that you will get up and help in the work, because the resolution and bills are before Congress, and we hope to have your help in getting together and organizing your Share Our Wealth society.

Now, that I have but a minute left, I want to say that I suppose my family is listening in on the radio in New Orleans, and I will say to my wife and three children that I am entirely well and hope to be home before many more days, and I hope they have listened to my speech tonight, and I wish them and all their neighbors and friends everything good that may be had.

I thank you, my friends, for your kind attention, and I hope you will enroll with us, take care of your own work in the work of this government, and share or help in our Share Our Wealth society.

I thank you.

28

BLOOD, TOIL, TEARS AND SWEAT

Winston Churchill

The speech commonly referred to as 'Blood, Toil, Tears and Sweat' was delivered by Sir Winston Churchill on 13 May 1940, shortly after he became the British prime minister. This powerful address marked the beginning of Churchill's leadership during World War II and outlined his vision for confronting the challenges posed by Nazi Germany. Churchill's speech was delivered to the House of Commons and set the tone for the tough road ahead. He acknowledged the gravity of the situation and the sacrifices that would be required to achieve victory. The phrase 'blood, toil, tears and sweat' captured the essence of the hardships and sacrifices that lay ahead for the British people.

Mr Speaker, on Friday evening last I received His Majesty's commission to form a new administration. It was the evident wish and will of Parliament and the nation that this should be conceived on the broadest possible basis and that it should include all parties, both those who supported the late government and also the parties of the Opposition. I have completed the most important part of this task. A War Cabinet has been formed of five members, representing, with the Liberal Opposition, the unity of the nation. The three party leaders have agreed to serve, either in the War Cabinet or in high executive office. The three fighting services have been filled. It was necessary that this should be done in one single day, on account of the extreme urgency and rigor of events. A number of other key positions were filled yesterday, and I am submitting a further list to His Majesty tonight. I hope to complete the appointment of the principal ministers during tomorrow. The appointment of the other ministers usually takes a little longer, but I trust that when Parliament meets again, this part of my task will be completed, and that the administration will be complete in all respects.

Sir, I considered it in the public interest to suggest that the House should be summoned to meet today. Mr Speaker agreed, and took the necessary steps, in accordance with the powers conferred upon him by the resolution of the House. At the end of the proceedings today, the adjournment of the House will be proposed until Tuesday, 21 May, with, of course, provision for earlier meeting, if need be. The business to be considered during that week will be notified to Members at the earliest opportunity. I now invite the House, by the resolution which stands in my name, to record its approval of the steps taken and to declare its confidence in the new government.

Sir, to form an administration of this scale and complexity is a serious undertaking in itself, but it must be remembered that we are in the preliminary stage of one of the greatest battles in history, that we are in action at many points in Norway and in Holland, that we have to be prepared in the Mediterranean, that the air battle is continuous and that many preparations have to be made here at home. In this crisis I hope I may be pardoned if I do not address the House at any length today. I hope that any of my friends and colleagues, or former colleagues, who are affected by the political reconstruction, will make all allowances for any lack of ceremony with which it has been necessary to act. I would say to the House, as I said to those who have joined the government: 'I have nothing to offer but blood, toil, tears and sweat.'

We have before us an ordeal of the most grievous kind. We have before us many, many long months of struggle and of suffering. You ask, what is our policy? I will say: it is to wage war, by sea, land and air, with all our might and with all the strength that God can give us; to wage war against a monstrous tyranny, never surpassed in the dark and lamentable catalogue of human crime. That is our policy. You ask, what is our aim? I can answer in one word: victory; victory at all costs, victory in spite of all terror, victory, however long and hard the road may be; for without victory, there is no survival. Let that be realized; no survival for the British Empire, no survival for all that the British Empire has stood for, no survival for the urge and impulse of the ages, that mankind will move forward towards its goal. But I take up my task with buoyancy and hope. I feel sure that our cause will not be suffered to fail among men. At this time I feel entitled to claim the aid of all, and I say, 'Come then, let us go forward together with our united strength.'

29

WE SHALL FIGHT ON THE BEACHES

Winston Churchill

'We Shall Fight on the Beaches' is an iconic phrase from one of Sir Winston Churchill's most famous speeches to the House of Commons during World War II, delivered on 4 June 1940. In a rapidly changing situation, with the Dunkirk rescue operation having just been pulled off by the skin of the Allies' teeth, Churchill had to reassure the public that France's tenuous situation would not impact the British resistance. He reassured their commitment to resist a potential Nazi invasion. The speech is remembered for its fierce and impactful conclusion, leaving no uncertainty about Churchill's and Britain's resolve.

From the moment that the French defenses at Sedan and on the Meuse were broken at the end of the second week of May, only a rapid retreat to Amiens and the south could have saved the British and French Armies who had entered Belgium at the appeal of the Belgian king; but this strategic fact was not immediately realized. The French High Command hoped they would be able to close the gap, and the armies of the north were under their orders. Moreover, a retirement of this kind would have involved almost certainly the destruction of the fine Belgian Army of over 20 divisions and the abandonment of the whole of Belgium. Therefore, when the force and scope of the German penetration were realized and when a new French generalissimo, General Weygand, assumed command in place of General Gamelin, an effort was made by the French and British armies in Belgium to keep on holding the right hand of the Belgians and to give their own right hand to a newly created French Army which was to have advanced across the Somme in great strength to grasp it.

However, the German eruption swept like a sharp scythe around the right and rear of the armies of the north. Eight or nine armored divisions, each of about 400 armoured vehicles of different kinds, but carefully assorted to be complementary and divisible into small self-contained units, cut off all communications between us and the main French Armies. It severed our own communications for food and ammunition, which ran first to Amiens and afterwards through Abbeville, and it shore its way up the coast to Boulogne and Calais, and almost to Dunkirk. Behind this armoured and mechanized onslaught came a number of German divisions in lorries, and behind them again there plodded comparatively slowly the dull brute mass of the ordinary German Army and German people, always so ready to be led to the trampling down in other lands of liberties and comforts which they have never known in their own.

I have said this armoured scythe-stroke almost reached Dunkirk—almost but not quite. Boulogne and Calais were the scenes of desperate fighting. The Guards defended Boulogne for a while and were then withdrawn by orders from this country. The Rifle Brigade, the 60th Rifles, and the Queen Victoria's Rifles, with a battalion of British tanks and 1,000 Frenchmen, in all about 4,000 strong, defended Calais to the last. The British Brigadier was given an hour to surrender. He spurned the offer, and four days of intense street fighting passed before silence reigned over Calais, which marked the end of a memorable resistance. Only 30 unwounded survivors were brought off by the Navy, and we do not know the fate of their comrades. Their sacrifice, however, was not in vain. At least two armoured divisions, which otherwise would have been turned against the British Expeditionary Force, had to be sent to overcome them. They have added another page to the glories of the light divisions, and the time gained enabled the Graveline water lines to be flooded and to be held by the French troops.

Thus it was that the port of Dunkirk was kept open. When it was found impossible for the armies of the north to reopen their communications to Amiens with the main French armies, only one choice remained. It seemed, indeed, forlorn. The Belgian, British and French armies were almost surrounded. Their sole line of retreat was to a single port and to its neighboring beaches. They were pressed on every side by heavy attacks and far outnumbered in the air.

When, a week ago today, I asked the House to fix this afternoon as the occasion for a statement, I feared it would be my hard lot to announce the greatest military disaster in our long history. I thought—and some good judges agreed with me—that perhaps 20,000 or 30,000 men might be re-embarked. But it certainly seemed that the whole of the French First Army and the whole of the British Expeditionary Force north of the Amiens–Abbeville gap would be broken up in the open field or else would have to capitulate for lack of food and ammunition. These were the hard and heavy tidings for which I called upon the House and the nation to prepare themselves a week ago. The whole root and core and brain of the British Army, on which and around which we were to build, and are to build, the great British armies in the later years of the war, seemed about to perish upon the field or to be led into an ignominious and starving captivity.

That was the prospect a week ago. But another blow which might well have proved final was yet to fall upon us. The king of the Belgians had called upon us to come to his aid. Had not this ruler and his government severed themselves from the Allies, who rescued their country from extinction in the late war, and had they not sought refuge in what was proved to be a fatal neutrality, the French and British armies might well at the outset have saved not only Belgium but perhaps even Poland. Yet at the last moment, when Belgium was already invaded, King Leopold called upon us to come to his aid, and even at the last moment we came. He and his brave, efficient army, nearly half a million strong, guarded our left flank and thus kept open our only line of retreat to the sea. Suddenly, without prior consultation, with the least possible notice, without the advice of his Ministers and upon his own personal act, he sent a plenipotentiary to the German Command, surrendered his army, and exposed our whole flank and means of retreat.

I asked the House a week ago to suspend its judgment because the facts were not clear, but I do not feel that any reason now exists why we should not form our own opinions upon this pitiful episode. The surrender of the Belgian Army compelled the British at the shortest notice to cover a flank to the sea more than 30 miles in length. Otherwise all would have been cut off, and all would have shared the fate to which King Leopold had condemned the finest army his country had ever formed. So in doing this and in exposing this flank, as anyone who followed the operations on the map will see, contact was lost between the British and two out of the three corps forming the First French Army, who were still farther from the coast than we were, and it seemed impossible that any large number of Allied troops could reach the coast.

The enemy attacked on all sides with great strength and fierceness, and their main power, the power of their far more numerous Air Force, was thrown into the battle or else concentrated upon Dunkirk and the beaches. Pressing in upon the narrow exit, both from the east and from the west, the enemy began to fire with cannon upon the beaches by which alone the shipping could approach or depart. They sowed magnetic mines in the channels and seas; they sent repeated waves of hostile aircraft, sometimes more than a hundred strong in one formation, to cast their bombs upon the single pier that remained, and upon the sand dunes upon which the troops had their eyes for shelter. Their U-boats, one of which was sunk, and their motor launches took their toll of the vast traffic which now began. For four or five days an intense struggle reigned. All their armored divisions—or what Was left of them—together with great masses of infantry and artillery, hurled themselves in vain upon the ever-narrowing, ever-contracting appendix within which the British and French armies fought.

Meanwhile, the Royal Navy, with the willing help of countless merchant seamen, strained every nerve to embark the British and Allied troops; 220 light warships and 650 other vessels were engaged. They had to operate upon the difficult coast, often in adverse weather, under an almost ceaseless hail of bombs and an increasing concentration of artillery fire. Nor were the seas, as I have said, themselves free from mines and torpedoes. It was in conditions such as these that our men carried on, with little or no rest, for days and nights on end, making trip after trip across the dangerous waters, bringing with them always men whom they had rescued. The numbers they have brought back are the measure of their devotion and their courage. The hospital ships, which brought off many thousands of British and French wounded, being so plainly marked were a special target for Nazi bombs; but the men and women on board them never faltered in their duty.

Meanwhile, the Royal Air Force, which had already been intervening in the battle, so far as its range would allow, from home bases, now used part of its main metropolitan fighter strength, and struck at the German bombers and at the fighters which in large numbers protected them. This struggle was protracted and fierce. Suddenly the scene has cleared, the crash and thunder has for the moment—but only for the moment—died away. A miracle of deliverance, achieved by valor, by perseverance, by perfect discipline, by faultless service, by resource, by skill, by unconquerable fidelity, is manifest to us all. The enemy was hurled back by the retreating British and French troops. He was so roughly handled that he did not hurry their departure seriously. The Royal Air Force engaged the main strength of the German Air Force, and inflicted upon them losses of at least four to one; and the Navy, using nearly

1,000 ships of all kinds, carried over 335,000 men, French and British, out of the jaws of death and shame, to their native land and to the tasks which lie immediately ahead. We must be very careful not to assign to this deliverance the attributes of a victory. Wars are not won by evacuations. But there was a victory inside this deliverance, which should be noted. It was gained by the air force. Many of our soldiers coming back have not seen the air force at work; they saw only the bombers which escaped its protective attack. They underrate its achievements. I have heard much talk of this; that is why I go out of my way to say this. I will tell you about it.

This was a great trial of strength between the British and German air forces. Can you conceive a greater objective for the Germans in the air than to make evacuation from these beaches impossible, and to sink all these ships which were displayed, almost to the extent of thousands? Could there have been an objective of greater military importance and significance for the whole purpose of the war than this? They tried hard, and they were beaten back; they were frustrated in their task. We got the army away; and they have paid fourfold for any losses which they have inflicted. Very large formations of German aeroplanes—and we know that they are a very brave race—have turned on several occasions from the attack of one-quarter of their number of the Royal Air Force, and have dispersed in different directions.

Twelve aeroplanes have been hunted by two. One aeroplane was driven into the water and cast away by the mere charge of a British aeroplane, which had no more ammunition. All of our types—the Hurricane, the Spitfire and the new Defiant—and all our pilots have been vindicated as superior to what they have at present to face.

When we consider how much greater would be our advantage in defending the air above this island against an overseas attack, I must say that I find in these facts a sure basis upon which practical and reassuring thoughts may rest. I will pay my tribute to these young airmen. The great French Army was very largely, for the time being, cast back and disturbed by the onrush of a few thousands of armoured vehicles. May it not also be that the cause of civilization itself will be defended by the skill and devotion of a few thousand airmen? There never has been, I suppose, in all the world, in all the history of war, such an opportunity for youth. The Knights of the Round Table, the Crusaders, all fall back into the past—not only distant but prosaic; these young men, going forth every morn to guard their native land and all that we stand for, holding in their hands these instruments of colossal and shattering power, of whom it may be said that

> 'Every morn brought forth a noble chance
> And every chance brought forth a noble knight,'

deserve our gratitude, as do all the brave men who, in so many ways and on so many occasions, are ready, and continue ready to give life and all for their native land.

I return to the army. In the long series of very fierce battles, now on this front, now on that, fighting on three fronts at once, battles fought by two or three divisions against an equal or somewhat larger number of the enemy, and fought fiercely on some of the old grounds that so many of us knew so well—in these battles our losses in men have exceeded 30,000 killed, wounded and missing. I take occasion to express the sympathy of the House to all who have suffered bereavement or who are still anxious. The president of the Board of Trade [Sir Andrew Duncan] is not here today. His son has been killed, and many in the House have felt the pangs of affliction in the sharpest form. But I will say this about the missing: we have had a large number of wounded come home safely to this country, but I would say about the missing that there may be very many reported missing who will come back home, some day, in one way or another. In the confusion of this fight it is inevitable that many have been left in positions where honor required no further resistance from them.

Against this loss of over 30,000 men, we can set a far heavier loss certainly inflicted upon the enemy. But our losses in material are enormous. We have perhaps lost one-third of the men we lost in the opening days of the battle of 21 March 1918, but we have lost nearly as many guns—nearly 1,000—and all our transport, all the armoured vehicles that were with the army in the north. This loss will impose a further delay on the expansion of our military strength. That expansion had not been proceeding as far as we had hoped. The best of all we had to give had gone to the British Expeditionary Force, and although they had not the numbers of tanks and some articles of equipment which were desirable, they were a very well and finely equipped army. They had the first-fruits of all that our industry had to give, and that is gone. And now here is this further delay. How long it will be, how long it will last, depends upon the exertions which we make in this island. An effort the like of which has never been seen in our records is now being made. Work is proceeding everywhere, night and day, Sundays and week days. Capital and Labor have cast aside their interests, rights and customs and put them into the common stock. Already the flow of munitions has leaped forward. There is no reason why we should not in a few months overtake the sudden and serious loss that has come upon us, without retarding the development of our general program.

Nevertheless, our thankfulness at the escape of our Army and so many men, whose loved ones have passed through an agonizing week, must not blind us to the fact that what has happened in France and Belgium is a colossal military disaster. The French Army has been weakened, the Belgian Army has been lost, a large part of those fortified lines upon which so much faith had been reposed is gone, many valuable mining districts and factories have passed into the enemy's possession, the whole of the Channel ports are in his hands, with all the tragic consequences that follow from that, and we must expect another blow to be struck almost immediately at us or at France. We are told that Herr Hitler has a plan for invading the British Isles. This has often been thought of before. When Napoleon lay at Boulogne for a year with his flat-bottomed boats and his Grand Army, he was told by someone, 'There are bitter weeds in England.' There are certainly a great many more of them since the British Expeditionary Force returned.

The whole question of home defence against invasion is, of course, powerfully affected by the fact that we have for the time being in this island incomparably more powerful military forces than we have ever had at any moment in this war or the last. But this will not continue. We shall not be content with a defensive war. We have our duty to our Ally. We have to reconstitute and build up the British Expeditionary Force once again, under its gallant commander-in-chief, Lord Gort. All this is in train; but in the interval we must put our defenses in this island into such a high state of organization that the fewest possible numbers will be required to give effective security and that the largest possible potential of offensive effort may be realized. On this we are now engaged. It will be very convenient, if it be the desire of the House, to enter upon this subject in a secret Session. Not that the government would necessarily be able to reveal in very great detail military secrets, but we like to have our discussions free, without the restraint imposed by the fact that they will be read the next day by the enemy; and the government would benefit by views freely expressed in all parts of the House by members with their knowledge of so many different parts of the country. I understand that some request is to be made upon this subject, which will be readily acceded to by His Majesty's Government.

We have found it necessary to take measures of increasing stringency, not only against enemy aliens and suspicious characters of other nationalities, but also against British subjects who may become a danger or a nuisance should the war be transported to the United Kingdom. I know there are a great many people affected by the orders which we have made who are the passionate enemies of Nazi Germany. I am very sorry for them, but we cannot, at the present time and under the present stress, draw all the distinctions which we should like to do. If parachute landings were attempted and fierce fighting attendant upon them followed, these unfortunate people would be far better out of the way, for their own sakes as well as for ours. There is, however, another class, for which I feel not the slightest sympathy. Parliament has given us the powers to put down fifth column activities with a strong hand, and we shall use those powers subject to the supervision and correction of the House, without the slightest hesitation until we are satisfied, and more than satisfied, that this malignancy in our midst has been effectively stamped out.

Turning once again, and this time more generally, to the question of invasion, I would observe that there has never been a period in all these long centuries of which we boast when an absolute guarantee against invasion, still less against serious raids, could have been given to our people. In the days of Napoleon the same wind which would have carried his transports across the Channel might have driven away the blockading fleet. There was always the chance, and it is that chance which has excited and befooled the imaginations of many Continental tyrants. Many are the tales that are told. We are assured that novel methods will be adopted, and when we see the originality of malice, the ingenuity of aggression, which our enemy displays, we may certainly prepare ourselves for every kind of novel stratagem and every kind of brutal and treacherous maneuver. I think that no idea is so outlandish that it should not be considered and viewed with a searching, but at the same time, I hope, with a steady eye. We must never forget the solid assurances of sea power and those which belong to air power if it can be locally exercised.

I have, myself, full confidence that if all do their duty, if nothing is neglected, and if the best arrangements are made, as they are being made, we shall prove ourselves once again able to defend our island home, to ride out the storm of war and to outlive the menace of tyranny, if necessary for years, if necessary alone. At any rate, that is what we are going to try to do. That is the resolve of His Majesty's Government—every man of them. That is the will of Parliament and the nation. The British Empire and the French Republic, linked together in their cause and in their need, will defend to the death their native soil, aiding each other like good comrades to the utmost of their strength. Even though large tracts of Europe and many old and famous States have fallen or may fall into the grip of the Gestapo and all the odious apparatus of Nazi rule, we shall not flag or fail. We shall go on to the end, we shall fight in France, we shall fight on the seas and oceans, we shall fight with growing confidence and growing strength in the air, we shall defend our island, whatever the cost may be, we shall fight on the beaches, we shall fight on the landing grounds, we shall fight in the fields and in the streets, we shall fight in the hills; we shall never surrender, and even if, which I do not for a moment believe, this island or a large part of it were subjugated and starving, then our Empire beyond the seas, armed and guarded by the British Fleet, would carry on the struggle, until, in God's good time, the New World, with all its power and might, steps forth to the rescue and the liberation of the old.

30

THEIR FINEST HOUR

Winston Churchill

'Their Finest Hour' is the title of a historic speech delivered by Sir Winston Churchill on 18 June 1940. This iconic address is considered one of Churchill's most powerful and memorable speeches, delivered during a critical time in World War II. At the time of the speech, the German forces had already conquered much of Western Europe, and Britain stood alone against the advancing Nazi war machine. The speech was delivered to the House of Commons, just weeks after the evacuation of British troops from Dunkirk, which had been a miraculous rescue operation. In 'Their Finest Hour,' Churchill acknowledged the grim reality of the situation, and the immense challenges and dangers faced by Britain. However, he expressed unwavering confidence in the British people, their resolve and their ability to resist the German onslaught.

I spoke the other day of the colossal military disaster which occurred when the French High Command failed to withdraw the northern Armies from Belgium at the moment when they knew that the French front was decisively broken at Sedan and on the Meuse. This delay entailed the loss of 15 or 16 French divisions and threw out of action for the critical period the whole of the British Expeditionary Force. Our Army and 120,000 French troops were indeed rescued by the British Navy from Dunkirk but only with the loss of their cannon, vehicles and modern equipment. This loss inevitably took some weeks to repair, and in the first two of those weeks the battle in France has been lost. When we consider the heroic resistance made by the French Army against heavy odds in this battle, the enormous losses inflicted upon the enemy and the evident exhaustion of the enemy, it may well be the thought that these 25 divisions of the best-trained and best-equipped troops might have turned the scale. However, General Weygand had to fight without them. Only three British divisions or their equivalent were able to stand in the line with their French comrades. They have suffered severely, but they have fought well. We sent every man we could to France as fast as we could re-equip and transport their formations.

I am not reciting these facts for the purpose of recrimination. That I judge to be utterly futile and even harmful. We cannot afford it. I recite them in order to explain why it was we did not have, as we could have had, between 12 and 14 British divisions fighting in the line in this great battle instead of only three. Now I put all this aside. I put it on the shelf, from which the historians, when they have time, will select their documents to tell their stories. We have to think of the future and not of the past. This also applies in a small way to our own affairs at home. There are many who would hold an inquest in the House of Commons on the conduct of the governments—and of parliaments, for they are in it, too—during the years which led up to this catastrophe. They seek to indict those who were responsible for the guidance of our affairs. This also would be a foolish and pernicious process. There are too many in it. Let each man search his conscience and search his speeches. I frequently search mine.

Of this I am quite sure, that if we open a quarrel between the past and the present, we shall find that we have lost the future. Therefore, I cannot accept the drawing of any distinctions between members of the present government. It was formed at a moment of crisis in order to unite all the parties and all sections of opinion. It has received the almost unanimous support of both Houses of Parliament. Its members are going to stand together, and, subject to the authority of the House of Commons, we are going to govern the country and fight the war. It is absolutely necessary at a time like this that every minister who tries each day to do his duty shall be respected; and their subordinates must know that their chiefs are not threatened men, men who are here today and gone tomorrow, but that their directions must be punctually and faithfully obeyed. Without this concentrated power we cannot face what lies before us. I should not think it would be very advantageous for the House to prolong this debate this afternoon under conditions of public stress. Many facts are not clear that will be clear in a short time. We are to have a secret session on Thursday, and I should think that would be a better opportunity for the many earnest expressions of opinion which members will desire to make and for the House to discuss vital matters without having everything read the next morning by our dangerous foes.

The disastrous military events which have happened during the past fortnight have not come to me with any sense of surprise. Indeed, I indicated a fortnight ago as clearly as I could to the House that the worst possibilities were open; and I made it perfectly clear then that whatever happened in France would make no difference to the resolve of Britain and the British Empire to fight on, if necessary for years, if necessary alone.

During the last few days we have successfully brought off the great majority of the troops we had on the line of communication in France; and seven-eighths of the troops we have sent to France since the beginning of the war—that is to say, about 350,000 out of 400,000 men—are safely back in this country. Others are still fighting with the French, and fighting with considerable success in their local encounters against the enemy. We have also brought back a great mass of stores, rifles and munitions of all kinds which had been accumulated in France during the last nine months.

We have, therefore, in this Island today a very large and powerful military force. This force comprises all our best-trained and our finest troops, including scores of thousands of those who have already measured their quality against the Germans and found themselves at no disadvantage. We have under arms at the present time in this Island over a million and a quarter men. Behind these we have the Local Defence Volunteers, numbering half a million, only a portion of whom, however, are yet armed with rifles or other firearms. We have incorporated into our Defence Forces every man for whom we have a weapon. We expect very large additions to our weapons in the near future, and in preparation for this we intend forthwith to call up, drill and train further large numbers. Those who are not called up, or else are employed during the vast business of munitions production in all its branches—and their ramifications are innumerable—will serve their country best by remaining at their ordinary work until they receive their summons. We have also over here Dominions armies. The Canadians had actually landed in France, but have now been safely withdrawn, much disappointed, but in perfect order, with all their artillery and equipment. And these very high-class forces from the Dominions will now take part in the defence of the Mother Country.

Lest the account which I have given of these large forces should raise the question: why did they not take part in the great battle in France? I must make it clear that, apart from the divisions training and organizing at home, only 12 divisions were equipped to fight upon a scale which justified their being sent abroad. And this was fully up to the number which the French had been led to expect would be available in France at the ninth month of the war. The rest of our forces at home have a fighting value for home defence which will, of course, steadily increase every week that passes. Thus, the invasion of Great Britain would at this time require the transportation across the sea of hostile armies on a very large scale, and after they had been so transported they would have to be continually maintained with all the masses of munitions and supplies which are required for continuous battle—as continuous battle it will surely be.

Here is where we come to the Navy—and after all, we have a Navy. Some people seem to forget that we have a Navy. We must remind them. For the last 30 years I have been concerned in discussions about the possibilities of oversea invasion, and I took the responsibility on behalf of the Admiralty, at the beginning of the last war, of allowing all regular troops to be sent out of the country. That was a very serious step to take, because our Territorials had only just been called up and were quite untrained. Therefore, this island was for several months particularly denuded of fighting troops. The Admiralty had confidence at that time in their ability to prevent a mass invasion even though at that time the Germans had a magnificent battle fleet in the proportion of 10 to 16, even though they were capable of fighting a general engagement every day and any day, whereas now they have only a couple of heavy ships worth speaking of—the Scharnhorst and the Gneisenau. We are also told that the Italian Navy is to come out and gain sea superiority in these waters. If they seriously intend it, I shall only say that we shall be delighted to offer Signor Mussolini a free and safeguarded passage through the Strait of Gibraltar in order that he may play the part to which he aspires. There is a general curiosity in the British Fleet to find out whether the Italians are up to the level they were at in the last war or whether they have fallen off at all.

Therefore, it seems to me that as far as sea-borne invasion on a great scale is concerned, we are far more capable of meeting it today than we were at many periods in the last war and during the early months of this war, before our other troops were trained, and while the BEF had proceeded abroad. Now, the Navy have never pretended to be able to prevent raids by bodies of 5,000 or 10,000 men flung suddenly across and thrown ashore at several points on the coast some dark night or foggy morning. The efficacy of sea power, especially under modern conditions, depends upon the invading force being of large size; it has to be of large size, in view of our military strength, to be of any use. If it is of large size, then the Navy have something they can find and meet and, as it were, bite on. Now, we must remember that even five divisions, however lightly equipped, would require 200 to 250 ships, and with modern air reconnaissance and photography it would not be easy to collect such an armada, marshal it, and conduct it across the sea without any powerful naval forces to escort it; and there would be very great possibilities, to put it mildly, that this armada would be intercepted long before it reached the coast, and all the men drowned in the sea or, at the worst blown to pieces with their equipment while they were trying to land. We also have a great system of minefields, recently strongly reinforced, through which we alone know the channels. If the enemy tries to sweep passages through these minefields, it will be the task of the Navy to destroy the mine-sweepers and any other forces employed to protect them. There should be no difficulty in this, owing to our great superiority at sea.

Those are the regular, well-tested, well-proved arguments on which we have relied during many years in peace and war. But the question is whether there are any new methods by which those solid assurances can be circumvented. Odd as it may seem, some attention has been given to this by the Admiralty, whose prime duty and responsibility is to destroy any large sea-borne expedition before it reaches, or at the moment when it reaches, these shores. It would not be a good thing for me to go into details of this. It might suggest ideas to other people which they have not thought of, and they would not be likely to give us any of their ideas in exchange. All I will say is that untiring vigilance and mind-searching must be devoted to the subject, because the enemy is crafty and cunning and full of novel treacheries and stratagems. The House may be assured that the utmost ingenuity is being displayed and imagination is being evoked from large numbers of competent officers, well-trained in tactics and thoroughly up to date, to measure and counterwork novel possibilities. Untiring vigilance and untiring searching of the mind is being, and must be, devoted to the subject, because, remember, the enemy is crafty and there is no dirty trick he will not do.

Some people will ask why, then, was it that the British Navy was not able to prevent the movement of a large army from Germany into Norway across the Skagerrak? But the conditions in the Channel and in the North Sea are in no way like those which prevail in the Skagerrak. In the Skagerrak, because of the distance, we could give no air support to our surface ships, and consequently, lying as we did close to the enemy's main air power, we were compelled to use only our submarines. We could not enforce the decisive blockade or interruption which is possible from surface vessels. Our submarines took a heavy toll but could not, by themselves, prevent the invasion of Norway. In the Channel and in the North Sea, on the other hand, our superior naval surface forces, aided by our submarines, will operate with close and effective air assistance.

This brings me, naturally, to the great question of invasion from the air, and of the impending struggle between the British and German air forces. It seems quite clear that no invasion on a scale beyond the capacity of our land forces to crush speedily is likely to take place from the air until our Air Force has been definitely overpowered. In the meantime, there may be raids by parachute troops and attempted descents of airborne soldiers. We should be able to give those gentry a warm reception both in the air and on the ground, if they reach it in any condition to continue the dispute. But the great question is: can we break Hitler's air weapon? Now, of course, it is a very great pity that we have not got an Air Force at least equal to that of the most powerful enemy within striking distance of these shores. But we have a very powerful Air Force which has proved itself far superior in quality, both in men and in many types of machine, to what we have met so far in the numerous and fierce air battles which have been fought with the Germans. In France, where we were at a considerable disadvantage and lost many machines on the ground when they were standing round the aerodromes, we were accustomed to inflict in the air losses of as much as two and two-and-a-half to one. In the fighting over Dunkirk, which was a sort of no-man's-land, we undoubtedly beat the German Air Force, and gained the mastery of the local air, inflicting here a loss of three or four to one day after day. Anyone who looks at the photographs which were published a week or so ago of the re-embarkation, showing the masses of troops assembled on the beach and forming an ideal target for hours at a time, must realize that this re-embarkation would not have been possible unless the enemy had resigned all hope of recovering air superiority at that time and at that place.

In the defence of this island the advantages to the defenders will be much greater than they were in the fighting around Dunkirk. We hope to improve on the rate of three or four to one which was realized at Dunkirk; and in addition all our injured machines and their crews which get down safely—and, surprisingly, a very great many injured machines and men do get down safely in modern air fighting—all of these will fall, in an attack upon these islands, on friendly soil and live to fight another day; whereas all the injured enemy machines and their complements will be total losses as far as the war is concerned.

During the great battle in France, we gave very powerful and continuous aid to the French Army, both by fighters and bombers; but in spite of every kind of pressure we never would allow the entire metropolitan fighter strength of the Air Force to be consumed. This decision was painful, but it was also right, because the fortunes of the battle in France could not have been decisively affected even if we had thrown in our entire fighter force. That battle was lost by the unfortunate strategical opening, by the extraordinary and unforeseen power of the armored columns, and by the great preponderance of the German Army in numbers. Our fighter Air Force might easily have been exhausted as a mere accident in that great struggle, and then we should have found ourselves at the present time in a very serious plight. But as it is, I am happy to inform the House that our fighter strength is stronger at the present time relatively to the Germans, who have suffered terrible losses, than it has ever been; and consequently we believe ourselves possessed of the capacity to continue the war in the air under better conditions than we have ever experienced before. I look forward confidently to the exploits of our fighter pilots—these splendid men, this brilliant youth—who will have the glory of saving their native land, their island home and all they love, from the most deadly of all attacks.

There remains, of course, the danger of bombing attacks, which will certainly be made very soon upon us by the bomber forces of the enemy. It is true that the German bomber force is superior in numbers to ours; but we have a very large bomber force also, which we shall use to strike at military targets in Germany without intermission. I do not at all underrate the severity of the ordeal which lies before us; but I believe our countrymen will show themselves capable of standing up to it, like the brave men of Barcelona, and will be able to stand up to it, and carry on in spite of it, at least as well as any other people in the world. Much will depend upon this; every man and every woman will have the chance to show the finest qualities of their race, and render the highest service to their cause. For all of us, at this time, whatever our sphere, our station, our occupation or our duties, it will be a help to remember the famous lines:

'He nothing common did or mean, Upon that memorable scene.'

I have thought it right upon this occasion to give the House and the country some indication of the solid, practical grounds upon which we base our inflexible resolve to continue the war. There are a good many people who say, 'Never mind. Win or lose, sink or swim, better die than submit to tyranny—and such a tyranny.' And I do not dissociate myself from them. But I can assure them that our professional advisers of the three Services unitedly advise that we should carry on the war, and that there are good and reasonable hopes of final victory. We have fully informed and consulted all the self-governing Dominions, these great communities far beyond the oceans who have been built up on our laws and on our civilization, and who are absolutely free to choose their course, but are absolutely devoted to the ancient Motherland, and who feel themselves inspired by the same emotions which lead me to stake our all upon duty and honour. We have fully consulted them, and I have received from their prime ministers, Mr Mackenzie King of Canada, Mr Menzies of Australia, Mr Fraser of New Zealand and General Smuts of South Africa—that wonderful man, with his immense profound mind, and his eye watching from a distance the whole panorama of European affairs—I have received from all these eminent men, who all have governments behind them elected on wide franchises, who are all there because they represent the will of their people, messages couched in the most moving terms in which they endorse our decision to fight on, and declare themselves ready to share our fortunes and to persevere to the end. That is what we are going to do.

We may now ask ourselves: in what way has our position worsened since the beginning of the war? It has worsened by the fact that the Germans have conquered a large part of the coast line of Western Europe, and many small countries have been overrun by them. This aggravates the possibilities of air attack and adds to our naval preoccupations. It in no way diminishes, but on the contrary definitely increases, the power of our long-distance blockade. Similarly, the entrance of Italy into the war increases the power of our long-distance blockade. We have stopped the worst leak by that. We do not know whether military resistance will come to an end in France or not, but should it do so, then of course the Germans will be able to concentrate their forces, both military and industrial, upon us. But for the reasons I have given to the House these will not be found so easy to apply. If invasion has become more imminent, as no doubt it has, we, being relieved from the task of maintaining a large army in France, have far larger and more efficient forces to meet it.

If Hitler can bring under his despotic control the industries of the countries he has conquered, this will add greatly to his already vast armament output. On the other hand, this will not happen immediately, and we are now assured of immense, continuous and increasing support in supplies and munitions of all kinds from the United States; and especially of aeroplanes and pilots from the Dominions and across the oceans coming from regions which are beyond the reach of enemy bombers.

I do not see how any of these factors can operate to our detriment on balance before the winter comes; and the winter will impose a strain upon the Nazi regime, with almost all Europe writhing and starving under its cruel heel, which, for all their ruthlessness, will run them very hard. We must not forget that from the moment when we declared war on 3 September it was always possible for Germany to turn all her Air Force upon this country, together with any other devices of invasion she might conceive, and that France could have done little or nothing to prevent her doing so. We have, therefore, lived under this danger, in principle and in a slightly modified form, during all these months. In the meanwhile, however, we have enormously improved our methods of defence, and we have learned what we had no right to assume at the beginning, namely, that the individual aircraft and the individual British pilot have a sure and definite superiority. Therefore, in casting up this dread balance sheet and contemplating our dangers with a disillusioned eye, I see great reason for intense vigilance and exertion, but none whatever for panic or despair.

During the first four years of the last war the Allies experienced nothing but disaster and disappointment. That was our constant fear: one blow after another, terrible losses, frightful dangers. Everything miscarried. And yet at the end of those four years the morale of the Allies was higher than that of the Germans, who had moved from one aggressive triumph to another, and who stood everywhere triumphant invaders of the lands into which they had broken. During that war we repeatedly asked ourselves the question: 'How are we going to win?' And no one was able ever to answer it with much precision, until at the end, quite suddenly, quite unexpectedly, our terrible foe collapsed before us, and we were so glutted with victory that in our folly we threw it away.

We do not yet know what will happen in France or whether the French resistance will be prolonged, both in France and in the French Empire overseas. The French government will be throwing away great opportunities and casting adrift their future if they do not continue the war in accordance with their treaty obligations, from which we have not felt able to release them. The House will have read the historic declaration in which, at the desire of many Frenchmen—and of our own hearts—we have proclaimed our willingness at the darkest hour in French history to conclude a union of common citizenship in this struggle. However matters may go in France or with the French government, or other French governments, we in this island and in the British Empire will never lose our sense of comradeship with the French people. If we are now called upon to endure what they have been suffering, we shall emulate their courage, and if final victory rewards our toils they shall share the gains, aye, and freedom shall be restored to all. We abate nothing of our just demands; not one jot or tittle do we recede. Czechs, Poles, Norwegians, Dutch, Belgians have joined their causes to our own. All these shall be restored.

What General Weygand called the Battle of France is over. I expect that the Battle of Britain is about to begin. Upon this battle depends the survival of Christian civilization. Upon it depends our own British life, and the long continuity of our institutions and our Empire. The whole fury and might of the enemy must very soon be turned on us.

Hitler knows that he will have to break us in this island or lose the war. If we can stand up to him, all Europe may be free and the life of the world may move forward into broad, sunlit uplands. But if we fail, then the whole world, including the United States, including all that we have known and cared for, will sink into the abyss of a new Dark Age made more sinister, and perhaps more protracted, by the lights of perverted science.

Let us therefore brace ourselves to our duties, and so bear ourselves that if the British Empire and its Commonwealth last for a thousand years, men will still say, 'This was their finest hour.'

31

THE FLAME OF FRENCH RESISTANCE

Charles de Gaulle

Between 18–22 June 1940, Charles de Gaulle conveyed a trio of speeches through the BBC radio in London. The period followed Nazi Germany's conquest of France in World War II, leading to the French opting for an armistice. De Gaulle staunchly opposed this decision. His famous speeches that encouraged the French to defend their country and rely on their international allies are believed to have kindled the French Resistance and inspired soldiers to continue the struggle despite the odds.

18 June 1940

The leaders who, for many years past, have been at the head of the French armed forces have set up a government.

Alleging the defeat of our armies, this government has entered into negotiations with the enemy with a view to bringing about a cessation of hostilities.

It is quite true that we were, and still are, overwhelmed by enemy mechanised forces, both on the ground and in the air. It was the tanks, the planes, and the tactics of the Germans, far more than the fact that we were outnumbered, that forced our armies to retreat. It was the German tanks, planes, and tactics that provided the element of surprise which brought our leaders to their present plight.

But has the last word been said? Must we abandon all hope?

Is our defeat final and irremediable? To those questions I answer—No!

Speaking in full knowledge of the facts, I ask you to believe me when I say that the cause of France is not lost. The very factors that brought about our defeat may one day lead us to victory.

For, remember this, France does not stand alone. She is not isolated. Behind her is a vast empire, and she can make common cause with the British empire, which commands the seas and is continuing the struggle. Like England, she can draw unreservedly on the immense industrial resources of the United States.

This war is not limited to our unfortunate country. The outcome of the struggle has not been decided by the battle of France. This is a world war. Mistakes have been made, there have been delays and untold suffering, but the fact remains that there still exists in the world everything we need to crush our enemies some day.

Today we are crushed by the sheer weight of mechanized force hurled against us, but we can still look to a future in which even greater mechanized force will bring us victory. The destiny of the world is at stake.

I, General de Gaulle, now in London, call on all French officers and men who are at present on British soil, or may be in the future, with or without their arms; I call on all engineers and skilled workmen from the armaments factories who are at present on British soil, or may be in the future, to get in touch with me.

Whatever happens, the flame of French resistance must not and shall not die.

Tomorrow I shall broadcast again from London.

19 June 1940

Frenchmen must now be fully aware that all ordinary forms of authority have disappeared.

Faced by the bewilderment of my countrymen, by the

disintegration of a government in thrall to the enemy, by the fact that the institutions of my country are incapable, at the moment, of functioning, I, General de Gaulle, a French soldier and military leader, realize that I now speak for France. In the name of France, I make the following solemn declaration: it is the bounden duty of all Frenchmen who still bear arms to continue the struggle. For them to lay down their arms, to evacuate any position of military importance, or agree to hand over any part of French territory, however small, to enemy control, would be a crime against our country. For the moment I refer particularly to French North Africa—to the integrity of French North Africa.

The Italian armistice is nothing but a clumsy trap. In the Africa of Clauzel, Bugeaud, Lyautey and Noguès, honour and duty strictly enjoin that the French should refuse to carry out the conditions imposed by the enemy.

The thought that the panic of Bordeaux could make itself felt across the sea is not to be borne.

Soldiers of France, wherever you may be, arise!

22 June 1940

The French government, after having asked for an armistice, now knows the conditions dictated by the enemy.

The result of these conditions would be the complete demobilization of the French land, sea and air forces, the surrender of our weapons and the total occupation of French territory. The French government would come under German and Italian tutelage.

It may therefore be said that this armistice would not only be a capitulation, but that it would also reduce the country to slavery. Now, a great many Frenchmen refuse to accept either capitulation or slavery, for reasons which are called: honour, common sense and the higher interests of the country.

I say honour, for France has undertaken not to lay down arms save in agreement with her allies. As long as the allies continue the war, her government has no right to surrender to the enemy. The Polish, Norwegian, Belgian, Netherlands and Luxemburg governments, though driven from their territories, have thus interpreted their duty. I say common sense, for it is absurd to consider the struggle as lost. True, we have suffered a major defeat. We lost the battle of France through a faulty military system, mistakes in the conduct of operations, and the defeatist spirit shown by the government during recent battles. But we still have a vast empire, our fleet is intact and we possess large sums in gold. We still have the gigantic potentialities of American industry. The same war conditions which caused us to be beaten by 5,000 planes and 6,000 tanks can tomorrow bring victory by means of 20,000 tanks and 20,000 planes.

I say the higher interests of the country, for this is not a Franco-German war to be decided by a single battle. This is a world war. No one can foresee whether the neutral countries of today will not be at war tomorrow, or whether Germany's allies will always remain her allies. If the powers of freedom ultimately triumph over those of servitude, what will be the fate of a France which has submitted to the enemy?

Honour, common sense and the interests of the country require that all free Frenchmen, wherever they be, should continue the fight as best they may.

It is therefore necessary to group the largest possible French force wherever this can be done. Everything which can be collected by way of French military elements and potentialities for armaments production must be organized wherever such elements exist.

I, General de Gaulle, am undertaking this national task here in England.

I call upon all French servicemen of the land, sea and air forces; I call upon French engineers and skilled armaments workers who are on British soil, or have the means of getting here, to come and join me.

I call upon the leaders, together with all soldiers, sailors, and airmen of the French land, sea and air forces, wherever they may now be, to get in touch with me.

I call upon all Frenchmen who want to remain free to listen to my voice and follow me.

Long live free France in honour and independence!

32

THE NAZI INVASION OF RUSSIA

Vyacheslav Molotov

On 22 June 1941, following Germany's surprise attack on the Soviet Union, known as Operation Barbarossa, Molotov addressed Russia through the radio. He condemned the aggression of Nazi Germany, emphasized the resilience and determination of the Soviet people to defend their homeland and called for unity and sacrifice in the face of the invasion.

Citizens of the Soviet Union:

The Soviet government and its head, Comrade Stalin, have authorized me to make the following statement:

Today at four o'clock a.m., without any claims having been presented to the Soviet Union, without a declaration of war, German troops attacked our country, attacked our borders at many points and bombed from their airplanes our cities; Zhitomir, Kiev, Sevastopol, Kaunas and some others, killing and wounding over 200 persons.

There were also enemy air raids and artillery shelling from Rumanian and Finnish territory.

This unheard-of attack upon our country is perfidy unparalleled in the history of civilized nations. The attack on our country was perpetrated despite the fact that a treaty of non-aggression had been signed between the USSR and Germany and that the Soviet government most faithfully abided by all provisions of this treaty.

The attack upon our country was perpetrated despite the fact that during the entire period of operation of this treaty, the German government could not find grounds for a single complaint against the USSR as regards observance of this treaty.

Entire responsibility for this predatory attack upon the Soviet Union falls fully and completely upon the German fascist rulers.

At 5:30 a.m.—that is, after the attack had already been perpetrated, Von der Schulenburg, the German ambassador in Moscow, on behalf of his government made the statement to me as People's Commissar of Foreign Affairs to the effect that the German government had decided to launch war against the USSR in connection with the concentration of Red Army units near the eastern German frontier.

In reply to this I stated on behalf of the Soviet government that, until the very last moment, the German government had not presented any claims to the Soviet government, that Germany attacked the USSR despite the peaceable position of the Soviet Union, and that for this reason fascist Germany is the aggressor.

On instruction of the government of the Soviet Union I also stated that at no point had our troops or our Air Force committed a violation of the frontier and therefore the statement made this morning by the Rumanian radio to the effect that Soviet aircraft allegedly had fired on Rumanian airdromes is a sheer lie and provocation.

Likewise a lie and provocation is the whole declaration made today by Hitler, who is trying belatedly to concoct accusations charging the Soviet Union with failure to observe the Soviet-German pact.

Now that the attack on the Soviet Union has already been committed, the Soviet government has ordered our troops to repulse the predatory assault and to drive German troops from the territory of our country.

This war has been forced upon us, not by the German people, not by German workers, peasants and intellectuals, whose sufferings we well understand, but by the clique of bloodthirsty fascist rulers of Germany who have enslaved Frenchmen, Czechs, Poles, Serbians,

Norway, Belgium, Denmark, Holland, Greece and other nations.

The government of the Soviet Union expresses its unshakable confidence that our valiant Army and Navy and brave falcons of the Soviet Air Force will acquit themselves with honour in performing their duty to the fatherland and to the Soviet people, and will inflict a crushing blow upon the aggressor.

This is not the first time that our people have had to deal with an attack of an arrogant foe. At the time of Napoleon's invasion of Russia our people's reply was war for the fatherland, and Napoleon suffered defeat and met his doom.

It will be the same with Hitler, who in his arrogance has proclaimed a new crusade against our country. The Red Army and our whole people will again wage victorious war for the fatherland, for our country, for honour, for liberty.

The government of the Soviet Union expresses the firm conviction that the whole population of our country, all workers, peasants and intellectuals, men and women, will conscientiously perform their duties and do their work. Our entire people must now stand solid and united as never before.

Each one of us must demand of himself and of others discipline, organization and self-denial worthy of real Soviet patriots, in order to provide for all the needs of the Red Army, Navy and Air Force, to insure victory over the enemy.

The government calls upon you, citizens of the Soviet Union, to rally still more closely around our glorious Bolshevist party, around our Soviet government, around our great leader and comrade, Stalin. Ours is a righteous cause. The enemy shall be defeated. Victory will be ours.

33

I AM STILL ALIVE

Subhas Chandra Bose

This speech of Subhas Chandra Bose aired in Germany, 25 March 1942, on radio and is very compelling and revealing. It shows how much the British government was afraid of Bose and his activities in Europe. They wanted to see him dead. The canard which the British propaganda spread about the death of Bose in an air crash on way to Tokyo, while he was still in Germany, was refuted by Bose himself through this broadcast which was heard by millions in India and throughout the world. There are millions of people in India who still do not believe that Bose died in an air crash over Formosa on 18 August 1945.

This is Subhas Chandra Bose, who is still alive, speaking to you over the Azad Hind radio. British news agencies have spread all over the world the report that I died in an aeroplane crash on my way to Tokyo to attend an important conference there. Ever since I left India, last year, British propaganda agencies have, from time to time, given contradictory reports of my whereabouts, while newspapers in England have not hesitated to use uncomplimentary language about me. The latest report about my death is perhaps an instance of wishful thinking. I can imagine that the British government would, at this critical hour in India's history; like to see me dead since they are now trying their level best to win India over to their side for the purpose of their imperialistic war. I do not have before me the full particulars of the aeroplane disaster referred to above. I cannot, therefore, say if it was the result of sabotage on the part of our enemy. In any case, I beg to offer my respectful homage to the memory of those who lost their lives in that tragic event. Their names will be written in letters of gold in the history of our struggle for independence.

I have considered very carefully the offer of the British government to India and the radio speech of Sir Stafford Cripps in that connection. I feel perfectly convinced that it is now quite clear that Sir Stafford has gone to India to try the age-long policy of British imperialism—'divide and rule'.

Many people in India did not expect Sir Stafford Cripps to play a role which might very well have been reserved for a conservative politician like Mr Amery. Sir Stafford has himself assured us that the terms offered to India are, in his opinion, the soundest and the best, and that the members of the British Cabinet were all unanimous over these proposals. This affords one further proof that, in Britain, all party differences disappear when the question of India comes up. Sir Stafford has told us that India is a subcontinent inhabited by many races and peoples. I would like to remind him that India was unified under the empire of Ashoka the Great, several centuries before the Christian era—more than a thousand years before England was unified. Britain has, in other parts of her Empire, for instance in Ireland and Palestine, used the religious issue in order to divide the people. She has been utilizing in India for that same purpose not only this issue but other imperial weapons like the Indian princes, depressed classes, etc. Now Sir Stafford is in India to use the same instruments for imperialistic ends. It is no less striking that he is applying the old imperialist policy for working out a compromise with one section of the people while simultaneously suppressing the other. This is why on one side Sir Stafford is conferring with one set of politicians, while on the other the fearless and uncompromising fighters for independence are safely lodged behind prison. The Indian people are fully aware of this nefarious policy of British politicians.

I have no doubt that the spirit of our freedom fighters will hurl down the prison walls and inspire the people of India to know that this is an insult to India's self-respect and honour. As the London paper, *The Daily Telegraph*, has remarked, Sir Stafford's proposals contain nothing that is fundamentally new. The essence is dominion status within the Empire, which will be realized only when the war is over. But according to the terms of the offer, the speech of Sir Stafford Cripps, and the comments of English papers like *The Manchester Guardian*, it is quite clear that the real intention of the British government is to split India into a number of states, just as Ireland was split up at the end of the last war. I am doubtful whether India will even look at such an offer. Indians by nature are hospitable, and Sir Stafford will be committing a grievous mistake if he interpreted such hospitality to mean the acceptance of his offer.

Sir Stafford reached the height of imperialist hypocrisy when, at a press conference at Delhi, he remarked that the Indians have not been able to produce an agreed constitution. But the Indian people know from their bitter experience that only the British government is responsible for the corruption and bribery in India. The Indian people are, therefore, convinced that they can no longer hope to win their freedom by discussion or argument, propaganda and passive resistance, but must now resort to other methods which are more effective and powerful.

Sir Stafford also mentioned that while the war is going on, a new constitution cannot be framed for India, and hence the inauguration of dominion status will begin on the termination of the war. I may remind Sir Stafford Cripps that, as early as October 1939, I replied to the British government by suggesting that a provisional national government, commanding the confidence of the majority of the people, should be set up at once. This provisional national government could be made responsible to the present Indian Legislative Assembly. This suggestion was first of all put forward by me on behalf of the Forward Bloc of the Congress, and being practicable and reasonable, the official Congress Committee also adopted it as their own demand. The fact, however, is that the British government is not ready to part with power at the present moment. By raising the issue of the minorities, princes or of the so-called depressed classes, they can at any time find a plea that the Indians are not united. Sir Stafford must be living in a fool's paradise if he thinks that by making such hopeless offers, he can satisfy India's hunger for freedom. In the last World War, with the help of India, the war was won by England, but India's reward was further suppression and massacre. India has not forgotten those episodes, and she will see that the present golden opportunity is not lost.

Since the beginning of this century, the British government has been using another organization as a counter-blast to the Congress in order to reject its demands. It has been using the Muslim League for this purpose, because that party is regarded as pro-British in its outlook. In fact, British propaganda has tried to create the impression that the Muslim League is almost as influential a body as the Congress, and that it represents the majority of India's Muslims. This, however, is far from the truth. In reality, there are several influential and important Muslim organizations which are thoroughly nationalist. Moreover, of the eleven provinces in British India, out of which only four have a majority of Muslims, only one, the Punjab, has a cabinet which may be regarded as a Muslim League Cabinet. But even the Punjab premier is strongly opposed to the main program of the Muslim League, namely the division of India. But even then it is said that the majority of the Muslims will not stand for Indian independence.

As far as the defence of India is concerned, it is stated in the British proposals that, so long as the war lasts, the full military control of India will be directly in the hands of Britain, not even in the hands of the viceroy or the commander-in-chief in India. By this policy, Britain wants to achieve a twofold purpose. She desires, on the one hand, to utilize to the fullest extent India's resources for the whole Empire, and on the other, to force thereby, the enemies of Britain to attack Britain's military base in India, so that the Indian people may be provoked into voluntarily entering the war as Britain's ally. I would like to affirm, with all the emphasis at my command, that all the pro-British Indians who are participating in Britain's war will alone be responsible if the war comes ultimately to India. Further, I would like to warn my countrymen that Britain's sole object flow is to drag the Indian people into the war. It has been a successful game of the British people to get other nations involved in the war. Up to the present time, they have been carrying out glorious retreats and successful evacuations.

Recently they have adopted a novel policy of burning and destroying everything before taking to their heels. If the British government apply these scorched earth tactics to their own county—that is no concern of ours. But I have every reason to believe that they have decided to apply these scorched earth tactics in Ceylon and India, should the war come there. Therefore, participation in Britain's war will not only hinder Britain's defeat and overthrow but will also delay the attainment of independence for Indians.

34

QUIT INDIA

Mohandas Karamchand Gandhi

Gandhiji addressed the AICC at Bombay on 8 August 1942, outlining his plan of action, in Hindi.

Before you discuss the resolution, let me place before you one or two things, I want you to understand two things very clearly and to consider them from the same point of view from which I am placing them before you. I ask you to consider it from my point of view, because if you approve of it, you will be enjoined to carry out all I say. It will be a great responsibility. There are people who ask me whether I am the same man that I was in 1920, or whether there has been any change in me. You are right in asking that question.

Let me, however, hasten to assure that I am the same Gandhi as I was in 1920. I have not changed in any fundamental respect. I attach the same importance to non-violence that I did then. If at all, my emphasis on it has grown stronger. There is no real contradiction between the present resolution and my previous writings and utterances.

Occasions like the present do not occur in everybody's and but rarely in anybody's life. I want you to know and feel that there is nothing but purest Ahimsa in all that I am saying and doing today. The draft resolution of the Working Committee is based on Ahimsa, the contemplated struggle similarly has its roots in Ahimsa. If, therefore, there is any among you who has lost faith in Ahimsa or is wearied of it, let him not vote for this resolution.

Let me explain my position clearly. God has vouchsafed to me a priceless gift in the weapon of Ahimsa. I and my Ahimsa are on our trail today. If in the present crisis, when the earth is being scorched by the flames of Himsa and crying for deliverance, I failed to make use of the God given talent, God will not forgive me and I shall be judged unworthy of the great gift. I must act now. I may not hesitate and merely look on, when Russia and China are threatened.

Ours is not a drive for power, but purely a non-violent fight for India's independence. In a violent struggle, a successful general has been often known to effect a military coup and to set up a dictatorship. But under the Congress scheme of things, essentially non-violent as it is, there can be no room for dictatorship. A non-violent soldier of freedom will covet nothing for himself, he fights only for the freedom of his country. The Congress is unconcerned as to who will rule, when freedom is attained. The power, when it comes, will belong to the people of India, and it will be for them to decide whom it placed in the entrusted. May be that the reins will be placed in the hands of the Parsis, for instance—as I would love to see happen—or they may be handed to some others whose names are not heard in the Congress today. It will not be for you then to object saying, 'This community is microscopic. That party did not play its due part in the freedom struggle; why should it have all the power?' Ever since its inception the Congress has kept itself meticulously free of the communal taint. It has thought always in terms of the whole nation and has acted accordingly...

I know how imperfect our Ahimsa is and how far away we are still from the ideal, but in Ahimsa there is no final failure or defeat. I have faith, therefore, that if, in spite of our shortcomings, the big thing does happen, it will be because God wanted to help us by crowning with success our silent, unremitting Sadhana for the last 22 years.

I believe that in the history of the world, there has not been a more genuinely democratic struggle for freedom than ours. I read Carlyle's *French Revolution* while I was in prison, and Pandit Jawaharlal has told me something about the Russian revolution. But it is my conviction that inasmuch as these struggles were fought with the weapon of violence, they failed to realize the democratic ideal. In the democracy which I have envisaged, a democracy established by non-violence, there will be equal freedom for all. Everybody will be his own master. It is to join a struggle for such democracy that I invite you today. Once you realize this you will forget the differences between the Hindus and Muslims, and think of yourselves as Indians only, engaged in the common struggle for independence.

Then, there is the question of your attitude towards the British. I have noticed that there is hatred towards the British among the people. The people say they are disgusted with their behaviour. The people make no distinction between British imperialism and the British people. To them, the two are one. This hatred would even make them welcome the Japanese. It is most dangerous. It means that they will exchange one slavery for another. We must get rid of this feeling. Our quarrel is not with the British people, we fight their imperialism. The proposal for the withdrawal of British power did not come out of anger. It came to enable India to play its due part at the present critical juncture. It is not a happy position for a big country like India to be merely helping with money and material obtained willy-nilly from her while the United Nations are conducting the war. We cannot evoke the true spirit of sacrifice and valour, so long as we are not free. I know the British government will not be able to withhold freedom from us, when we have made enough self-sacrifice. We must, therefore, purge ourselves of hatred. Speaking for myself, I can say that I have never felt any hatred. As a matter of fact, I feel myself to be a greater friend of the British now than ever before. One reason is that they are today in distress. My very friendship, therefore, demands that I should try to save them from their mistakes. As I view the situation, they are on the brink of an abyss. It, therefore, becomes my duty to warn them of their danger even though it may, for the time being, anger them to the point of cutting off the friendly hand that is stretched out to help them. People may laugh, nevertheless that is my claim. At a time when I may have to launch the biggest struggle of my life, I may not harbour hatred against anybody.

35

GIVE ME BLOOD, AND I SHALL GIVE YOU FREEDOM

Subhas Chandra Bose

During the 1940s, Bose led the Indian National Army (INA) and delivered several speeches to inspire and mobilize his troops. His speeches focused on the themes of nationalism, sacrifice and the fight for independence. Bose's words encouraged his followers to dedicate themselves to the cause of freedom and to be willing to make great sacrifices for the sake of their country. This speech became the most popular of them all, and also popularized the phrase 'Give Me Blood, and I Shall Give You Freedom.'

Friends! 12 months ago a new programme of total mobilization or maximum sacrifice was placed before Indians in East Asia. Today I shall give you an account of our achievements during the past year and shall place before you our demands for the coming year. But, before I do so, I want you to realize once again what a golden opportunity you have for winning freedom. The British are engaged in a worldwide struggle and in the course of struggle they have suffered defeat after defeat on so many fronts. The enemy having been thus considerably weakened, our fight for liberty has become very much easier than it was five years ago. Such a rare and God-given opportunity comes once in a century for liberating our motherland from the British yoke.

I am so very hopeful and optimistic about the outcome of our struggle, because I do not rely merely on the efforts of three million Indians in East Asia. There is a gigantic movement going on inside

India and millions of our countrymen are prepared for maximum suffering and sacrifice in order to achieve liberty. Unfortunately, ever since the great fight of 1857, our countrymen are disarmed, whereas the enemy is armed to the teeth. Without arms and without a modern army it is impossible for a disarmed people to win freedom in this modern age. Through the grace of Providence and through the help of generous Nippon, it has become possible for Indians in East Asia to get arms to build up a modern army. Moreover. Indians in East Asia are united to a man in the endeavour to win freedom and all the religious and other differences that the British tried to engineer inside India, simply do not exist in East Asia. Consequently, we have now an ideal combination of circumstances favoring the success of our struggle—and all that is wanted is that Indians should themselves come forward to pay the price of liberty. According to the programme of 'total mobilization', I demanded of you men, money and materials. Regarding men, I am glad to tell you that I have obtained sufficient recruits already. Recruits have come to us from every corner of east Asia—China, Japan, Indo-China, Philippines, Java, Borneo, Celebes, Sumatra, Malaya, Thailand and Burma...You must continue the mobilization of men, money and materials with greater vigour and energy, in particular, the problem of supplies and transport has to be solved satisfactorily.

We require more men and women of all categories for administration and reconstruction in liberated areas. We must be prepared for a situation in which the enemy will ruthlessly apply the scorched earth policy, before withdrawing from a particular area and will also force the civilian population to evacuate as was attempted in Burma.

The most important of all is the problem of sending reinforcements in men and in supplies to the fighting fronts. If we do not do so, we cannot hope to maintain our success at the fronts. Nor can we hope to penetrate deeper into India.

Those of you who will continue to work on the Home Front should never forget that East Asia—and particularly Burma—form our base for the war of liberation. If this base is not strong, our fighting forces can never be victorious. Remember that this is a 'total war'—and not merely a war between two armies. That is why for a full one year I have been laying so much stress on 'total mobilization' in the East.

There is another reason why I want you to look after the Home Front properly. During the coming months I and my colleagues on the war committee of the Cabinet desire to devote our whole attention to the fighting front—and also to the task of working up the revolution inside India. Consequently, we want to be fully assured that the work at the base will go on smoothly and uninterruptedly even in our absence.

Friends, one year ago, when I made certain demands of you, I told you that if you give me 'total mobilization', I would give you a 'second front'. I have redeemed that pledge. The first phase of our campaign is over. Our victorious troops, fighting side by side with Nipponese troops, have pushed back the enemy and are not fighting bravely on the sacred soil of our dear motherland.

Gird up your loins for the task that now lies ahead. I had asked you for men, money and materials. I have got them in generous measure. Now I demand more of you. Men, money and materials cannot by themselves bring victory or freedom. We must have the motive power that will inspire us to brave deeds and heroic exploits.

It will be a fatal mistake for you to wish to live and see India free simply because victory is now within reach. No one here should have the desire to live to enjoy freedom. A long fight is still in front of us. We should have but one desire today—the desire to die so that India may live—the desire to face a martyr's death, so that the path to freedom may be paved with the martyr's blood.

Friends! My comrades in the War of Liberation! Today I demand of you one thing, above all. I demand of you blood. It is blood alone that can avenge the blood that the enemy has spilt. It is blood alone that can pay the price of freedom. Give me blood and I promise you freedom!

36

A TRYST WITH DESTINY

Jawaharlal Nehru

One of the most iconic speeches of India, 'A Tryst with Destiny' was delivered by Jawaharlal Nehru on the night of 14 August 1947, right after the British colonizers finally left India. Nehru talks about a hopeful future for the country, and unity as the tool for change and progress.

Long years ago, we made a tryst with destiny; and now the time comes when we shall redeem our pledge, not wholly or in full measure, but very substantially. At the stroke of the midnight hour, when the world sleeps, India will awake to life and freedom.

A moment comes, which comes but rarely in history, when we step out from the old to the new—when an age ends, and when the soul of a nation, long suppressed, finds utterance. It is fitting that at this solemn moment we take the pledge of dedication to the service of India, and her people, and to the still larger cause of humanity.

At the dawn of history, India started on her unending quest, and trackless centuries are filled with her striving and the grandeur of her successes and her failures. Through good and ill fortune alike, she has never lost sight of that quest or forgotten the ideals which gave her strength. We end today a period of ill fortune and India discovers herself again.

The achievement we celebrate today is but a step, an opening of opportunity, to the greater triumphs and achievements that await us. Are we brave enough and wise enough to grasp this opportunity and accept the challenge of the future?

Freedom and power bring responsibility. That responsibility rests upon this assembly, a sovereign body representing the sovereign people of India. Before the birth of freedom, we have endured all the pains of labor, and our hearts are heavy with the memory of this sorrow. Some of those pains continue even now. Nevertheless, the past is over, and it is the future that beckons to us now.

That future is not one of ease or resting but of incessant striving so that we might fulfill the pledges we have so often taken and the one we shall take today. The service of India means the service of the millions who suffer. It means the ending of poverty and ignorance and disease and inequality of opportunity.

The ambition of the greatest man of our generation has been to wipe 'every tear from every eye.' That may be beyond us, but so long as there are tears and suffering, so long our work will not be over.

And so we have to labor and to work, and work hard, to give reality to our dreams. Those dreams are for India, but they are also for the world, for all the nations and peoples are too closely knit together today for any one of them to imagine that it can live apart.

Peace has been said to be indivisible; so is freedom; so is prosperity now; and so also is disaster in this one world that can no longer be split into isolated fragments.

To the people of India, whose representatives we are, we make appeal to join us with faith and confidence in this great adventure. This is no time for petty and destructive criticism, no time for ill will or blaming others. We have to build the noble mansion of free India where all her children may dwell.

37

QUEEN ADDRESSES THE UNITED NATIONS

Elizabeth II

In 1957, Queen Elizabeth II addressed the General Assembly of the United Nations for the first time.

I thank you, Mr President, for your words of welcome.

I wish first to express to you, to the Secretary-General and to the General Assembly of the United Nations, my great pleasure at being here today.

This Assembly was born of the endeavours of countless men and women from different nations who, over the centuries, have pursued the aims of the preservation of peace between nations, equality of justice for all before the law and the right of the peoples of the world to live their lives in freedom and security.

The Charter of the United Nations was framed with a view to giving expression to these great purposes and so forming a fitting memorial to the men and women whose toil and sacrifices turned those ideas into articles of faith for the nations of today.

Time has in fact made the task of the United Nations more difficult than it seemed when the terms of the charter were agreed at San Francisco 12 years ago. We are still far from the achievement of the ideals which I have mentioned but we must not be discouraged. The peoples of the world expect the United Nations to persevere in its efforts.

Ten Commonwealth countries are represented in this Assembly—countries which form a free association of fully independent states and which have widely different histories, cultures and traditions. Common ideals and hopes, not formal bonds, unite the members of the Commonwealth and promote that association between them which, in my belief, has contributed significantly to the cause of human freedom.

The countries of the Commonwealth regard their continuing association with one another and joint service to their high ideals as still an essential contribution to world peace and justice. They add and will continue to add to a tried element of strength, and of accumulated experience.

The United Nations is an organization, dedicated to peace, where representatives from all over the world meet to examine the problems of the time. In it men and women from all these countries—large or small, powerful or weak—can exercise an influence that might otherwise be denied them. The United Nations also originates and inspires a wide range of social and economic activities for the benefit of the whole human race.

But, Mr President, the future of this Organization will be determined, not only by the degree to which its members observe strictly the provisions of the charter and cooperate in its practical activities, but also by the strength of its people's devotion to the pursuit of those great ideals to which I have referred. When justice and respect for obligations are firmly established, the United Nations will the more confidently achieve the goal of a world at peace, law-abiding and prosperous, for which men and women have striven so long and which is the heart's desire of every nation here represented. I offer you my best wishes in your task and pray that you may be successful.

38

INAUGURAL ADDRESS

John Fitzgerald Kennedy

John F. Kennedy delivered his inaugural address on 20 January 1961, following his election as the thirty-fifth president of the United States. His inaugural address is regarded as one of the most iconic and memorable speeches in American history. Kennedy's speech is perhaps best remembered for its famous quote, 'Ask not what your country can do for you—ask what you can do for your country.' This call to public service became an enduring and powerful statement, encapsulating his vision of civic engagement and the shared responsibility of all Americans to contribute to the well-being of their nation.

We observe today not a victory of party, but a celebration of freedom—symbolizing an end, as well as a beginning—signifying renewal, as well as change. For I have sworn before you and Almighty God the same solemn oath our forebears prescribed nearly a century and three quarters ago.

The world is very different now. For man holds in his mortal hands the power to abolish all forms of human poverty and all forms of human life. And yet the same revolutionary beliefs for which our forebears fought are still at issue around the globe—the belief that the rights of man come not from the generosity of the state, but from the hand of God.

We dare not forget today that we are the heirs of that first revolution. Let the word go forth from this time and place, to friend and foe alike, that the torch has been passed to a new generation of Americans—born in this century, tempered by war, disciplined by a hard and bitter peace, proud of our ancient heritage—and unwilling to witness or permit the slow undoing of those human rights to which this nation has always been committed, and to which we are committed today at home and around the world.

Let every nation know, whether it wishes us well or ill, that we shall pay any price, bear any burden, meet any hardship, support any friend, oppose any foe, in order to assure the survival and the success of liberty.

This much we pledge—and more.

To those old allies whose cultural and spiritual origins we share, we pledge the loyalty of faithful friends. United, there is little we cannot do in a host of cooperative ventures. Divided, there is little we can do—for we dare not meet a powerful challenge at odds and split asunder.

To those new states whom we welcome to the ranks of the free, we pledge our word that one form of colonial control shall not have passed away merely to be replaced by a far more iron tyranny. We shall not always expect to find them supporting our view. But we shall always hope to find them strongly supporting their own freedom—and to remember that, in the past, those who foolishly sought power by riding the back of the tiger ended up inside.

To those peoples in the huts and villages across the globe struggling to break the bonds of mass misery, we pledge our best efforts to help them help themselves, for whatever period is required—not because the Communists may be doing it, not because we seek their votes, but because it is right. If a free society cannot help the many who are poor, it cannot save the few who are rich.

To our sister republics south of our border, we offer a special pledge—to convert our good words into good deeds—in a new alliance for progress—to assist free men and free governments in casting off the chains of poverty.

But this peaceful revolution of hope cannot become the prey

of hostile powers. Let all our neighbors know that we shall join with them to oppose aggression or subversion anywhere in the Americas. And let every other power know that this hemisphere intends to remain the master of its own house.

To that world assembly of sovereign states, the United Nations, our last best hope in an age where the instruments of war have far outpaced the instruments of peace, we renew our pledge of support—to prevent it from becoming merely a forum for invective—to strengthen its shield of the new and the weak—and to enlarge the area in which its writ may run.

Finally, to those nations who would make themselves our adversary, we offer not a pledge but a request: that both sides begin anew the quest for peace, before the dark powers of destruction unleashed by science engulf all humanity in planned or accidental self-destruction.

We dare not tempt them with weakness. For only when our arms are sufficient beyond doubt can we be certain beyond doubt that they will never be employed.

But neither can two great and powerful groups of nations take comfort from our present course—both sides overburdened by the cost of modern weapons, both rightly alarmed by the steady spread of the deadly atom, yet both racing to alter that uncertain balance of terror that stays the hand of mankind's final war.

So let us begin anew—remembering on both sides that civility is not a sign of weakness, and sincerity is always subject to proof. Let us never negotiate out of fear. But let us never fear to negotiate.

Let both sides explore what problems unite us instead of belaboring those problems which divide us.

Let both sides, for the first time, formulate serious and precise proposals for the inspection and control of arms—and bring the absolute power to destroy other nations under the absolute control of all nations. Let both sides seek to invoke the wonders of science instead of its terrors.

Together let us explore the stars, conquer the deserts, eradicate disease, tap the ocean depths and encourage the arts and commerce.

Let both sides unite to heed in all corners of the earth the command of Isaiah—to 'undo the heavy burdens, and to let the oppressed go free.'

And if a beachhead of cooperation may push back the jungle of suspicion, let both sides join in creating a new endeavor, not a new balance of power, but a new world of law, where the strong are just and the weak secure and the peace preserved.

All this will not be finished in the first 100 days. Nor will it be finished in the first 1,000 days, nor in the life of this administration, nor even perhaps in our lifetime on this planet. But let us begin.

In your hands, my fellow citizens, more than in mine, will rest the final success or failure of our course. Since this country was founded, each generation of Americans has been summoned to give testimony to its national loyalty. The graves of young Americans who answered the call to service surround the globe.

Now the trumpet summons us again—not as a call to bear arms, though arms we need; not as a call to battle, though embattled we are—but a call to bear the burden of a long twilight struggle, year in and year out, 'rejoicing in hope, patient in tribulation'—a struggle against the common enemies of man: tyranny, poverty, disease and war itself.

Can we forge against these enemies a grand and global alliance, North and South, East and West, that can assure a more fruitful life for all mankind? Will you join in that historic effort?

In the long history of the world, only a few generations have been granted the role of defending freedom in its hour of maximum danger. I do not shrink from this responsibility—I welcome it. I do not believe that any of us would exchange places with any other people or any other generation. The energy, the faith, the devotion which we bring to this endeavor will light our country and all who serve it—and the glow from that fire can truly light the world.

And so, my fellow Americans: ask not what your country can do for you—ask what you can do for your country.

My fellow citizens of the world: ask not what America will do for you, but what together we can do for the freedom of man.

Finally, whether you are citizens of America or citizens of the world, ask of us the same high standards of strength and sacrifice which we ask of you. With a good conscience our only sure reward, with history the final judge of our deeds, let us go forth to lead the land we love, asking His blessing and His help, but knowing that here on earth God's work must truly be our own.

39

IT'S ABOUT DUTY, HONOR, COUNTRY

Douglas MacArthur

This is a famous speech delivered by General Douglas MacArthur on 12 May 1962, at the United States Military Academy at West Point. In his speech, General Douglas MacArthur addresses the cadets at West Point, emphasizing the fundamental values of duty, honor and country. He begins by highlighting the significance of the occasion, acknowledging the rich history and esteemed tradition of West Point as a renowned institution that molds future leaders of the United States Armed Forces.

General Westmoreland, General Grove, distinguished guests, and gentlemen of the Corps!

As I was leaving the hotel this morning, a doorman asked me, 'Where are you bound for, General?' And when I replied, 'West Point,' he remarked, 'Beautiful place. Have you ever been there before?'

No human being could fail to be deeply moved by such a tribute as this [Thayer Award]. Coming from a profession I have served so long, and a people I have loved so well, it fills me with an emotion I cannot express. But this award is not intended primarily to honor a personality, but to symbolize a great moral code—the code of conduct and chivalry of those who guard this beloved land of culture and ancient descent. That is the animation of this medallion. For all eyes and for all time, it is an expression of the ethics of the American soldier. That I should be integrated in this way with so noble an ideal, arouses a sense of pride and yet of humility which will be with me always.

Duty, Honor, Country: those three hallowed words reverently dictate what you ought to be, what you can be, what you will be. They are your rallying points: to build courage when courage seems to fail; to regain faith when there seems to be little cause for faith; to create hope when hope becomes forlorn.

Unhappily, I possess neither that eloquence of diction, that poetry of imagination, nor that brilliance of metaphor to tell you all that they mean.

The unbelievers will say they are but words, but a slogan, but a flamboyant phrase. Every pedant, every demagogue, every cynic, every hypocrite, every troublemaker, and I am sorry to say, some others of an entirely different character, will try to downgrade them even to the extent of mockery and ridicule.

But these are some of the things they do; they build your basic character. They mold you for your future roles as the custodians of the nation's defense. They make you strong enough to know when you are weak, and brave enough to face yourself when you are afraid. They teach you to be proud and unbending in honest failure, but humble and gentle in success; not to substitute words for actions, not to seek the path of comfort, but to face the stress and spur of difficulty and challenge; to learn to stand up in the storm but to have compassion on those who fall; to master yourself before you seek to master others; to have a heart that is clean, a goal that is high; to learn to laugh, yet never forget how to weep; to reach into the future yet never neglect the past; to be serious yet never to take yourself too seriously; to be modest so that you will remember the simplicity of true greatness, the open mind of true wisdom, the meekness of true strength. They give you a temper of the will, a quality of the imagination, a vigor of the emotions, a freshness of the deep springs of life, a temperamental predominance of courage over timidity, of an appetite for adventure over love of ease. They create in your heart the sense of wonder, the unfailing hope of what next, and the joy and inspiration of life. They teach you in this way to be an officer and a gentleman.

And what sort of soldiers are those you are to lead? Are they reliable? Are they brave? Are they capable of victory? Their story is known to all of you.

It is the story of the American man-at-arms. My estimate of him was formed on the battlefield many, many years ago, and has never changed. I regarded him then as I regard him now—as one of the world's noblest figures, not only as one of the finest military characters, but also as one of the most stainless. His name and fame are the birthright of every American citizen. In his youth and strength, his love and loyalty, he gave all that mortality can give.

He needs no eulogy from me or from any other man. He has written his own history and written it in red on his enemy's breast. But when I think of his patience under adversity, of his courage under fire, and of his modesty in victory, I am filled with an emotion of admiration I cannot put into words. He belongs to history as furnishing one of the greatest examples of successful patriotism. He belongs to posterity as the instructor of future generations in the principles of liberty and freedom. He belongs to the present, to us, by his virtues and by his achievements. In twenty campaigns, on a hundred battlefields, around a thousand campfires, I have witnessed that enduring fortitude, that patriotic self-abnegation, and that invincible determination which have carved his statue in the hearts of his people. From one end of the world to the other he has drained deep the chalice of courage.

As I listened to those songs [of the glee club], in memory's eye I could see those staggering columns of the First World War, bending under soggy packs, on many a weary march from dripping dusk to drizzling dawn, slogging ankle-deep through the mire of shell-shocked roads, to form grimly for the attack, blue-lipped, covered with sludge and mud, chilled by the wind and rain, driving home to their objective, and for many, to the judgment seat of God.

I do not know the dignity of their birth, but I do know the glory of their death. They died unquestioning, uncomplaining, with faith in their hearts, and on their lips the hope that we would go on to victory. Always, for them: Duty, Honor, Country; always their blood and sweat and tears, as we sought the way and the light and the truth.

And 20 years after, on the other side of the globe, again the filth of murky foxholes, the stench of ghostly trenches, the slime of dripping dugouts; those boiling suns of relentless heat, those torrential rains of devastating storms; the loneliness and utter desolation of jungle trails; the bitterness of long separation from those they loved and cherished; the deadly pestilence of tropical disease; the horror of stricken areas of war; their resolute and determined defense, their swift and sure attack, their indomitable purpose, their complete and decisive victory—always victory. Always through the bloody haze of their last reverberating shot, the vision of gaunt, ghastly men reverently following your password of: Duty, Honor, Country.

The code which those words perpetuate embraces the highest moral laws and will stand the test of any ethics or philosophies ever promulgated for the uplift of mankind. Its requirements are for the things that are right, and its restraints are from the things that are wrong.

The soldier, above all other men, is required to practice the greatest act of religious training—sacrifice.

In battle and in the face of danger and death, he discloses those divine attributes which his Maker gave when he created man in his own image. No physical courage and no brute instinct can take the place of the divine help which alone can sustain him. However horrible the incidents of war may be, the soldier who is called upon to offer and to give his life for his country is the noblest development of mankind.

You now face a new world—a world of change. The thrust into outer space of the satellite, spheres and missiles mark the beginning of another epoch in the long story of mankind. In the five or more billions of years the scientists tell us it has taken to form the earth, in the three or more billion years of development of the human race, there has never been a more abrupt or staggering evolution. We deal now not with things of this world alone, but with the illimitable distances and as yet unfathomed mysteries of the universe. We are reaching out for a new and boundless frontier.

We speak in strange terms: of harnessing the cosmic energy; of making winds and tides work for us; of creating unheard synthetic materials to supplement or even replace our old standard basics; to purify sea water for our drink; of mining ocean floors for new fields of wealth and food; of disease preventatives to expand life into the hundreds of years; of controlling the weather for a more equitable distribution of heat and cold, of rain and shine; of space ships to the moon; of the primary target in war, no longer limited to the armed forces of an enemy, but instead to include his civil populations; of ultimate conflict between a united human race and the sinister forces of some other planetary galaxy; of such dreams and fantasies as to make life the most exciting of all time.

And through all this welter of change and development, your mission remains fixed, determined, inviolable: it is to win our wars. Everything else in your professional career is but corollary to this vital dedication. All other public purposes, all other public projects, all other public needs, great or small, will find others for their accomplishment. But you are the ones who are trained to fight. Yours is the profession of arms, the will to win, the sure knowledge that in war there is no substitute for victory; that if you lose, the nation will be destroyed; that the very obsession of your public service must be: Duty, Honor, Country.

Others will debate the controversial issues, national and international, which divide men's minds; but serene, calm, aloof, you stand as the nation's war-guardian, as its lifeguard from the raging tides of international conflict, as its gladiator in the arena of battle. For a century and a half you have defended, guarded, and protected its hallowed traditions of liberty and freedom, of right and justice.

Let civilian voices argue the merits or demerits of our processes of government; whether our strength is being sapped by deficit financing, indulged in too long, by federal paternalism grown too mighty, by power groups grown too arrogant, by politics grown too corrupt, by crime grown too rampant, by morals grown too low, by taxes grown too high, by extremists grown too violent; whether our personal liberties are as thorough and complete as they should be. These great national problems are not for your professional participation or military solution. Your guidepost stands out like a ten-fold beacon in the night: Duty, Honor, Country.

You are the leaven which binds together the entire fabric of our national system of defense. From your ranks come the great captains who hold the nation's destiny in their hands the moment the war tocsin sounds. The Long Gray Line has never failed us. Were you to do so, a million ghosts in olive drab, in brown khaki, in blue and gray, would rise from their white crosses thundering those magic words: Duty, Honor, Country. This does not mean that you are war mongers.

On the contrary, the soldier, above all other people, prays for peace, for he must suffer and bear the deepest wounds and scars of war. But always in our ears ring the ominous words of Plato, that wisest of all philosophers: Only the dead have seen the end of war.

The shadows are lengthening for me. The twilight is here. My days of old have vanished, tone and tint. They have gone glimmering through the dreams of things that were. Their memory is one of wondrous beauty, watered by tears, and coaxed and caressed by the smiles of yesterday. I listen vainly, but with thirsty ears, for the witching melody of faint bugles blowing reveille, of far drums beating the long roll. In my dreams, I hear again the crash of guns, the rattle of musketry, the strange, mournful mutter of the battlefield.

But in the evening of my memory, always I come back to West Point. Always there echoes and re-echoes: Duty, Honor, Country.

Today marks my final roll call with you, but I want you to

know that when I cross the river my last conscious thoughts will be of the Corps, and the Corps, and the Corps.

I bid you farewell.

40

I HAVE A DREAM

Martin Luther King Jr

'I Have a Dream' is a renowned speech delivered by Dr Martin Luther King Jr on 28 August 1963, during the March on Washington for Jobs and Freedom. It has become one of the most iconic speeches in American history and a defining moment in the Civil Rights Movement.

In his speech, Dr King expressed his vision and hope for racial equality and justice in the United States. He spoke passionately about his dream of a future where people would not be judged by the colour of their skin but by the content of their character. He called for an end to racial segregation and discrimination, advocating for equal rights and opportunities for all individuals, regardless of their race or background.

I am happy to join with you today in what will go down in history as the greatest demonstration for freedom in the history of our nation.

Five score years ago, a great American, in whose symbolic shadow we stand today, signed the Emancipation Proclamation. This momentous decree came as a great beacon light of hope to millions of Negro slaves who had been seared in the flames of withering injustice. It came as a joyous daybreak to end the long night of their captivity.

But one hundred years later, the Negro still is not free. One hundred years later, the life of the Negro is still sadly crippled by the manacles of segregation and the chains of discrimination. One hundred years later, the Negro lives on a lonely island of poverty in the midst of a vast ocean of material prosperity. One hundred years later, the Negro is still languished in the corners of American society and finds himself an exile in his own land. And so we've come here today to dramatize a shameful condition.

In a sense we've come to our nation's capital to cash a check. When the architects of our republic wrote the magnificent words of the Constitution and the Declaration of Independence, they were signing a promissory note to which every American was to fall heir. This note was a promise that all men, yes, black men as well as white men, would be guaranteed the 'unalienable Rights' of 'Life, Liberty and the pursuit of Happiness.' It is obvious today that America has defaulted on this promissory note, insofar as her citizens of color are concerned. Instead of honoring this sacred obligation, America has given the Negro people a bad check, a check which has come back marked 'insufficient funds.' But we refuse to believe that the bank of justice is bankrupt. We refuse to believe that there are insufficient funds in the great vaults of opportunity of this nation. And so, we've come to cash this check, a check that will give us upon demand the riches of freedom and the security of justice.

We have also come to this hallowed spot to remind America of the fierce urgency of Now. This is no time to engage in the luxury of cooling off or to take the tranquilizing drug of gradualism. Now is the time to make real the promises of democracy. Now is the time to rise from the dark and desolate valley of segregation to the sunlit path of racial justice. Now is the time to lift our nation from the quicksands of racial injustice to the solid rock of brotherhood. Now is the time to make justice a reality for all of God's children.

It would be fatal for the nation to overlook the urgency of the moment. This sweltering summer of the Negro's legitimate discontent will not pass until there is an invigorating autumn of freedom and equality. 1963 is not an end, but a beginning. And those who hope that the Negro needed to blow off steam and will now be content will have a rude awakening if the nation returns to business as usual. And there will be neither rest nor tranquility in America until the Negro is granted his citizenship rights. The whirlwinds of revolt will continue to shake the foundations of our nation until the bright day of justice emerges.

But there is something that I must say to my people, who stand on the warm threshold which leads into the palace of justice: in the process of gaining our rightful place, we must not be guilty of wrongful deeds. Let us not seek to satisfy our thirst for freedom by drinking from the cup of bitterness and hatred. We must forever conduct our struggle on the high plane of dignity and discipline. We must not allow our creative protest to degenerate into physical violence. Again and again, we must rise to the majestic heights of meeting physical force with soul force.

The marvelous new militancy which has engulfed the Negro community must not lead us to a distrust of all white people, for many of our white brothers, as evidenced by their presence here today, have come to realize that their destiny is tied up with our destiny. And they have come to realize that their freedom is inextricably bound to our freedom.

We cannot walk alone.

And as we walk, we must make the pledge that we shall always march ahead.

We cannot turn back.

There are those who are asking the devotees of civil rights, 'When will you be satisfied?' We can never be satisfied as long as the Negro is the victim of the unspeakable horrors of police brutality. We can never be satisfied as long as our bodies, heavy with the fatigue of travel, cannot gain lodging in the motels of the highways and the hotels of the cities. We cannot be satisfied as long as the negro's basic mobility is from a smaller ghetto to a larger one. We can never be satisfied as long as our children are stripped of their self-hood and robbed of their dignity by signs stating: 'For Whites Only.' We cannot be satisfied as long as a Negro in Mississippi cannot vote and a Negro in New York believes he has nothing for which to vote. No, no, we are not satisfied, and we will not be satisfied until 'justice rolls down like waters, and righteousness like a mighty stream.' I am not unmindful that some of you have come here out of great trials and tribulations. Some of you have come fresh from narrow jail cells. And some of you have come from areas where your quest for freedom left you battered by the storms of persecution and staggered by the winds of police brutality. You have been the veterans of creative suffering. Continue to work with the faith that unearned suffering is redemptive. Go back to Mississippi, go back to Alabama, go back to South Carolina, go back to Georgia, go back to Louisiana, go back to the slums and ghettos of our northern cities, knowing that somehow this situation can and will be changed.

Let us not wallow in the valley of despair, I say to you today, my friends.

And so even though we face the difficulties of today and tomorrow, I still have a dream. It is a dream deeply rooted in the American dream.

I have a dream that one day this nation will rise up and live out the true meaning of its creed: 'We hold these truths to be self-evident, that all men are created equal.' I have a dream that one day on the red hills of Georgia, the sons of former slaves and the sons of former slave owners will be able to sit down together at the table of brotherhood.

I have a dream that one day even the state of Mississippi, a state sweltering with the heat of injustice, sweltering with the heat of oppression, will be transformed into an oasis of freedom and justice.

I have a dream that my four little children will one day live in a nation where they will not be judged by the color of their skin but by the content of their character.

I have a dream today!

I have a dream that one day, down in Alabama, with its vicious racists, with its governor having his lips dripping with the words of 'interposition' and 'nullification'—one day right there in Alabama little black boys and black girls will be able to join hands with little white boys and white girls as sisters and brothers.

I have a dream today!

I have a dream that one day every valley shall be exalted, and every hill and mountain shall be made low, the rough places will be made plain, and the crooked places will be made straight; 'and the glory of the Lord shall be revealed and all flesh shall see it together.' This is our hope, and this is the faith that I go back to the South with.

With this faith, we will be able to hew out of the mountain of despair a stone of hope. With this faith, we will be able to transform the jangling discords of our nation into a beautiful symphony of brotherhood. With this faith, we will be able to work together, to pray together, to struggle together, to go to jail together, to stand up for freedom together, knowing that we will be free one day.

And this will be the day—this will be the day when all of God's children will be able to sing with new meaning:

My country 'tis of thee, sweet land of liberty, of thee I sing. Land where my fathers died, land of the Pilgrim's pride, from every mountainside, let freedom ring!

And if America is to be a great nation, this must become true.

And so let freedom ring from the prodigious hilltops of New Hampshire.

Let freedom ring from the mighty mountains of New York.

Let freedom ring from the heightening Alleghenies of Pennsylvania.

Let freedom ring from the snow-capped Rockies of Colorado.

Let freedom ring from the curvaceous slopes of California.

But not only that:

Let freedom ring from Stone Mountain of Georgia.

Let freedom ring from Lookout Mountain of Tennessee.

Let freedom ring from every hill and molehill of Mississippi.

From every mountainside, let freedom ring.

And when this happens, and when we allow freedom ring, when we let it ring from every village and every hamlet, from every state and every city, we will be able to speed up that day when all of God's children, black men and white men, Jews and Gentiles, Protestants and Catholics, will be able to join hands and sing in the words of the old Negro spiritual:

Free at last! Free at last!

Thank God Almighty, we are free at last!

41

THE BALLOT OR THE BULLET

Malcolm X

'The Ballot or the Bullet' is a famous speech delivered by Malcolm X on 3 April 1964, in Cleveland, Ohio. This speech is considered one of Malcolm X's most influential and powerful addresses, as it encapsulates his evolving perspective on civil rights, racial equality and the struggle for African American liberation.

Mr Moderator, Brother Lomax, brothers and sisters, friends and enemies: I just can't believe everyone in here is a friend, and I don't want to leave anybody out. The question tonight, as I understand it, is 'The Negro Revolt, and Where Do We Go From Here?' or 'What Next?' In my little humble way of understanding it, it points toward either the ballot or the bullet.

Before we try and explain what is meant by the ballot or the bullet, I would like to clarify something concerning myself. I'm still a Muslim; my religion is still Islam. That's my personal belief. Just as Adam Clayton Powell is a Christian minister who heads the Abyssinian Baptist Church in New York, but at the same time takes part in the political struggles to try and bring about rights to the black people in this country; and Dr Martin Luther King is a Christian minister down in Atlanta, Georgia, who heads another organization fighting for the civil rights of black people in this country; and Reverend Galamison, I guess you've heard of him, is another Christian minister in New York who has been deeply involved in the school boycotts to eliminate segregated education; well, I myself am a minister, not a Christian minister, but a Muslim minister; and I believe in action on all fronts by whatever means necessary.

Although I'm still a Muslim, I'm not here tonight to discuss my religion. I'm not here to try and change your religion. I'm not here to argue or discuss anything that we differ about, because it's time for us to submerge our differences and realize that it is best for us to first see that we have the same problem, a common problem, a problem that will make you catch hell whether you're a Baptist, or a Methodist, or a Muslim, or a nationalist. Whether you're educated or illiterate, whether you live on the boulevard or in the alley, you're going to catch hell just like I am. We're all in the same boat and we all are going to catch the same hell from the same man. He just happens to be a white man. All of us have suffered here, in this country, political oppression at the hands of the white man, economic exploitation at the hands of the white man, and social degradation at the hands of the white man.

Now in speaking like this, it doesn't mean that we're anti-white, but it does mean we're anti-exploitation, we're anti-degradation, we're anti-oppression. And if the white man doesn't want us to be anti-him, let him stop oppressing and exploiting and degrading us. Whether we are Christians or Muslims or nationalists or agnostics or atheists, we must first learn to forget our differences. If we have differences, let us differ in the closet; when we come out in front, let us not have anything to argue about until we get finished arguing with the man. If the late President Kennedy could get together with Khrushchev and exchange some wheat, we certainly have more in common with each other than Kennedy and Khrushchev had with each other.

If we don't do something real soon, I think you'll have to agree that we're going to be forced either to use the ballot or the bullet. It's one or the other in 1964. It isn't that time is running out—time has run out!

1964 threatens to be the most explosive year America has ever witnessed. The most explosive year. Why? It's also a political year.

It's the year when all of the white politicians will be back in the so-called Negro community jiving you and me for some votes. The year when all of the white political crooks will be right back in your and my community with their false promises, building up our hopes for a letdown, with their trickery and their treachery, with their false promises which they don't intend to keep. As they nourish these dissatisfactions, it can only lead to one thing, an explosion; and now we have the type of black man on the scene in America today—I'm sorry, Brother Lomax—who just doesn't intend to turn the other cheek any longer.

Don't let anybody tell you anything about the odds are against you. If they draft you, they send you to Korea and make you face 800 million Chinese. If you can be brave over there, you can be brave right here. These odds aren't as great as those odds. And if you fight here, you will at least know what you're fighting for.

I'm not a politician, not even a student of politics; in fact, I'm not a student of much of anything. I'm not a Democrat. I'm not a Republican, and I don't even consider myself an American. If you and I were Americans, there'd be no problem. Those Honkies that just got off the boat, they're already Americans; Polacks are already Americans; the Italian refugees are already Americans. Everything that came out of Europe, every blue-eyed thing, is already an American. And as long as you and I have been over here, we aren't Americans yet.

Well, I am one who doesn't believe in deluding myself. I'm not going to sit at your table and watch you eat, with nothing on my plate, and call myself a diner. Sitting at the table doesn't make you a diner, unless you eat some of what's on that plate. Being here in America doesn't make you an American. Being born here in America doesn't make you an American. Why, if birth made you American, you wouldn't need any legislation; you wouldn't need any amendments to the Constitution; you wouldn't be faced with civil-rights filibustering in Washington, DC, right now. They don't have to pass civil-rights legislation to make a Polack an American.

No, I'm not an American. I'm one of the 22 million black people who are the victims of Americanism. One of the 22 million black people who are the victims of democracy, nothing but disguised hypocrisy. So, I'm not standing here speaking to you as an American, or a patriot, or a flag-saluter, or a flag-waver—no, not I. I'm speaking as a victim of this American system. And I see America through the eyes of the victim. I don't see any American dream; I see an American nightmare.

These 22 million victims are waking up. Their eyes are coming open. They're beginning to see what they used to only look at. They're becoming politically mature. They are realizing that there are new political trends from coast to coast. As they see these new political trends, it's possible for them to see that every time there's an election the races are so close that they have to have a recount. They had to recount in Massachusetts to see who was going to be governor, it was so close. It was the same way in Rhode Island, in Minnesota, and in many other parts of the country. And the same with Kennedy and Nixon when they ran for president. It was so close they had to count all over again. Well, what does this mean? It means that when white people are evenly divided, and black people have a bloc of votes of their own, it is left up to them to determine who's going to sit in the White House and who's going to be in the dog house.

It was the black man's vote that put the present administration in Washington, DC. Your vote, your dumb vote, your ignorant vote, your wasted vote put in an administration in Washington, DC, that has seen fit to pass every kind of legislation imaginable, saving you until last, then filibustering on top of that. And your and my leaders have the audacity to run around clapping their hands and talk about how much progress we're making. And what a good president we have. If he wasn't good in Texas, he sure can't be good in Washington, DC. Because Texas is a lynch state. It is in the same breath as Mississippi, no different; only they lynch you in Texas with a Texas accent and lynch you in Mississippi with a Mississippi accent. And these Negro leaders have the audacity to go and have some coffee in the White House with a Texan, a Southern cracker—that's all he is—and then come out and tell you and me that he's going to be better for us because, since he's from the South, he knows how to deal with the Southerners. What kind of logic is that? Let Eastland be president, he's from the South too. He should be better able to deal with them than Johnson.

In this present administration they have in the House of Representatives 257 Democrats to only 177 Republicans. They control two-thirds of the House vote. Why can't they pass something that will help you and me? In the Senate, there are 67 senators who are of the Democratic Party. Only 33 of them are Republicans. Why, the Democrats have got the government sewed up, and you're the one who sewed it up for them. And what have they given you for it? Four years in office, and just now getting around to some civil-rights legislation. Just now, after everything else is gone, out of the way, they're going to sit down now and play with you all summer long—the same old giant con game that they call filibuster. All those are in cahoots together. Don't you ever think they're not in cahoots together, for the man that is heading the civil-rights filibuster is a man from Georgia named Richard Russell. When Johnson became president, the first man he asked for when he got back to Washington, DC, was 'Dicky'—that's how tight they are. That's his boy, that's his pal, that's his buddy. But they're playing that old con game. One of them makes believe he's for you, and he's got it fixed where the other one is so tight against you, he never has to keep his promise.

So it's time in 1964 to wake up. And when you see them coming up with that kind of conspiracy, let them know your eyes are open. And let them know you got something else that's wide open too. It's got to be the ballot or the bullet. The ballot or the bullet. If you're afraid to use an expression like that, you should get on out of the country; you should get back in the cotton patch; you should get back in the alley. They get all the Negro vote, and after they get it, the Negro gets nothing in return. All they did when they got to Washington was give a few big Negroes big jobs. Those big Negroes didn't need big jobs, they already had jobs. That's camouflage, that's trickery, that's treachery, window-dressing. I'm not trying to knock out the Democrats for the Republicans. We'll get to them in a minute. But it is true; you put the Democrats first and the Democrats put you last.

Look at it the way it is. What alibis do they use, since they control Congress and the Senate? What alibi do they use when you and I ask, 'Well, when are you going to keep your promise?' They blame the Dixiecrats. What is a Dixiecrat? A Democrat. A Dixiecrat is nothing but a Democrat in disguise. The titular head of the Democrats is also the head of the Dixiecrats, because the Dixiecrats are a part of the Democratic Party. The Democrats have never kicked the Dixiecrats out of the party. The Dixiecrats bolted themselves once, but the Democrats didn't put them out. Imagine, these lowdown Southern segregationists put the Northern Democrats down. But the Northern Democrats have never put the Dixiecrats down. No, look at that thing the way it is. They have got a con game going on, a political con game, and you and I are in the middle. It's time for you and me to wake up and start looking at it like it is, and trying to understand it like it is; and then we can deal with it like it is.

The Dixiecrats in Washington, DC, control the key committees that run the government. The only reason the Dixiecrats control these committees is because they have seniority. The only reason they have seniority is because they come from states where Negroes can't vote. This is not even a government that's based on democracy. It is not a government that is made up of representatives of the people. Half of the people in the South can't even vote. Eastland is not even supposed to be in Washington. Half of the senators and congressmen who occupy these key positions in Washington, DC, are there illegally, are there unconstitutionally.

I was in Washington, DC, a week ago Thursday, when they

were debating whether or not they should let the bill come onto the floor. And in the back of the room where the Senate meets, there's a huge map of the United States, and on that map it shows the location of Negroes throughout the country. And it shows that the Southern section of the country, the states that are most heavily concentrated with Negroes, are the ones that have senators and congressmen standing up filibustering and doing all other kinds of trickery to keep the Negro from being able to vote. This is pitiful. But it's not pitiful for us any longer; it's actually pitiful for the white man, because soon now, as the Negro awakens a little more and sees the vise that he's in, sees the bag that he's in, sees the real game that he's in, then the Negro's going to develop a new tactic.

These senators and congressmen actually violate the constitutional amendments that guarantee the people of that particular state or county the right to vote. And the Constitution itself has within it the machinery to expel any representative from a state where the voting rights of the people are violated. You don't even need new legislation. Any person in Congress right now, who is there from a state or a district where the voting rights of the people are violated, that particular person should be expelled from Congress. And when you expel him, you've removed one of the obstacles in the path of any real meaningful legislation in this country. In fact, when you expel them, you don't need new legislation, because they will be replaced by black representatives from counties and districts where the black man is in the majority, not in the minority.

If the black man in these Southern states had his full voting rights, the key Dixiecrats in Washington, DC, which means the key Democrats in Washington, DC, would lose their seats. The Democratic Party itself would lose its power. It would cease to be powerful as a party. When you see the amount of power that would be lost by the Democratic Party if it were to lose the Dixiecrat wing, or branch, or element, you can see where it's against the interests of the Democrats to give voting rights to Negroes in states where the Democrats have been in complete power and authority ever since the Civil War. You just can't belong to that Party without analysing it.

I say again, I'm not anti-Democrat, I'm not anti-Republican, I'm not anti-anything. I'm just questioning their sincerity, and some of the strategy that they've been using on our people by promising them promises that they don't intend to keep. When you keep the Democrats in power, you're keeping the Dixiecrats in power. I doubt that my good Brother Lomax will deny that. A vote for a Democrat is a vote for a Dixiecrat. That's why, in 1964, it's time now for you and me to become more politically mature and realize what the ballot is for; what we're supposed to get when we cast a ballot; and that if we don't cast a ballot, it's going to end up in a situation where we're going to have to cast a bullet. It's either a ballot or a bullet.

In the North, they do it a different way. They have a system that's known as gerrymandering, whatever that means. It means when Negroes become too heavily concentrated in a certain area, and begin to gain too much political power, the white man comes along and changes the district lines. You may say, 'Why do you keep saying white man?' Because it's the white man who does it. I haven't ever seen any Negro changing any lines. They don't let him get near the line. It's the white man who does this. And usually, it's the white man who grins at you the most, and pats you on the back, and is supposed to be your friend. He may be friendly, but he's not your friend.

So, what I'm trying to impress upon you, in essence, is this: you and I in America are faced not with a segregationist conspiracy, we're faced with a government conspiracy. Everyone who's filibustering is a senator—that's the government. Everyone who's finagling in Washington, DC, is a congressman—that's the government. You don't have anybody putting blocks in your path but people who are a part of the government. The same government that you go abroad to fight for and die for is the government that is in a conspiracy to deprive you of your voting rights, deprive you of your economic opportunities, deprive you of decent housing, deprive you of decent education. You don't need to go to the employer alone, it is the government itself, the government of America, that is responsible for the oppression and exploitation and degradation of black people in this country. And you should drop it in their lap. This government has failed the Negro. This so-called democracy has failed the Negro. And all these white liberals have definitely failed the Negro.

So, where do we go from here? First, we need some friends. We need some new allies. The entire civil-rights struggle needs a new interpretation, a broader interpretation. We need to look at this civil-rights thing from another angle—from the inside as well as from the outside. To those of us whose philosophy is black nationalism, the only way you can get involved in the civil-rights struggle is give it a new interpretation. That old interpretation excluded us. It kept us out. So, we're giving a new interpretation to the civil-rights struggle, an interpretation that will enable us to come into it, take part in it. And these handkerchief-heads who have been dillydallying and pussyfooting and compromising—we don't intend to let them pussyfoot and dillydally and compromise any longer.

How can you thank a man for giving you what's already yours? How then can you thank him for giving you only part of what's already yours? You haven't even made progress, if what's being given to you, you should have had already. That's not progress. And I love my Brother Lomax, the way he pointed out we're right back where we were in 1954. We're not even as far up as we were in 1954. We're behind where we were in 1954. There's more segregation now than there was in 1954. There's more racial animosity, more racial hatred, more racial violence today in 1964, than there was in 1954. Where is the progress?

And now you're facing a situation where the young Negro's coming up. They don't want to hear that 'turn-the-other-cheek' stuff, no. In Jacksonville, those were teenagers, they were throwing Molotov cocktails. Negroes have never done that before. But it shows you there's a new deal coming in. There's new thinking coming in. There's new strategy coming in. It'll be Molotov cocktails this month, hand grenades next month, and something else next month. It'll be ballots, or it'll be bullets. It'll be liberty, or it will be death. The only difference about this kind of death— it'll be reciprocal. You know what is meant by 'reciprocal'? That's one of Brother Lomax's words. I stole it from him. I don't usually deal with those big words because I don't usually deal with big people. I deal with small people. I find you can get a whole lot of small people and whip hell out of a whole lot of big people. They haven't got anything to lose, and they've got everything to gain. And they'll let you know in a minute: 'It takes two to tango; when I go, you go.'

The black nationalists, those whose philosophy is black nationalism, in bringing about this new interpretation of the entire meaning of civil rights, look upon it as meaning, as Brother Lomax has pointed out, equality of opportunity. Well, we're justified in seeking civil rights, if it means equality of opportunity, because all we're doing there is trying to collect for our investment. Our mothers and fathers invested sweat and blood. 310 years we worked in this country without a dime in return—I mean without a dime in return. You let the white man walk around here talking about how rich this country is, but you never stop to think how it got rich so quick. It got rich because you made it rich.

You take the people who are in this audience right now. They're poor. We're all poor as individuals. Our weekly salary individually amounts to hardly anything. But if you take the salary of everyone in here collectively, it'll fill up a whole lot of baskets. It's a lot of wealth. If you can collect the wages of just these people right here for a year, you'll be rich—richer than rich. When you look at it like that, think how rich Uncle Sam had to become, not with this handful, but millions of black people. Your and my mother and father, who didn't work an eight-hour shift, but worked from 'can't see' in the morning until 'can't see' at night, and worked for nothing, making the white man rich, making Uncle Sam rich. This is our investment. This is our contribution, our blood.

Not only did we give of our free labor, we gave of our blood. Every time he had a call to arms, we were the first ones in uniform. We died on every battlefield the white man had. We have made a greater sacrifice than anybody who's standing up in America today. We have made a greater contribution and have collected less. Civil rights, for those of us whose philosophy is black nationalism, means: 'Give it to us now. Don't wait for next year. Give it to us yesterday, and that's not fast enough.'

I might stop right here to point out one thing. Whenever you're going after something that belongs to you, anyone who's depriving you of the right to have it is a criminal. Understand that. Whenever you are going after something that is yours, you are within your legal rights to lay claim to it. And anyone who puts forth any effort to deprive you of that which is yours, is breaking the law, is a criminal. And this was pointed out by the Supreme Court decision. It outlawed segregation.

Which means segregation is against the law. Which means a segregationist is breaking the law. A segregationist is a criminal. You can't label him as anything other than that. And when you demonstrate against segregation, the law is on your side. The Supreme Court is on your side.

Now, who is it that opposes you in carrying out the law? The police department itself. With police dogs and clubs. Whenever you demonstrate against segregation, whether it is segregated education, segregated housing, or anything else, the law is on your side, and anyone who stands in the way is not the law any longer. They are breaking the law; they are not representatives of the law. Any time you demonstrate against segregation and a man has the audacity to put a police dog on you, kill that dog, kill him, I'm telling you, kill that dog. I say it, if they put me in jail tomorrow, kill that dog. Then you'll put a stop to it. Now, if these white people in here don't want to see that kind of action, get down and tell the mayor to tell the police department to pull the dogs in. That's all you have to do. If you don't do it, someone else will.

If you don't take this kind of stand, your little children will grow up and look at you and think 'shame.' If you don't take an uncompromising stand, I don't mean go out and get violent; but at the same time you should never be non-violent unless you run into some non-violence. I'm non-violent with those who are non-violent with me. But when you drop that violence on me, then you've made me go insane, and I'm not responsible for what I do. And that's the way every Negro should get. Any time you know you're within the law, within your legal rights, within your moral rights, in accord with justice, then die for what you believe in. But don't die alone. Let your dying be reciprocal. This is what is meant by equality. What's good for the goose is good for the gander.

When we begin to get in this area, we need new friends, we need new allies. We need to expand the civil-rights struggle to a higher level—to the level of human rights. Whenever you are in a civil-rights struggle, whether you know it or not, you are confining yourself to the jurisdiction of Uncle Sam. No one from the outside world can speak out in your behalf as long as your struggle is a civil-rights struggle. Civil rights comes within the domestic affairs of this country. All of our African brothers and our Asian brothers and our Latin-American brothers cannot open their mouths and interfere in the domestic affairs of the United States. And as long as it's civil rights, this comes under the jurisdiction of Uncle Sam.

But the United Nations has what's known as the charter of human rights; it has a committee that deals in human rights. You may wonder why all of the atrocities that have been committed in Africa and in Hungary and in Asia and in Latin America are brought before the UN, and the Negro problem is never brought before the UN. This is part of the conspiracy. This old, tricky blue-eyed liberal who is supposed to be your and my friend, supposed to be in our corner, supposed to be subsidizing our struggle, and supposed to be acting in the capacity of an adviser, never tells you anything about human rights. They keep you wrapped up in civil rights. And you spend so much time barking up the civil-rights tree, you don't even know there's a human-rights tree on the same floor.

When you expand the civil-rights struggle to the level of human rights, you can then take the case of the black man in this country before the nations in the UN. You can take it before the General Assembly. You can take Uncle Sam before a world court. But the only level you can do it on is the level of human rights. Civil rights keeps you under his restrictions, under his jurisdiction. Civil rights keeps you in his pocket. Civil rights means you're asking Uncle Sam to treat you right. Human rights are something you were born with. Human rights are your God-given rights. Human rights are the rights that are recognized by all nations of this earth. And any time any one violates your human rights, you can take them to the world court.

Uncle Sam's hands are dripping with blood, dripping with the blood of the black man in this country. He's the earth's number-one hypocrite. He has the audacity—yes, he has—imagine him posing as the leader of the free world. The free world! And you over here singing 'We Shall Overcome.' Expand the civil-rights struggle to the level of human rights. Take it into the United Nations, where our African brothers can throw their weight on our side, where our Asian brothers can throw their weight on our side, where our Latin-American brothers can throw their weight on our side, and where 800 million Chinamen are sitting there waiting to throw their weight on our side.

Let the world know how bloody his hands are. Let the world know the hypocrisy that's practiced over here. Let it be the ballot or the bullet. Let him know that it must be the ballot or the bullet.

When you take your case to Washington, DC, you're taking it to the criminal who's responsible; it's like running from the wolf to the fox. They're all in cahoots together. They all work political chicanery and make you look like a chump before the eyes of the world. Here you are walking around in America, getting ready to be drafted and sent abroad, like a tin soldier, and when you get over there, people ask you what are you fighting for, and you have to stick your tongue in your cheek. No, take Uncle Sam to court, take him before the world.

By ballot I only mean freedom. Don't you know—I disagree with Lomax on this issue—that the ballot is more important than the dollar? Can I prove it? Yes. Look in the UN. There are poor nations in the UN; yet those poor nations can get together with their voting power and keep the rich nations from making a move. They have one nation—one vote, everyone has an equal vote. And when those brothers from Asia, and Africa and the darker parts of this earth get together, their voting power is sufficient to hold Sam in check. Or Russia in check. Or some other section of the earth in check. So, the ballot is most important.

Right now, in this country, if you and I, 22 million African Americans—that's what we are—Africans who are in America. You're nothing but Africans. Nothing but Africans. In fact, you'd get farther calling yourself African instead of Negro. Africans don't catch hell. You're the only one catching hell. They don't have to pass civil-rights bills for Africans. An African can go anywhere he wants right now. All you've got to do is tie your head up. That's right, go anywhere you want. Just stop being a Negro. Change your name to Hoogagagooba. That'll show you how silly the white man is. You're dealing with a silly man. A friend of mine who's very dark put a turban on his head and went into a restaurant in Atlanta before they called themselves desegregated. He went into a white restaurant, he sat down, they served him, and he said, 'What would happen if a Negro came in here?' And there he's sitting, black as night, but because he had his head wrapped up the waitress looked back at him and says, 'Why, there wouldn't no nigger dare come in here.'

So, you're dealing with a man whose bias and prejudice are making him lose his mind, his intelligence, every day. He's frightened. He looks around and sees what's taking place on this earth, and he sees that the pendulum of time is swinging in your direction. The dark people are waking up. They're losing their fear of the white man. No place where he's fighting right now is he winning. Everywhere he's fighting, he's fighting someone your and my complexion. And they're beating him. He can't win any more. He's won his last battle. He failed to win the Korean War. He couldn't win it. He had to sign a truce. That's a loss.

Any time Uncle Sam, with all his machinery for warfare, is held to a draw by some rice-eaters, he's lost the battle. He had to sign a truce. America's not supposed to sign a truce. She's supposed to be bad. But she's not bad any more. She's bad as long as she can use her hydrogen bomb, but she can't use hers for fear Russia might use hers. Russia can't use hers, for fear that Sam might use his. So, both of them are weapon-less. They can't use the weapon because each's weapon nullifies the other's. So the only place where action can take place is on the ground. And the white man can't win another war fighting on the ground. Those days are over. The black man knows it, the brown man knows it, the red man knows it and the yellow man knows it. So they engage him in guerrilla warfare. That's not his style. You've got to have heart to be a guerrilla warrior, and he hasn't got any heart. I'm telling you now.

I just want to give you a little briefing on guerrilla warfare because, before you know it, before you know it. It takes heart to be a guerrilla warrior because you're on your own. In conventional warfare you have tanks and a whole lot of other people with you to back you up—planes over your head and all that kind of stuff. But a guerrilla is on his own. All you have is a rifle, some sneakers and a bowl of rice, and that's all you need—and a lot of heart. The Japanese on some of those islands in the Pacific, when the American soldiers landed, one Japanese sometimes could hold the whole army off. He'd just wait until the sun went down, and when the sun went down they were all equal. He would take his little blade and slip from bush to bush, and from American to American. The white soldiers couldn't cope with that. Whenever you see a white soldier that fought in the Pacific, he has the shakes, he has a nervous condition, because they scared him to death.

The same thing happened to the French up in French Indochina. People who just a few years previously were rice farmers got together and ran the heavily-mechanized French Army out of Indochina. You don't need it—modern warfare today won't work. This is the day of the guerrilla. They did the same thing in Algeria. Algerians, who were nothing but Bedouins, took a rifle and sneaked off to the hills, and de Gaulle and all of his highfalutin' war machinery couldn't defeat those guerrillas. Nowhere on this earth does the white man win in a guerrilla warfare. It's not his speed. Just as guerrilla warfare is prevailing in Asia and in parts of Africa and in parts of Latin America, you've got to be mighty naive, or you've got to play the black man cheap, if you don't think some day he's going to wake up and find that it's got to be the ballot or the bullet.

I would like to say, in closing, a few things concerning the Muslim Mosque, Inc., which we established recently in New York City. It's true we're Muslims and our religion is Islam, but we don't mix our religion with our politics and our economics and our social and civil activities—not any more. We keep our religion in our mosque. After our religious services are over, then as Muslims we become involved in political action, economic action and social and civic action. We become involved with anybody, anywhere, any time and in any manner that's designed to eliminate the evils, the political, economic and social evils that are afflicting the people of our community.

The political philosophy of black nationalism means that the black man should control the politics and the politicians in his own community; no more. The black man in the black community has to be re-educated into the science of politics so he will know what politics is supposed to bring him in return. Don't be throwing out any ballots. A ballot is like a bullet. You don't throw your ballots until you see a target, and if that target is not within your reach, keep your ballot in your pocket.

The political philosophy of black nationalism is being taught in the Christian church. It's being taught in the NAACP. It's being taught in CORE meetings. It's being taught in SNCC (Student Nonviolent Coordinating Committee) meetings. It's being taught in Muslim meetings. It's being taught where nothing but atheists and agnostics come together. It's being taught everywhere. Black people are fed up with the dillydallying, pussyfooting, compromising approach that we've been using toward getting our freedom. We want freedom now, but we're not going to get it saying 'We Shall Overcome.' We've got to fight until we overcome.

The economic philosophy of black nationalism is pure and simple. It only means that we should control the economy of our community. Why should white people be running all the stores in our community? Why should white people be running the banks of our community? Why should the economy of our community be in the hands of the white man? Why? If a black man can't move his store into a white community, you tell me why a white man should move his store into a black community. The philosophy of black nationalism involves a re-education program in the black community in regards to economics. Our people have to be made to see that any time you take your dollar out of your community and spend it in a community where you don't live, the community where you live will get poorer and poorer, and the community where you spend your money will get richer and richer.

Then you wonder why where you live is always a ghetto or a slum area. And where you and I are concerned, not only do we lose it when we spend it out of the community, but the white man has got all our stores in the community tied up; so that though we spend it in the community, at sundown the man who runs the store takes it over across town somewhere. He's got us in a vise.

So the economic philosophy of black nationalism means in every church, in every civic organization, in every fraternal order, it's time now for our people to become conscious of the importance of controlling the economy of our community. If we own the stores, if we operate the businesses, if we try and establish some industry in our own community, then we're developing to the position where we are creating employment for our own kind. Once you gain control of the economy of your own community, then you don't have to picket and boycott and beg some cracker downtown for a job in his business.

The social philosophy of black nationalism only means that we have to get together and remove the evils, the vices, alcoholism, drug addiction and other evils that are destroying the moral fiber of our community. We ourselves have to lift the level of our community, the standard of our community to a higher level, make our own society beautiful so that we will be satisfied in our own social circles and won't be running around here trying to knock our way into a social circle where we're not wanted. So I say, in spreading a gospel such as black nationalism, it is not designed to make the black man re-evaluate the white man—you know him already—but to make the black man re-evaluate himself. Don't change the white man's mind—you can't change his mind, and that whole thing about appealing to the moral conscience of America—America's conscience is bankrupt. She lost all conscience a long time ago. Uncle Sam has no conscience.

They don't know what morals are. They don't try and eliminate an evil because it's evil, or because it's illegal, or because it's immoral; they eliminate it only when it threatens their existence. So you're wasting your time appealing to the moral conscience of a bankrupt man like Uncle Sam. If he had a conscience, he'd straighten this thing out with no more pressure being put upon him. So it is not necessary to change the white man's mind. We have to change our own mind. You can't change his mind about us. We've got to change our own minds about each other. We have to see each other with new eyes. We have to see each other as brothers and sisters. We have to come together with warmth so we can develop unity and harmony that's necessary to get this problem solved ourselves. How can we do this? How can we avoid jealousy? How can we avoid the suspicion and the divisions that exist in the community? I'll tell you how.

I have watched how Billy Graham comes into a city, spreading what he calls the gospel of Christ, which is only white nationalism. That's what he is. Billy Graham is a white nationalist; I'm a black nationalist. But since it's the natural tendency for leaders to be jealous and look upon a powerful figure like Graham with suspicion and envy, how is it possible for him to come into a city and get all the cooperation of the church leaders? Don't think because they're church leaders that they don't have weaknesses that make them envious and jealous—no, everybody's got it. It's not an accident that when they want to choose a cardinal, as Pope over there in Rome, they get in a closet so you can't hear them cussing and fighting and carrying on.

Billy Graham comes in preaching the gospel of Christ. He evangelizes the gospel. He stirs everybody up, but he never tries to start a church. If he came in trying to start a church, all the churches would be against him. So, he just comes in talking about Christ and tells everybody who gets Christ to go to any church where Christ is; and in this way the church cooperates with him. So we're going to take a page from his book.

Our gospel is black nationalism. We're not trying to threaten the existence of any organization, but we're spreading the gospel of black nationalism. Anywhere there's a church that is also preaching and practicing the gospel of black nationalism, join that church. If the NAACP is preaching and practicing the gospel of black nationalism, join the NAACP. If CORE is spreading and practicing the gospel of black nationalism, join CORE. Join any organization that has a gospel that's for the uplift of the black man. And when you get into it and see them pussyfooting or compromising, pull out of it because that's not black nationalism. We'll find another one.

And in this manner, the organizations will increase in number and in quantity and in quality, and by August, it is then our intention to have a black nationalist convention which will consist of delegates from all over the country who are interested in the political, economic and social philosophy of black nationalism. After these delegates convene, we will hold a seminar; we will hold discussions; we will listen to everyone. We want to hear new ideas and new solutions and new answers. And at that time, if we see fit then to form a black nationalist party, we'll form a black nationalist party. If it's necessary to form a black nationalist army, we'll form a black nationalist army. It'll be the ballot or the bullet. It'll be liberty or it'll be death.

It's time for you and me to stop sitting in this country, letting some cracker senators, Northern crackers and Southern crackers, sit there in Washington, DC, and come to a conclusion in their mind that you and I are supposed to have civil rights. There's no white man going to tell me anything about my rights. Brothers and sisters, always remember, if it doesn't take senators and congressmen and presidential proclamations to give freedom to the white man, it is not necessary for legislation or proclamation or Supreme Court decisions to give freedom to the black man. You let that white man know, if this is a country of freedom, let it be a country of freedom; and if it's not a country of freedom, change it.

We will work with anybody, anywhere, at any time, who is genuinely interested in tackling the problem head-on, non-violently as long as the enemy is non-violent, but violent when the enemy gets violent. We'll work with you on the voter-registration drive, we'll work with you on rent strikes, we'll work with you on school boycotts; I don't believe in any kind of integration; I'm not even worried about it, because I know you're not going to get it anyway; you're not going to get it because you're afraid to die; you've got to be ready to die if you try and force yourself on the white man, because he'll get just as violent as those crackers in Mississippi, right here in Cleveland. But we will still work with you on the school boycotts because we're against a segregated school system. A segregated school system produces children who, when they graduate, graduate with crippled minds. But this does not mean that a school is segregated because it's all black. A segregated school means a school that is controlled by people who have no real interest in it whatsoever.

Let me explain what I mean. A segregated district or community is a community in which people live, but outsiders control the politics and the economy of that community. They never refer to the white section as a segregated community. It's the all-Negro section that's a segregated community. Why? The white man controls his own school, his own bank, his own economy, his own politics, his own everything, his own community; but he also controls yours. When you're under someone else's control, you're segregated. They'll always give you the lowest or the worst that there is to offer, but it doesn't mean you're segregated just because you have your own. You've got to control your own. Just like the white man has control of his, you need to control yours.

You know the best way to get rid of segregation? The white man is more afraid of separation than he is of integration. Segregation means that he puts you away from him, but not far enough for you to be out of his jurisdiction; separation means you're gone. And the white man will integrate faster than he'll let you separate. So we will work with you against the segregated school system because it's criminal, because it is absolutely destructive, in every way imaginable, to the minds of the children who have to be exposed to that type of crippling education.

Last but not least, I must say this concerning the great controversy over rifles and shotguns. The only thing that I've ever said is that in areas where the government has proven itself either unwilling or unable to defend the lives and the property of Negroes, it's time for Negroes to defend themselves. Article number two of the constitutional amendments provides you and me the right to own a rifle or a shotgun. It is constitutionally legal to own a shotgun or a rifle. This doesn't mean you're going to get a rifle and form battalions and go out looking for white folks, although you'd be within your rights—I mean, you'd be justified; but that would be illegal and we don't do anything illegal. If the white man doesn't want the black man buying rifles and shotguns, then let the government do its job.

That's all. And don't let the white man come to you and ask you what you think about what Malcolm says—why, you old Uncle Tom. He would never ask you if he thought you were going to say, 'Amen!' No, he is making a Tom out of you. So, this doesn't mean forming rifle clubs and going out looking for people, but it is time, in 1964, if you are a man, to let that man know. If he's not going to do his job in running the government and providing you and me with the protection that our taxes are supposed to be for, since he spends all those billions for his defense budget, he certainly can't begrudge you and me spending $12 or $15 for a single-shot, or double-action. I hope you understand. Don't go out shooting people, but any time—brothers and sisters, and especially the men in this audience; some of you wearing Congressional Medals of Honor, with shoulders this wide, chests this big, muscles that big—any time you and I sit around and read where they bomb a church and murder in cold blood, not some grownups, but four little girls while they were praying to the same God the white man taught them to pray to, and you and I see the government go down and can't find who did it.

Why, this man—he can find Eichmann hiding down in Argentina somewhere. Let two or three American soldiers, who are minding somebody else's business way over in South Vietnam, get killed, and he'll send battleships, sticking his nose in their business. He wanted to send troops down to Cuba and make them have what he calls free elections—this old cracker who doesn't have free elections in his own country.

No, if you never see me another time in your life, if I die in the morning, I'll die saying one thing: the ballot or the bullet, the ballot or the bullet.

If a Negro in 1964 has to sit around and wait for some cracker senator to filibuster when it comes to the rights of black people, why, you and I should hang our heads in shame. You talk about a march on Washington in 1963, you haven't seen anything. There's some more going down in '64.

And this time they're not going like they went last year. They're not going singing 'We Shall Overcome.' They're not going with white friends. They're not going with placards already painted for them. They're not going with round-trip tickets. They're going with one-way tickets. And if they don't want that non-nonviolent army going down there, tell them to bring the filibuster to a halt.

The black nationalists aren't going to wait. Lyndon B. Johnson is the head of the Democratic Party. If he's for civil rights, let him go into the Senate next week and declare himself. Let him go in there right now and declare himself. Let him go in there and denounce the Southern branch of his party. Let him go in there right now and take a moral stand—right now, not later. Tell him, don't wait until election time. If he waits too long, brothers and sisters, he will be responsible for letting a condition develop in this country which will create a climate that will bring seeds up out of the ground with vegetation on the end of them looking like something these people never dreamed of. In 1964, it's the ballot or the bullet.

Thank you.

42

WE SHALL OVERCOME

Lyndon Baines Johnson

On 15 March 1965, Johnson delivered a televised address to a joint session of Congress, known as the 'We Shall Overcome' speech. In this speech, he called for the passing of the Voting Rights Act, a crucial piece of legislation aimed at combating racial discrimination in voting practices.

Mr Speaker, Mr President, Members of the Congress:

I speak tonight for the dignity of man and the destiny of democracy. I urge every member of both parties, Americans of all religions and of all colors, from every section of this country, to join me in that cause.

At times history and fate meet at a single time in a single place to shape a turning point in man's unending search for freedom. So it was at Lexington and Concord. So it was a century ago at Appomattox. So it was last week in Selma, Alabama. There, long-suffering men and women peacefully protested the denial of their rights as Americans. Many were brutally assaulted. One good man, a man of God, was killed.

There is no cause for pride in what has happened in Selma. There is no cause for self-satisfaction in the long denial of equal rights of millions of Americans. But there is cause for hope and for faith in our democracy in what is happening here tonight. For the cries of pain and the hymns and protests of oppressed people have summoned into convocation all the majesty of this great government—the government of the greatest nation on earth. Our mission is at once the oldest and the most basic of this country: to right wrong, to do justice, to serve man.

In our time we have come to live with the moments of great crisis. Our lives have been marked with debate about great issues—issues of war and peace, issues of prosperity and depression. But rarely in any time does an issue lay bare the secret heart of America itself. Rarely are we met with a challenge, not to our growth or abundance, or our welfare or our security, but rather to the values, and the purposes, and the meaning of our beloved nation.

The issue of equal rights for American Negroes is such an issue.

And should we defeat every enemy, and should we double our wealth and conquer the stars, and still be unequal to this issue, then we will have failed as a people and as a nation. For with a country as with a person, 'What is a man profited, if he shall gain the whole world, and lose his own soul?'

There is no Negro problem. There is no Southern problem. There is no Northern problem. There is only an American problem. And we are met here tonight as Americans—not as Democrats or Republicans. We are met here as Americans to solve that problem.

This was the first nation in the history of the world to be founded with a purpose. The great phrases of that purpose still sound in every American heart, North and South: 'All men are created equal,' 'government by consent of the governed,' 'give me liberty or give me death.' Well, those are not just clever words, or those are not just empty theories. In their name Americans have fought and died for two centuries, and tonight around the world they stand there as guardians of our liberty, risking their lives.

Those words are a promise to every citizen that he shall share in the dignity of man. This dignity cannot be found in a man's possessions; it cannot be found in his power, or in his position. It really rests on his right to be treated as a man equal in opportunity to all others. It says that he shall share in freedom, he shall choose his leaders, educate his children, provide for his family according to his ability and his merits as a human being. To apply any other test—to deny a man his hopes because of his color, or race, or his religion, or the place of his birth is not only to do injustice, it is to deny America and to dishonor the dead who gave their lives for American freedom.

Our fathers believed that if this noble view of the rights of man was to flourish, it must be rooted in democracy. The most basic right of all was the right to choose your own leaders. The history of this country, in large measure, is the history of the expansion of that right to all of our people. Many of the issues of civil rights are very complex and most difficult. But about this there can and should be no argument.

Every American citizen must have an equal right to vote.

There is no reason which can excuse the denial of that right. There is no duty which weighs more heavily on us than the duty we have to ensure that right.

Yet the harsh fact is that in many places in this country men and women are kept from voting simply because they are Negroes. Every device of which human ingenuity is capable has been used to deny this right. The Negro citizen may go to register only to be told that the day is wrong, or the hour is late, or the official in charge is absent. And if he persists, and if he manages to present himself to the registrar, he may be disqualified because he did not spell out his middle name or because he abbreviated a word on the application. And if he manages to fill out an application, he is given a test. The registrar is the sole judge of whether he passes this test. He may be asked to recite the entire Constitution, or explain the most complex provisions of State law. And even a college degree cannot be used to prove that he can read and write.

For the fact is that the only way to pass these barriers is to show a white skin. Experience has clearly shown that the existing process of law cannot overcome systematic and ingenious discrimination. No law that we now have on the books—and I have helped to put three of them there—can ensure the right to vote when local officials are determined to deny it. In such a case our duty must be clear to all of us. The Constitution says that no person shall be kept from voting because of his race or his color. We have all sworn an oath before God to support and to defend that Constitution. We must now act in obedience to that oath.

Wednesday, I will send to Congress a law designed to eliminate illegal barriers to the right to vote.

The broad principles of that bill will be in the hands of the Democratic and Republican leaders tomorrow. After they have reviewed it, it will come here formally as a bill. I am grateful for this opportunity to come here tonight at the invitation of the leadership to reason with my friends, to give them my views, and to visit with my former colleagues. I've had prepared a more comprehensive analysis of the legislation which I had intended to transmit to the clerk tomorrow, but which I will submit to the clerks tonight. But I want to really discuss with you now, briefly, the main proposals of this legislation.

This bill will strike down restrictions to voting in all elections—federal, state, and local—which have been used to deny Negroes the right to vote. This bill will establish a simple, uniform standard which cannot be used, however ingenious the effort, to flout our Constitution. It will provide for citizens to be registered by officials of the United States government, if the State officials refuse to register them. It will eliminate tedious, unnecessary lawsuits which delay the right to vote. Finally, this legislation will ensure that properly registered individuals are not prohibited from voting.

I will welcome the suggestions from all of the members of Congress—I have no doubt that I will get some—on ways and means to strengthen this law and to make it effective. But experience has plainly shown that this is the only path to carry out the command of the Constitution.

To those who seek to avoid action by their national government in their own communities, who want to and who seek to maintain purely local control over elections, the answer is simple: open your polling places to all your people.

Allow men and women to register and vote whatever the color of their skin.

Extend the rights of citizenship to every citizen of this land.

There is no constitutional issue here. The command of the Constitution is plain. There is no moral issue. It is wrong—deadly wrong—to deny any of your fellow Americans the right to vote in this country. There is no issue of states' rights or national rights. There is only the struggle for human rights. I have not the slightest doubt what will be your answer.

But the last time a president sent a civil rights bill to the Congress, it contained a provision to protect voting rights in federal elections. That civil rights bill was passed after eight long months of debate. And when that bill came to my desk from the Congress for my signature, the heart of the voting provision had been eliminated. This time, on this issue, there must be no delay, or no hesitation, or no compromise with our purpose.

We cannot, we must not, refuse to protect the right of every American to vote in every election that he may desire to participate in. And we ought not, and we cannot, and we must not wait another eight months before we get a bill. We have already waited a hundred years and more, and the time for waiting is gone.

So I ask you to join me in working long hours—nights and weekends, if necessary—to pass this bill. And I don't make that request lightly. For from the window where I sit with the problems of our country, I recognize that from outside this chamber is the outraged conscience of a nation, the grave concern of many nations, and the harsh judgment of history on our acts.

But even if we pass this bill, the battle will not be over. What happened in Selma is part of a far larger movement which reaches into every section and state of America. It is the effort of American Negroes to secure for themselves the full blessings of American life. Their cause must be our cause too. Because it's not just Negroes, but really it's all of us, who must overcome the crippling legacy of bigotry and injustice.

And we shall overcome.

As a man whose roots go deeply into Southern soil, I know how agonizing racial feelings are. I know how difficult it is to reshape the attitudes and the structure of our society. But a century has passed, more than a hundred years since the Negro was freed. And he is not fully free tonight.

It was more than a hundred years ago that Abraham Lincoln, a great president of another party, signed the Emancipation Proclamation; but emancipation is a proclamation, and not a fact. A century has passed, more than a hundred years, since equality was promised. And yet the Negro is not equal. A century has passed since the day of promise. And the promise is un-kept.

The time of justice has now come. I tell you that I believe sincerely that no force can hold it back. It is right in the eyes of man and God that it should come. And when it does, I think that day will brighten the lives of every American. For Negroes are not the only victims. How many white children have gone uneducated? How many white families have lived in stark poverty? How many white lives have been scarred by fear, because we've wasted our energy and our substance to maintain the barriers of hatred and terror?

And so I say to all of you here, and to all in the nation tonight, that those who appeal to you to hold on to the past do so at the cost of denying you your future.

This great, rich, restless country can offer opportunity and education and hope to all, all black and white, all North and South, sharecropper and city dweller. These are the enemies: poverty, ignorance, disease. They're our enemies, not our fellow man, not our neighbor. And these enemies too—poverty, disease and ignorance: we shall overcome.

Now let none of us in any section look with prideful righteousness on the troubles in another section, or the problems of our neighbors. There's really no part of America where the promise of equality has been fully kept. In Buffalo as well as in Birmingham, in Philadelphia as well as Selma, Americans are struggling for the fruits of freedom. This is one nation. What happens in Selma or in Cincinnati is a matter of legitimate concern to every American. But let each of us look within our own hearts and our own communities, and let each of us put our shoulder to the wheel to root out injustice wherever it exists.

As we meet here in this peaceful, historic chamber tonight, men from the South, some of whom were at Iwo Jima, men from the North who have carried Old Glory to far corners of the world and brought it back without a stain on it, men from the East and from the West, are all fighting together without regard to religion, or color, or region, in Vietnam. Men from every region fought for us across the world 20 years ago.

And now in these common dangers and these common sacrifices, the South made its contribution of honor and gallantry no less than any other region in the Great Republic—and in some instances, a great many of them, more.

And I have not the slightest doubt that good men from everywhere in this country, from the Great Lakes to the Gulf of Mexico, from the Golden Gate to the harbors along the Atlantic, will rally now together in this cause to vindicate the freedom of all Americans.

For all of us owe this duty; and I believe that all of us will respond to it. Your president makes that request of every American.

The real hero of this struggle is the American Negro. His actions and protests, his courage to risk safety and even to risk his life, have awakened the conscience of this nation. His demonstrations have been designed to call attention to injustice, designed to provoke change, designed to stir reform. He has called upon us to make good the promise of America. And who among us can say that we would have made the same progress were it not for his persistent bravery, and his faith in American democracy.

For at the real heart of battle for equality is a deep-seated belief in the democratic process. Equality depends not on the force of arms or tear gas but depends upon the force of moral right; not on recourse to violence but on respect for law and order.

And there have been many pressures upon your president and there will be others as the days come and go. But I pledge you tonight that we intend to fight this battle where it should be fought—in the courts, and in the Congress, and in the hearts of men.

We must preserve the right of free speech and the right of free assembly. But the right of free speech does not carry with it, as has been said, the right to holler fire in a crowded theater. We must preserve the right to free assembly. But free assembly does not carry with it the right to block public thoroughfares to traffic.

We do have a right to protest, and a right to march under conditions that do not infringe the constitutional rights of our neighbors. And I intend to protect all those rights as long as I am permitted to serve in this office.

We will guard against violence, knowing it strikes from our hands the very weapons which we seek: progress, obedience to law and belief in American values.

In Selma, as elsewhere, we seek and pray for peace. We seek order. We seek unity. But we will not accept the peace of stifled rights, or the order imposed by fear, or the unity that stifles protest. For peace cannot be purchased at the cost of liberty.

In Selma tonight—and we had a good day there—as in every city, we are working for a just and peaceful settlement. And we must all remember that after this speech I am making tonight, after the police and the FBI and the Marshals have all gone, and after you have promptly passed this bill, the people of Selma and the other cities of the nation must still live and work together. And when the attention of the nation has gone elsewhere, they must try to heal the wounds and to build a new community.

This cannot be easily done on a battleground of violence, as the history of the South itself shows. It is in recognition of this that men of both races have shown such an outstandingly impressive responsibility in recent days—last Tuesday, again today.

The bill that I am presenting to you will be known as a civil rights bill. But, in a larger sense, most of the program I am recommending is a civil rights program. Its object is to open the city of hope to all people of all races.

Because all Americans just must have the right to vote. And we are going to give them that right. All Americans must have the privileges of citizenship—regardless of race. And they are going to have those privileges of citizenship—regardless of race.

But I would like to caution you and remind you that to exercise these privileges takes much more than just legal right. It requires a trained mind and a healthy body. It requires a decent home, and the chance to find a job, and the opportunity to escape from the clutches of poverty.

Of course, people cannot contribute to the nation if they are never taught to read or write, if their bodies are stunted from hunger, if their sickness goes untended, if their life is spent in hopeless poverty just drawing a welfare check. So we want to open the gates to opportunity. But we're also going to give all our people, black and white, the help that they need to walk through those gates.

My first job after college was as a teacher in Cotulla, Texas, in a small Mexican-American school. Few of them could speak English, and I couldn't speak much Spanish. My students were poor and they often came to class without breakfast, hungry. And they knew, even in their youth, the pain of prejudice. They never seemed to know why people disliked them. But they knew it was so, because I saw it in their eyes. I often walked home late in the afternoon, after the classes were finished, wishing there was more that I could do. But all I knew was to teach them the little that I knew, hoping that it might help them against the hardships that lay ahead.

And somehow you never forget what poverty and hatred can do when you see its scars on the hopeful face of a young child.

I never thought then, in 1928, that I would be standing here in 1965. It never even occurred to me in my fondest dreams that I might have the chance to help the sons and daughters of those students and to help people like them all over this country.

But now I do have that chance—and I'll let you in on a secret—I mean to use it.

And I hope that you will use it with me.

This is the richest and the most powerful country which ever occupied this globe. The might of past empires is little compared to ours. But I do not want to be the president who built empires, or sought grandeur, or extended dominion.

I want to be the president who educated young children to the wonders of their world.

I want to be the president who helped to feed the hungry and to prepare them to be tax-payers instead of tax-eaters.

I want to be the president who helped the poor to find their own way and who protected the right of every citizen to vote in every election.

I want to be the president who helped to end hatred among his fellow men, and who promoted love among the people of all races and all regions and all parties.

I want to be the president who helped to end war among the brothers of this earth.

And so, at the request of your beloved Speaker, and the senator from Montana, the majority leader, the senator from Illinois, the minority leader, Mr McCulloch, and other Members of both parties, I came here tonight—not as President Roosevelt came down one time, in person, to veto a bonus bill, not as President Truman came down one time to urge the passage of a railroad bill—but I came down here to ask you to share this task with me, and to share it with the people that we both work for. I want this to be the Congress, Republicans and Democrats alike, which did all these things for all these people.

Beyond this great chamber, out yonder in fifty states, are the people that we serve. Who can tell what deep and unspoken hopes are in their hearts tonight as they sit there and listen. We all can guess, from our own lives, how difficult they often find their own pursuit of happiness, how many problems each little family has. They look most of all to themselves for their futures. But I think that they also look to each of us.

Above the pyramid on the great seal of the United States it says in Latin: 'God has favored our undertaking.' God will not favor everything that we do. It is rather our duty to divine His will.

But I cannot help believing that He truly understands and that He really favors the undertaking that we begin here tonight.

43

I'VE BEEN TO THE MOUNTAINTOP

Martin Luther King Jr'

'I've Been to the Mountaintop' is a speech by Dr Martin Luther King Jr, delivered on 3 April 1968, the day before his assassination. In this speech, he spoke about his commitment to the civil rights movement and the potential for transformative change in society.

Thank you very kindly, my friends. As I listened to Ralph Abernathy in his eloquent and generous introduction and then thought about myself, I wondered who he was talking about. It's always good to have your closest friend and associate say something good about you. And Ralph is the best friend that I have in the world.

I'm delighted to see each of you here tonight in spite of a storm warning. You reveal that you are determined to go on anyhow. Something is happening in Memphis; something is happening in our world.

And you know, if I were standing at the beginning of time, with the possibility of taking a general and panoramic view of the whole human history up to now, and the Almighty said to me, 'Martin Luther King, which age would you like to live in?'—I would take my mental flight by Egypt and I would watch God's children in their magnificent trek from the dark dungeons of Egypt through, or rather across the Red Sea, through the wilderness on toward the Promised Land. And in spite of its magnificence, I wouldn't stop there. I would move on by Greece, and take my mind to Mount Olympus. And I would see Plato, Aristotle, Socrates, Euripides and Aristophanes assembled around the Parthenon as they discussed the great and eternal issues of reality.

But I wouldn't stop there. I would go on, even to the great heyday of the Roman Empire. And I would see developments around there, through various emperors and leaders. But I wouldn't stop there. I would even come up to the day of the Renaissance, and get a quick picture of all that the Renaissance did for the cultural and esthetic life of man. But I wouldn't stop there. I would even go by the way that the man for whom I'm named had his habitat. And I would watch Martin Luther as he tacked his ninety-five theses on the door at the church in Wittenberg.

But I wouldn't stop there. I would come on up even to 1863, and watch a vacillating president by the name of Abraham Lincoln finally come to the conclusion that he had to sign the Emancipation Proclamation. But I wouldn't stop there. I would even come up to the early thirties, and see a man grappling with the problems of the bankruptcy of his nation. And come with an eloquent cry that we have nothing to fear but fear itself.

But I wouldn't stop there. Strangely enough, I would turn to the Almighty, and say, 'If you allow me to live just a few years in the second half of the twentieth century, I will be happy.' Now that's a strange statement to make, because the world is all messed up. The nation is sick. Trouble is in the land. Confusion all around. That's a strange statement. But I know, somehow, that only when it is dark enough, can you see the stars. And I see God working in this period of the twentieth century in a way that men, in some strange way, are responding—something is happening in our world. The masses of people are rising up. And wherever they are assembled today, whether they are in Johannesburg, South Africa; Nairobi, Kenya; Accra, Ghana; New York City; Atlanta, Georgia; Jackson, Mississippi; or Memphis, Tennessee—the cry is always the same—'We want to be free.' And another reason that I'm happy to live in this period is that we have been forced to a point where we're going to have to grapple with the problems that men have been trying to grapple with through history, but the demand didn't force them to do it. Survival demands that we grapple with them. Men, for years now, have been talking about war and peace. But now, no longer can they just talk about it. It is no longer a choice between violence and non-violence in this world; it's non-violence or non-existence.

That is where we are today. And also in the human rights revolution, if something isn't done, and in a hurry, to bring the colored peoples of the world out of their long years of poverty, their long years of hurt and neglect, the whole world is doomed. Now, I'm just happy that God has allowed me to live in this period, to see what is unfolding. And I'm happy that He's allowed me to be in Memphis.

I can remember, I can remember when Negroes were just going around as Ralph has said, so often, scratching where they didn't itch, and laughing when they were not tickled. But that day is all over. We mean business now, and we are determined to gain our rightful place in God's world.

And that's all this whole thing is about. We aren't engaged in any negative protest and in any negative arguments with anybody. We are saying that we are determined to be men. We are determined to be people. We are saying that we are God's children. And that we don't have to live like we are forced to live.

Now, what does all of this mean in this great period of history? It means that we've got to stay together. We've got to stay together and maintain unity. You know, whenever Pharaoh wanted to prolong the period of slavery in Egypt, he had a favorite, favorite formula for doing it. What was that? He kept the slaves fighting among themselves. But whenever the slaves get together, something happens in Pharaoh's court, and he cannot hold the slaves in slavery. When the slaves get together, that's the beginning of getting out of slavery. Now let us maintain unity.

Secondly, let us keep the issues where they are. The issue is injustice. The issue is the refusal of Memphis to be fair and honest in its dealings with its public servants, who happen to be sanitation workers. Now, we've got to keep attention on that. That's always the problem with a little violence. You know what happened the other day, and the press dealt only with the window-breaking. I read the articles. They very seldom got around to mentioning the fact that 1,300 sanitation workers were on strike, and that Memphis is not being fair to them, and that Mayor Loeb is in dire need of a doctor. They didn't get around to that.

Now we're going to march again, and we've got to march again, in order to put the issue where it is supposed to be. And force everybody to see that there are 1,300 of God's children here suffering, sometimes going hungry, going through dark and dreary nights wondering how this thing is going to come out. That's the issue. And we've got to say to the nation: we know it's coming out. For when people get caught up with that which is right and they are willing to sacrifice for it, there is no stopping point short of victory.

We aren't going to let any mace stop us. We are masters in our non-violent movement in disarming police forces; they don't know what to do, I've seen them so often. I remember in Birmingham, Alabama, when we were in that majestic struggle there, we would move out of the Sixteenth Street Baptist Church day after day; by the hundreds we would move out. And Bull Connor would tell them to send the dogs forth and they did come; but we just went before the dogs singing, 'Ain't gonna let nobody turn me round.' Bull Connor next would say, 'Turn the fire hoses on.' And as I said to you the other night, Bull Connor didn't know history. He knew a kind of physics that somehow didn't relate to the transphysics that we knew about. And that was the fact that there was a certain kind of fire that no water could put out. And we went before the fire hoses; we had known water. If we were Baptist or some other denomination, we had been immersed. If we were Methodist, and some others, we had been sprinkled, but we knew water.

That couldn't stop us. And we just went on before the dogs and we would look at them; and we'd go on before the water hoses and we would look at it, and we'd just go on singing 'Over my head I see freedom in the air.' And then we would be thrown in the paddy wagons, and sometimes we were stacked in there like sardines in a can. And they would throw us in, and old Bull would say, 'Take them off,' and they did; and we would just go in the paddy wagon singing, 'We Shall Overcome.' And every now and then we'd get in the jail, and we'd see the jailers looking through the windows being moved by our prayers, and being moved by our words and our songs. And there was a power there which Bull Connor couldn't adjust to; and so we ended up transforming Bull into a steer, and we won our struggle in Birmingham.

Now we've got to go on to Memphis just like that. I call upon you to be with us Monday. Now about injunctions: we have an injunction and we're going into court tomorrow morning to fight this illegal, unconstitutional injunction. All we say to America is, 'Be true to what you said on paper.' If I lived in China or even Russia, or any totalitarian country, maybe I could understand the denial of certain basic First Amendment privileges, because they hadn't committed themselves to that over there. But somewhere I read of the freedom of assembly. Somewhere I read of the freedom of speech. Somewhere I read of the freedom of the press. Somewhere I read that the greatness of America is the right to protest for right. And so just as I say, we aren't going to let any injunction turn us around. We are going on.

We need all of you. And you know what's beautiful to me, is to see all of these ministers of the Gospel. It's a marvelous picture. Who is it that is supposed to articulate the longings and aspirations of the people more than the preacher? Somehow the preacher must be an Amos, and say, 'Let justice roll down like waters and righteousness like a mighty stream.' Somehow, the preacher must say with Jesus, 'The spirit of the Lord is upon me, because he hath anointed me to deal with the problems of the poor.' And I want to commend the preachers, under the leadership of these noble men: James Lawson, one who has been in this struggle for many years; he's been to jail for struggling; but he's still going on, fighting for the rights of his people. Revd Ralph Jackson, Billy Kiles; I could just go right on down the list, but time will not permit. But I want to thank them all. And I want you to thank them, because so often, preachers aren't concerned about anything but themselves. And I'm always happy to see a relevant ministry.

It's all right to talk about 'long white robes over yonder,' in all of its symbolism. But ultimately people want some suits and dresses and shoes to wear down here. It's all right to talk about 'streets flowing with milk and honey,' but God has commanded us to be concerned about the slums down here, and his children who can't eat three square meals a day. It's all right to talk about the new Jerusalem, but one day, God's preachers must talk about the New York, the new Atlanta, the new Philadelphia, the new Los Angeles, the new Memphis, Tennessee. This is what we have to do.

Now the other thing we'll have to do is this: always anchor our external direct action with the power of economic withdrawal. Now, we are poor people, individually, we are poor when you compare us with white society in America. We are poor. Never stop and forget that collectively, that means all of us together, collectively we are richer than all the nations in the world, with the exception of nine. Did you ever think about that? After you leave the United States, Soviet Russia, Great Britain, West Germany, France, and I could name the others, the Negro collectively is richer than most nations of the world. We have an annual income of more than $30 billion a year, which is more than all of the exports of the United States, and more than the national budget of Canada. Did you know that? That's power right there, if we know how to pool it.

We don't have to argue with anybody. We don't have to curse and go around acting bad with our words. We don't need any bricks and bottles, we don't need any Molotov cocktails, we just need to go around to these stores, and to these massive industries in our country, and say, 'God sent us by here, to say to you that you're not treating his children right. And we've come by here to ask you to make the first item on your agenda fair treatment, where God's children are concerned. Now, if you are not prepared to do that, we do have an agenda that we must follow. And our agenda calls for withdrawing economic support from you.' And so, as a result of this, we are asking you tonight, to go out and tell your neighbors not to buy Coca-Cola in Memphis. Go by and tell them not to buy Sealtest milk. Tell them not to buy—what is the other bread?—Wonder Bread. And what is the other bread company, Jesse? Tell them not to buy Hart's bread. As Jesse Jackson has said, up to now, only the garbage men have been feeling pain; now we must kind of redistribute the pain. We are choosing these companies because they haven't been fair in their hiring policies; and we are choosing them because they can begin the process of saying they are going to support the needs and the rights of these men who are on strike. And then they can move on downtown and tell Mayor Loeb to do what is right.

But not only that, we've got to strengthen black institutions. I call upon you to take your money out of the banks downtown and deposit your money in Tri-State Bank—we want a 'bank-in' movement in Memphis. So go by the savings and loan association. I'm not asking you something we don't do ourselves at SCLC. Judge Hooks and others will tell you that we have an account here in the savings and loan association from the Southern Christian Leadership Conference. We're just telling you to follow what we're doing. Put your money there. You have six or seven black insurance companies in Memphis. Take out your insurance there. We want to have an 'insurance-in.' Now these are some practical things we can do. We begin the process of building a greater economic base. And at the same time, we are putting pressure where it really hurts. I ask you to follow through here.

Now, let me say as I move to my conclusion that we've got

to give ourselves to this struggle until the end. Nothing would be more tragic than to stop at this point, in Memphis. We've got to see it through. And when we have our march, you need to be there. Be concerned about your brother. You may not be on strike. But either we go up together, or we go down together.

Let us develop a kind of dangerous unselfishness. One day a man came to Jesus; and he wanted to raise some questions about some vital matters in life. At points, he wanted to trick Jesus, and show him that he knew a little more than Jesus knew, and through this, throw him off base. Now that question could have easily ended up in a philosophical and theological debate. But Jesus immediately pulled that question from mid-air, and placed it on a dangerous curve between Jerusalem and Jericho. And he talked about a certain man, who fell among thieves. You remember that a Levite and a priest passed by on the other side. They didn't stop to help him. And finally a man of another race came by. He got down from his beast, decided not to be compassionate by proxy. But he got down with him, administering first aid, and helped the man in need. Jesus ended up saying, this was the good man, this was the great man, because he had the capacity to project the 'I' into the 'thou,' and to be concerned about his brother. Now you know, we use our imagination a great deal to try to determine why the priest and the Levite didn't stop. At times we say they were busy going to church meetings—an ecclesiastical gathering—and they had to get on down to Jerusalem so they wouldn't be late for their meeting. At other times we would speculate that there was a religious law that 'One who was engaged in religious ceremonials was not to touch a human body twenty-four hours before the ceremony.' And every now and then we begin to wonder whether maybe they were not going down to Jerusalem, or down to Jericho, rather to organize a 'Jericho Road Improvement Association.' That's a possibility. Maybe they felt that it was better to deal with the problem from the causal root, rather than to get bogged down with an individual effort.

But I'm going to tell you what my imagination tells me. It's possible that these men were afraid. You see, the Jericho road is a dangerous road. I remember when Mrs King and I were first in Jerusalem. We rented a car and drove from Jerusalem down to Jericho. And as soon as we got on that road, I said to my wife, 'I can see why Jesus used this as a setting for his parable.' It's a winding, meandering road. It's really conducive for ambushing. You start out in Jerusalem, which is about 1,200 miles, or rather 1,200 feet above sea level. And by the time you get down to Jericho, 15 or 20 minutes later, you're about 2,200 feet below sea level. That's a dangerous road. In the days of Jesus it came to be known as the 'Bloody Pass.' And you know, it's possible that the priest and the Levite looked over that man on the ground and wondered if the robbers were still around. Or it's possible that they felt that the man on the ground was merely faking. And he was acting like he had been robbed and hurt, in order to seize them over there, lure them there for quick and easy seizure. And so the first question that the Levite asked was, 'If I stop to help this man, what will happen to me?' But then the Good Samaritan came by. And he reversed the question: 'If I do not stop to help this man, what will happen to him?' That's the question before you tonight. Not, 'If I stop to help the sanitation workers, what will happen to all of the hours that I usually spend in my office every day and every week as a pastor?' The question is not, 'If I stop to help this man in need, what will happen to me?' 'If I do not stop to help the sanitation workers, what will happen to them?' That's the question.

Let us rise up tonight with a greater readiness. Let us stand with a greater determination. And let us move on in these powerful days, these days of challenge to make America what it ought to be. We have an opportunity to make America a better nation. And I want to thank God, once more, for allowing me to be here with you.

You know, several years ago, I was in New York City autographing the first book that I had written. And while sitting there autographing books, a demented black woman came up. The only question I heard from her was, 'Are you Martin Luther King?' And I was looking down writing, and I said yes. And the next minute I felt something beating on my chest. Before I knew it, I had been stabbed by this demented woman. I was rushed to Harlem Hospital. It was a dark Saturday afternoon. And that blade had gone through, and the X-rays revealed that the tip of the blade was on the edge of my aorta, the main artery. And once that's punctured, you drown in your own blood—that's the end of you.

It came out in *The New York Times* the next morning, that if I had sneezed, I would have died. Well, about four days later, they allowed me, after the operation, after my chest had been opened, and the blade had been taken out, to move around in the wheel chair in the hospital. They allowed me to read some of the mail that came in, and from all over the states, and the world, kind letters came in. I read a few, but one of them I will never forget. I had received one from the President and the Vice-President. I've forgotten what those telegrams said. I'd received a visit and a letter from the governor of New York, but I've forgotten what the letter said. But there was another letter that came from a little girl, a young girl who was a student at the White Plains High School. And I looked at that letter, and I'll never forget it. It said simply, 'Dear Dr King: I am a ninth-grade student at the White Plains High School.' She said, 'While it should not matter, I would like to mention that I am a white girl. I read in the paper of your misfortune, and of your suffering. And I read that if you had sneezed, you would have died. And I'm simply writing you to say that I'm so happy that you didn't sneeze.' And I want to say tonight, I want to say that I am happy that I didn't sneeze. Because if I had sneezed, I wouldn't have been around here in 1960, when students all over the South started sitting-in at lunch counters. And I knew that as they were sitting in, they were really standing up for the best in the American dream. And taking the whole nation back to those great wells of democracy which were dug deep by the Founding Fathers in the Declaration of Independence and the

Constitution. If I had sneezed, I wouldn't have been around in 1962, when Negroes in Albany, Georgia, decided to straighten their backs up. And whenever men and women straighten their backs up, they are going somewhere, because a man can't ride your back unless it is bent. If I had sneezed, I wouldn't have been here in 1963, when the black people of Birmingham, Alabama, aroused the conscience of this nation, and brought into being the Civil Rights Bill. If I had sneezed, I wouldn't have had a chance later that year, in August, to try to tell America about a dream that I had had. If I had sneezed, I wouldn't have been down in Selma, Alabama, been in Memphis to see the community rally around those brothers and sisters who are suffering. I'm so happy that I didn't sneeze.

And they were telling me, now it doesn't matter now. It really doesn't matter what happens now. I left Atlanta this morning, and as we got started on the plane, there were six of us, the pilot said over the public address system, 'We are sorry for the delay, but we have Dr Martin Luther King on the plane. And to be sure that all of the bags were checked, and to be sure that nothing would be wrong with the plane, we had to check out everything carefully. And we've had the plane protected and guarded all night.' And then I got to Memphis. And some began to say the threats, or talk about the threats that were out. What would happen to me from some of our sick white brothers?

Well, I don't know what will happen now. We've got some difficult days ahead. But it doesn't matter with me now. Because I've been to the mountaintop. And I don't mind. Like anybody, I would like to live a long life. Longevity has its place. But I'm not concerned about that now. I just want to do God's will. And He's allowed me to go up to the mountain. And I've looked over. And I've seen the Promised Land. I may not get there with you. But I want you to know tonight, that we, as a people, will get to the Promised Land. And I'm happy, tonight. I'm not worried about anything. I'm not fearing any man. Mine eyes have seen the glory of the coming of the Lord.

44

WHAT EDUCATED WOMEN CAN DO

Indira Gandhi

Indira Gandhi delivered a speech at the Golden Jubilee Celebrations of Indraprastha College for Women on 23 November 1974, in which she talked about the importance of educating Indian women and how education would set them free from a patriarchal society.

An ancient Sanskrit saying says, woman is the home and the home is the basis of society. It is as we build our homes that we can build our country. If the home is inadequate—either inadequate in material goods and necessities or inadequate in the sort of friendly, loving atmosphere that every child needs to grow and develop—then that country cannot have harmony and no country which does not have harmony can grow in any direction at all.

That is why women's education is almost more important than the education of boys and men. We—and by 'we' I do not mean only we in India but all the world—have neglected women education. It is fairly recent. Of course, not to you but when I was a child, the story of early days of women's education in England, for instance, was very current. Everybody remembered what had happened in the early days.

I remember what used to happen here. I still remember the days when living in old Delhi even as a small child of seven or eight. I had to go out in a doli if I left the house. We just did not walk. Girls did not walk in the streets. First, you had your sari with which you covered your head, then you had another shawl or something with which you covered your hand and all the body, then you had a white shawl, with which every thing was covered again although your face was open fortunately. Then you were in the doli, which again was covered by another cloth. And this was in a family or community which did not observe purdah of any kind at all. In fact, all our social functions always were mixed functions but this was the atmosphere of the city and of the country.

Now, we have got education and there is a debate all over the country whether this education is adequate to the needs of society or the needs of our young people. I am one of those who always believe that education needs a thorough overhauling. But at the same time, I think that everything in our education is not bad, that even the present education has produced very fine men and women, specially scientists and experts in different fields, who are in great demand all over the world and even in the most affluent countries. Many of our young people leave us and go abroad because they get higher salaries, they get better conditions of work.

But it is not all a one-sided business because there are many who are persuaded and cajoled to go even when they are reluctant. We know of first class students, especially in medicine or nuclear energy for instance, they are approached long before they have passed out and offered all kinds of inducements to go out. Now, that shows that people do consider that they have a standard of knowledge and capability which will be useful any where in the world.

So, that is why I say that there is something worthwhile. It also shows that our own ancient philosophy has taught us that nothing in life is entirely bad or entirely good. Everything is somewhat of a mixture and it depends on us and our capability how we can extract the good, how we can make use of what is around us. There are people who through observation can learn from anything that is around them. There are others who can be surrounded by the most fascinating people, the most wonderful books, and other things and who yet remain quite closed in and they are unable to take anything from this wealth around them.

Our country is a very rich country. It is rich in culture, it is rich in many old traditions—old and even modern tradition. Of course, it has a lot of bad things too and some of the bad things are in the society—superstition, which has grown over the years and which sometimes clouds over the shining brightness of ancient thought and values, eternal values. Then, of course, there is the physical poverty of large numbers of our people. That is something which is ugly and that hampers the growth of millions of young boys and girls. Now, all these bad things we have to fight against and that is what we are doing since independence.

But, we must not allow this dark side of the picture which, by the way, exists in every country in the world. Even the most rich country in the world has its dark side, but usually other people hide their dark sides and they try to project the shining side or the side of achievement. Here in India, we seem to want to project the worst side of society. Before anybody does anything, he has to have, of course, knowledge and capability, but along with it he has to have a certain amount of pride in what he or she is doing. He has to have self-confidence in his own ability. If your teacher tells, 'You cannot do this,' even if you are a very bright student I think every time you will find, it will be more and more difficult for you to do it. But if your teacher encourages saying, 'Go along, you have done very good work, now try a little harder,' then you will try a little harder and you will be able to do it. And it is the same with societies and with countries.

This country, India, has had remarkable achievements to its credit, of course in ancient times, but even in modern times, I think there are a few modern stories, success stories, which are as fascinating as the success story of our country. It is true that we have not banished poverty, we have not banished many of our social ills, but if you compare us to what we were just about 27 years ago, I think that you will not find a single other country that has been able to achieve so much under the most difficult circumstances.

Today, we are passing through specially dark days. But these are not dark days for India alone. Except for the countries which call themselves socialist and about which we do not really know very much, every other country has the same sort of economic problems, which we have. Only a few countries, which have very small populations, have no unemployment. Otherwise, the rich countries also today have unemployment. They have shortages of essential articles. They have shortages even of food.

I do not know how many of you know that the countries of Western Europe and Japan import 41 per cent of their food needs, whereas India imports just under two per cent. Yet, somehow we ourselves project an image that India is out with the begging bowl. And naturally when we ourselves say it, other people will say it much louder and much stronger. It is true, of course, that our two per cent is pretty big because we are a very big country and we have a far bigger population than almost any country in the world with the exception of China. We have to see and you, the educated women, because it is great privilege for you to have higher education, you have to try and see our problems in the perspective of what has happened here in this country and what is happening all over the world.

There is today great admiration for certain things that have happened in other countries where the society is quite differently formed, where no dissent is allowed. The same people who admire that system or the achievements of that system are the ones who say there is dictatorship here even though, I think, nobody has yet been able to point out to me which country has more freedom of expression or action. So, something is said and a lot of people without thinking keep on repeating it with additions until an entirely distorted picture of the country and of our people is presented.

As I said, we do have many shortcomings, whether it is the government, whether it is the society. Some are due to our traditions because, as I said, not all tradition is good. And one of the biggest responsibilities of the educated women today is how to synthesize what has been valuable and timeless in our ancient traditions with what is good and valuable in modern thought. All that is modern is not good just as all that is old is neither all good nor all bad. We have to decide, not once and for all but almost every week, every month what is coming out that is good and useful to our country and what of the old we can keep and enshrine in our society. To be modern, most people think that it is something of a manner of dress or a manner of speaking or certain habits and customs, but that is not really being modern. It is a very superficial part of modernity.

For instance, when I cut my hair, it was because of the sort of life that I was leading. We were all in the movement. You simply could not have long hair and go in the villages and wash it every day. So, when you lead a life, a particular kind of life, your clothes, your everything has to fit into that life if you are to be efficient. If you have to go in the villages and you have to bother whether your clothes are going to be dirty, then you cannot be a good worker. You have to forget everything of that kind. That is why, gradually, clothes and so on have changed in some countries because of the changes in the life-style. Does it suit our life-style or what we want to do or not? If it does, maybe we have to adopt some of these things not merely because it is done in another country and perhaps for another purpose. But what clothes we wear is really quite unimportant. What is important is how we are thinking.

Sometimes, I am very sad that even people who do science are quite unscientific in their thinking and in their other actions—not what they are doing in the laboratories but how they live at home or their attitudes towards other people. Now, for India to become what we want it to become with a modern, rational society and firmly based on what is good in our ancient tradition and in our soil, for this we have to have a thinking public, thinking young women who are not content to accept what comes from any part of the world but are willing to listen to it, to analyse it and to decide whether it is to be accepted or whether it is to be thrown out and this is the sort of education which we want, which enables our young people to adjust to this changing world and to be able to contribute to it.

Some people think that only by taking up very high jobs, you are doing something important or you are doing national service. But we all know that the most complex machinery will be ineffective if one small screw is not working as it should and that screw is just as important as any big part. It is the same in national life. There is no job that is too small; there is no person who is too small. Everybody has something to do. And if he or she does it well, then the country will run well.

In our superstition, we have thought that some work is dirty work. For instance, sweeping has been regarded as dirty. Only some people can do it; others should not do it. Now we find that manure is the most valuable thing that the world has today and many of the world's economies are shaking because there is not enough fertilizer—and not just the chemical fertilizer but the ordinary manure, night-soil and all that sort of thing, things which were considered dirty.

Now it shows how beautifully balanced the world was with everything fitted in with something else. Everything, whether dirty or small, had a purpose. We, with our science and technology, have tried to—not purposely, but somehow, we have created an imbalance and that is what is troubling, on a big scale, the economies of the world and also people and individuals. They are feeling alienated from their societies, not only in India but almost in every country in the world, except in places where the whole purpose of education and government has to be to make the people conform to just one idea. We are told that people there are very happy in whatever they are doing. If they are told to clean the streets, well, if he is a professor he has to clean the streets, if he is a scientist he has to do it, and we were told that they are happy doing it. Well, if they are happy, it is alright.

But I do not think in India we can have that kind of society where people are forced to do things because we think that they can be forced maybe for 25 years, maybe for 50 years, but sometime or the other there will be an explosion. In our society, we allow lots of smaller explosions because we think that that will guard the basic stability and progress of society and prevent it from having the kind of chaotic explosion which can retard our progress and harmony in the country.

So, I hope that all of you who have this great advantage of education will not only do whatever work you are doing keeping the national interests in view, but you will make your own contribution to creating peace and harmony, to bringing beauty in the lives of our people and our country. I think this is the special responsibility of the women of India. We want to do a great deal for our country, but we have never regarded India as isolated from the rest of the world. What we want to do is to make a better world. So, we have to see India's problems in the perspective of the larger world problems.

It has given me great pleasure to be with you here. I give my warm congratulations to those who are doing well and my very good wishes to all the others that they will also do much better. This college has had a high reputation but we must always see that we do better than those who were there before us. So, good luck and good wishes to you.

45

THE HOPE SPEECH

Harvey Milk

Harvey Milk, an American politician and gay rights activist, delivered a famous speech known as the 'Hope Speech' on 10 March 1978, as the keynote address at a meeting of the gay caucus of the California Democratic Council (CDC) in San Diego. This speech is remembered as one of his most powerful and inspiring addresses. In his speech, Milk spoke about the significance of hope and its transformative power in the LGBTQ+ community's fight for equality. He acknowledged the challenges and discrimination faced by the community but emphasized the importance of remaining hopeful and resilient in the face of adversity.

My name is Harvey Milk and I'm here to recruit you.

I've been saying this one for years. It's a political joke. I can't help it—I've got to tell it. I've never been able to talk to this many political people before, so if I tell you nothing else you may be able to go home laughing a bit.

This ocean liner was going across the ocean and it sank. And there was one little piece of wood floating and three people swam to it and they realized only one person could hold on to it. So they had a little debate about which was the person. It so happened that the three people were the Pope, the President and Mayor Daley. The Pope said he was titular head of one of the greatest religions of the world and he was spiritual adviser to many, many millions and he went on and pontificated and they thought it was a good argument. Then the President said he was leader of the largest and most powerful nation of the world. What takes place in this country affects the whole world and they thought that was a good argument. And Mayor Daley said he was mayor of the backbone of the United States and what took place in Chicago affected the world, and what took place in the archdiocese of Chicago affected Catholicism. And they thought that was a good argument. So they did it the democratic way and voted. And Daley won, seven to two.

About six months ago, Anita Bryant in her speaking to God said that the drought in California was because of the gay people. On November 9, the day after I got elected, it started to rain. On the day I got sworn in, we walked to City Hall and it was kinda nice, and as soon as I said the word 'I do,' it started to rain again. It's been raining since then and the people of San Francisco figure the only way to stop it is to do a recall petition. That's the local joke.

So much for that. Why are we here? Why are gay people here? And what's happening? What's happening to me is the antithesis of what you read about in the papers and what you hear about on the radio. You hear about and read about this movement to the Right. That we must band together and fight back this movement to the Right. And I'm here to go ahead and say that what you hear and read is what they want you to think because it's not happening. The major media in this country has talked about the movement to the Right so the legislators think that there is indeed a movement to the right and that the Congress and the legislators and the city councils will start to move to the Right the way the major media want them. So they keep on talking about this move to the Right.

So let's look at 1977 and see if there was indeed a move to the Right. In 1977, gay people had their rights taken away from them in Miami. But you must remember that in the week before Miami and the week after that, the word homosexual or gay appeared in every single newspaper in this nation in articles both pro and con. In every radio station, in every TV station and every household.

For the first time in the history of the world, everybody was talking about it, good or bad. Unless you have dialogue, unless you open the walls of dialogue, you can never reach to change people's opinion. In those two weeks, more good and bad, but more about the word homosexual and gay was written than probably in the history of mankind. Once you have dialogue starting, you know you can break down prejudice. In 1977 we saw a dialogue start. In 1977, we saw a gay person elected in San Francisco. In 1977 we saw the state of Mississippi decriminalize marijuana. In 1977, we saw the convention of conventions in Houston. And I want to know where the movement to the Right is happening.

What that is, is a record of what happened last year. What we must do is make sure that 1978 continues the movement that is really happening that the media don't want you to know about. That is the movement to the Left. It's up to CDC to put the pressures on Sacramento—but to break down the walls and the barriers so the movement to the Left continues and progress continues in the nation. We have before us coming up several issues we must speak out on. Probably the most important issue outside the Briggs—which we will come to—but we do know what will take place this June. We know there's an issue on the ballot called Jarvis-Gann. We hear the taxpayers talk about it on both sides. But what you don't hear is that it's probably the most racist issue on the ballot in a long time. In the city and county of San Francisco, if it passes and we indeed have to lay off people, who will they be? The last in, and the first in, and who are the last in but the minorities? Jarvis-Gann is a racist issue. We must address that issue. We must not talk away from it. We must not allow them to talk about the money it's going to save, because look at who's going to save the money and who's going to get hurt.

We also have another issue that we've started in some of the north counties and I hope in some of the south counties it continues. In San Francisco elections we're asking—at least we hope to ask—that the US government put pressure on the closing of the South African consulate. That must happen. There is a major difference between an embassy in Washington which is a diplomatic bureau and a consulate in major cities. A consulate is there for one reason only—to promote business, economic gains, tourism, investment. And every time you have business going to South Africa, you're promoting a regime that's offensive.

In the city of San Francisco, if everyone of 51 per cent of that city were to go to South Africa, they would be treated as second-class citizens. That is an offense to the people of San Francisco and I hope all my colleagues up there will take every step we can to close down that consulate and hope that people in other parts of the state follow us in that lead. The battles must be started some place and CDC is the greatest place to start the battles. I know we are pressed for time so I'm going to cover just one more little point. That is to understand why it is important that gay people run for office and that gay people get elected. I know there are many people in this room who are running for central committee who are gay. I encourage you. There's a major reason why. If my non-gay friends and supporters in this room understand it, they'll probably understand why I've run so often before I finally made it. Y'see right now, there's a controversy going on in this convention about the gay governor. Is he speaking out enough? Is he strong enough for gay rights? And there is controversy and for us to say it is not would be foolish. Some people are satisfied and some people are not.

You see there is a major difference—and it remains a vital difference—between a friend and a gay person, a friend in office and a gay person in office. Gay people have been slandered nationwide. We've been tarred and we've been brushed with the picture of pornography. In Dade County, we were accused of child molestation. It's not enough anymore just to have friends represent us. No matter how good that friend may be.

The black community made up its mind to that a long time ago. That the myths against blacks can only be dispelled by electing black leaders, so the black community could be judged by the leaders and not by the myths or black criminals. The Spanish community must not be judged by Latin criminals or myths. The Asian community must not be judged by Asian criminals or myths. The Italian community must not be judged by the mafia myths. And the time has come when the gay community must not be judged by our criminals and myths.

Like every other group, we must be judged by our leaders and by those who are themselves gay, those who are visible. For invisible, we remain in limbo—a myth, a person with no parents, no brothers, no sisters, no friends who are straight, no important positions in employment. A tenth of the nation supposedly composed of stereotypes and would-be seducers of children—and no offense meant to the stereotypes. But today, the black community is not judged by its friends, but by its black legislators and leaders. And we must give people the chance to judge us by our leaders and legislators. A gay person in office can set a tone, can command respect not only from the larger community, but from the young people in our own community who need both examples and hope.

The first gay people we elect must be strong. They must not be content to sit in the back of the bus. They must not be content to accept pablum. They must be above wheeling and dealing. They must be—for the good of all of us—independent, unbought. The anger and the frustrations that some of us feel is because we are misunderstood, and friends can't feel the anger and frustration. They can sense it in us, but they can't feel it. Because a friend has never gone through what is known as coming out. I will never forget what it was like coming out and having nobody to look up toward. I remember the lack of hope—and our friends can't fulfill it.

I can't forget the looks on faces of people who've lost hope. Be they gay, be they seniors, be they blacks looking for an almost-impossible job, be they Latins trying to explain their problems and aspirations in a tongue that's foreign to them. I personally will never forget that people are more important than buildings. I use the word 'I' because I'm proud. I stand here tonight in front of my gay sisters, brothers and friends because I'm proud of you. I think it's time that we have many legislators who are gay and proud of that fact and do not have to remain in the closet. I think that a gay person, up-front, will not walk away from a responsibility and be afraid of being tossed out of office. After Dade County, I walked among the angry and the frustrated night after night and I looked at their faces. And in San Francisco, three days before Gay Pride Day, a person was killed just because he was gay. And that night, I walked among the sad and the frustrated at City Hall in San Francisco and later that night as they lit candles on Castro Street and stood in silence, reaching out for some symbolic thing that would give them hope. These were strong people, whose faces I knew from the shop, the streets, meetings and people who I never saw before but I knew. They were strong, but even they needed hope.

And the young gay people in the Altoona, Pennsylvanias, and the Richmond, Minnesotas, who are coming out and hear Anita Bryant on television and her story. The only thing they have to look forward to is hope. And you have to give them hope. Hope for a better world, hope for a better tomorrow, hope for a better place to come to if the pressures at home are too great. Hope that all will be all right. Without hope, not only gays, but the blacks, the seniors, the handicapped, the us'es, the us'es will give up. And if you help elect to the central committee and other offices, more gay people, that gives a green light to all who feel disenfranchised, a green light to move forward. It means hope to a nation that has given up, because if a gay person makes it, the doors are open to everyone.

So if there is a message I have to give, it is that I've found one overriding thing about my personal election, it's the fact that if a gay person can be elected, it's a green light. And you and you and you, you have to give people hope. Thank you very much.

46

TEAR DOWN THIS WALL

Ronald Reagan

'Tear down this wall' is a famous phrase from a speech delivered by President Ronald Reagan on 12 June 1987, in West Berlin, near the iconic Brandenburg Gate. This address is widely regarded as a pivotal moment in Cold War history and became synonymous with the call for the reunification of Germany and the end of the Berlin Wall.

Chancellor Kohl, Governing Mayor Diepgen, ladies and gentlemen: 24 years ago, President John F. Kennedy visited Berlin, speaking to the people of this city and the world at the City Hall. Well, since then two other presidents have come, each in his turn, to Berlin. And today I, myself, make my second visit to your city.

We come to Berlin, we American presidents, because it's our duty to speak, in this place, of freedom. But I must confess, we're drawn here by other things as well: by the feeling of history in this city, more than 500 years older than our own nation; by the beauty of the Grunewald and the Tiergarten; most of all, by your courage and determination. Perhaps the composer Paul Lincke understood something about American presidents. You see, like so many presidents before me, I come here today because wherever I go, whatever I do: 'Ich hab noch einen Koffer in Berlin.' [I still have a suitcase in Berlin.]

Our gathering today is being broadcast throughout Western Europe and North America. I understand that it is being seen and heard as well in the East. To those listening throughout Eastern

Europe, a special word: although I cannot be with you, I address my remarks to you just as surely as to those standing here before me. For I join you, as I join your fellow countrymen in the West, in this firm, this unalterable belief: Es gibt nur ein Berlin. [There is only one Berlin.]

Behind me stands a wall that encircles the free sectors of this city, part of a vast system of barriers that divides the entire continent of Europe. From the Baltic, south, those barriers cut across Germany in a gash of barbed wire, concrete, dog runs and guard towers. Farther south, there may be no visible, no obvious wall. But there remain armed guards and checkpoints all the same—still a restriction on the right to travel, still an instrument to impose upon ordinary men and women the will of a totalitarian state. Yet it is here in Berlin where the wall emerges most clearly; here, cutting across your city, where the news photo and the television screen have imprinted this brutal division of a continent upon the mind of the world. Standing before the Brandenburg Gate, every man is a German, separated from his fellow men. Every man is a Berliner, forced to look upon a scar.

President von Weizsacker has said, 'The German question is open as long as the Brandenburg Gate is closed.' Today I say: as long as the gate is closed, as long as this scar of a wall is permitted to stand, it is not the German question alone that remains open, but the question of freedom for all mankind. Yet I do not come here to lament. For I find in Berlin a message of hope, even in the shadow of this wall, a message of triumph.

In this season of spring in 1945, the people of Berlin emerged from their air-raid shelters to find devastation. Thousands of miles away, the people of the United States reached out to help. And in 1947 Secretary of State—as you've been told—George Marshall announced the creation of what would become known as the Marshall Plan. Speaking precisely 40 years ago this month, he said: 'Our policy is directed not against any country or doctrine, but against hunger, poverty, desperation and chaos.' In the Reichstag a few moments ago, I saw a display commemorating this fortieth anniversary of the Marshall Plan. I was struck by the sign on a burnt-out, gutted structure that was being rebuilt. I understand that Berliners of my own generation can remember seeing signs like it dotted throughout the western sectors of the city. The sign read simply: 'The Marshall Plan is helping here to strengthen the free world.' A strong, free world in the West, that dream became real. Japan rose from ruin to become an economic giant. Italy, France, Belgium—virtually every nation in Western Europe saw political and economic rebirth; the European Community was founded.

In West Germany and here in Berlin, there took place an economic miracle, the Wirtschaftswunder. Adenauer, Erhard, Reuter and other leaders understood the practical importance of liberty—that just as truth can flourish only when the journalist is given freedom of speech, so prosperity can come about only when the farmer and businessman enjoy economic freedom. The German leaders reduced tariffs, expanded free trade, lowered taxes. From 1950 to 1960 alone, the standard of living in West Germany and Berlin doubled.

Where four decades ago there was rubble, today in West Berlin there is the greatest industrial output of any city in Germany—busy office blocks, fine homes and apartments, proud avenues and the spreading lawns of parkland. Where a city's culture seemed to have been destroyed, today there are two great universities, orchestras and an opera, countless theaters and museums. Where there was want, today there's abundance—food, clothing, automobiles—the wonderful goods of the Ku'damm. From devastation, from utter ruin, you Berliners have, in freedom, rebuilt a city that once again ranks as one of the greatest on earth. The Soviets may have had other plans. But my friends, there were a few things the Soviets didn't count on—Berliner Herz, Berliner Humor, ja, und Berliner Schnauze. [Berliner heart, Berliner humor, yes, and a Berliner Schnauze.]

In the 1950s, Khrushchev predicted: 'We will bury you.' But

in the West today, we see a free world that has achieved a level of prosperity and well-being unprecedented in all human history. In the Communist world, we see failure, technological backwardness, declining standards of health, even want of the most basic kind—too little food. Even today, the Soviet Union still cannot feed itself. After these four decades, then, there stands before the entire world one great and inescapable conclusion: freedom leads to prosperity. Freedom replaces the ancient hatreds among the nations with comity and peace. Freedom is the victor.

And now the Soviets themselves may, in a limited way, be coming to understand the importance of freedom. We hear much from Moscow about a new policy of reform and openness. Some political prisoners have been released. Certain foreign news broadcasts are no longer being jammed. Some economic enterprises have been permitted to operate with greater freedom from state control.

Are these the beginnings of profound changes in the Soviet state? Or are they token gestures, intended to raise false hopes in the West, or to strengthen the Soviet system without changing it? We welcome change and openness; for we believe that freedom and security go together, that the advance of human liberty can only strengthen the cause of world peace. There is one sign the Soviets can make that would be unmistakable, that would advance dramatically the cause of freedom and peace.

General Secretary Gorbachev, if you seek peace, if you seek prosperity for the Soviet Union and Eastern Europe, if you seek liberalization: come here to this gate! Mr Gorbachev, open this gate! Mr Gorbachev, tear down this wall!

I understand the fear of war and the pain of division that afflict this continent—and I pledge to you my country's efforts to help overcome these burdens. To be sure, we in the West must resist Soviet expansion. So we must maintain defenses of unassailable strength. Yet we seek peace; so we must strive to reduce arms on both sides.

each other. And our differences are not about weapons but about liberty. When President Kennedy spoke at the City Hall those 24 years ago, freedom was encircled, Berlin was under siege. And today, despite all the pressures upon this city, Berlin stands secure in its liberty. And freedom itself is transforming the globe.

In the Philippines, in South and Central America, democracy has been given a rebirth. Throughout the Pacific, free markets are working miracle after miracle of economic growth. In the industrialized nations, a technological revolution is taking place—a revolution marked by rapid, dramatic advances in computers and telecommunications.

In Europe, only one nation and those it controls refuse to join the community of freedom. Yet in this age of redoubled economic growth, of information and innovation, the Soviet Union faces a choice: it must make fundamental changes, or it will become obsolete.

Today thus represents a moment of hope. We in the West stand ready to cooperate with the East to promote true openness, to break down barriers that separate people, to create a safe, freer world. And surely there is no better place than Berlin, the meeting place of East and West, to make a start. Free people of Berlin: today, as in the past, the United States stands for the strict observance and full implementation of all parts of the Four Power Agreement of 1971. Let us use this occasion, the 750th anniversary of this city, to usher in a new era, to seek a still fuller, richer life for the Berlin of the future. Together, let us maintain and develop the ties between the Federal Republic and the Western sectors of Berlin, which is permitted by the 1971 agreement.

And I invite Mr Gorbachev: let us work to bring the Eastern and Western parts of the city closer together, so that all the inhabitants of all Berlin can enjoy the benefits that come with life in one of the great cities of the world.

To open Berlin still further to all Europe, East and West, let us expand the vital air access to this city, finding ways of making commercial air service to Berlin more convenient, more comfortable, and more economical. We look to the day when West Berlin can become one of the chief aviation hubs in all central Europe.

With our French and British partners, the United States is prepared to help bring international meetings to Berlin. It would be only fitting for Berlin to serve as the site of United Nations meetings, or world conferences on human rights and arms control or other issues that call for international cooperation.

There is no better way to establish hope for the future than to enlighten young minds, and we would be honored to sponsor summer youth exchanges, cultural events, and other programs for young Berliners from the East. Our French and British friends, I'm certain, will do the same. And it's my hope that an authority can be found in East Berlin to sponsor visits from young people of the Western sectors.

One final proposal, one close to my heart: sport represents a source of enjoyment and ennoblement, and you may have noted that the Republic of Korea—South Korea—has offered to permit certain events of the 1988 Olympics to take place in the North. International sports competitions of all kinds could take place in both parts of this city. And what better way to demonstrate to the world the openness of this city than to offer in some future year to hold the Olympic games here in Berlin, East and West? In these four decades, as I have said, you Berliners have built a great city. You've done so in spite of threats—the Soviet attempts to impose the East-mark, the blockade. Today the city thrives in spite of the challenges implicit in the very presence of this wall. What keeps you here? Certainly there's a great deal to be said for your fortitude, for your defiant courage. But I believe there's something deeper, something that involves Berlin's whole look and feel and way of life—not mere sentiment. No one could live long in Berlin without being completely disabused of illusions. Something instead, that has seen the difficulties of life in Berlin but chose to accept them,

ANC even under the most difficult circumstances.

I salute the rank and file members of the ANC. You have sacrificed life and limb in the pursuit of the noble cause of our struggle.

I salute combatants of Umkhonto we Sizwe, like Solomon Mahlangu and Ashley Kriel who have paid the ultimate price for the freedom of all South Africans.

I salute the South African Communist Party for its sterling contribution to the struggle for democracy. You have survived 40 years of unrelenting persecution. The memory of great communists like Moses Kotane, Yusuf Dadoo, Bram Fischer and Moses Mabhida will be cherished for generations to come.

I salute General Secretary Joe Slovo, one of our finest patriots. We are heartened by the fact that the alliance between ourselves and the Party remains as strong as it always was. I salute the United Democratic Front, the National Education Crisis Committee, the South African Youth Congress, the Transvaal and Natal Indian Congresses and COSATU and the many other formations of the Mass Democratic Movement.

I also salute the Black Sash and the National Union of South African Students. We note with pride that you have acted as the conscience of white South Africa. Even during the darkest days in the history of our struggle you held the flag of liberty high. The largescale mass mobilisation of the past few years is one of the key factors which led to the opening of the final chapter of our struggle.

I extend my greetings to the working class of our country. Your organized strength is the pride of our movement. You remain the most dependable force in the struggle to end exploitation and oppression.

I pay tribute to the many religious communities who carried the campaign for justice forward when the organisations for our people were silenced. I greet the traditional leaders of our country—many of you continue to walk in the footsteps of great heroes like Hintsa and Sekhukune.

I pay tribute to the endless heroism of youth, you, the young lions. You, the young lions, have energised our entire struggle.

I pay tribute to the mothers and wives and sisters of our nation. You are the rock-hard foundation of our struggle. Apartheid has inflicted more pain on you than on anyone else.

On this occasion, we thank the world community for their great contribution to the anti-apartheid struggle. Without your support our struggle would not have reached this advanced stage. The sacrifice of the frontline states will be remembered by South Africans forever.

My salutations would be incomplete without expressing my deep appreciation for the strength given to me during my long and lonely years in prison by my beloved wife and family. I am convinced that your pain and suffering was far greater than my own.

Before I go any further I wish to make the point that I intend making only a few preliminary comments at this stage. I will make a more complete statement only after I have had the opportunity to consult with my comrades.

Today the majority of South Africans, black and white, recognise that apartheid has no future. It has to be ended by our own decisive mass action in order to build peace and security. The mass campaign of defiance and other actions of our organisation and people can only culminate in the establishment of democracy. The destruction caused by apartheid on our sub-continent is incalculable. The fabric of family life of millions of my people has been shattered. Millions are homeless and unemployed. Our economy lies in ruins and our people are embroiled in political strife. Our resort to the armed struggle in 1960 with the formation of the military wing of the ANC, Umkhonto we Sizwe, was a purely defensive action against the violence of apartheid. The factors which necessitated the armed struggle still exist today. We have no option but to continue. We express the hope that a climate conducive to a negotiated settlement will be created soon so that

and free society in which all persons live together in harmony and with equal opportunities. It is an ideal which I hope to live for and to achieve. But if needs be, it is an ideal for which I am prepared to die.'

48

I AM AN AFRICAN

Thabo Mbeki

In Thabo Mbeki's 'I am an African' speech, delivered on 8 May 1996, during the adoption of the new South African Constitution, he emphasized the unity and shared identity of the diverse people of South Africa. Mbeki highlighted the struggles, achievements and aspirations of the African people, expressing pride in their heritage and determination to overcome challenges.

Chairperson, Esteemed President of the democratic Republic, Honourable Members of the Constitutional Assembly, our distinguished domestic and foreign guests, friends, on an occasion such as this, we should, perhaps, start from the beginning. So, let me begin. I am an African. I owe my being to the hills and the valleys, the mountains and the glades, the rivers, the deserts, the trees, the flowers, the seas and the ever-changing seasons that define the face of our native land. My body has frozen in our frosts and in our latter-day snows. It has thawed in the warmth of our sunshine and melted in the heat of the midday sun. The crack and the rumble of the summer thunders, lashed by startling lightening, have been a cause both of trembling and of hope. The fragrances of nature have been as pleasant to us as the sight of the wild blooms of the citizens of the veld. The dramatic shapes of the Drakensberg, the soil-coloured waters of the Lekoa, iGqili noThukela, and the sands of the Kgalagadi, have all been panels of the set on the natural stage on which we act out the foolish deeds of the theatre of our day. At times, and in fear, I have wondered whether I should

death is directly proportional to their personal welfare. And so, like pawns in the service of demented souls, they kill in furtherance of the political violence in KwaZulu-Natal. They murder the innocent in the taxi wars. They kill slowly or quickly in order to make profits from the illegal trade in narcotics. They are available for hire when husband wants to murder wife and wife, husband. Among us prowl the products of our immoral and amoral past—killers who have no sense of the worth of human life, rapists who have absolute disdain for the women of our country, animals who would seek to benefit from the vulnerability of the children, the disabled and the old, the rapacious who brook no obstacle in their quest for self-enrichment.

All this I know and know to be true because I am an African! Because of that, I am also able to state this fundamental truth that I am born of a people who are heroes and heroines. I am born of a people who would not tolerate oppression. I am of a nation that would not allow that fear of death, torture, imprisonment, exile or persecution should result in the perpetuation of injustice. The great masses who are our mother and father will not permit that the behaviour of the few results in the description of our country and people as barbaric. Patient because history is on their side, these masses do not despair because today the weather is bad. Nor do they turn triumphalist when, tomorrow, the sun shines. Whatever the circumstances they have lived through and because of that experience, they are determined to define for themselves who they are and who they should be.

We are assembled here today to mark their victory in acquiring and exercising their right to formulate their own definition of what it means to be African. The constitution whose adoption we celebrate constitutes an unequivocal statement that we refuse to accept that our Africanness shall be defined by our race, colour, gender of historical origins. It is a firm assertion made by ourselves that South Africa belongs to all who live in it, black and white. It gives concrete expression to the sentiment we share as Africans, and will defend to the death, that the people shall govern. It recognizes the fact that the dignity of the individual is both an objective which society must pursue, and is a goal which cannot be separated from the material well-being of that individual. It seeks to create the situation in which all our people shall be free from fear, including the fear of the oppression of one national group by another, the fear of the disempowerment of one social echelon by another, the fear of the use of state power to deny anybody their fundamental human rights and the fear of tyranny. It aims to open the doors so that those who were disadvantaged can assume their place in society as equals with their fellow human beings without regard to colour, race, gender, age or geographic dispersal. It provides the opportunity to enable each one and all to state their views, promote them, strive for their implementation in the process of governance without fear that a contrary view will be met with repression. It creates a law-governed society which shall be inimical to arbitrary rule. It enables the resolution of conflicts by peaceful means rather than resort to force. It rejoices in the diversity of our people and creates the space for all of us voluntarily to define ourselves as one people.

As an African, this is an achievement of which I am proud, proud without reservation and proud without any feeling of conceit. Our sense of elevation at this moment also derives from the fact that this magnificent product is the unique creation of African hands and African minds. But it also constitutes a tribute to our loss of vanity that we could, despite the temptation to treat ourselves as an exceptional fragment of humanity, draw on the accumulated experience and wisdom of all humankind, to define for ourselves what we want to be. Together with the best in the world, we too are prone to pettiness, petulance, selfishness and shortsightedness. But it seems to have happened that we looked at ourselves and said the time had come that we make a super-human effort to be other than human, to respond to the call to create for ourselves a glorious future, to remind ourselves of the

whether we hail from Iowa or New Hampshire, Nevada or South Carolina, we are ready to take this country in a fundamentally new direction. That is what's happening in America right now. Change is what's happening in America.

You can be the new majority who can lead this nation out of a long political darkness—Democrats, independents and Republicans who are tired of the division and distraction that has clouded Washington; who know that we can disagree without being disagreeable; who understand that if we mobilize our voices to challenge the money and influence that's stood in our way and challenge ourselves to reach for something better, there's no problem we can't solve—no destiny we cannot fulfill.

Our new American majority can end the outrage of unaffordable, unavailable health care in our time. We can bring doctors and patients, workers and businesses, Democrats and Republicans together; and we can tell the drug and insurance industry that while they'll get a seat at the table, they don't get to buy every chair. Not this time. Not now.

Our new majority can end the tax breaks for corporations that ship our jobs overseas and put a middle-class tax cut into the pockets of the working Americans who deserve it.

We can stop sending our children to schools with corridors of shame and start putting them on a pathway to success. We can stop talking about how great teachers are and start rewarding them for their greatness. We can do this with our new majority.

We can harness the ingenuity of farmers and scientists, citizens and entrepreneurs to free this nation from the tyranny of oil and save our planet from a point of no return.

And when I am president, we will end this war in Iraq and bring our troops home; we will finish the job against Al Qaeda in Afghanistan; we will care for our veterans; we will restore our moral standing in the world; and we will never use 9/11 as a way to scare up votes, because it is not a tactic to win an election, it is a challenge that should unite America and the world against the common threats of the twenty-first century: terrorism and nuclear weapons, climate change and poverty, genocide and disease.

All of the candidates in this race share these goals. All have good ideas. And all are patriots who serve this country honorably.

But the reason our campaign has always been different is because it's not just about what I will do as president, it's also about what you, the people who love this country, can do to change it.

That's why tonight belongs to you. It belongs to the organizers and the volunteers and the staff who believed in our improbable journey and rallied so many others to join.

We know the battle ahead will be long, but always remember that no matter what obstacles stand in our way, nothing can withstand the power of millions of voices calling for change.

We have been told we cannot do this by a chorus of cynics who will only grow louder and more dissonant in the weeks to come. We've been asked to pause for a reality check. We've been warned against offering the people of this nation false hope.

But in the unlikely story that is America, there has never been anything false about hope. For when we have faced down impossible odds; when we've been told that we're not ready, or that we shouldn't try, or that we can't, generations of Americans have responded with a simple creed that sums up the spirit of a people.

Yes we can.

It was a creed written into the founding documents that declared the destiny of a nation.

Yes we can.

It was whispered by slaves and abolitionists as they blazed a trail toward freedom through the darkest of nights.

Yes we can.

It was sung by immigrants as they struck out from distant shores and pioneers who pushed westward against an unforgiving wilderness.

Yes we can.

It was the call of workers who organized, women who reached

diving into harm's way to save others...flying across the country to put out a fire...driving for hours to bail out a flooded town.

And I've seen it in our men and women in uniform and our proud military families...in wounded warriors who tell me they're not just going to walk again, they're going to run, and they're going to run marathons...in the young man blinded by a bomb in Afghanistan who said, simply, '...I'd give my eyes 100 times again to have the chance to do what I have done and what I can still do.'

Every day, the people I meet inspire me...every day, they make me proud...every day they remind me how blessed we are to live in the greatest nation on earth.

Serving as your First Lady is an honor and a privilege...but back when we first came together four years ago, I still had some concerns about this journey we'd begun.

While I believed deeply in my husband's vision for this country...and I was certain he would make an extraordinary president...like any mother, I was worried about what it would mean for our girls if he got that chance.

How would we keep them grounded under the glare of the national spotlight?

How would they feel being uprooted from their school, their friends, and the only home they'd ever known?

Our life before moving to Washington was filled with simple joys...Saturdays at soccer games, Sundays at grandma's house...and a date night for Barack and me was either dinner or a movie, because as an exhausted mom, I couldn't stay awake for both.

And the truth is, I loved the life we had built for our girls...I deeply loved the man I had built that life with...and I didn't want that to change if he became president.

I loved Barack just the way he was.

You see, even though back then Barack was a Senator and a presidential candidate...to me, he was still the guy who'd picked me up for our dates in a car that was so rusted out, I could actually see the pavement going by through a hole in the passenger side door...he was the guy whose proudest possession was a coffee table he'd found in a dumpster, and whose only pair of decent shoes was half a size too small.

But when Barack started telling me about his family—that's when I knew I had found a kindred spirit, someone whose values and upbringing were so much like mine.

You see, Barack and I were both raised by families who didn't have much in the way of money or material possessions but who had given us something far more valuable—their unconditional love, their unflinching sacrifice, and the chance to go places they had never imagined for themselves.

My father was a pump operator at the city water plant, and he was diagnosed with multiple sclerosis when my brother and I were young.

And even as a kid, I knew there were plenty of days when he was in pain... I knew there were plenty of mornings when it was a struggle for him to simply get out of bed.

But every morning, I watched my father wake up with a smile, grab his walker, prop himself up against the bathroom sink, and slowly shave and button his uniform.

And when he returned home after a long day's work, my brother and I would stand at the top of the stairs to our little apartment, patiently waiting to greet him...watching as he reached down to lift one leg, and then the other, to slowly climb his way into our arms.

But despite these challenges, my dad hardly ever missed a day of work...he and my mom were determined to give me and my brother the kind of education they could only dream of.

And when my brother and I finally made it to college, nearly all of our tuition came from student loans and grants.

But my dad still had to pay a tiny portion of that tuition himself.

And every semester, he was determined to pay that bill right on time, even taking out loans when he fell short.

He was so proud to be sending his kids to college...and he

That's why he signed the Lilly Ledbetter Fair Pay Act to help women get equal pay for equal work.

That's why he cut taxes for working families and small businesses and fought to get the auto industry back on its feet.

That's how he brought our economy from the brink of collapse to creating jobs again—jobs you can raise a family on, good jobs right here in the United States of America.

When it comes to the health of our families, Barack refused to listen to all those folks who told him to leave health reform for another day, another president.

He didn't care whether it was the easy thing to do politically—that's not how he was raised—he cared that it was the right thing to do.

He did it because he believes that here in America, our grandparents should be able to afford their medicine...our kids should be able to see a doctor when they're sick...and no one in this country should ever go broke because of an accident or illness.

And he believes that women are more than capable of making our own choices about our bodies and our health care...that's what my husband stands for.

When it comes to giving our kids the education they deserve, Barack knows that like me and like so many of you, he never could've attended college without financial aid.

And believe it or not, when we were first married, our combined monthly student loan bills were actually higher than our mortgage.

We were so young, so in love and so in debt.

That's why Barack has fought so hard to increase student aid and keep interest rates down, because he wants every young person to fulfill their promise and be able to attend college without a mountain of debt.

So in the end, for Barack, these issues aren't political—they're personal.

Because Barack knows what it means when a family struggles.

He knows what it means to want something more for your kids and grandkids.

Barack knows the American Dream because he's lived it...and he wants everyone in this country to have that same opportunity, no matter who we are, or where we're from, or what we look like, or who we love.

And he believes that when you've worked hard, and done well, and walked through that doorway of opportunity...you do not slam it shut behind you...you reach back, and you give other folks the same chances that helped you succeed.

So when people ask me whether being in the White House has changed my husband, I can honestly say that when it comes to his character, and his convictions, and his heart, Barack Obama is still the same man I fell in love with all those years ago.

He's the same man who started his career by turning down high paying jobs and instead working in struggling neighborhoods where a steel plant had shut down, fighting to rebuild those communities and get folks back to work...because for Barack, success isn't about how much money you make, it's about the difference you make in people's lives.

He's the same man who, when our girls were first born, would anxiously check their cribs every few minutes to ensure they were still breathing, proudly showing them off to everyone we knew.

That's the man who sits down with me and our girls for dinner nearly every night, patiently answering their questions about issues in the news, and strategizing about middle school friendships.

That's the man I see in those quiet moments late at night, hunched over his desk, poring over the letters people have sent him.

The letter from the father struggling to pay his bills...from the woman dying of cancer whose insurance company won't cover her care...from the young person with so much promise but so few opportunities.

I see the concern in his eyes...and I hear the determination in his voice as he tells me, 'You won't believe what these folks are

about whether Barack and I were doing what's best for our girls.

Because today, I know from experience that if I truly want to leave a better world for my daughters, and all our sons and daughters...if we want to give all our children a foundation for their dreams and opportunities worthy of their promise...if we want to give them that sense of limitless possibility—that belief that here in America, there is always something better out there if you're willing to work for it...then we must work like never before...and we must once again come together and stand together for the man we can trust to keep moving this great country forward...my husband, our president, President Barack Obama.

Thank you, God bless you, and God bless America.